Indeterminate Creatures

Alan Apperley

**Tindal
Street
Press**

First published in UK March 2010
by Tindal Street Press Ltd
217 The Custard Factory, Gibb Street,
Birmingham, B9 4AA
www.tindalstreet.co.uk

A CIP catalogue reference for this book is available
from the British Library

ISBN: 978 0 9556476 8 0

Typeset by Alma Books Ltd
Printed and bound in Great Britain by
CPI Cox & Wyman, Reading

Butterflies . . . not quite birds, as they were not quite flowers, mysterious and fascinating as are all indeterminate creatures.

Elizabeth Goudge, *The Child from the Sea*

PART ONE

FIRST TRIMESTER

JUNE 2002

I

The heavens had opened. A sheet of water enveloped them as they left the bar, and thunder reverberated above them in the dark. The street was a marine spectacle of light drizzling through the dense rain, gaudy as a harbour. Cars gushed past them, cutting heavily through the flooding road like tugboats, lifting water on to the kerb where they stood.

'Where are we?' she said, and tottered under the weight of the rain – and the alcohol.

'God knows,' he said. 'I'm drunk. We'd better find a taxi.'

But after a few seconds of arbitrary walking they were soaked through to the skin and the search had become less urgent. The weather reports that morning had predicted rainstorms for the evening but they'd paid no attention. They hadn't planned to go out at all, but the heat and humidity and the cajoling of friends had easily drawn them. What is more, he – Michael – and she – Hope – had been living together now for exactly one year to the day. There was an excuse for celebration.

As the rain eased and the thunder withdrew into the distance, their walking slowed to a lovers' stroll. They held hands and wondered how, after the heavy rain, the smell of earth could lift to them through the weight of concrete and tarmac.

'Buildings float,' he said.

'They do after that rain,' she replied.

'No, I mean it, they *float*. The soil that they're on, right, it gives off vapours, and the earth's sort of insulated by them. Or it's electromagnetic or something.'

'You're pissed,' she said. 'You're the only thing that's floating around here.'

'Look, I'll prove it to you.'

They were walking beside a low wall that separated the cathedral from the banks and shops lining the street. Two giant spotlights flooded the building's front end with orange light. Along its side, hemmed in behind the low wall, were dim sarcophagi; the last remains of the city's Victorian dignitaries. Michael skipped over the wall and came back carrying a handful of stones. He sat down on the wall and began to take off one of his shoes.

'What the bloody hell are you doing?' Hope asked, standing over him.

'I'm giving you,' he said, 'a scientific demonstration.'

He took his sock off and laid it lengthways along the wall. He then carefully selected four stones and lay them at what appeared to be strategic positions on the garment.

'I don't get it,' she said, puzzled.

'Well, my sock's wet, right?'

'Yeah, so?'

'Well, as the moisture leaves the sock it'll lift the stones. Thus,' he said, grandly.

'*Thus?*' she said, snorting with laughter. 'Did you say *thus?*'

'Thus,' he insisted, 'proving my point. QED.'

'*QED?* You don't know what that means. Anyway, the only thing that'll lift those stones will be the stench from your feet.'

'It'll take a while,' he said, and put his arm around her wet shoulders. Her dark hair looked untouched by the downpour, but it dropped diamonds into her lap and shone like patent leather under the street lamps.

'Diamonds and patent leather,' he said. She turned her head, showering his lap with gems.

'What did you say? You're babbling, you drunkard.'

She slurred her words slightly; an attractive lisp. He pictured her tongue against her lips and, despite the alcohol, felt the blood begin to pour into his groin. He shifted his hips slightly to facilitate this, though he was hardly aware of doing so. But she immediately understood his body language, and despite the sodden ghosts drifting past them as they sat on the wall, she cupped his groin in her hand.

'What's this then?' she asked with a leer.

'Christ, Hope! Not here,' he said, genuinely embarrassed.

'Where then? Here?' And saying this, she hiked his legs upwards, causing him to fall backwards on to the grass border behind the wall. She followed him over, and fell on him.

'Come on, sexy,' she ordered, 'get your pants off! You know you want it! I bet you're dying for it! You men are all the same!' And she pretended to tear at his flimsy summer trousers.

'Get off!' he shouted, more tickled than aroused. 'You tart! You big slapper! You slut!'

'More!' she yelled. 'I love it when you talk dirty!'

Michael grabbed her wrists in an effort to regain his composure.

'Anyway,' she said, 'where did you learn words like that?'

By this time she'd straddled him and he felt the full weight of her across his hips. The blood beat back into his groin, and this time his thoughts were concentrated on her. She felt him harden against her and she responded, tightening her buttocks against him.

'My word!' she breathed. 'We'd better get you home.'

She dismounted and climbed the wall, leaving him to recover himself. He watched her sodden cotton dress cleaving to her as though the air had been sucked out of it by a vacuum. Her limbs pulled at the garment as she manoeuvred herself on to the street. He imagined he could see her muscles as they worked her body over the wall.

Michael envied Hope her controlled freedom of movement. As he pushed himself clumsily upright, he felt the weight of gravity bearing down upon him as though he'd just climbed out from a swimming pool. He found it difficult to lift his arms; his hands were sandbags. Drunken panic gripped him; he was unable to keep up with her, though she hadn't gone far.

'Wait, Hope. Where are you going?' he shouted.

'I'm going to hail a taxi,' she replied, and shot an arm in the air.

'They won't stop,' he shouted back. 'It's not legal any more.'

The vehicle slushed past Hope without stopping. Michael checked his pockets – his money and his keys seemed to be there but his phone had fallen out during his tussle with Hope. He bent over the wall to investigate; there it was. But then he stopped and turned to Hope.

'Quick! Come quickly,' he shouted.

She idled back towards him. 'What?' she asked.

'Look,' he hissed, faking excitement. 'Look!'

'What?' she asked again, not understanding him.

'The stones. Look!'

He was, by now, affecting awe, pointing at the 'experiment'. The sock, so far as they could tell, was still in its place, but the stones had vanished. They looked over the wall for them, but if they were there, they were indistinguishable from all the other stones that lay on the thin gravel strip that kept the foot of the wall from the grass.

'My experiment!' he yelled, adopting a pseudo-German accent befitting of Nobel Prize winners. 'It vos a zuccess! A schtupendous zuccess!'

'Bollocks,' Hope replied. 'Put your sock on.'

She returned to the kerbside and within seconds had flagged a taxi down. Michael hobbled across to the open door, struggling to put his sock on.

The car sped through the industrial belt, along roads still awash with rainwater. Michael and Hope huddled together on the back seat of the saloon. The driver had introduced herself as Parmjit before the car had pulled away. She kept up a constant barrage of chatter, as though contracted to do so.

'Have you been out drinking? Great! Got caught in the rain? Bloody terrible wasn't it? I thought it was great! I couldn't see a thing! Don't worry though – I'm a good driver, me. Only crashed twice this evening. Nah seriously, where is it you want? Call me Pam, by the way.'

'Potters Road,' the passengers chimed in unison.

'Potters Road? Which end? It's a long road, you know. Of course you do. You live there! Are you hungry? I could take you to a good restaurant not far from there. It's my uncle's.'

'Which one's that?' said Michael, suddenly animated at the thought of food.

Pam turned to answer him and at that moment the taxi ploughed into a pond that had formed in a trough in the road. There was an explosion, like the amplified beat of a heart. Water enveloped the car, sealing the occupants in an aquatic universe, an amniotic sac.

Then the waters broke. There was a grinding sound – metal on metal – and when the water subsided the passengers realized that the car had come to a halt. There was an incongruous moment of calm, and then Pam spoke.

'Oh shit. I've hit him.'

For all the sound and fury, the impact had been mild. Hope and Michael had been jolted but nothing more. The water drained from the windows to reveal a car facing in the opposite direction, sandwiched like a Siamese twin against their own. Driver faced driver, both unable to leave their cars. Pam tried to lower her window but the door had buckled against the mechanism. The other driver had no such problem. He'd got his window down and was bellowing obscenities at Pam.

'You fucking stupid Paki bitch! Are you blind? Stupid fucking woman driver.'

Ignoring the tirade, Pam turned to her passengers. 'Are you all right? Don't worry, I'll radio in for help.'

She picked up her handset and spoke coolly, seemingly oblivious to the tirade being levelled at her from behind her window. The call took seconds; a location and a code-word. Meanwhile, the other driver had decided to leave his car by the passenger door. As he sank up to his ankles in water, the level of insults rose even higher.

'Oh dear,' said Pam, stifling her laughter. 'He is *not* having a good day.'

As the driver began to wade around the breadth of the two cars, Hope and Michael heard the clunk of the central locking mechanism.

'Don't open the doors,' whispered Pam. 'He'll probably kill me if he gets in. Did you see what happened?'

By this time Hope and Michael were warming to their driver, siding with her against the Neanderthal trying to attack her. It hadn't been anyone's fault.

'Can you give me a statement for the insurance? If I need one?'

By now, the driver was rapping on the passenger window. Pam lowered the window an inch and coolly told the driver that she was going to pull back out of the water.

'I'm not getting my feet wet,' she said to her passengers and, starting the engine, she eased her car back out of the water on to the shore.

By the time she'd reached dry land, a second taxi had arrived. Three men got out. One walked over to Pam's taxi, while the other two stood imposingly, staring at the sodden, angry driver of the other car.

'I'm just going to sort this out,' Pam said to her passengers. 'Don't leave, will you? I'll see you get home all right. I'll leave the engine running.'

She left the car and closed the door. The air conditioning whirred cool air into the body of the vehicle.

'Nice of the taxi company to lay on this entertainment for us,' said Michael.

It began to rain again, as heavily as before. The windows of the car were a varicose network of rivulets. It was difficult to see what was going on outside, and difficult to hear with the rain thrumming on the body of the car. Inside, the windows began to film over. Hope's dress was beginning to irritate her as it dried against her skin. She hiked the edge of the garment up to the top of her thighs and slid her bottom forward on the seat so that she could flap cool air along the length of her body. Michael, still drunk, watched her. His own clothes were beginning to irritate him but he could do nothing about it, short of undressing himself. He remembered, for the first time in many years, a childhood envy of girls' clothes, particularly the freedom of dresses.

'Good god,' he said. 'I've just remembered trying on my sister's dresses!' His voice slurred, a cocktail of alcohol and weariness.

'*What?* You pervert! When was this?' Hope chortled at the thought, a thick inebriated giggle. She too was beginning to feel the weight of the day in her limbs.

'Oh, ages ago. When I was a kid.'

'Thank god, I thought you were going to say last week.'

'I think my bones are saturated,' he said. 'I feel really heavy.'

Michael lay back alongside Hope. He lifted his hand on to her exposed thigh. Hope moved her hand to his, laced his fingers in her own.

'Where do memories come from?' he asked, distantly.

'Where do they go to?' she mimicked, waving her arm airily across the width of the car. But she responded to his bewilderment and moved closer to him. 'We're in a world of water here,' she said, as a volley of thick raindrops rattled across the roof of the car.

'We're in a womb,' he said. 'Brother and sister.'

'Twins,' she said.

The drumming on the roof softened for a moment, and then the cannonade resumed, as heavy as before.

'Can I try your dress on later?' he whispered.

The door opened and Pam climbed into her seat. Her hair and clothes were sodden but she seemed oblivious to this fact.

'All sorted,' she said. 'Potters Road, wasn't it? Sorry about the delay. No charge for the ride.'

'I'm starving,' pleaded Michael. 'Take us to your uncle's restaurant.'

'Don't!' said Hope.

In spite of his desire for food, Michael seemed increasingly the worse for wear.

'Is he all right?' said Pam, directly to Hope. 'I've got a plastic bag in the front here if he needs it.'

'He's all right,' said Hope, calmly. 'Let's just get him home.'

'Food!' protested Michael. 'Uncle's home cooking. Now!'

'Shut up, you oaf!'

'Too late,' said Pam. 'We're there.'

Hope insisted on paying the fare while Michael lolled against the door of their terraced house, washed by the unearthly yellow light from the street lamp above them. The rain had eased again and a belligerent moon had broken through the troubled clouds above the city. The taxi pulled away from the kerb and slipped along the street to the corner where it passed out of view, taking all motion with it. As a palpable emptiness settled on the street, Hope stood for a moment on the kerb, listening. In the distance she could hear the low rumble of city traffic, tyres screeching on tarmac, the shriek of a siren, the faltering drone of an aeroplane somewhere behind the clouds. There was so much going on, even at this late hour. Life never stopped.

She looked over at Michael, now sitting on the doorstep, head in hands. Life, it seemed, did occasionally slow down.

'I'm so *tired!*' he moaned in self-absorption.

'You're such a prima donna,' she whispered. She found her key and let them in.

The room they stepped into was tinted with the same eerie yellow light from the street lamp outside, until Hope reached the light switch and flooded the room with their familiar decor. Michael immediately slopped down into an armchair, his head lolling backwards, mouth open. He groaned again and watched the room rotate around him for a moment before closing his eyes in an effort to centre his spinning universe.

Hope watched him with concern. How drunk was he really? Would he be all right sitting there if she left him? He was so pathetic, and yet she knew that this was partly what attracted her to him. She knew that he was essentially weak, that the world would almost always beat him down. But she sensed that he knew this himself, and she admired his refusal to give up on that world, the naïve optimism with which he faced the uncertainties of life.

Hope knew how uncertain life could be. Her parents had been killed in a car crash on their way to the airport five years before she met Michael, just as she was beginning to repair the damage that years of teenage rebelliousness had caused to their relationship. Her father had worked in the City, her mother as a solicitor. They'd met as students in Cambridge and had married shortly after graduating. Neither had been keen to let a child get in the way of their respective careers, and so Hope had been looked after by a series of nannies. She'd grown up, she now realized, with a chip on her shoulder, nursing a resentment towards her parents and their 'materialistic' lifestyle. After graduating, she'd calmed down, and while she'd still felt that her parents had been more interested in their own careers than in her, she'd begun to build a bridge back to them. But that had all come to nothing, and it still hurt that they'd died before she could make her peace with them.

Maybe it was the difficulties she'd had with her own parents that made it so easy for Hope to get on with Michael's. After all, she'd come to understand something of why she'd failed to get on with her own folks. But Michael's parents were just Michael's parents. There was no baggage there to be unpacked. They'd accepted Hope for who she was, and she'd done the same with them. They'd taken her into their family, and made her feel like she was one of their own daughters, and she loved them all the more for this.

Hope closed the curtains and locked the door, then climbed the stairs to their bedroom, leaving Michael whirling in his pool of self-pity.

Michael had made it to the kitchen, where he stood drinking water. He'd dozed for no more than half an hour, a restless dream-ridden sleep so vivid that he was finding it difficult to unpick his memories of the day's events from his memories of the dreams he'd just had. Most of his confusions centred around Evette: had she really spent the entire evening watching him from underneath her copper fringe? She'd certainly kept herself in reserve, sitting quietly on the edge of the conversation. But Michael was sure that every time he'd looked over at her, she'd been silently regarding him, though almost every time he did so she'd averted her eyes from his.

Except once, when she'd stared at him with a frankness that now intrigued him. He'd been drawn into the shadows beneath her fringe as though in pursuit of a mysterious animal retreating into the velvet depths of her dark pupils. And then she'd calmly turned her head aside to make some brief comment, leaving Michael abandoned at the edge of the forest. This sudden flight had jolted him. He'd continued to pursue her gaze, had watched her eyelids flicker across her irises like butterflies coveting attractive flowers, but she hadn't returned to him.

Or had he dreamed all this?

Michael was no longer sure, but he'd realized in this unreliable memory just how alluring Evette was. He thought of her lips, made full by the wet-look gloss of her red lipstick, and wished he were kissing them now. He remembered the tight black sweater she'd worn, and wished he could run his hands across the velveteen material, mapping the body beneath. Desire pulsed through his body, cutting through the alcohol polluting his system. He wanted Evette, and not having her right now was torture. He thought of the phone in his pocket, and for a brief moment considered sending her a text. Any contact would be better than none. But he was sober enough now to admit that Evette was his best friend's girlfriend, and that she would be tucked up in bed with him by now.

Instead, he went upstairs to Hope, who lay naked on the bed. The quilt had slipped on to the floor in the cloying summer heat of the bedroom. She lay on her side, her hip bone-white in the refracted moonlight. Michael was steady now, drunk but not incapable. Hope rolled easily on to her back and Michael watched the moonlight break like surf across the peaks of her body. Her eyes opened on him.

'Hello.' Her voice was thick with sleep. 'What time is it? Are you OK?

'I'm all right. It's about half-two, I think.'

He went to the bathroom. Hope reached for the clock and squinted briefly, then took a sip of water from the glass beside her. She heard him cleaning his teeth, then using the toilet. The alcohol in her bloodstream hadn't yet begun to sour. She lay back, her head momentarily swimming in the moonlight, and then she saw Michael standing at the foot of the bed. He was looking down at her and had the stirrings of an erection, his penis nodding up and down.

'I agree,' she said lewdly, and Michael moved to lie with her.

2

Jeffrey Chancredy walked across the lounge bar carrying two tall glasses of beer. Dressed completely in black, except for the slash of luminous-white dress shirt visible through the curtains of his jacket, and with long blond hair framing his hawkish features, Jeffrey Chancredy was incongruous in the traditional pub surroundings. He walked with grace and rhythm, his body balanced around the glasses he carried. He placed one in front of Michael and sipped from his own as he lowered into his seat.

'Cheers, J,' said Michael.

They were in a city centre pub. Michael had taken the afternoon off for no reason other than that he'd the time available to take. Jeffrey, Michael's closest friend, had taken the whole day off work. It was now that quiet time between afternoon and evening. A few stalwart drinkers stood at the bar indefinitely extending their lunchtime session, and a couple of old gents sat staring morosely into their flat beers. Now and then laughter sputtered from the group at the bar, quickly receding, leaving only a murmur of conversation, and the occasional fanfare from the slot machines, positioned by the entrance to the toilet. A fanfare sounded as Michael replaced his glass.

'I wish she'd get rid of those machines,' said Michael, idly. They hadn't been annoying him especially.

'She'd like to,' said Jeffrey. 'It's the brewery though. She has no control over fixtures and fittings. She does, however . . .'

And Jeffrey paused for a moment to savour another example of the individual subverting a corporate strategy. His sharp blue eyes locked directly on to Michael's, a conspiratorial smile suffusing his face.

'. . . have control over *where* they go.'

'I don't follow,' said Michael.

'They're by the toilets.'

'So?'

'The association. Where you go to piss, and where you go to piss your money away.'

'Very subtle,' said Michael, who was much more impressed by Jeffrey's easy ability to glean this information from someone he'd never spoken to before. Michael, who worked within walking distance of the city centre, used the pub regularly at lunchtimes and after work, but he'd never passed more than money or requests for drinks across the bar.

'Let us drink to the success of her campaign!' said Jeffrey, grandly.

Both replaced their glasses simultaneously and relaxed back into their seats.

'What are you in town for?' asked Michael.

Michael knew that Jeffrey's favourite topic of conversation was his own plans and projects, and he didn't mind leaving openings into which Jeffrey could insert himself. Michael was never comfortable talking about himself, and so was always happy to defer to someone who had something interesting to say. Jeffrey yawned, and stretched himself out before sitting upright. Only when he'd adopted this imperious posture did he reply. Michael always had the sense that Jeffrey would prefer to be standing up when outlining his plans and projects, as though the additional height would give them more authority.

'Oh, nothing really. I ordered some leads for the studio and had to pick them up. Bought some guitar strings, too. I get through strings like a prostitute gets through condoms. Still, the wiring's nearly done now and I just need to finish the soundproofing.'

'This is the recording studio, or the editing suite?'

'Both. I don't see them as separate projects.'

Jeffrey then went on to explain, once again, what his overall project was. It was a story that Michael knew well, and although details had changed as Jeffrey developed his project, the core of the plan remained unaltered.

As far as the world at large was concerned, Jeffrey Chancredy made a living working as a graphic artist for a small advertising agency. But as far as Jeffrey was concerned, his job was only a means by which to finance his *real* creative endeavours. For in Jeffrey's universe, true creativity could not be harnessed to such mundane ends as earning a living wage, or maximizing profit on behalf of some faceless corporation. Arts Council grants weren't an option either, and those artists who were awarded them simply became lackeys of a system which ultimately both feared and resented true creative expression. The very phrase 'creative *industries*' was, for Jeffrey, an oxymoron.

Jeffrey had set himself the task of freeing himself from these enemies of true artistic expression. Converting the suburban, between-the-wars semi he shared with Evette into a multimedia artist's studio was an essential step towards allowing Jeffrey complete artistic freedom of expression.

As an artist, Jeffrey felt no compulsion to restrict himself to any one field of expertise. He planned extravagant projects for his nascent production company, projects in which he developed the storylines, scripted them, and drew the storyboards. He was writer, designer, scenic artist, cameraman, producer and director. He also wrote the music for his own productions and, since he played a variety of musical instruments competently, was able to realize his own compositions by a clever mixture of multi-tracking and computer-programmed digitized instrumentation. The only aspect of the entire process that Jeffrey didn't appear to do himself was acting in his own productions. No one was really sure how Jeffrey dealt with this particular problem, since no one had yet seen anything other than brief snatches of Jeffrey's work – a half-finished song here; a few moments of film there; artfully-done sketches for proposed DVD or CD covers – fragments suggestive of a complex, multi-faceted multimedia artwork.

But, although Jeffrey delighted in outlining the projects upon which he was working, he would never let anyone see them. It was as though he believed that no single item would make sense unless the entire overarching project was brought simultaneously to completion. For example, Jeffrey had written a suite of novels which were somehow linked to the master project. His friends had seen evidence of these novels – titles, outlines, a page or so of writing – enough to reassure them that Jeffrey was, in principle, capable of writing. But in spite of this evidence, Jeffrey had refused to allow anyone to read any of the completed manuscripts. Except, that is, Evette. Having no reason to doubt Evette's word, Jeffrey's friends had no reason to doubt that these novels existed. But they remained unread, encoded on Jeffrey's hard drive.

'I've named the production company at last.'

Jeffrey paused, waiting for Michael to catch up with him. Michael, who had been watching the moisture beading on the side of his glass, realized that Jeffrey was addressing him.

'At last,' he agreed. 'Something witty? Poignant? Short?'

Jeffrey, who had evidently prepared himself for such a moment, coolly handed Michael a leaflet, A5 size. It was a flyer. In the centre of the leaflet was a reproduction of Leonardo da Vinci's *Vitruvian Man*, digitally doctored by Jeffrey. The architecture within which the Christ-like figure was usually suspended, and with which Leonardo had sought to demonstrate the ideal geometric proportions of the human body, had been replaced by the screen of a mobile phone. A logo, fashioned from the letters CMC, was positioned in the bottom left-hand corner of the leaflet, along with a web link, an email address, and a mobile phone number. The legend along the full length of the left-hand margin, and at a right-angle to the image, read: CHANCREDY MULTIMEDIA COLLECTIVE.

'Collective?' said Michael, quizzically.

'I'm late,' said Hope, from behind her cup.

She sipped her tea and looked guardedly around the café. She worked as a librarian at the city's university. It was the summer vacation, and it would be another three weeks at least before the students returned to the campus. Even so, the café was full where Hope was sitting with Alex, her friend and colleague. The patrons were mostly men and women in suits, each sporting a prominent name tag. They would be on campus for one of the many conferences the university sought to finance itself with during the long vacation.

'What do you mean?' Alex was puzzled; she and Hope had arrived together nearly half an hour before. If Hope had an appointment elsewhere, she was making no move to finish her tea.

'I'm late,' Hope said again. This time the directness of her stare spoke eloquently. She sipped her tea again, as if to cover up the remark.

'Are you sure?' said Alex, cautiously.

'Sure about what?'

'Sure that you're . . . you know, *late*?'

There was a moment's baffled silence and then the tension snapped as they caught up with each other, and they found themselves laughing together.

'Only a week,' said Hope, regaining her composure. 'I'm not sure what to do.'

Hope had been late before and hadn't worried about it. But this was the first time it had happened since she and Michael had set up home together and, while they had occasionally talked of children, their discussions had always been inconclusive. And yet, Hope had continued the discussion in private, with herself. She would be thirty years old in just under two months, and time was pressing.

'Have you told Michael yet?'

'No. I mean, I'm not really sure what I'd be telling him.'

Alex looked at Hope with an exaggerated expression of astonishment.

'You know what I mean,' said Hope, bashfully. 'I thought I might get one of those kits?'

It was both a statement and a plea for advice. Alex thought for a moment, then took a drag on her cigarette. She exhaled, and spoke through the smoke. 'Save your money. Go see a doctor.'

'I'm worried though. Going to the doctor would be like confirming it.'

'Oh no,' said Alex, looking up at the ceiling. 'She's already in denial!'

'I deny that,' countered Hope, weakly. 'I don't know, though. What should I do?'

'Are you particularly stressed at the moment?'

'I've thought of that. I've thought of everything.'

'Is it Michael's? Is that why you won't tell him?'

'Oh really!'

Hope explained about the rain-soaked evening of three weeks before. She'd been drinking; Michael had been drinking; they hadn't used a condom.

'So you must be three weeks gone then,' said Alex. 'You must tell him. Before you do the test. It wouldn't be fair to spring it on him.'

Hope looked at her watch. 'Shit! I *am* late. I've got to rush.'
She hugged Alex briefly, and she was gone. With a single
corporate mind, the business community rose to resume their
conference. Alex quietly lit herself another cigarette.

Michael had drunk three pints and felt slightly the worse for
wear. Daytime drinking always tired him, so having left Jeffrey
he wandered slowly through town. Hope's university was
only a short distance from the centre by train. Michael knew
she would be leaving work soon, and he planned to intercept
her as she emerged from the railway station on her way to
the bus stop. He dawdled along the pedestrianized streets,
remembering when people had crowded under the wings of
the buildings as traffic roared through their midst. In those
days, people had spent as little time as possible in the city
centre and planned their shopping like a military campaign;
now, they relaxed. Pedestrianization had reclaimed the streets
for the people, and music and the smell of food filled the
summer air. Michael sat down on a vacant bench, dazed by it
all. The sun beat on the back of his neck and he drowsed with
boozy weariness. He closed his eyes, and all the smells and all
the sounds merged with the light behind his closed eyelids,
and he knew with an utter certainty that he was happy as he'd
never been before.

'Hello.' It was Hope's voice. Michael opened his eyes. 'How
was your drink?'

'Good. I think I'm pissed.'

'No you're not. Let's go for a drink.'

They stood together, and looked around. The smartly-
dressed people who had stalked purposefully to their offices
that morning were now emerging, crumpled and creased by
the day's exertions. The human rush hour was in full flow,
and Hope and Michael would usually allow themselves to

be carried out of the city on the monochrome-suited tide, anaesthetized by the breath and the hum of thousands of fellow travellers. When they made the journey together, they didn't talk. When they made it alone, they didn't think. Today, they would step out of the stream. Hope needed to talk.

'I need something to eat,' said Michael.

'Pizza,' said Hope.

The restaurant was decorated in the style of an American log cabin, with sepia-tinted posters advertising rodeos and offering rewards for various smoke-dried desperados. They were shown to a table by a pale, thin young man. His greeting was mechanical, and he managed to avoid any form of eye-contact with his customers.

'Poor kid,' said Hope, as soon as the youth was out of earshot. 'Straight out of school into a shit job. Where to from here?'

'Come on, Hope. It's still a job.'

'It's a crap job though, badly paid with no union representation and no prospects.'

Michael began to feel uncomfortable, as he always did when confronted with life's injustices.

'But you don't know what he gets paid, or what prospects there are.'

Hope was tired and hot. 'Oh, come off it, Michael! It's a shitty job and you know it. The turnover of staff in places like this is phenomenal. Does that suggest to you a contented workforce?'

'But it's just a stepping stone, isn't it? A first job, like a paper round or something.'

'That's not the point.'

'Yes it is. Kids . . .'

'No, it's *not* the point!' Hope slapped her hand firmly down on the table, crushing the end of Michael's sentence. 'The point is that the conditions are crap for however long you work here. A year, a month, a day. It doesn't matter. If you're exploited you're exploited, and these kids are exploited. They have no protection from unscrupulous managers, they're paid a pittance, and if they speak up against anything, they're out on their ear with no compensation. They're . . .'

In a calmer moment, Michael would have thrown his weight behind Hope's argument because, after all, he thought that Hope was probably right. But having been slapped down by her, Michael's defensiveness was colouring into crossness. He poked his finger at her to emphasize his own point and inadvertently knocked over a precariously wilting menu. It toppled towards Hope, taking a condiment set with it. Unfortunately, some previous diner had unscrewed the tops of both shakers, and cajun-spiced salt and dried oregano scattered across the table. Michael looked at the blast-area in disbelief, his riposte to Hope forgotten. Where had all that salt came from? And the oregano? The particles were everywhere.

He made to rise, thinking he should get a cloth or something, but a figure appeared at their table.

'No need for violence. I'll have it cleared up in a sec.'

Michael looked up at the waitress. He'd expected it to be the same young man who had unknowingly initiated their argument a few minutes earlier. But this was a young Asian woman who looked familiar. Hope, pushing the particles into a heap using a napkin, looked up at her and the waitress voiced Hope's thoughts. 'I know you, don't I?' she said, looking at Hope.

'And you,' she said, looking at Michael.

'I think so,' he answered. 'But I . . .'

'You're the taxi driver,' said Hope. 'Last month. The crash. You're Pam.'

'Parmjit. That's right.'

'I've got it,' said Michael, catching up. 'Your uncle owned a restaurant.'

'Still does. And it wasn't really a crash.'

'A scrape, then,' said Hope, laughing. 'How are you? What are you doing here?'

'Being exploited?' said Pam, laughing too.

'Oh no.' Hope groaned and sank her head into her hands. 'Were we really that loud?'

'Yep!' said Pam, cheerfully. 'It's all right. We all know the score here. Don't think that we don't know how to make the most of it.'

'Sorry,' said Hope, embarrassed.

'What happened to the taxi?' said Michael, changing the subject out of genuine curiosity.

'Still got it. I only work here four nights out of seven. Sometimes I do a stretch in the cab after I finish here.'

Michael was impressed. 'Where on earth do you get the energy?' he asked.

As she spoke, Pam swept the spilled condiments into a dustpan using a damp cloth.

'It's not difficult. I sleep late. I'm saving to go to university.'

'What, locally?' asked Hope.

'Yeah. I have to be near to my family. I need to help my grandmother.'

'Your grandmother?' said Hope.

'My mom died a couple of years back.'

Hope could see, in Parmjit's silent, downward glance, that the memory was still painful to her.

'Hope works at the university,' said Michael, changing the subject again.

'Doing what?'

'In the library,' said Hope. 'Sorry, "Learning Centre". I'm what used to be called a librarian, when it used to be called a library!'

'Well, whatever it's called, I'll see you there in October. I start my degree then.'

'What will you be studying?'

'History and Politics. Look, I've got to get on. I'll hand you back to Piers. I'm only on cleaning duties until it gets busy. It's really nice to see you again. Don't forget my uncle's restaurant!'

Parmjit winked through her smile, and moved away. When she seemed out of earshot Hope leaned forward and whispered to Michael.

'I like her. She seems to be nobody's fool.'

'I'd forgotten all about that taxi journey,' said Michael. 'Until now. That's odd, isn't it?'

Hope turned her immediate attention to the menu, but part of her wondered just how much of the rest of the evening Michael remembered.

Michael's lips left Hope's and travelled down to her neck where they slowly circled around her earlobes. He wasn't so much kissing her as touching her lightly with his mouth, and she loved the delicacy of his touch. When he reached her earlobes at last, the combination of ticklishness and sensuality had frozen her. She could barely breathe and held her breath, her eyes closed in concentration. But behind her eyes, other concerns vied with her desires.

Michael moved on, tracing her collarbone to the centre of her chest. Hope thought of her conversation with Alex. She'd tried to tell Michael during the meal but couldn't find the words. On the train journey home, Michael had read his paper while Hope stared out at the urban landscape unfurling against the translucent autumn sky, stalled in her attempt to communicate.

Michael cupped Hope's breast in his hand, pushing her nipple upwards. He took the small knot between his lips and drew it between his tongue and the roof of his mouth, sucking gently. Hope looked down at him in the dim light. She rolled slightly to one side and folded her arms around his head, watching him nuzzle her. She ran fingers through his thick, dark hair and wondered whether or not the baby would inherit this. His hands cupped and stroked her backside, his fingers tracing the crack from the small of her back to the moist folds of flesh between her legs. His fingers stroked her secret lips, and slowly pushed inside. As he did this, he moved his head down to her stomach, kissing her there.

For no reason that she could understand, Hope suddenly felt exposed and vulnerable. It was as though Michael had deserted her and her body had been invaded by a stranger. She wanted Michael back where she could hold him and she wanted *him* inside her. She rolled on to her back, pulling him back up to her, feeling for his penis. Michael sensed her urgency.

'I'll get my thingy,' he said, attempting to pull himself clear of her.

'No!' Hope's voice was a whisper and a roar. 'Do it now!'

She pulled his penis towards her. Michael, shocked and excited by the force of Hope's demands, allowed himself to enter her. She came easily and quickly, and Michael followed shortly after.

They lay together for a while. They held each other, both sensing that something had passed between them; an obscure understanding which neither understood. In the dim light, and into the calm silence of the room, Hope spoke softly. 'I think I might be pregnant.'

Michael lay still and silent. Hope needed some response.

'Are you OK with that?'

'I think so,' he replied sleepily.

3

Michael stared blankly at the computer screen. The phrase BE HONEST WITH YOURSELF tumbled slowly around the screen. Every week a different phrase cajoled the employees of Farsight Plastic Mouldings plc to work harder, or lavished false praise upon them, or treated them to enigmatic snatches of classical texts. He touched a key on the keyboard and the phrase disappeared, revealing the spreadsheet that recorded the stock for which he was responsible. A cup of coffee appeared under his nose.

'You look like you need this.'

The voice belonged to Preston Sinclair, an office colleague of Michael's.

'Cheers, Preston.'

Michael took the cup and sipped the vending-machine coffee. It was liquid, but it tasted like cardboard and seemed to suck the moisture from his mouth.

'Everything OK?'

'I'm just tired. Had a late night last night.'

Preston rolled a chair over to Michael's desk and sat down. 'Then you won't want to go for a drink after work?'

'Christ, Preston, I've only just got here!'

Preston laughed his deep, chuckling laugh, *yukyukyuk*, and Michael laughed too.

'Yeah, I might,' he said. 'Why not? Life's too short not to drink. Where?'

'I'll let you know. There's a few of us are going. Bring Hope along.'

Michael liked Preston a lot, admired his ingrained cheerfulness and his energy – he was always organizing outings for his colleagues, to pubs and clubs and concerts – and whatever Michael's mood, Preston usually cheered him up. But today Michael was impervious to Preston's sunshine, and the mention of Hope caused a phrase to tumble unbidden from Michael's lips.

'Hope's pregnant.'

The words seemed to come from somewhere else, and Michael realized instantly how odd they sounded. It was as though he were revealing the information to himself for the first time. Preston, however, smiled a big, wide smile.

'Nah? Really? Mikey, that's great!'

He said it and he meant it. Michael basked for a moment in the warmth of Preston's response, allowing himself a smile. He was surprised at Preston's enthusiasm and suddenly felt the need to qualify his confession.

'She *thinks* she is at any rate. She did one of those home test things and it came up positive. She's gone to the doc's to get it confirmed.'

The phone on Michael's desk rang and, as he reached for it, Preston scooted his chair back in the direction of his own desk, smiling his big smile and waving.

'Catch you later,' he said, and disappeared behind a row of filing cabinets.

Michael picked up the phone.

'Michael?' It was Hope, her voice controlled, steady. He knew why she was calling.

'What was it?'

'Positive,' she said.

There was silence on both ends of the phone. At last Michael spoke. 'So what happens now?'

Another silence. This time Hope spoke first. 'Michael?'

'Yeah?'

'I don't know what to do about this.'

Hope's voice seemed to come from a long way off.

'Are you all right?' Michael asked.

'I think so.' The voice was frail now. 'I just don't know what to do.'

'We'll talk later, OK? I told Preston.'

'Told him what?' Now her voice sounded edgy.

'That you think you're pregnant. He thinks it's great.'

'Don't tell anyone else,' she snapped.

'Why?'

'Just don't. I don't know what I want to do about it yet. Just don't tell anyone anything. Tell Preston to keep it to himself.'

The note of anger in Hope's voice unsettled Michael. 'OK, OK. I'll tell him.' Michael wasn't sure what the problem was, but he didn't want to talk about it over the phone. 'Let's talk later,' he said. 'Preston wants us to go for a drink after work. Are you on for that?'

'I'll phone later,' she said, flatly. 'You go if you want.'

They said their goodbyes, and Michael replaced the handset. He felt tired and unsettled. He wasn't sure what Hope thought about all of this, and so he wasn't sure how he should view the matter for himself. He picked up the handset again, and dialled Preston's number.

'Yeah?'

'Preston, don't tell anyone else yet, will you? Hope wants to keep it a secret for the time being.'

'No problem, Mikey.'

Michael hung up. He mechanically tapped the keyboard again and the tumbling phrase disappeared. But as it did so, Michael's mind registered a change. The phrase had read BE

Hope put the phone down on the coffee table. She felt heavy, almost dizzy with the weight of herself. She held her belly and took deep, steady draughts of air, expanding her chest to give the heart that battered against her ribcage more room. She was angry at Michael for betraying her to someone else, but she was also angry at him for forcing her to consider that she might have options other than having the baby. The phone rang, and Hope picked it up with effort. It was Alex. 'Hope?'

'Alex, I can't get my breath.'

'OK, OK,' said Alex quietly. 'You're having a panic attack. Just do as I say and you'll be all right. Starting from twenty, I want you to count backwards slowly. I'll help. By the time you get to one, you'll be fine.'

Hope colluded, and with Alex's gentle prompting she reached a state of calm until she was laughing with Alex, in a mixture of embarrassment and relief.

'Where did you learn that technique?' she asked.

'The truth? I made it up just now.'

More laughter.

'You fraud,' said Hope.

'So what brought it on?'

Hope told Alex about her positive pregnancy test result, and that Michael had told Preston. 'I didn't want anyone to know. Suppose I want to get rid of it, I don't want everyone knowing about it.'

'You're not going to, are you?' Alex's voice was toneless. 'Get rid of it, I mean.'

Hope hadn't even thought about it until Michael had mentioned telling Preston.

'Would you though?' Alex persisted.

Hope didn't know. She'd so little knowledge of maternity, of babies, of the practicalities of abortion. Since the test had shown up positive all her thoughts had been turned towards the idea of actually going through with the pregnancy.

'I don't know, Alex. I'm not sure that I'd want to. I'm not sure that I could.'

'What about Michael?'

Hope was silent again. She had no idea what Michael thought about abortion.

'I don't know. I think he'd probably want to keep it. We've talked about babies before. He'd like children. I would too. But I don't know. This is different. It's not what –'

'You need to talk to him.'

'I know, I know. I will.'

'This evening. Do it this evening. Don't put it off.'

Alex's tone was unusually urgent, and something troubled Hope about this. But she was too exhausted to pursue the matter now.

'He's going out with Preston for a drink. I'm not sure I will.'

'I'll come round to see you then. After work.'

'OK.'

And Alex rang off, leaving Hope to the sharpened silence of the room.

Alex put the phone down beside her on the sofa. She felt cold in spite of the central heating. She looked around her neat, sparsely furnished living room – at the stark vase on the angular, low bookcase, both jet black against the hard white of the wall, and her eyes came to rest on the solitary print, framed above the fireplace. It was Turner's *Steamer in a Snowstorm*, a maelstrom of smoke, snow and spray, the steamship barely visible at the heart of the picture.

As Alex contemplated the painting the whole scene seemed, as it always did, to swirl chaotically before her eyes, drawing her towards the still centre of the work. But as always, that centre eluded her, and she found herself caught up in the frantic motion of the painting, drawn not to calm waters but instead into a vortex. She knew that if she kept still and focused, that the vortex would grow, consuming her field of vision and dissipating her as it did so. The phone rang, and the vortex relinquished its hold on her.

'Alex, baby! How are ya?' The breezy Hollywood director's voice was Jeffrey's.

'Hello, Jeffrey. What do you want?'

The faintly impatient tone in Alex's voice appeared not to register with Jeffrey. 'Baby,' he wheedled, still in character, 'I wanna make you a star! I rilly rilly do! I see you naked, on a beach, surrounded by paparazzi, adorers, admirers, hangers-on . . .'

'Naked on a beach, eh? Not really my style, Jeffrey.'

'All right then,' persisted Jeffrey, now in his own accent, 'How about just naked? Here, in the studio?' And suddenly his accent was that of Groucho Marx. 'If I said you'd got a great body, kid, would you hold it against me?'

'Here,' said Alex, tiring of this. 'Are you making a pass at me? I'll tell Evette, young man!'

'Oh say it again, call me a young man again, I love flattery!'

'Oh get on with it, Jeffrey! What do you want? I'm busy,' Alex lied. The relentlessness of Jeffrey's humour annoyed her; he seemed to use humour as a mask. Alex preferred people not to hide themselves from her; though she knew that she herself hid from most of the people she knew.

'It's about Hope.'

'Go on,' she said, quietly.

'Her birthday, she's the big three-oh in six weeks, or whenever. I don't know what to get her.'

Alex relaxed. This subject was safe. 'You know about the party?' Alex inquired.

'Yeah, yeah. I'll be there. But I can't come empty-handed.'

'Oh you can, Jeffrey, you can!'

'*Oh Matron!*' exclaimed Jeffrey, in his Kenneth Williams *Carry On* voice. 'Seriously though, what can I get her? What would she like?'

Alex thought for a moment. 'Buy her some art. She likes watercolours. Buy her something decent in watercolour. Something a bit antiquey, with trees, mountains.'

'Something Lake Districtish?'

'Wordsworth. The Romantics. That kind of thing. I don't like it myself, but Hope does. I'll be seeing her later. If you like, I'll probe her to see if there's anything in particular she'd like.'

'You'll *probe* her? Ding Dong! Can I watch?'

'Jeffrey, get off the phone.'

'OK,' he said, laughing. 'I know when I'm not wanted. *Ciao* baby!'

The line went dead, leaving Jeffrey's breezy voice ringing in Alex's head. She settled back once more into the emptiness of the room.

Jeffrey ended the call and speed-dialled another. 'Hello?'

'It's me,' he said. 'Can you talk?'

Jeffrey reminded Evette about Hope's thirtieth birthday, and reported his conversation with Alex. Evette knew that Jeffrey was indirectly asking her to buy the present from them both. This wasn't solidarity on Jeffrey's part. It was a background assumption of his relationship with Evette that she carried out the domestic tasks, while he got on with the important task of creative labour. Evette appeared to accept this assumption; whether this was out of laziness, cowardice, or devotion to Jeffrey, no one knew.

'I suppose we could get some prints framed for her.'

'Something antiquey,' he specified, focusing her mind for her. 'You know, lakes, mountains, trees. Pretty baa-lambs.'

'I'll give Michael a ring. See if I can get any ideas from him,' she said.

Jeffrey rang off and Evette immediately phoned Michael.

'Hello. It's me.'

'Hope?' asked Michael, not sure of the voice.

'Evette.'

With relief, Michael said hello. Evette explained the reason for the call; Michael promised to think about it. He knew of an antique shop that Hope liked. 'It's a second-hand shop really,' he explained. 'A bit of a junk shop.'

Before Evette rang off, Michael mentioned that he would be going for a drink later that evening if she and Jeffrey wanted to join them. When he put the handset down, he thought about the offer he'd made to take Evette to the antique shop so that she could see for herself what it was like. It hadn't been a definite arrangement; he didn't want Evette to feel that she had to go with him if she didn't want to. But she'd sounded keen and had said that she would get back to him about it. He hoped she would.

Michael looked at the screen of his computer. The phrase had changed back again: BE HONEST WITH YOURSELF.

Michael shut down his PC and turned from his desk. He wondered whether or not to phone Hope before he left the office. She hadn't phoned him back as she'd said she would, and he was now torn, part worried about her, part angry at her, and part pleased to defer discussion of the issue. He decided not to phone her. Already he felt that their relationship had altered, though he was reluctant to face this feeling now. He was tired and needed to wind down. He put on his coat and left the office.

4

Hope felt bloated, as though her stomach contained a medium-sized balloon.

'Jesus,' she said to Alex. 'It can't be big enough to feel yet.'

They were sitting in one of the cafeterias on the campus, having a mid-morning break from work.

'You're imagining it,' said Alex, drawing on her cigarette before carefully blowing the smoke away from Hope. 'You know it's in there and you think that it's causing any sensation you might have in your stomach.'

Hope instinctively rubbed her abdomen.

'I've never had a bad stomach in my life,' she said morosely.

'Have some more coffee, sorry . . . tea.'

'No. I think I'd like some water.'

Alex rose and sauntered across the body of the crowded café, watched by Hope, who realized more than ever before just how beautiful her friend was. She walked sensually, her undulating hips caressed by her slacks, her waist – wasp-thin in spite of her love affair with the confectionery counter – swaying like a salsa dancer's. Her shoulders were strong, but didn't undermine the powerfully feminine figure that bent slightly and erotically forward to flirt with the young counter attendant who couldn't do enough to assist her as she assembled her tray. Hope watched with envy as several young male heads tracked Alex as she swayed back across the floor to their table. None of these young men looked in Hope's direction. She felt dowdy – a pregnant, dull, nearly-thirty-year-old woman who no one would give a second glance to. And this was only the beginning.

'Are you all right?' said Alex, noticing Hope's glum expression.

'It's my indigestion,' she said.

Hope knew that Alex meant well, but she was in no mood for being handled like a sickly child. Moreover, Alex's sympathizing only accentuated Hope's sense that she was fading in the light of her friend's effortless beauty. Alex lit another cigarette.

'Do you have to smoke?' said Hope, sharply.

This took Alex by surprise, and she immediately extinguished the cigarette. 'Sorry,' she said, inwardly excusing her friend on the grounds of her condition. 'I wasn't thinking. Let's move to the No Smoking area.'

Hope immediately regretted her outburst.

'No, I'm all right. I'm just not at my best.'

Hope felt even worse now. She stared down at the fingernail she'd chipped while opening a cupboard earlier that morning.

'No, you're right,' said Alex. 'I shouldn't make you a passive smoker. Come on, we'll move.'

Now, on top of everything else, Hope felt controlled. Everything she thought, everything she heard, everything she saw seemed to exacerbate her sense of worthlessness – and the more helpful and considerate Alex tried to be, the more Hope felt diminished by her attentions. She was close to tears.

'Please, Alex,' she pleaded. 'I'm OK. Honestly. I'll be all right.' And the tears momentarily spilled over.

Alex watched her friend, not knowing what to do next. Hope briefly and self-consciously dabbed at her eyes with a serviette. Alex wanted to reach over and touch Hope's hand, but she knew that she was somehow implicated in Hope's turmoil. She waited for Hope to compose herself.

'Sorry,' said Hope. 'I don't know what's happening to me. I feel like shit.'

'Hormones,' said Alex. 'It's not you. You're being dictated to by your biology.'

'Great,' said Hope, recovering herself a little. 'And me a democrat too.'

At that moment her phone sounded; a text from Michael.

evrythng ok? am in mtg bored stoopid

Hope thought of him sitting in a meeting composing text messages, keeping in touch. She felt a sudden and profound love for him, a feeling that hit her so forcefully that her head swam. The sensation quickly passed, but Hope remained buoyed by the thought that Michael was thinking of her in his meeting, that at random moments throughout his day she would be on his mind.

Michael thought of Hope. He thought of her in order to reassure himself that he wasn't going to do anything that would hurt her in any way. Not that he *would* do anything, of course. But just in case anything happened that shouldn't happen. He hadn't mentioned to Hope that he would be meeting Evette this afternoon, but he reasoned that, as he was meeting her in order to help her purchase Hope's birthday present, to have told Hope would surely have spoiled the surprise. That he'd booked the entire afternoon off in order to do this might have seemed excessive, but he hadn't mentioned this to Evette, so he wasn't expecting to spend the entire afternoon with her, was he?

In truth, Michael had already spent much longer than an afternoon with Evette. He'd lived with her in his head ever since that night in the bar, the night that Hope thought she'd become pregnant. He remembered hazily, but surely, that he'd fantasized that night that it was Evette beneath him as he'd made love with Hope. He'd closed his eyes and looked into Evette's and, this time, instead of leaving him stranded at the edge of the forest, her butterfly eyes had drawn him into the mysterious darkness beneath her copper fringe. He'd been lost in the forest with her since then.

And now, shadowed from the pale September sunshine, Michael stood on the steps of the old Town Hall, waiting for Evette. He was nervous, and cold in spite of the sunshine. He felt awkward and he tried to keep himself out of sight of the crowds surging across the square in front of him. Evette was already ten minutes late, and Michael's discomfort increased with each passing minute. He knew that there would shortly come a time when he would have to decide on a course of action. He would either have to abandon his vigil and head home, or he would have to phone Evette. He felt the slender bulk of the phone in his pocket, and decided to wait another ten minutes before calling her.

Another fifteen minutes passed. The phone trilled in his pocket – a reply from Hope to his last text.

poor u. njoy yr lunch. having mine w alex xx

Michael sat down on the steps. He thought of the gap between his fantasies about Evette and his importance to her, and felt foolish. She had his mobile number. She could have called to say that she was going to be late, or apologized for not turning up. He told himself that he was annoyed with Evette, and his annoyance became his excuse for not phoning her himself. He stood up to leave.

'Hello.'

He hadn't seen her hurrying up to him. She looked immaculate and officious in her dark, plum-coloured suit and patent shoes. Her copper hair was meticulously straight and her eyes regarded him from behind rimless lenses suspended beneath her razor-sharp fringe.

'So, where's this antique shop?'

Michael stepped out from the shadow into the sunshine and looked at her, his mood shifting as instantly from dark to light.

'Where were you? I was just about to call,' said Michael, without reproach.

'I got stuck in a meeting. Sorry. Let's go. I've got to get back for three.'

Michael registered this deadline but didn't dwell on it. 'We'd better get a taxi there then. You'll never get back in time if we walk.'

'We can drive if you like. My car's parked in town.'

'OK,' said Michael. 'Let's go.'

The car journey passed in pleasantries. They pulled up opposite the antique shop, and got out of the car. They stood on the pavement, looking across the road at the shabby exterior of the shop and at the jaded, peeling sign – CHARRINGTON'S – suspended precariously over a dirty window crammed with glass cases full of old toy cars and trains, grubby glassware and militaria. The shop was in the middle of a terrace of old shops, most of which were closed and boarded up, sealed with layers of tattered fly-posters advertising long-forgotten gigs by defunct bands. In the air there hung a faint but distinct aroma of roasting spices, its richness and complexity jarring with the seediness of the surroundings. Michael could not see the restaurant and wondered briefly whether or not he should suggest trying to find it. But when he looked at Evette, the idea instantly evaporated. He immediately sensed Evette's dislike of the area.

'That's not an antique shop,' she said curtly. 'It's a junk shop.'

Feeling responsible for this shift in Evette's mood, Michael sought to placate her. 'It's not all junk. It's a bit of a mix, but that's good because the bloke who runs it doesn't charge too much for the good stuff.'

Evette was having none of it. She scowled at Michael, said, 'Let's get this over with,' and walked off across the road towards the shop. Michael rushed after her. At the door, Evette stepped aside to let Michael open it, as though she'd no intention of touching anything in the shop if she could get away with it. They stepped into the gloom of the interior and paused to allow their eyes to adjust. The shop was crammed with dark, massive furniture receding towards a narrow doorway through which artificial light shone weakly. It seemed to make the room seem even darker.

'Christ, we'll never find anything in here,' said Evette, incredulously.

'I know where the pictures are,' said Michael.

He edged forward towards the door at the back of the shop and stepped through it. Inside was a small desk cluttered with scuffed lever-arch files, dog-eared books, old newspapers, and gently-drifting cigarette ash. A small man sat behind the desk – aged anything from fifty to ninety, Michael thought – brittle and bent, with a mottled purple nose, and weak eyes distorted by bottle-end glasses. His hair was the colour of sellotape, and it was greased back thinly over his head. A cigarette butt drooped from the corner of his mouth, and he wheezed as he smoothed his crumpled newspaper down on to the desktop. When he spoke, his voice rattled through thick layers of tar-filled mucus.

'Need any help?'

The situation for Michael wasn't getting any better. As Evette followed him through the doorway and caught sight of the lone proprietor, her distaste of the place increased. Michael knew he had to get her away.

'Erm . . . we're just browsing,' said Michael, trying to retreat past Evette.

'No we're not,' said Evette bluntly, pushing by him. 'We want to look at pictures. Paintings. Whatever. Where are they?'

'There's a room upstairs,' the old man wheezed. He made to get up, failed, and sank back into his seat, coughing. He pointed in the direction of a wooden staircase in the corner of the small room. 'Take a look if you like.'

The sentence tailed off into a racking cough. Michael watched the old man, appalled and embarrassed. He'd been here before with Hope, but the squalor of the place, and of its occupant, had never struck him so forcefully. He wished that he'd never invited Evette along. Evette, meanwhile, made straight for the stairs, and so Michael followed her.

The room upstairs was lighter than the one below. No heavy furniture could be brought this far up to block the light from the windows. Evette seemed to relax a little here. Michael watched her for a moment as she bent over several dark-framed paintings stacked against the wall, and he felt the beat of desire as her suit stretched across the curve of her hips. He turned away, embarrassed by his lust, and began looking through another stack of paintings.

'What kind of thing are we looking for?' asked Evette, regarding a painting of cows in a field. 'Not this, for sure.'

Michael pulled paintings forward. A seaside landscape, but clumsily executed and with too much blue. A harbour scene, with small fishing boats. An estuary. All seemed painted by the same amateurish hand. He moved on to the next stack.

'Landscapes,' he said. 'Watercolours. Like this.'

He pulled a small painting out from behind a stack of six larger ones. It was a lakeland scene, a hill forested to one side, with a lake in the middle distance and mountains beyond. Michael was no expert, but there was something about the quality of the painting, the richness of the colours, that set it apart from anything else he'd seen so far. He took it across to Evette and tilted it towards the light. 'What do you think?' he asked.

The picture – no more than twelve inches across by eight inches high – was in a plain, dark-varnished frame that looked to be in reasonably good condition. The back of the picture was sealed with broad parcel tape, brown and stained with age, and beginning to peel in places.

Evette scrutinized it. 'Not bad,' she said. 'What about this one?'

She lifted a slightly larger picture up to the light, and held it beside Michael's. Evette's was also a landscape, but both could see immediately that Michael's painting was the more accomplished of the two; the detail was finer, the colour richer, and they both agreed that it had something indescribable that Evette's lacked.

'The more you look at it, the deeper you seem to go into it,' Michael said. 'You're sort of drawn into the landscape. With that one, all you see is a painting.'

Evette looked again at the painting in her hand, and then at Michael's. 'I think you're right,' she said, finally. 'But will Hope like it?'

'I think so,' said Michael.

'I hope so,' said Evette.

To Michael, this sounded unnervingly like a warning.

It was Monday morning, almost noon, and Hope sat in the toilet cubicle taking long, slow breaths. Was this morning sickness? She didn't think so; she wasn't nauseous. It felt more like disorientation, a loss of self, like the faintness brought on by lack of food, though she knew that she couldn't eat anything now. She felt on the verge of tears, and the thought of dissolving in front of her colleagues fuelled her self-contempt, but also her resolve to harden herself before returning to her desk. Feeling no dizziness, Hope stood up and left the cubicle.

'Hello,' said a familiar voice. 'Are you all right? You look a bit wobbly?'

Hope had stood up too quickly. Suddenly light-headed and dizzy again, she tottered back towards the cubicle.

'Woah, steady,' said Parmjit, taking Hope by the arm.

'Parmjit,' said Hope, weakly. 'What are you doing here?

'I'm enrolling. Come on, let's get you some sweet tea.'

Hope sipped the sweetest tea she'd ever tasted, and felt better. They sat in the utilitarian surroundings of the learning centre canteen.

'Can I ask you something?' said Parmjit, cautiously.

'Ask me anything,' said Hope. 'You bought the tea.'

'OK. This will sound stupid, but . . . can I ask, are you pregnant?'

Hope's first impulse was to deny that she was. But she knew that even if she wanted to keep it a secret, in a few months' time her body would betray her condition to anyone who saw her.

'You are, aren't you?' said Parmjit, increasingly sure of her ground.

'Yes,' said Hope. The answer tumbled out in spite of herself and made her blush; she realized that she'd entered a new world, a world in which she was a pregnant woman.

'Wow,' said Parmjit. 'Well done! You're so lucky!'

'Am I?' said Hope, hardly aware of the sullen tone in her voice.

'Of course you are,' said Parmjit. 'I love kids! I'd like dozens of them!'

'Wouldn't they wear you down? One seems like it might be enough trouble to me.'

'No, no. You should never only have one child. Only children are always so self-centred. They don't learn in the same way as you do when you have brothers and sisters to contend with

– social skills and stuff. How many brothers and sisters have you got?'

'Well,' said Hope, deliberately drawing out her answer. 'None, actually.'

Parmjit, suddenly embarrassed, held her hand to her mouth.

'Oh, I'm sorry, I didn't mean . . . God, I'm such a prat!'

Hope wasn't offended. She liked Parmjit and wanted to reassure her. 'Michael has a sister though. She has two kids.' Parmjit didn't look reassured, so Hope changed the subject. 'What made you think I was pregnant?'

'Dunno,' said Parmjit sheepishly. 'Woman's intuition?'

Over tea, Hope learned that Parmjit was the only girl among four brothers. She also learned that, with the exception of the second brother – Kamaljit, or 'Kammi' – they expected her to remain at home with their grandmother, or at least to help out in the family shop or restaurant.

'They want me to be a waitress,' she said bitterly. 'At home and at work. They don't even want me to wait on tables in the restaurant because that's what they employ young men to do. They just want me to serve drinks. It's demeaning.'

'But you drive a taxi,' said Hope, confused.

'Yeah, but I had to fight for that. Even now it's not a topic of conversation. My brothers tolerate it, but my father never mentions it. He resents his daughter driving a cab. I can't believe that I just used 'tolerate' and 'brothers' in the same sentence!' She paused and then laughed briefly, sadly. 'Kammi's good to me, though. We watch out for each other. He's at university in London studying medicine. None of the others could be bothered to go to university. They all wanted to be businessmen.'

'What does your mother say?' said Hope. Even as she said it, she remembered Parmjit telling her in the pizza restaurant that her mother had died recently. Now it was Hope who was embarrassed. 'Oh, Pam! I'm sorry, I forgot.'

'It's all right. My gran lives with us. We're very close, me and my gran. She doesn't say much. She's a bit timid, you know? Knows her place in a man's world? It's the way she was brought up. She's learned to keep her own counsel. Talks to me, though.'

'What about your father?'

'Oh, he talks all the time. Mostly pontificating on things he knows very little about. He's the most narrow-minded, reactionary, conservative . . .'

'Steady on, Pam!'

'We don't get on well. He's a bigot. It's almost as though he proves his British credentials by being more bigoted than the natives. You should hear him going on about immigrants invading this country . . .'

'He just sounds insecure.'

'That's no excuse. He's so completely right wing.'

Hope saw, for the first time since she'd known Parmjit, the world of sadness that lay behind her breezy facade.

'Anyway, the most important thing in my life at the moment is to get my degree.'

'What did you say you were going to study?'

'History and Politics. All those jobs I do, it's to help pay my way. My dad won't give me the money; says it's a waste of time. But I've saved a lot of money now, and he's not going to stop me.'

Hope registered the determination in Parmjit's voice and was genuinely impressed. She thought of her own parents, how their initial supportiveness had receded when she chose to attend a modern Midlands university instead of the Oxford or Cambridge they'd expected. She thought of them now, sitting in judgement upon her constant failure to live up to their expectations. They would have considered her job as a librarian demeaning, like working in a shop but without even the responsibility of handling money. They would surely, too, have found some reason to disapprove of Michael, so heaven knows what they would have made of her being pregnant with his child. But maybe she was underestimating them. After all, she was pregnant with their first grandchild . . .

'Everything all right?' said Parmjit. 'You drifted off.'

'Sorry,' said Hope. Then she had an idea. 'Listen, I'm having a party to celebrate my thirtieth birthday this weekend. Would you come? I'd really like you to.'

'I don't know,' said Parmjit, surprised. 'I wouldn't know anyone.'

'You know me. And you know Michael. We'll look after you. Please say yes.'

Parmjit hesitated still.

'Bring a friend,' said Hope, urging her to acceptance. She had no idea why, but it was suddenly very important to her that Parmjit be there. 'Bring your gran, if she'll come.'

Michael sat in his office. The phone on his desk rang simultaneously with the mobile in his breast pocket. He picked up the landline: 'Hold on please.'

He pressed the 'mute' button. The mobile told him that Evette was calling him. 'Hold on a sec,' he said to her. 'Got another call.'

He picked up the landline, cancelled the mute. 'Sorry about that. Can you call back?'

'It's Jeffrey,' the voice said. 'Give me a bell when you can.'

Michael hung up and returned his attention to Evette.

'Busy man,' she said in a neutral voice.

'In demand, as usual,' said Michael. 'Everything OK?'

She told him that Jeffrey had looked over the picture and thought it quite impressive. She'd wanted to dismantle the painting to clean up the frame, maybe get a new one, but Jeffrey had thought that Hope might enjoy doing any necessary renovation herself.

'Yes, she'd like that,' said Michael.

'I cleaned it up anyway. Just superficially. I hope that's OK.'

'It'll be fine,' said Michael. 'OK for Saturday?'

'We'll be there.'

Michael registered the plural. Was she warning him off? Was she even aware that he was interested in her?

When he said goodbye, he turned to his landline to return Jeffrey's call. Jeffrey asked exactly the same question as Evette had, and Michael gave him the same answer. As he turned back to his computer screen, he realized that he hadn't told Jeffrey that he'd just spoken to Evette.

5

In the small galley kitchen, Michael stood wreathed in steam, momentarily bewildered amid the clutter of food preparation. He'd lost track of what he was doing. There was food on every available surface, dumbly awaiting some sentient being to pull it all together and provide coherence. Michael stared dumbly back. He'd been preparing food for Hope's birthday party later that evening. But he could not bring the food back into focus. Giving up for the moment, he poured himself a fresh glass of red wine and gulped a mouthful down.

In his mind the idea of fatherhood was slowly gestating. So abstract was the prospect, so indeterminate the idea, that in a certain light it could seem quite attractive. He could see himself holding the bundle, bottle-feeding it, changing its nappies, pushing the pushchair – the many things he'd seen his sister do for her two children. He even quite liked the idea of having someone call him 'dad'. Fatherhood was a remote but pleasant idea.

Yet something nagged him. Through the curtains of steam that hung about the tiny room, Michael caught sight of an egg box, lying open on a worktop. Half a dozen flesh-coloured domes sat in orderly rows, and suddenly each one was a hairless cancer victim ravaged by chemotherapy. He gulped down another mouthful of wine. Maybe somewhere, in the dark recesses of his mind, he was frightened by the idea that his child could be born with some awful disease ticking away inside it. He remembered that his grandfather had died of a brain tumour, or cancer, or something like that (he wasn't quite sure of the details). And his father had suffered an attack of angina only last year. Cancer and heart disease rife in the family! Perhaps he'd already sentenced his child to death? And suppose that it were born with Down's syndrome, or a cleft palate, or three legs, or no ears, or webbed fingers. Would he love it? *Could* he love it?

Michael realized that he was sweating. He took another swig of wine, put his glass down on the work surface, and reached up to open the window directly above the eggs. As he did this, his elbow caught an empty beer bottle that had been left on top of the tall refrigerator. This small green article fell sideways and then rolled off the edge on to the eggs.

'Oh shit!' said Michael, stepping backwards to avoid scrambled egg all over his trousers.

But as he back-pedalled, his elbow toppled his wine glass, emptying the ruby-red contents on to his jeans.

'Shit! Fucking shit!'

Once again, Michael encountered at first hand the curious phenomenon of how a small amount of liquid seems to multiply its volume a hundredfold as it flattens across a plane.

'Fuckshitbollocks!' he exclaimed. 'Shitshitshit!'

Hope appeared in the doorway. She leaned against the door jamb and watched Michael frantically dabbing at his backside with a tea towel.

'Everything all right?' she said, making no attempt to conceal her amusement at the sight.

Michael refocused his venom on this living target. 'What the fuck does it look like, Hope? I'm glad I'm entertaining you while you stand there doing fuck all!'

The sight of Michael's wine-dark seat was too amusing for his barbs to have any effect.

'Come on, Michael,' she said mischievously. 'You can't expect me to help. It's my birthday.'

The doorbell sounded.

'I'll get it,' she said. 'I wouldn't want you to lose your concentration.'

With Michael's 'fuck off' echoing along the hallway behind her, Hope guffawed her way to the front door.

Alex's throaty laugh pierced the thick atmosphere of Michael's kitchen long before she appeared in the doorway. By the time she got there, Michael had cleared up the mess, recharged his glass and was now standing with his wine-soaked backside turned away from the door. Alex stood in the doorway, grinning wickedly.

'What's cooking, Michael?'

'Hello, Alex. How goes it? I've actually forgotten what's cooking.'

By now Michael was feeling sorry for his outburst, and Hope sensed this. Alex, however, continued to stir the waters.

'I find that wine usually goes straight to my *head*,' she said, very evidently craning her neck in order to ogle the massive stain on Michael's trousers. Hope swallowed her laughter in the doorway behind Alex.

'Aren't you going to wring me out a glass then?' She edged closer to him in the narrow space, twisting her mouth into a playful drool. 'If you took them off I could just . . . *suck* them myself,' she breathed, casting a conspiratorial glance back at Hope. 'It'd save on the washing-up,' she added, brightly.

'Now, now, Alex,' said Hope, mock-seriously. 'It's not a good vintage you know. He's had those trousers on for a week. They have, erm . . . an *unusual* bouquet.'

Alex gave Michael the mandatory hug and kiss, and grabbed herself a glass from the shelf.

'Light me!' she said, and held the glass out to him.

'I'll have to open another bottle. I'll bring you a glass through. Hope?'

Hope declined, but the connection between them had been re-established; everything was all right again, for the moment.

It was eight-fifteen. A decorating table had been set up in the front room, now supporting a mound of food; sofas and chairs had been cleared of their mundane clutter; candles burned throughout the two rooms; the kitchen work surfaces were covered with a regiment of wines and spirits, soft drinks and glasses. The fridge had been cleared of as much food as possible to make way for beer and white wine. Hope and Alex sat watching TV in the living room, sipping drinks and critiquing the game-show contestants. Michael – now shaved and dressed in clean trousers – stood in the kitchen, mobile phone in hand. He sent a text to Preston:

where r u?

Though Michael had suggested that people arrive at around eight-thirty, he knew that no one would come that early. He expected people to meet for a drink or two in a pub before coming to the party. Preston's reply confirmed his suspicion.

in pub on way 20 mins or so

Michael picked up his wine glass and left the kitchen for the living room. As he crossed the hallway, the doorbell rang. He opened the door and was met by Parmjit, dressed in jeans and a black vest short enough to expose her pierced navel; and an older, smaller woman, dressed in a vivid blue sari trimmed with ornate gold edging.

'Are we late?' said Parmjit.

Michael had no idea that she'd been invited, and his surprise registered with Parmjit.

'Sorry,' she said. 'Hope invited us. Honest. We've brought food. Is that OK?'

Michael looked down at the plastic bags hanging from Parmjit's hand. The woman standing behind her held a shallow cardboard box, a sheet of aluminium foil concealing its contents.

'Sorry,' said Michael, swiftly adjusting to the idea that Parmjit had arrived. 'Sorry. Come on in. You're the first to arrive. Well, almost.'

Michael stepped aside to make way for the two women. He felt oddly pleased to see Parmjit again, who never failed to surprise him.

'This is my grandmother,' she said as she stepped past him into the hallway. 'Gran, this is Michael.'

The woman nodded at Michael respectfully, briefly making eye contact with him, before following her granddaughter into the house.

'Her English is not so good,' said Parmjit over her shoulder. 'In fact, it's almost non-existent. Where's the kitchen?'

As Parmjit passed the living room she met Hope, who had heard the unfamiliar voices at the door and had come to investigate. Michael watched the two women hug, bemused at the affection between them. Where had this come from, he wondered? It was going to be an interesting evening.

At its height, there had been around twenty-five people crammed into the small terraced house, but now – at half an hour past midnight – a hard core of eleven remained. Preston, Michael, Jeffrey and Alex were in the kitchen, standing amid the anarchy of empty and near-empty bottles, used and abandoned glasses, and the detritus – corks, bottle tops, half-eaten food on strewn paper plates – produced in the course of the evening. Michael, who was sozzled, was being held up by the kitchen unit against which he leaned. Animated by alcohol, the other three were talking loudly to each other, but Michael could barely follow their conversation. His head was spinning, and the attempt to stabilize his world absorbed him. Hope appeared in the doorway.

'Everyone all right?'

Hope had agreed with Michael earlier in the day that she would announce her pregnancy during the course of the party. She'd done this in her own way, person to person, and had received warm congratulations – and some ribbing – from the guests. She thought it odd to be telling their friends when they hadn't yet said anything to Michael's parents, but for some reason Michael was reluctant, just yet, to tell them the good news. She didn't want to push him too hard on this – they were *his* parents, after all – and he had now agreed that they should tell them soon after the party. But she sensed that Michael was uncomfortable about the whole business of telling people, and she'd noticed that his consumption of alcohol, already fairly heavy, had increased as people began to congratulate him. As she stepped into the kitchen Hope, who hadn't been drinking alcohol at all, could see that Michael had had enough.

'We're in the garden,' she said to the others. 'It's lovely outside. Karl's spliffing up. Come on out.'

The room emptied, leaving Hope and Michael together.

'Are you OK? You look like you're about to collapse.'

Michael's answer was slurred, but just about comprehensible. He was all right; just a bit pissed.

'Well, don't drink any more, OK? Drink a glass or three of water. I'm going to go outside. Come out when you've drunk some water. The fresh air might do you some good.'

As Hope left the kitchen, she inadvertently switched off the light. Finding himself in the dark all alone, Michael's attempt to appear sober and upright gave way. He slid down to the floor, dumbfounded by an overwhelming weariness.

The pull of the earth seemed for a moment to steady him in his whirling universe, and a strange euphoria washed through him. He realized that he was happy where he was, there on the floor of the kitchen, and didn't want to ever move again. It was in this position that he received a series of visitors.

Hope was in the living room with Parmjit, Evette and Ben – a librarian she worked with. Parmjit's grandmother sat on a chair by the table with her hands folded in her lap. She said nothing, but she didn't look bored. Throughout the evening, Parmjit had spoken to her quietly, in Gujarati, giving her information about the guests when she could. Occasionally Mrs Patel would leave the room, returning with a small plate of food, or a glass of water.

'Is your gran OK?' asked Hope.

Parmjit turned, spoke briefly and confidentially to her grandmother, and received a small wave in return accompanied by a brief nod of the head.

'She's fine.'

'I'm not trying to throw you out, but she doesn't mind being out this late, does she?'

Hope was worried that in spite of Parmjit's assurance, her grandmother might be wanting to get off home.

'Honestly Hope, she's enjoying herself. Dad wouldn't approve – her being out this late – but he's away at a business convention in Nottingham with my brothers. We've got the run of the house till next Tuesday. Believe me, she loves being out.'

Hope leaned forward conspiratorially.

'They're smoking dope in the back garden. Will she mind?'

'Not if she doesn't go out there. I don't know. She probably wouldn't know what it was. And if she did, she'd probably want to try it!'

'The food was great by the way. You didn't have to bring anything.'

Parmjit and her grandmother's food had proved very popular with the guests, especially with Hope, whose appetite of late had stalled on account of a strange taint to her palate, as though she'd been sucking an old coin.

'I hope Michael wasn't offended. He must have been at it for hours getting that lot ready.'

Michael, worried that he hadn't prepared enough food, had actually been pleased that additional supplies had arrived.

'Believe me, Michael ate more of it than anyone else. He loves Indian food. But he can't cook it for toffee. Maybe you could teach him. Those samosas . . .'

'I hope you like the chocolates,' said Parmjit, catching sight of the presents strewn around the room. 'I wasn't really sure what to get you. I really like that painting, though.'

Michael had propped Evette and Jeffrey's painting against the chimney breast on the mantelpiece. Hope was pleased with the painting – watercolours could be rather lifeless but this one had a luminosity which she liked. It wasn't an easy trick to pull off, though it was the effect that most watercolourists sought.

'I wasn't expecting a present,' said Hope. 'I'm just glad you came. You and your gran.'

As they spoke together, Mrs Patel got up and left the room, glass in hand.

Michael sat with his eyes closed. But in his mind's eye he could see that each individual brain cell had separated from all the others and, glowing bright orange for no reason that he could think of, they had all begun to whirl around in his head, like a million autumn leaves caught in a whirlwind.

The effect was exhilarating. Then the swarm of cells began to eddy to and fro, twisting and looping like a flock of birds, directed by a primordial collective intelligence. The fragments of intelligence swarmed this way and that through what seemed to be a forest, though he could see no trees and no undergrowth distinctly. He followed wherever the swarm went, strangely attracted by the fluidity with which it manoeuvred, not quite able to keep up with the rapidity of movement. And so he was unprepared when the swarm turned and flew straight at him, suddenly and completely enveloping him. Then, just as suddenly, and as completely, the swarm had gone and a face hovered before him, indistinct but somehow familiar all the same. It was Parmjit's grandmother, Mrs Patel, her face glowing in the warm half-light pouring from the fridge. She held a glass of clear liquid in her hand, which she offered to Michael. He took it and drank it down.

'It's nectar,' she said. 'You'll need it for strength.'

'Huh?' said Michael, not understanding at all.

'You've begun a long journey and there will be many obstacles and detours along the way. You will need strength and wisdom, and you will need to make many decisions about which path to follow.'

'What?'

'You must decide what it is that you want with Evette.'

'*Evette?*'

'And you must decide what it is that you want with Hope.'

'*Hope?*'

'But you must also realize that the most important thing is no longer what *you* want. There is another now who has needs that must be attended to. You must find some way to unite the needs of this person with your own desires. This is not easy, but it can be done. Drink up. You will need the nectar for the journey.'

'*Nectar?*' said Michael, still befuddled. 'What are you talking about?'

The face before him remained resolutely irresolute.

'Nectar,' it said.

'But . . . but *you can't speak English!*' Michael splurted out in exasperation. He'd no idea what the old woman was talking to him about.

'But I'm not speaking to you,' she said. 'You're drunk and you're talking to yourself. Just don't blame me if I say anything that you don't want to hear.'

'Such as?'

'Such as: Hope's pregnant now and you should support her and not run around after Evette.'

'Christ, you sound like my mother. At least, you sound like she would if she knew that Hope was pregnant and that I was running around after Evette.'

'But I probably *am* your mother talking to you. You only see *me* because I'm Asian, an exotic outsider, a perfect vehicle for this mystical exchange about butterflies and nectar.'

'*Butterflies?*' said Michael.

'It's your lurking racism that's put me here in front of you talking about this stuff.'

'You've lost me,' said Michael.

'That's the truest thing you've said to yourself for a long time now.'

'I don't know what you're talking about. Am I really saying all this to myself? Surely if I *were* talking to myself, I'd understand what I was saying, wouldn't I?'

'Sadly, no. We do not always understand what we are saying, even to ourselves. And then of course we do not always want to *hear* what we are saying to ourselves.'

Michael fell silent at this. After a moment, Mrs Patel spoke again quietly.

'I must go now. We've talked long enough and people will begin to miss us. But don't forget. *Nectar!*'

And with that, the face exploded into a million shards and poured once more into the forest.

As Mrs Patel came into the room, glass of water in hand, Evette stood up and left for the garden. The night air was cool after the closeness of the living room. Preston and Alex sat together on an old wooden bench, while Jeffrey and Karl sat close by on chairs. Jeffrey was drawing on a freshly-rolled joint, while Karl was busy rolling another. Preston shuffled along the seat, and Evette sat down between him and Alex. Jeffrey, holding his breath, passed the joint to Alex who took a long draw.

'I couldn't cope. I'd be all over the place. Your life wouldn't be your own,' said Karl, without lifting his head from the object of his labours. 'Fuck that.'

Jeffrey had exhaled at last. 'Well, you can say that. But if you were pregnant – say you got pregnant by accident – you'd immediately change. You'd be swamped by hormones and you'd love the idea.'

'That's not necessarily true,' said Alex.

'I couldn't get pregnant even by accident,' protested Karl.

'Rubbish!' said Jeffrey, responding to Alex. 'Of course you would. None of us are really in control of our emotional lives. If it's not hormones, it's genes . . .'

'And if it's not jeans, it's little black mini-dresses,' said Karl.

'Or it's socialization,' said Preston, thickly. 'Or acculturation.' He stumbled over the word 'acculturation'.

'Is that a word?' said Evette.

'Not any more,' said Karl, amused at how quickly Preston seemed to be getting stoned.

'But seriously,' continued Jeffrey. 'It's the biological imperative, isn't it. Men can avoid it; women can't. Women are programmed to love the kid from the word go. It's that simple. Women are slaves to their hormones, but men can act autonomously . . .'

'What?' said Alex, the faint tone of hostility not registering with the others, least of all with Jeffrey.

'It's true!' said Preston. 'Look at me. Every evening after work I autonomously decide that I need a drink. It's an act of will. I say to myself, "Preston, you *will* have a drink!"'

Preston's lightness of tone passed Alex by. 'So you're saying that I'm a slave but you're not,' she glowered.

As his friends generally understood, Jeffrey's ideas about the world were not opinions that might be defeated by argument and evidence. Jeffrey not only believed in a natural order of things, but that he alone understood what this order was. His opinions had the status of foundational beliefs, and as foundational beliefs it was difficult to challenge Jeffrey on them. But Alex was in a mood to try. Evette, who'd had very little to drink and very little to smoke, could see what was occurring between Alex and Jeffrey. She was in no mood for the impending confrontation.

'I'm going to get a drink,' she said, breaking into the conversation. 'Anyone else need anything?'

Michael had been abandoned by the swarm and he wandered alone now in the darkened forest. The trees and undergrowth were so thick he felt himself ensnared, though he couldn't clearly discern any actual vegetation; yet there was a palpable sense that, whatever was about him, it was a living entity. He heard noises. Deep moans seemed to emanate from the fibrous surfaces around him, and the whispering of the canopy somewhere high overhead seemed indistinctly to be muttering to him. He strained to hear what the trees might want to say to him.

'Hello.'

The voice came from behind him. He turned and saw the hazy outline of a figure in the distance. It was Evette, though none of her features were clear to him from that far away.

'Hello,' he replied. 'I can't seem to move.'

'No. You're caught.'

Although Evette seemed no closer, her voice was a whisper in his ear. Startled, Michael tried to turn in the direction of the sound but couldn't.

'Where are you?' he said, though he could still see the indistinct figure shimmering ahead of him.

'Oh, here and there.'

This time the voice seemed to phase from left to right. He turned his head to follow and when he looked back Evette's face was in front of his. She looked beautiful, ethereal. Her skin was the colour of moonlight, her hair a deep copper, like metal dug from the deepest folds and recesses of ancient mountains. Her eyes were dark, velvet wombs in which, far off, something moved. Michael strained to see what it was. It flickered like a star dying, far off and thousands of years ago, in a vast prehistoric sky.

'Now I'm here,' she said.

Michael was unable to look away from her eyes. The flickering fascinated him. Was it a flame, or something else?

'Do you want me?' she said, and again the voice seemed not to come from her mouth. It was all around him, suffocating him. Breathless and exhilarated by this, Michael gasped his reply.

'Yes.'

'What do you want me for?' The tone was measured, serious. Michael had no idea what to say. He thought of Evette's body which he'd never seen naked, of her breasts which he'd never touched, and he thought of her pubic hair glistening with sweat. 'Do you want to kiss me?'

'Yes.'

'Do you want to lick me?'

'Yes.'

'Where?'

'All over.'

Michael's answers came without hesitation, betraying his premeditations. He could no longer see Evette's face. His head was now crammed with erotic images of Evette's body, bending, stretching, unfurling. He wanted to do everything possible to her. It was agony. He was sure that he would come if he didn't get the images out of his head, and standing there in front of Evette he didn't want to embarrass himself. He was at the centre of a storm of images when suddenly he was aware of Evette's face again. He looked into her fathomless eyes, and this time he could see that in each deep recess an insect flicked its large, orange wings. Michael recognized immediately the markings of the Monarch butterfly.

'*Butterflies!*' he said, astounded. 'Why are you all going on about butterflies?'

'I can't answer that,' said Evette. 'But I can give you nectar.'

'*Nectar?* I don't get it. What are you all saying to me?'

'We're trying to tell you something. It's kind of a riddle.'

Suddenly Evette's voice was chatty, and it now came from her mouth. Her face had receded, and Michael could at last see her clearly, dressed in the clothes she'd worn to Hope's party. She was crouching in front of him with a glass of water in her hand.

'Come on,' she said. 'Drink this.'

Michael realized that he was still sitting on the floor of the kitchen. The light was on and Evette was trying to get him to drink some water.

'I have to lick you,' he slurred. 'I have to lick you all over.'

'Well, I should drink this first,' she replied, laughing.

'I need nectar,' he rambled.

'Of course you do.'

'No, no. I *really* do. Everyone says so.'

Evette put the glass to Michael's lips and he drank sloppily. 'Is he OK?'

The voice was Hope's. She'd come to see how Michael was. He looked pathetic sitting on the floor being fed water, but Hope felt a pang of love for him all the same.

'Are you going to be sick?' said Evette.

Michael realized that he was.

'Let's get him to the bathroom,' said Hope.

'It's all right. I'll sort him out. You go back down.'

Michael heard Hope say this to Evette as he stumbled towards the bathroom, panicking as the spinning of the room grew in violence and his gorge rose. He no sooner made the toilet bowl than he was spewing violently into the increasingly vivid depths, his body racked with spasms. Then came relief, accompanied by a cold sweat and a chance to clear his flooded mouth and nose. He blindly fumbled for toilet paper, unable to lift his head out of the bowl against which he now leaned. It was a single, stable point in his wildly rotating universe.

'Here.'

Hope handed him a wad of toilet paper. He wiped his forehead and eyes, then blew his nose. He could barely perform these simple operations. Appalled at the mess below him, he reached clumsily for the handle.

'Here,' said Hope. 'Let me.'

The toilet flushed in his face, but Michael could not move. He didn't care at that moment what happened to him. He'd become solely concerned with getting from one moment to the next with as little incident as possible.

As the water below him settled, he could see what he assumed was the shape of his own head reflected in the water. But then it spoke to him.

'Well now, what have you been up to?'

Michael managed only an astonished 'huh?' in response. He tried to raise his head from the toilet but Hope, who had heard Michael's exclamation and who thought he was about to throw up again, pressed his head back to the bowl.

'No you don't,' she said. 'Not all over the bathroom floor.'

'No indeed,' said the voice from below. 'And not over me either!'

There was silence, as though the voice expected Michael to say something. He peered into the bowl, the indeterminate face floating beneath him.

'Here,' said Hope, from behind him. She pressed another wad of tissue into his hand. 'I've put some water on the shelf just above you. Drink it, won't you? I'm going back downstairs.'

'OK,' muttered Michael. He listened as Hope left the room.

'Alone at last,' said the voice.

The tone was playful, even mocking. There was something about its sound that was very familiar to Michael. It seemed to contain something of everyone he knew in it, though it sounded like no one in particular. Neither distinctly male nor female, it was a curiously comforting voice all the same.

'Who are you? What do you want?' said Michael. 'What's going on?'

'So many questions,' said the voice. 'Let's see. I don't want anything. I'm just visiting. I wanted to see what you're up to. You know, getting to know you and all that stuff. You can't start too early, I say. And one of us had to make the first move. You've been too preoccupied, so I thought I'd better . . .'

'Preoccupied?'

'Come on. You've been running around after that woman.'

'Who? Hope?'

'Come off it, Dad. You know who we're talking about.'

Michael, addressed as 'Dad' for the first time, realized who it was he was talking to. He was shocked by this, and also by the idea that his unborn child might know about his most secret thoughts.

'It's none of your business,' said Michael defensively. 'You're not even born yet. You're just a . . . a *fish!*'

'Nice try, Dad, but the question is not what I *am*. It's what do I have the potential to *become?* You need to start thinking outside of the present. You need to start thinking about the future. And you need to start thinking about the consequences of *your* actions, too.'

'Don't you lecture me! You don't know what it's like out here.'

'True, but what worries me is that you don't seem to know what it's like out there either. When do you ever think about what you're doing or what's happening to you? You must be the least self-aware person of all the people at the party tonight.'

'You were there?' said Michael.

'See what I mean?'

'But I *do* think about you,' protested Michael. 'I was thinking about you earlier this evening while I was cooking.'

'Yes that was a start. I accept that. But you've got to start taking more responsibility for what's happening to you. You're not a helpless victim things just happen to. Remember what Mrs Patel said to you earlier in the kitchen . . .'

'You were there too?'

'My point is, Dad, that you only seem to be able to acknowledge what's happening to you through a third party. You need to start communicating with yourself more directly. I mean, what are you doing talking to me now? I'm not even born yet.'

'But you started it.'

There was silence.

'Hey! Where are have you gone?'

Silence again.

'Aren't you going to mention butterflies?' Michael called out.

Hope met Preston at the foot of the stairs.

'I was just on my way out,' she said.

'I wouldn't,' said Preston. 'Alex and Jeffrey are at each other's throats.'

'Why?'

'Who knows. They're both stoned I think, or drunk, or both. Bad karma. It's a bit cold too. Who's Ben? I haven't seen him before.'

'He's the new boy in the office. Seems nice enough so I thought I'd invite him along. Why?'

'Just wondering. I was talking to him outside just now.'

'Oh well, if Alex is arguing with Jeffrey, then at least Ben's safe for the moment.'

'For the moment,' said Preston, smiling along with Hope.

As they stepped into the living room, Mrs Patel rose from her seat and Parmjit rose from the floor. Ben stood by the mantelpiece, inspecting the watercolour painting. Only Madge, Karl's partner, remained on the floor, leaning heavily against an armchair.

'We're off now,' said Parmjit. 'Gotta get Gran to bed.'

Hope walked them to the door. She felt the need to apologize for Michael's absence.

'He's a bit the worse for wear,' said Hope. 'I hope your gran enjoyed herself.'

'She had a brilliant time. Me too. Thanks for inviting us.'

At that moment Michael, pale but steady on his feet, appeared in the hallway. He carried the glass of water Hope had left for him, drained and now refilled.

'Michael,' said Parmjit. 'Are you all right? We're just off.'

'Thanks for coming,' he replied, his voice thick but coherent. 'Sorry I got so pissed. I hope I didn't disgrace myself too much.'

He was looking at Mrs Patel as he said this. She was smiling wordlessly and shaking Hope's hand.

'Don't worry about it,' said Parmjit. 'Anyway, better get off.'

Hope and Michael stood watching them as they walked down the road to the end of the street.

'Will they be all right walking? Didn't they want to get a taxi?'

'Pam said her gran loves walking. Anyway, she's probably had enough of taxis.'

Michael waved to them as they turned the corner at the end of the street. Hope turned down the hall, leaving Michael to close the door.

'Did Pam say that her grandmother can't speak at all, or just that she can't speak English?'

Hope turned in response to Michael's question. 'Well, she seemed to do quite a lot of talking to Parmjit. Why?'

'I just wondered,' he said.

Back in the living room, Preston had joined Ben at the mantelpiece, and both now pored over the painting.

'It looks like an 8,' said Preston, squinting at the bottom right-hand corner of the painting.

'No. It's more like the *eszett*,' said Ben.

'The what?' Preston looked at Ben.

'The *eszett* – it's a character from the old German alphabet, the Teutonic alphabet. It used to stand in for the combination of the letters s and z – the word *eszett* is literally the German letters *es* and *zett* stuck together – but it's more often used to represent the double s. The symbol is shaped like an italicized capital B that's tottering to the right. Only there are two of them here, joined back to back.'

Hope joined them at the mantelpiece. Michael sat down in the armchair against which Madge leaned. At that moment Karl and Alex entered the room.

'No no, I'm going home,' said Alex, in response to Karl's solicitations. She was clearly upset, though as ever seeking to play down in public what she was really feeling. 'I'm tired and it's late. Where's my phone?'

With five people now standing in the small room, it was suddenly very crowded. Karl smiled at Madge and motioned his head to say that they should be going. Madge nodded briefly, and Karl joined the group at the mantelpiece peering at the painting.

'Is it a signature?' said Hope.

Alex had found her phone and was requesting a taxi. 'Can you drop us off on your way?' said Madge. Alex nodded and closed her phone. 'Fifteen, twenty minutes,' she said.

'It's a symbol. It's too small for a signature,' said Preston.

Evette stepped into the room. 'I think we're going,' she said. 'Anyone need a lift?'

Michael looked up at her. She looked beautiful, not at all tired. Her copper hair was perfect, as though she'd just that moment brushed it. He remembered his drunken encounter with her and felt a bit embarrassed, though Evette seemed not even to notice him sitting there.

'We're OK,' said Madge. 'Thanks anyway.'

'*Is* it an 8?' said Ben.

There was a moment's silence.

'I know what it is,' said Karl, suddenly, triumphantly. 'It's not an 8 – it's a butterfly.'

6

Michael said goodbye to Hope at the railway station and took the escalator to street level. It was a cold but bright October morning, and an autumnal gold flecked the buildings and pavements, unnoticed by Michael as he dawdled along. He was preoccupied with Hope's party and, his own drunkenness apart, felt a certain pride at the fact that it had all gone so well. He was particularly pleased by Hope's reaction to the painting that he and Evette had chosen together. He remembered the day he and Evette had chosen the picture, how appalled she'd been on arriving at Charrington's junk shop, and how bad he'd felt for bringing her there. And although the visit had been a success, he'd thought – or imagined – that she'd been a bit frosty with him on the way back into town. There'd been no further contact between them until Hope's party on Saturday night. But Hope had *really* liked the painting, and Evette had taken him aside at the party to thank him again for helping her choose it. There was no trace of malice or resentment in her voice, and this had been a huge relief to him. Moreover, he'd really liked the conspiratorial way Evette had approached him; he liked the fact that he and Evette shared a secret together. Maybe he'd send his co-conspirator a text, just (so he told himself) to be keeping in touch with her.

Michael reached into his pocket for his phone. But as he did so he suddenly remembered, with shocking clarity, the moment at Hope's party on Saturday night when, in his drunken, semi-hallucinatory state, he'd made a lewd suggestion to Evette. Embarrassment flooded his body and he dropped his phone back into his pocket. What on earth had made him do it? At least Evette hadn't slapped his face, and she'd been laughing at the time, so maybe she'd taken it in good spirit. But then people laugh for lots of reasons – embarrassment, discomfort, mockery even – and Michael's memory was too clouded by alcohol to be sure that Evette wasn't laughing *at* him, rather than *with* him. Even if he was misremembering what he'd said to Evette, which was entirely possible given the state he'd been in, she'd nevertheless seen him at his worst, collapsed on the floor of the kitchen, barely able to focus his eyes on her, and probably dribbling down his chin too. How could she possibly think anything good about him after witnessing that?

As he passed through the wrought-iron gates of Farsight Plastic Mouldings plc, his pride at the success of the painting slipped behind the clouds.

Hope walked from the station out on to the campus. The rolling parklands of the university looked beautiful in the morning sunshine, the cluster of tall buildings rising out of the trees as though they themselves were organic structures reaching for the last rays of sunlight before the onset of winter. Fallen leaves flecked the grass with shades of gold, copper, and bronze, adding to the richness of the tableau before her. The cold air was sharp against her face, stinging every minute pore into life. And Hope suddenly felt a pang of hunger. Her queasiness had subsided earlier than usual this morning. She felt like a convict *en route* to jail, momentarily deserted by her prison guards. She made straight for the campus supermarket in search of chocolate.

Michael sat at his desk, his stock control spreadsheets hidden behind another window. He was checking the Monarch Watch website, as he did frequently at this time of year, because this was the time when millions of Monarch butterflies would be funnelling through the narrow waist of the American continent on their way to their Mexican wintering sites. They would be tired, ragged, low on fuel, but still magnificent after their thousand-mile journey. At journey's end, they would roost in their millions, hanging from the bark and branches of trees high in the Mexican mountains, clustered together like bright autumn leaves refusing to fall. Occasionally, a sharp breeze would shake a branch-load free from their roost and they would billow out, like a loosely blown orange scarf, before returning to clothe the branch again. Michael knew this, not because he'd seen it for himself – though he dreamed that one day he would do exactly that – but through documentaries, and what literature he could find on these astonishing and beautiful creatures.

As a child he'd been fascinated by insects, but particularly by flying insects. The humble housefly – the bluebottle – had been astounding to his youthful eyes in the versatility of its flight. Going nowhere, with no apparent sense of purpose, bluebottles chicaned from room to room at breakneck speed, crashing recklessly into windows and switching direction of flight in the beat of a wing. When one stopped for rest, Michael would creep slowly in its direction, to find the creature squatting on a work surface rubbing its front legs together, its abdomen iridescent as an oil slick in a puddle. It would remain there until his face was inches from it, unmoved and unhurried, confident in its ability to evade Michael's attempt to catch it with his bare hands. As he lunged, it would rise effortlessly as though passing through one dimension into another, to appear instantaneously in another place, out of reach.

But it was the butterflies that thronged his mother's garden that had fascinated him more than any other insect. The garden was a small plot at the back of their council house, but his mother had worked tirelessly on it every summer for as long as he could remember. He knew almost nothing of the flowers and shrubs that grew there, with the exception of the buddleia which, at the height of summer, drowsed under the weight of heavy flowers that drooped like purple ash from the end of neglected cigarettes. These flowers seemed to mesmerize butterflies. He would watch their coy trajectory as they flicked their wings against the buffeting of invisible and subtle breezes, as though trying to give the impression that they were not really interested in the sumptuous flowers that were the secret goal of their journey. Yet, in spite of their evasive flight, the insects would finally alight on the bush, their sun-heavy wings slowly, reverently parting and drawing together in an act of devotion, their heads swimming ecstatically with the secret incense that had drawn them inexorably towards the plant.

Sometimes, at the height of summer, there would be so many butterflies gently flickering there that they themselves looked like the plant's flowers. They looked like candle flames guttering in a draught, and every so often they would rise from the plant, disturbed from their devotions by the force of the breeze, or by Michael's mother brushing against the plant as she worked in the border. Then they would settle back to their roost, descending like tongues of flame anointing the bush. But impressive as this spectacle was to his young eyes, it paled when compared to the astonishing sight of millions of butterflies cloaking the trees high in the Mexican mountains. There would surely be no sight on earth to rival the surreal beauty of this spectacle.

Hope had inducted her first cohort of students into the secrets of the library and now had time to kill. She thought of the campus she'd walked across that morning, glowing in the early-autumn sunshine with the vibrant colours of a pre-Raphaelite painting. Through the window the sky was clear again. The clouds that for a while had blotted out the sun had rolled on, and once again sunshine shimmered across the glass and steel buildings surrounding the library. Excitement welled up inside her. Not the nervous kind that might precede a job interview. More, the excitement of anticipation, of waiting for the roller coaster to reach its first summit before the headlong plunge towards earth. She felt happy, in a way that she hadn't done for some time. It must be hormones, she thought to herself, amused at the frequency with which she used this reason to explain her mood-changes. But whatever the reason for her exhilaration, she meant to ride the wave while it lasted, and so she headed outside to sit in the sunshine.

The campus was livelier than it had been when she'd arrived that morning. Students and staff milled about, some walking purposefully, others strolling and talking, smoking and laughing, drinking and sitting – a self-contained and cosmopolitan community of beautiful, healthy and mostly young people. Hope sat on a bench, feeling the warmth of the sun on the back of her head. She closed her eyes and listened to the distant roar of the city, the hazy chatter from the campus, the drone of a leaf-collecting machine and the clattering of a dump truck going to or from the latest building site on the campus. Time seemed to slow as Hope sat there, her body stilled and calmed. Michael was in her thoughts, but in an indistinct way, a background noise, or a wash applied to a canvas before painting begins. She felt him more than thought of him, and the world floated through her in waves, making her lighter and lighter.

Then she heard a voice. 'I think she fainted,' it said.

A man's voice. An accent, Japanese but spoken with an American intonation. Hope wondered to whom the voice was referring.

'Come on now,' said another voice, this time English, local, a Midlands twang. This voice seemed to address her directly.

She felt someone touch her face gently, and she became aware of an unpleasant sensation at the back of her head.

'Give her some water,' said a third voice. Female, European, but difficult to place, perhaps Scandinavian. 'Do any of you have water?'

Hope opened her eyes to see three people's faces floating above her, framed by the vivid blue sky.

'She's opened her eyes,' said the local voice. 'Give her a bit of room.'

'Give her some water,' repeated the Scandinavian voice.

A bottle was pressed gently but insistently to Hope's lips. She refused, panicking a little, and tried to sit up.

'I'm all right,' she said automatically, bewildered at finding herself the centre of attention.

'I think you fainted, or something,' said the Scandinavian, who Hope could now see was a middle-aged woman whose immaculately-cut grey hair was so fine that it looked like strands of silk reflecting the sun. She wore a crisp, blue business suit, and Hope recognized her as one of the mature students she'd shown around the library that morning.

'I'm sorry,' said Hope, focusing her attention on this woman as she tried to get herself up.

'Don't apologize. You couldn't help it.'

The woman assisted Hope on to the bench from which she'd slipped.

'Are you hurt?' she enquired.

'I don't think so,' said Hope. 'My head feels a bit sore at the back, but I don't know how that could be.'

A small crowd of concerned onlookers had gathered around the bench. These began to drift away on seeing that Hope was all right. Hope found herself alone on the bench, sitting beside her dapper part-time student.

'Did you miss breakfast?'

Hope pulled her thoughts away from her head and made herself address the woman's question.

'Yes,' she said. 'I mean no. I had some chocolate when I got to work.'

'I'd see a doctor if I were you,' said the woman, registering Hope's hesitance. 'Just to be sure. Get the bump on your head checked. You might have concussion.'

Hope thought this a bit extravagant, but then remembered her condition. 'I'm pregnant,' she said, more to herself than to the woman.

'Then you certainly must get yourself looked at,' the woman said. 'It's probably nothing, but better safe than sorry. Such a lot can go wrong in your condition. You mustn't take chances. I know.'

Hope, who was now beginning to feel weary, resisted the invitation to press the woman about her own experience of pregnancy.

'I'm sorry,' she said again. 'But I need to go and lie down for a while. You've been very kind.'

'OK, but see a doctor. Won't you?'

'I will,' said Hope, more to end the conversation than to take the woman's advice.

The woman rose and walked away. Hope put her head in her hands, and once more felt the warm sun on the back of her head, though this time the heat accentuated the soreness there. She could feel a slight swelling when she probed it with her fingers, but it didn't seem serious, and there was no blood. In spite of the soreness and the sudden weariness, the strange euphoria she'd experienced prior to fainting remained and she sat for a few moments longer, letting the sun warm her back, taking what strength she could from its rays. As soon as she felt able, she walked back to the library, ordered a taxi home, and took the rest of the day off.

It was lunchtime, and Michael was bored. He sat at his desk eating a sandwich and drinking a cup of vending-machine coffee. He'd still not sent a text to Evette, though he'd fretted over the idea until the start of his lunch break. By then it was too late, and Michael felt relieved that the decision had been placed beyond him. Woven in with this sensation of relief was a thread of self-righteousness, for Michael believed, in a vague way, that by deferring the decision he'd brought about a moral victory over his baser instincts. He had, so he told himself, remained faithful to Hope. This was preferable to admitting that he'd suffered an acute attack of fear.

Faced with the prospect of sitting around in his office for an hour, he looked for company closer to home and went in search of Preston. But Preston's desk was vacant, and his computer hadn't been switched on. No one had seen Preston since Friday, and no one could tell Michael where Preston was. Preston was usually meticulous about his timekeeping but he hadn't booked a day's leave or phoned in sick, and Michael's curiosity increased even more when he rang Preston's mobile and only reached his answering service. Michael returned to his desk, resigned to his own company. He checked his email and saw that he'd received one from Jeffrey, a mail-shot announcing the launch of the Chancredy Multimedia Collective's website. As he clicked on the link to the website, a text arrived from Hope. She'd been trying to phone him but had got no answer. Would he phone her at home, as soon as he could?

Michael picked up his landline and called home. His computer screen reported that the requested webpage could not be found. Typical Jeffrey, Michael thought for a second, before Hope picked up.

'It's me,' he said. 'What's up? I thought you were at work today.'

Hope told Michael about her fainting fit.

As Michael began to ask her what had happened he heard her mobile phone chime.

'Jesus!' said Hope. 'It's Preston, he's in hospital.'

'What? Why?'

'The message doesn't say. I don't even recognize the number. I'll find out what I can and call you back.'

Michael turned back to his screen. He was unsettled and wanted to lose himself in work, but his mind wouldn't focus. Preston was in hospital. Was it a car crash? A heart attack? It could be anything. And Hope, what had happened to her? He went over in his mind what she'd said: *I thought I'd better take it easy*.

With a shock, Michael suddenly understood that Hope meant that she'd better take it easy *in her condition*. He realized that when Hope had told him of her faint he hadn't thought at all of her pregnancy, hadn't considered that the fall might have damaged the child growing within her – *their* child. Was it all right? Had her pregnancy somehow contributed to her fainting fit?

While he knew, of course, that Hope was pregnant, so far there'd been almost no physical evidence of this fact and so it had been easy to ignore her condition. When he thought about the child, he did so in an uneasy and distant way, and not as something actually growing within her. It was the *physicality* of it that now most forcefully struck him. The child was *there* inside her, and Michael suddenly felt a pang of jealousy. This passed quickly, but it left him with an uncomfortable feeling that he was somehow becoming extraneous to the process. He was beginning to feel left out.

Hope stood naked, looking at herself in the mirror. She thought her face seemed a little flushed. She'd often heard people remark that pregnant women seemed to 'bloom', developing rosy cheeks in response to the life blossoming inside them. But Hope looked more like someone who had spent a little too long in the sun – a faint but discernible reddening across her brow, along the bridge of her nose and across the tops of her cheeks. She hadn't noticed the ruddiness earlier in the morning as she prepared herself for work. Maybe the 'glow' was connected in some way with her fainting fit. Hope had made an appointment with her doctor for the following morning; she would mention it to her.

She turned sideways on to look at her stomach. No change, yet. Her breasts seemed unaltered too, though her nipples, always pale and modest, might, she thought, have become a little darker than usual. She ran her hands over her stomach, pressing gently. Nothing. No sensation, no swelling that she could feel, no sense that there was a human being growing inside her. She felt desolate. Was it still there? Perhaps her faint had been caused by a miscarriage, though she'd checked herself for bleeding and found nothing. She thought again of her mother, and felt even more alone. She remembered having read somewhere that her emotional state during pregnancy could affect the personality of her unborn child. Would this dark mood somehow imprint itself on the child's character? Would it grow up miserable, uncomfortable with life and unable to accommodate to an irrational world?

Hope felt she'd already failed to equip her child for the trials it would have to face. It would be inadequate like her, incapable of seeing the light in dark places.

She wanted to crawl into bed but forced herself to normality. Once dressed, she phoned the number of the person who'd sent the text about Preston. To her surprise, it was Ben, the colleague who'd been at her party on Saturday. She had no idea why Ben, who hadn't met Preston before the party, was the one telling her about his hospitalization, but she was so shocked by the news that she didn't think to ask. Ben told her that Preston had been attacked and severely beaten up in the early hours of Sunday morning after leaving the party. He'd been taken to hospital, semi-conscious, and had been kept in under observation. 'He's in pretty bad shape,' said Ben. 'But they say he's stable.'

The word 'stable' brought home to Hope just how serious the attack must have been. When she'd finished talking to Ben she phoned Michael. They agreed that they should visit Preston that evening.

'I'll phone Jeffrey. And Evette, too. I'll let people know.'

'He might not want many visitors,' said Hope. 'We should find out what condition he's in before we all descend on him.'

Michael could see the sense in this, but still thought that Preston's friends should be told.

'Are you OK?' he asked. 'How's the head?'

'I'm OK,' she said. 'Just a bit low.'

'Well, take it easy this afternoon. Put your feet up. I'll be home in an hour.'

With a cup of tea in her hand, Hope went into the living room and sat on the sofa, at a loss as to what to do until Michael came home.

She glanced up at the fireplace, and her eyes came to rest on the painting Evette and Jeffrey had given her on Saturday. Against the neutral colour of the wall, the painting stood out, as though it were lit from within by a faint but natural light.

She rose, and stood in front of the fireplace looking closely at the painting, lost in its subtle beauty.

Picking up the painting, she sat down and inspected the frame. The thick dark-brown varnish was unflattering and would need to be stripped back to the wood; perhaps finished with polish, or a lighter varnish. The glass looked all right, no chips or fractures. She noticed again the curious butterfly-shaped mark in the bottom right-hand corner of the painting; a clue to the artist's identity, perhaps? She turned the painting over. The back of the picture had been covered with thick brown paper, sealed all the way round to the outer edge of the frame with broad parcel tape, which was lifting here and there, so old was the adhesive gum. The brown paper and the parcel tape were stained with grease and dirt. Two eye-hooks had been screwed into the back of the frame, one at each side, and thick string had been tied loosely across from one to the other. The eye-hooks were rusty and the string, once white, was now grey.

Hope went to the kitchen for scissors and pincers, and sat down again. She cut the string and unscrewed the eye-hooks, putting them aside. Then she tugged gently at the raised edges of the parcel tape. It came away easily, the adhesive having all but perished with age. She lifted the brown paper backing, thick like vellum and stiff like parchment. Hope laid it aside; it was somehow part of the picture, and she intended to replace it when she'd finished renovating the frame. With the tape and brown paper removed, she could see both the unvarnished back of the frame and the stiffening board that held the picture itself in place. The frame looked good – there were no worm holes, and the wood was of good quality with a dense grain to it.

The stiffening board was held in place by half a dozen sprigs. Hope removed these with the pincers and eased the stiffening board up from its rebated bed. She wanted to get at the picture itself, and at the glass through which she'd viewed it. The board came up without any difficulty, revealing the back of the painting underneath. But as she turned the board over, intending to lay it aside, her attention was caught.

Taped to the back of the board was an envelope, yellowing with age and with a handwritten address scrawled in black ink across the width of the visible area. Hope was amazed. The picture forgotten, she sat back with the board on her lap and, with infinite care, slowly removed the tape that held the envelope in place. As she took it in her hands, she heard Michael's key fumble in the lock.

'Hope?' called Michael, closing the door behind him.

'In here,' replied Hope.

But before he could enter the room, Hope did something that she couldn't, at that moment, have explained to anyone, slipping the unopened letter under the sofa.

'Hello,' said Michael, stepping into the living room. 'How's the head?'

7

Hope and Michael walked past a small group of smokers cupping cigarettes against the autumnal chill, and stepped up to what looked more like a side door than the main entrance of a major city hospital. They passed through the sliding glass into a dingy, colour-coded corridor, and looked for the signs to Ward C8.

'We follow the green arrows,' said Hope, and walked off, trailing Michael in her wake. This was the hospital where Hope would deliver her baby, and she was not impressed. The walls were grubby and needed repainting, and here and there strip lights were out. A couple of security guards stalked along the corridor ahead of her, and the sheer fact of their presence made the place seem menacing.

'Christ, Michael, why would a hospital need security guards?'

'Dunno. Drug addicts trying to pinch drugs?'

'I don't want to have our baby in this place. It's horrible.'

Hope led the way into the ward. Unlike the corridor, this was brightly lit and clean – the hospital was clearly focusing its limited resources where they mattered most – and Hope took some comfort from this. She walked slowly with Michael along the ward, scrutinizing the various tableaux arranged around each bed. Visitors sat awkwardly with bedridden friends or relatives, not quite knowing how to fill the time until the end of visiting hours. Preston lay almost at the end of the ward, flanked by his parents. In a chair beside Preston's father slouched a sullen but beautiful teenage boy holding a baseball cap on his knee. He'd clearly been told to take it off, and he wore his resentment like a skin, as only a teenager can. There was also a younger boy dressed, as the teenager was, in ostentatiously labelled baggy casuals. He stood shyly, half-hidden behind his mother. Preston lay on the bed, propped up at a shallow angle.

Hope looked at him after acknowledging his visitors, and when she did, she felt that she physically jumped. She blushed, realizing that everyone must have seen her, including Preston. Nor could Michael quite believe that he was looking at Preston. The area around Preston's eyes was so swollen that Michael wasn't even sure if Preston could see him. A raw gash, stretching from the top of Preston's left ear to his chin, had been sealed with butterfly stitches. His lower lip was split and swollen, and blood had congealed on it. His forehead had been bandaged, the medical cleanliness of the material jarring with the battleground of Preston's face. His left arm was in a sling, raised across his chest.

'It's hard for him to speak,' said Preston's mother, without meeting the eyes of Preston's friends.

'What happened?'

'He was beaten up,' said Preston's father, quietly stating the obvious. 'By a group of white boys.'

It sounded to Michael like an accusation, though it was directed at Preston rather than himself. But why would Preston's father want to accuse his own son? Having spoken his piece, the old man dropped his gaze again.

'But why?' asked Michael. 'What happened?'

Preston's parents raised their eyes to look at each other, and in this brief exchange Hope could see the full force of the father's resentment levelled at the mother, whose own eyes seemed to be pleading silently with her husband. It was as though they'd had a searing argument moments before she and Michael arrived. Hope made their excuses and ushered Michael away, promising to visit tomorrow in the hope that Preston would be feeling better.

'Christ,' said Michael when they were out of earshot in the corridor. 'Whoever it was gave him a right going-over. I've never seen anyone that badly beaten before.'

Michael glanced sideways at Hope for reassurance.

But Hope, suddenly crowded by the senseless violence of the world, walked on in silence, head down, aware of her own vulnerability and that of the life inside her. Preston was one of the loveliest men she knew; kind and gentle. Why would anyone want to beat him up? She was puzzled, too, by the wordless exchange between his mother and father.

As she and Michael walked through the grubby sliding doors and away from the building, an ambulance careered past them heading for the emergency entrance, swirling dead leaves in its wake, its crazed lights fracturing the darkness.

The next day, Hope phoned in sick and took the day off work. She felt fine physically, but she couldn't stop thinking about Preston's shocking injuries. She was also thinking of the Scandinavian woman who had spoken to her as she sat on the bench recovering from her fainting fit. The simple words – 'I know' – uttered by the woman, hinting at a dark personal experience of pregnancy, had grown steadily louder in Hope's mind. She wished that she'd pressed the woman for her story: *What* did she know? As a new student, she wouldn't be hard to find. Hope would seek her out.

She'd at least taken her advice about seeing a doctor. That morning, Hope had been examined at the local health centre by a new addition to the medical staff. Dr Dangerfield was about Hope's age, wore no wedding ring, and smiled what looked like a genuine rather than a professional smile. She'd asked Hope a series of questions – had she felt faint on previous occasions? Had she generally been feeling well? Had she experienced any bleeding? – and Hope had answered them all in the negative. But she did reveal that she'd been suffering from bad morning sickness, and that yesterday – the day of the fainting fit – she'd somehow known that it was over.

'I don't know how I knew it had passed, but I did. I'm afraid I went and bought a bar of chocolate to celebrate.'

As these questions were asked and answered, Dr Dangerfield took Hope's temperature and blood pressure, and looked closely into her eyes. 'Chocolate is good,' she said laughing easily. 'One bar good; two bars better! You are pigging out for two now, you know?'

'Actually,' said Hope touching her still-flat stomach, 'I can't quite explain it but I'm beginning to feel like two people now. I mean, like there really is someone else, in here.'

'Well, that certainly seems to be the case. Have you been under the sunlamp?'

Hope was surprised by the question. 'Do people still have sunlamps?'

'It's a fair cop,' said the doctor. 'I know you haven't been under a sunlamp. Have you noticed any other changes in pigmentation? Nipples darkening? That sort of thing?'

'They seem a little bigger, but I don't think they're darker.'

'You can sometimes get a dark line from the navel down to your pubes.'

'Nope. Nothing there.'

'Sometimes it's the face. Rarely. I've never seen it before myself, but then I'm in general practice. If I were a gynae I'd probably see it more.'

'Rare?' said Hope, faintly worried.

'It's nothing to worry about. It'll fade. It's hormonal. There's a fancy medical name, but those infamous Old Wives generally call it a butterfly mask. It's not permanent.'

'Pity,' said Hope. 'I thought it made me look flushed and healthy.'

'A ruddy-cheeked peasant girl? No, it'll fade sooner or later. Sorry.'

'No need to apologize,' said Hope. 'A butterfly mask? I like the sound of that.'

Hope was standing in the bathroom, looking at her face in the mirror when the phone rang.

'How are you feeling today?' asked Alex. 'What did the doctor have to say?'

Hope filled her in about the visit to Dr Dangerfield.

'A butterfly mask?' said Alex.

'It looks more like a suntan than a mask. I look as though I've caught the sun.'

'Maybe you did,' said Alex. 'You were sitting on that bench in the sun, weren't you?'

'No, it's the baby. It's trying to announce itself by changing the way I look. It's impatient. It can't wait to push my belly out.'

'But you must look radiant, my dear, glowing – '

'Yawn. Cliché city,' said Hope. 'I look like I've been in a nuclear attack. Like I've been roasted by radiation. And my hair's greasy. And I'm exhausted all the time. And –'

'All right, all right.' Alex, laughing, conceded the debate to Hope.

'Do you fancy lunch? I'm rattling around here on my own. I can't settle.'

'Sorry,' said Alex. 'Got a lunch date already. What about a drink later? Or coffee? Tea, rather?'

'Anyone I know?' said Hope, her curiosity engaged.

'No. I'll probably stay till five-thirtyish, so we could meet in town a bit later and see where we go from there. We could get something to eat.'

Distracted from questioning her further, Hope arranged to meet Alex in town after she'd visited Preston. She hung up, and in the space of quiet that followed, her shapeless anxieties resumed their haunting of her. She needed to do something to distract herself. It was then that she remembered the letter she'd found in the painting, and went downstairs to the living room where she'd hidden it under the sofa.

Parmjit sat in her first seminar, among a group of fifteen students fresh from their first lecture of the year. The seminar was due to begin at twelve o'clock, but at ten past students were still drifting into the room. By the time the group had assembled, two of them had already received calls on their mobiles. At a quarter past twelve the seminar tutor, shuffling papers at the front of the room, had coughed loudly, and a reluctant and restless silence had descended on the group. Another five minutes passed while the chairs were rearranged in a circle so that all sixteen people, tutor included, could face each other. Another call drew a plea from the tutor for all to switch their phones off for the duration of the seminar. They did so grudgingly, reluctant to disconnect themselves from the digital world in which they felt so at home. Parmjit, who'd switched off her phone before entering the room, looked around at her fellow students.

One in particular caught Parmjit's eye, a stocky male with a shock of natural blond hair cut very short at the back and sides. He looked fresh from his first day in the army. He sat quietly, with head tilted back and his eyes closed, at the point in the circle directly facing the tutor. When he spoke to introduce himself, as they each did in turn at the tutor's request, he opened his eyes and levelled his head at the group.

'Naumov, Gyorgy. My father was KGB. Is now businessman. He has sent me to UK for education because Russian education system is in crap.'

Having delivered this brief account of himself, he slowly closed his eyes and tilted his head back to its former position, seemingly oblivious to the introductions offered by his fellow students.

Parmjit, fascinated by this act of apparent disdain towards the others, was still looking at him when she realized it was her turn to speak. Flustered by the sudden attention and with all the group's eyes on her except Gyorgy's, Parmjit's mind raced so quickly to pull her back to herself that she stumbled over her name.

'I'm sorry?' The tutor leaned forward and cupped his hand over his ear.

Parmjit gave her name again.

'And?' Her tutor waited for her to say a little more about herself.

Parmjit, still flustered, was unsure what to say. 'Er . . . I . . . I'm a student.'

She immediately felt stupid. The tutor looked baffled.

'Good. Yes. Thank you.' He spoke with a waver of panic in his voice, as though not at all sure what to do next.

Seeing that he appeared to be in difficulties, and feeling responsible, Parmjit tried to rescue them both by carrying on talking. 'Sorry. Of course I'm a student. Wouldn't be here if I wasn't, would I? How stupid. I mean, I *am* a student, but I do other things too. Lots of different jobs. I'm a waitress, and a taxi driver. And I work for my uncle in his restaurant. Oh, and I look after my gran, and –'

'Yes. Yes. Thank you, Parmjit.'

'. . . and I'm a mature student too, though you wouldn't think to look at me, I hope!'

'Yes, thank you, Parmjit. Thank you.'

'Also, I –'

'Parmjit!'

As Parmjit shrank back into her chair she noticed that Gyorgy's eyes had opened slightly, though his head remained at its disdainful angle. A smile flickered briefly at the corners of his mouth.

Having completed the introductions, the tutor introduced himself as Ed Frampton, and then began to distribute reading material. This led to a lot of paper-shuffling, and another ten-minute delay. Parmjit glanced at the clock at the front of the room. It was half-past twelve, and the seminar proper had yet to begin.

Michael sat at his desk, mobile phone in hand, looking at a text message from Evette.

1 2 meet 4 lunch?

Why was Evette asking him? What did she want? He wouldn't confront what he *hoped* she wanted. He decided to accept; it seemed such an insignificant thing, to type *where? what time?* into his phone and to press send. It was almost as though the phone had answered Evette's question all by itself. As the message spiralled off into the ether, Michael felt a surge of excitement, though he was half-convinced that Evette would reply saying that something had suddenly come up and that she could no longer make lunch. Or any other rendezvous with him. Ever.

But he was wrong. The reply came back within minutes.

tea room, art gallery 1pm c u there

It was twelve-thirty. It would take Michael about twenty minutes to walk there. Leaving nothing to chance, he left his desk immediately, stopping only at the washroom to check his appearance in the full-length mirror. As usual, he regretted this; the disappointing, slightly untidy figure staring back at him could only dent his confidence.

Hope sat on the sofa holding the envelope, trying to read the address. She could make out the title – Herr – a letter addressed to a German or possibly an Austrian – and the initial J, and she could tell that the surname of the addressee began with an S and ended in ing, but the unfamiliarity of the handwriting and the marks of age smudging the ink made it difficult be sure of the remaining letters. She was fairly sure that the name began with Sch. So the name was Sch – something – ing. Schellering, perhaps, or Schnellering? The address was as difficult to decipher. The number was clear enough – 137 – though the street name was indecipherable. But the name of the city was clearly Wien, and Hope, who'd studied German at school, recognized this as Vienna. So the letter had been sent to Herr J something, in Vienna. But when, and by whom?

She turned the envelope over and drew out several sheets of folded paper. They were covered in the same handwriting as the envelope and were equally difficult to read. There were five sheets altogether. The first sheet began with a brief but illegible two-line address in the top, right-hand corner, while the final sheet concluded with a single, for once clearly legible word – *Immer* – and a single name – Klara, or perhaps Klare. Though Hope could remember little of her German now, she recognized the word *immer*: *always*. The only other text she could immediately understand was the date, written just beneath the address – *16. Juli 1898*.

'Any questions? Anyone?'

Although they had reached the point at which, it seemed, no one could think of any more ways to delay the start of the seminar, still their tutor seemed reluctant to set the discussion going. Met with more silence, he seemed at last to decide that the game was up.

'OK. Right. Let's make a start. Now, we all hate politics, don't we?'

Since they had all signed up specifically to study politics, this seemed, to Parmjit, to be an odd question. It met with yet another silence.

'Right. OK. Let's just break the ice here by saying something about the *reasons* why we hate politics.'

There was another painful silence, before a young woman with oriental features and a thick Scouse accent spoke timidly, unsure of herself. 'Erm, because we don't trust politicians?'

Ed Frampton, who was little more than her own age, sat up in his chair, evidently relieved to have finally prompted a response. 'Great. Great. Yes. Erm . . . *Emily*, isn't it? Great. Yes. Go on with that.'

Silence again. Nobody seemed sure as to what they should be going on with. Emily spoke again. 'Me?'

'Yes! Well, I mean, *anyone*. What do the rest of you think?'

He threw the question open but he was looking at Emily. She'd come to his rescue once already and this simple act of charity had created a special bond between them. She looked at Ed Frampton and his eyes seemed to will her on. Emily, confidence boosted by the supportive, pleading eyes of the young tutor, warmed to her role.

'I mean, it's politicians isn't it? We don't trust them, do we?' As she spoke, she looked around the group for confirmation of what seemed to her to be a self-evident truth. One or two heads nodded hesitantly.

'I mean, they're only out for themselves, aren't they? I mean, even when they're sincere, they're not really, are they? I mean, look at that Tony Blair. He seems nice enough, but really he's just like all the rest, isn't he? I mean, it's obvious. Isn't it?'

Emily's voice trailed away as she realized that her impassioned speech had failed to energize the rest of the group.

She looked around at her fellow students. They were all looking down, avoiding her gaze. All, that is, except Gyorgy, who still sat with arms folded, eyes closed and head tilted back. Parmjit, who was watching him slyly, out of the corners of her eyes, noticed that the thin spectre of a smile was once more haunting the corners of his mouth.

Having concluded her conversation with Hope, Alex put down the phone and returned her gaze to her computer screen. She needed a cigarette, but the office building in which she worked was smoke-free and she would have to wait until lunchtime before she could appease her body's craving. Alex worked in the university Registry and her job involved the input of data concerning the new intake of students. The job had a low-intelligence and high-boredom quotient and Alex, who had a degree in American Studies, resented having to do it, and resented it all the more as the nicotine levels in her body fell.

She was meeting Jeffrey for lunch. He'd phoned her at work early that morning and, very cagily Alex thought, had suggested they might have lunch to discuss a project that Jeffrey had in mind. 'Something artistic' he'd said, refusing to elaborate over the phone. Alex was both puzzled and intrigued by Jeffrey. There was no doubt that he was interesting and, in his maverick way, likeable. He had a sense of humour, and Alex quite liked the way Jeffrey always seemed to be baiting her when they were together; she liked the fact that he kept her on her toes, something her job manifestly failed to do. And he was a striking and stylish figure; tall, but not overbearingly so, and slim. He'd a curious, slightly dissipated aspect, like an aristocrat who'd disdained his ancestral duties for the bohemian life.

Alex looked at the clock. It was twelve-fifty. She lifted her bag on to the desk and fished out her cigarettes and lighter in readiness for the stroke of one.

Michael arrived ten minutes early. The art gallery bar was crowded, but there were a couple of discreet tables free here and there. He bought a drink from the bar to justify his occupying a table, and sat down to wait.

Parmjit left the room along with her fellow students, promptly at one o'clock. Five minutes earlier, and in spite of the fact that several of the students had just then begun to open up and discuss what might or might not count as 'politics', a general restlessness had erupted, with some students clearly craving communication every bit as badly as the nicotine addicts were craving their cigarettes – mobile phones had been reconnected to the grid even before Ed Frampton had finished trying to summarize the discussion, such as it was. Several were out of the door before he'd finished reminding them of their task for the next week. As she left the room, Parmjit looked back at her tutor. He sat leaning forward, elbows resting on his knees, face buried in his cupped hands.

'That was crap, yes?'

Parmjit recognized the voice before she turned around. Gyorgy stood, looking over Parmjit's head at their tutor. He dropped his gaze to look at her, and the smile returned to the corners of his mouth. 'We are going for food. Do you want to come?'

As he spoke, he nodded towards two other students lurking by the doorway. One was Emily, the oriental Liverpudlian, the other a shy-looking male whose name Parmjit had already forgotten. Aware that she would need to leave soon to get ready for an early-evening waitressing stint, she agreed nevertheless. As the four of them walked off across the campus to the refectory, Parmjit sensed that the seminar was only just beginning.

Alex, dragging on her cigarette, sat on a bench outside the Old Varsity Tavern, a pub on the perimeter of campus. Jeffrey was late. The October sun tilted off to one side, threading long shadows through the increasingly leafless trees surrounding the car park. The pub was a favourite lunchtime haunt of students and academics alike. Inside it was book-lined and oak-panelled, leather-seated and gold-fitted, with alabaster busts of intellectual giants strategically placed in alcoves here and there. Aristotle sat in his alcove, contemplating the admiring gaze of John Stuart Mill. Shakespeare brooded across the lounge towards the array of whiskies behind the bar. Voltaire who, perhaps because he was French, had been placed overlooking the entrance to the lavatories, tried to maintain a dignified expression as he watched the daily procession of his drunken intellectual progeny, stumbling towards the basest form of relief.

As she sat smoking, Alex felt the chill air seeping through the layers of her clothes. The attenuated sunshine now lit up the world, but didn't warm it. But the sharp air refreshed her after the recycled air of the office. The smoke she inhaled relaxed her, opening up the capillaries throughout her body and helping to make her experience of the scene altogether more sensuous. In the office Alex was an automaton, a slave in the service of the machines which required a constant supply of fresh data. In the office, her moods and emotions counted for nothing. But here, sitting on this bench, feeling the warm smoke and the cool air mingling in her throat, she could once more assert her humanity.

As she drew the last dregs of smoke from her cigarette, Alex saw Jeffrey's car turn into the car park. She dropped the stub at her feet, grinding it into the tarmac as she stood up.

It was nearly quarter-past when Evette finally walked through the door. She was dressed immaculately in a midnight-blue two-piece suit, skirt well above the knee. She wore sheer stockings or tights, and patent shoes with sharp toes and sharper stiletto heels. Under her jacket she had on a white shirt, and the whole outfit looked fresh and uncreased, as though she'd been dressed by her tailor five minutes before stepping through the door. Her copper hair, with its fringe as sharply defined as her stiletto heels, was perfect. On seeing her, the slightly dishevelled image staring back at Michael from the washroom mirror immediately returned to embarrass him. He wished he hadn't accepted her invitation.

Michael could not see her eyes – Evette had walked into the tea room still wearing her sunglasses. She saw Michael and sauntered over, unhurried, and unconcerned at having kept Michael waiting.

'Am I late?' She said it with a grin, knowing full well that she was.

'Don't worry about it. I've only just got here myself.'

As he said this, Michael was conscious of the almost-empty glass of lager that sat brazenly in front of him.

'Have you eaten?' As she spoke, she sat down at the table opposite him and took off her sunglasses. Michael, caught in the glare of her eyes, wished he could put his on without seeming rude.

'No. You?'

Michael was already on his feet. He'd have bought her a banquet if she'd asked for it. She didn't.

'Actually, I had a sandwich before I left the office. I'd kill for a drink though.'

'I'm not hungry myself,' said Michael, lying. 'What would you like?'

Evette stood up and told Michael to sit down. 'I'm buying,' she said.

Michael could tell from the firmness of her voice that it would be pointless to argue. 'Same again,' was all he could manage, pointing to his glass. 'Lager.'

He watched Evette walk to the bar, the sway of her hips and the backs of her legs sending him messages in a code as ancient as the human race itself.

Hope had put the letter aside – in the absence of a translator or a dictionary she could get no more out of it – and had turned to the painting itself. A landscape, skilfully done, but nothing there that she could see to explain the letter tucked into the back. The curious butterfly-shaped mark in the bottom right-hand corner of the painting told her nothing. She turned the painting over. On the back, in the top left-hand corner of the parchment, barely legible, was a date – *16/7/88* – and a name – *Braunau*. Hope looked at the date, and something echoed at the back of her mind. She picked up the first page of the letter and compared the date: *16. Juli* – July, the seventh month – *1898*. It was the same month and day, exactly ten years later.

Hope immediately sensed that there was a story to be told here. She could already see that the connection between the two dates was meaningful, though she didn't yet know exactly why. Perhaps it was a birthday, or some other anniversary. Perhaps the painting was a gift to mark the tenth anniversary of something. Braunau, she assumed, was a place; the spelling looked German, though she knew that it could as easily be Austrian. Maybe Braunau, wherever it might be, was the place represented in the painting. Did this place then have some significance to the anniversary, perhaps to remind the recipient of a holiday spent there?

The letter was addressed to a man, of that she was sure. But who was the sender? The handwriting seemed feminine to Hope, but she knew that men could sometimes have 'feminine' handwriting styles, too. Perhaps the word *immer* – 'always' – might be a clue to the identity of the writer. After all, the word hinted at something more than simply a familial relationship; it was the kind of thing a lover might put at the end of a letter. Maybe that was it; maybe this was a love letter from Klara, or Klare, to Herr J Schellering, or whatever his name was. Hope was intrigued now; she wanted to know more. She looked again at the letter, but the rest of the text remained mute to her secondary school German. Then a thought occurred. She worked at a university, after all; surely it wouldn't be too difficult to find someone in the language department who'd be willing to translate it for her?

Hope was quietly excited. She loved the painting that Jeffrey and Evette had given her for her thirtieth birthday, but this was an unexpected bonus. They'd inadvertently given her not just a painting, but also a puzzle to solve. As she put the letter down on the coffee table, she felt a brief and delicate fluttering sensation in the pit of her stomach which she took to be a physical manifestation of the excitement she was feeling. It took her a few moments more to realize that the sensation was much more than excitement; Hope realized that she'd experienced, for the first time, a direct act of communication from the child growing inside her.

It was eight o'clock in the evening, and Hope and Michael sat on the bus as it wound its way out of the city centre. The pavements glistened under the orange glow of the street lamps overhead. Neither spoke, both lost in their separate worlds.

As arranged, Hope had met Alex at six o'clock. Hope had talked mostly about Michael, who rarely seemed to acknowledge her pregnancy. Alex thought Michael's apparent lack of interest was just a 'man thing', pointing out that Michael had been spared the physical, hormonal and psychological changes that Hope was undergoing.

'Believe me, he'll get used to the idea,' Alex had said. 'He will. He's a good bloke, is Michael, even if he's not always as up to speed as he could be.'

It was said with affection, and Hope had laughed along with Alex. She knew that Alex was almost certainly right about Michael, though knowing it wasn't the same as feeling it. She stole a glance at Michael now, who sat with his eyes closed, head slowly nodding down towards his chest. He looked exhausted and vulnerable, and Hope instantly felt protective towards him. In that moment, she knew that she loved him; it was as though the DNA in every cell in her body had suddenly been re-inscribed with the knowledge. She realized again the implications of loving someone as she loved Michael; the responsibility which loving someone brought with it; the pain and sadness that lay ahead of her, should she ever lose him. She thought of her parents, dying in their wrecked car, and she thought of Preston lying in hospital – victims to the random violence of the world. So far, Michael was safe, but could she keep him safe for ever?

Forcing herself to think of other things, she remembered how she'd failed to discover who Alex had met for lunch earlier on. She'd asked Alex how her lunchtime rendezvous had gone, but received only the vaguest of replies. Alex wasn't usually reluctant to talk about her various lovers and friends, so perhaps in this case there really wasn't anything to tell.

And Hope in turn had kept something from Alex – she hadn't said anything about the letter she'd discovered tucked into the back of the painting. She'd now concealed her discovery from her two closest friends. She could rationalize this easily enough; after all, in the absence of a translation of the letter, there was really nothing to tell them yet. She knew that she'd tell them at some point, but for now Hope wanted to hold on to her secret puzzle. It was as though her inability to protect those whom she loved could be compensated for by protecting this one small secret thing that was hers and no one else's.

Michael, slightly drunk after his evening with Jeffrey and weary after his day's work, sat drowsing by Hope's side. The motion of the bus lulled him. The growl of its engine reverberated gently throughout his body, and the warmth of the bus cosseted him after the chill of the city streets. He could have been back in the womb.

Teetering on the edge of sleep, his thoughts drifted in and out of focus. His lunchtime drink with Evette – of which he'd said nothing to either Hope or Jeffrey – teased Michael by its inconclusiveness. Why had Evette invited him? She'd said that it was to thank him for taking the time and trouble to help her find Hope's birthday present, but that seemed a bit odd. After all, she'd already thanked him at Hope's party. If Evette was flirting with him, it wasn't obvious; she'd mostly talked about what Jeffrey was up to with his Chancredy project, and in truth Michael had found this a bit boring. Was it that she *wanted* to flirt with him, but wasn't sure how to go about it? She'd allowed him to kiss her as they parted and he'd foolishly, clumsily sought her lips with their rich coating of gloss, but she'd offered only her cheek to him. Surely if she was flirting, she would have let him kiss her on the mouth.

Evette's mouth. He'd spent quite a lot of their lunchtime together trying not to stare at her mouth. The deep, red gloss that made Evette's lips seem wet made him want, more than anything, to touch them with his tongue. He'd watched her lips, parting, meeting, briefly revealing sharp white teeth, occasionally embracing the tip of her tongue . . .

'Michael.'

It was Hope's voice. As he surfaced to the warm haven of the bus, he saw her moving to stand up. Dutifully, Michael followed her out into the night.

PART TWO

SECOND TRIMESTER

OCTOBER 2002

8

Michael's parents – Doreen and Ernest – sat opposite each other on armchairs, while Hope and Michael sat between them on the settee. The room was clean and orderly, as Michael's mother had always tried to keep it. The wall-unit, the mantelpiece, and the top of the TV all bore testament to the family that had flown. There were photographs of Michael and his sister as children, and of his sister's children now; a photograph of Michael with Hope, a family snapshot of Doreen, Ernest, Michael and his sister on holiday in Tenby when Michael was a moody teenager, and there was a stern, formally-posed studio photograph, sepia tinted, of Michael's maternal grandparents. There wasn't a speck of dust on any of them.

The TV in the corner of the room was on, though the sound was turned down. Michael's father sat watching it anyway, leaving the conversation to Michael's mother – who spoke mostly to Hope. Michael had broken the news of Hope's pregnancy over the phone a few days earlier and his mother had sounded delighted, immediately insisting that they come for tea the following Sunday. And so here they were, sitting in the small living room in his parents' council house, eating sandwiches off plates they held on their laps. The house had a front room with a small dining table, chairs and a sideboard, but this was too formal a setting for such close family as her son and his girlfriend. Doreen kept this room meticulously clean and tidy, refusing to abandon it to more mundane uses: 'You never know when the Queen's going to drop in for tea.' She would say this jokingly, but the point was a serious one: that however humble her surroundings might be, she could hold her head up with the highest in the land when it came to the maintenance of standards. Michael thought her silly and pretentious, but Hope saw Doreen's point, and admired her spirit.

'I must say, you're looking very well on it!' said Doreen. 'You've lovely rosy cheeks. Have you had a scan yet? It must be nearly time now, mustn't it?'

'A few weeks yet,' said Hope.

'Are you excited?'

'Well, yes I am,' said Hope, realizing that, yes, she was. 'If there's anything there to see yet.'

Always the note of caution, as though preparing herself for eventual disappointment.

'What about you, Michael? Are you looking forward to it?'

Michael had been watching the silent TV screen with his father. 'Huh? Sorry,' he said. 'What did you say?'

'The scan. Are you looking forward to it?' his mother persisted.

'I don't know,' he answered, the tone of his voice like a shrug of his shoulders. 'I've never seen one.'

'You have,' insisted his mother. 'You've seen Linnie's haven't you?'

Linnie – Linda – was Michael's sister. She lived a short walk from their parents' house, in a second-floor council flat. She had two children: Jade, nine, and Kyle, seven. Their father Gavin, a long-distance lorry driver, had abandoned them all three years ago and gone underground to avoid paying maintenance. Since then Linnie had survived on state benefits and the occasional loan from her parents, fighting depression, assisted by medication, daytime TV, and cigarettes.

Michael didn't like Jade and Kyle very much. He saw far too much of their father in them. Neither was particularly bright and they were excessively self-centred, even for children. When not at school, they seemed to spend most of their time watching TV.

'They're not like photographs. Everything's blurred. They're like Rorschach tests. You see what you want to see.'

Michael was referring to his sister's ultrasound pictures.

'That's not true,' protested Doreen. 'Linnie's scans were lovely.'

Hope thought that Michael was protesting too much. Was it further evidence of his lack of interest in their baby?

'Well, *I'm* looking forward to it,' said Hope.

Michael failed to pick up on the reproachful note in Hope's voice, and returned to watching the silent TV with his father.

Later, as Michael washed up the dishes at the kitchen sink, he watched Hope and his mother wandering around the small back garden in the fading evening light. Their visits to his parents would usually, weather permitting, culminate in Doreen taking Hope around her garden, showing off her new plantings, pointing out her successes and her failures, outlining her plans for the next year.

Michael heard a noise behind him. His father had brought a couple of mugs into the kitchen for washing and was now fumbling about, as though looking for something.

'Ta,' said Michael, turning back to the washing up. But he could feel his father remain standing beside him.

'Everything all right, Dad?' he said.

'Yes, son.'

He joined Michael at the sink, and together they watched the women in the garden.

'Your mother,' he said. 'She loves that garden.'

Michael waited. He wasn't sure what his father was trying to tell him, though he expected him to tell him something, since this had been the basis of their relationship for many years. If the family went on holiday, his father would point out sights or buildings of note, always explaining to Michael their significance. Or he would identify a species of bird, explaining to Michael how it hunted and where it nested. Watching TV, his father would keep up a running commentary on the actors who populated the screen – who they were, who they'd married, what films or programmes they'd previously starred in. His father was a fount of knowledge, a walking encyclopaedia, and as a child Michael had been impressed.

But as Michael had grown older, he'd found his father more and more irritating. In his father's constant desire to explain the world there was an implicit assumption that his son knew very little. Increasingly, Michael saw his father's insistence on categorizing the world for him as a way of keeping him in his place. And so, throughout Michael's teenage years, a tetchiness had grown between them.

On his father's side, the tetchiness towards his son lay in the complex mixture of rejection and loss of status and authority in his son's eyes. When the arguments had thinned out and finally ceased between them, Ernest had retreated behind the shield of a resentful silence. Their relationship now was cordial, not intimate, each unsure of his status in the other's eyes. Had they been closer, they could have talked out their differences and got over them. But to get closer, they would have needed to talk, and so their relationship had reached an impasse.

'I'll make some more tea,' said Ernest.

'Good idea,' said Michael.

In the garden, Doreen and Hope were talking about babies. Doreen was delighted by Hope's pregnancy. She'd never made a secret of the fact that she believed that Hope and Michael were 'right for each other', or that she hoped that they would eventually get married and have children. Before Hope, Michael had rarely managed to hold on to a girlfriend for more than a few months, so it was a good sign that they'd been together for so long. Michael needed stability, she thought, and Hope certainly seemed to have brought him that. But her son apart, Doreen liked Hope; they got on well together, which hadn't always been the case with Michael's previous girlfriends. Like Hope, Doreen's own parents had died when she was young, and she recognized in Hope something of the loneliness she'd experienced back then – though Hope was always reluctant to talk about herself. Doreen hadn't really come to terms with her loss until she'd met, and eventually married, Ernest and had a family of her own to look after. It was as though having her own family had allowed her to face the future, rather than remain chained to the past. Whatever Hope's pain was like on the inside, Doreen hoped that the child she was carrying would help her to come to terms with her loss. And she hoped that Michael would be as good for Hope as his father had been for her.

Back home that night, Michael sat on the bed watching TV. He was morose, as he always was following a Sunday visit to his parents. What was it about these visits that made him so unsettled, so depressed? Was it the sense of being pulled backwards towards the dependencies of youth?

But perhaps the visits were not so much a reminder of what he used to be, as a harbinger of what he might one day become. He'd come to loathe the way his parents had become set in their ways, their lives governed by ingrained routines. His parents' lives had become boring and predictable. Were he to surprise them with a visit, he knew exactly where they would be sitting; he knew what they'd be doing; he knew the times of day his mother would prepare meals for his father and he knew what they'd be eating. It was as though they had ceased living altogether; that they had been replaced by robots, their free will overwritten by a simple, repetitive programme. What was the point of their lives now? Their house was like a waiting room for death.

Yet he could distinguish between his loathing of what their lives had become, and the people to whom this had happened. What puzzled him was *why* it had happened. His parents, after all, had been teenagers during the 1960s and had witnessed first-hand the flowering of youth culture with all its creativity and anti-establishment rebelliousness; its Beatles and its Stones, its Woodstock and its Altamont. What had happened to them since those times? He looked at Hope, naked after her shower and pregnant with their child – their future – and he hoped that what happened to his parents wasn't called Linda and Michael.

9

Hope sat in a café in town, drinking a cup of coffee. She'd stopped drinking coffee as soon as she'd found out she was pregnant, but today she felt so tired and depressed that she'd decided to treat herself. A newspaper lay open on the table in front of her, its pages swimming before her eyes. She was thinking about how much Michael's parents' approval of her pregnancy meant to her. What would her own parents have made of it? What would they have made of Michael? And what, she wondered, would he have made of them?

Hope's phone rang, breaking her train of thought. It was Ben, calling from work; he'd found someone in the European Studies department who was willing to translate Hope's letter. 'His name's Gareth. He lectures on Germany for the European Studies people.'

'Brilliant! I wish I'd got the letter with me now.'

'Wouldn't do you much good; he's just gone off to Germany for a few weeks. Some sort of exchange thing. Look, I'll see you when you get on to campus. OK?'

Hope put her phone away. She hadn't thought very much about the letter since her visit to Michael's parents, but the thought that she might have found someone who could unravel its mysteries brought a surge of excitement. Would she really find out what the dates signified? Why the letter had been hidden in the back of the painting? What would she find out about the writer of the letter, or its recipient?

Hope's fingers trembled. Was it caffeine, or excitement? She rose, almost involuntarily, and made for the door.

Michael sat at his desk, checking the Monarch Watch website. The butterflies would soon be reaching the pine forests high in the mountains of the Sierra Madre, where they would see out the winter in a state of suspended animation – the cool mountain air slowing down their metabolism and helping to preserve their body fat, necessary fuel for the journey north next spring. And in the spring, the return of warm air wouldn't only wake the hibernating butterflies, but it would also trigger their dormant fertility, so that before they left the forests for the warmer northern climate they would mate, depositing eggs along the route.

Whether it was the thought of the Monarchs, so fragile in appearance, flying so doggedly for such an incomprehensible distance, or whether it was for some other reason he couldn't fathom, Michael felt restless and uncomfortable in his skin. He viewed his life, it seemed, as if from a distance; felt in danger of losing sight of himself. Compounding this sense of alienation was the fact that he hadn't seen any of his friends for some time. He saw Hope every day, preoccupied, lost in her own world; he hadn't seen Jeffrey for nearly two weeks, or had any contact with him. When he'd spoken to Preston, now recuperating at home, a week ago, he'd sounded depressed and reluctant to talk. The last time Michael had seen Alex, she'd been talking seriously and quietly to Hope and he'd felt excluded from their conversation.

Then there was Evette. Though he'd heard and seen nothing of her since their lunch at the gallery a few weeks ago, he thought of her constantly. In the midst of his strange mood, he'd fastened on to Evette as the only person who could bring him back to himself. The self he was increasingly detached from knew that this was fantasy – after all, Evette had shown no definite interest in him whatsoever. She'd been friendly towards him and nothing more. The person he was leaving behind berated him for persisting in his fantasies, reminding him that he loved Hope, and that she was expecting their child.

But the restless self, the detached self, the self emerging from the chrysalis of his routine life with Hope told him that Evette wasn't ignoring him, but *being cagey*, or *playing hard to get*, or *teasing him*. The man that Michael was becoming was only too keen to believe anything and everything, just so long as it ended in Evette finally dropping all pretence of reticence, and coming to him.

That evening, Michael and Hope sat side by side on the sofa watching a film. They had barely said a word to each other all evening. Michael's arms were folded, his legs drawn up under him at one end of the sofa; Hope mirrored him at the other end. She'd decided to tell Michael about the letter she'd found in the back of the painting Evette had given her. Ben's news that he'd found someone to translate it had provided her with a reason to break the news to Michael. But now she wasn't so sure that she wanted to. Michael was withdrawn. Was he cross with her for some reason? She couldn't think why he would be. Then she felt the fluttering sensation in her stomach, and the fear that Michael's reticence might be caused by the child growing inside her erupted forcefully from where she'd suppressed it. Michael didn't want to be a father after all. And he didn't want her now she was going to be a mother. She had to say something to him, get him to open up about how he really felt about her being pregnant. But she couldn't just come out and ask him – that would sound like an accusation.

'I think I felt the baby move,' she said, as an opening gambit.

'Hmm? What?'

'I think I felt it move.'

'What?'

'The baby,' Hope persevered.

'How do you mean?' Michael barely took his eyes from the TV screen.

'Here.' She pulled her T-shirt up above her stomach, and the top of her jogging pants below it. That got Michael's attention. 'Give me your hand.'

She knew that it was too early for Michael to be able to feel the baby moving, but she wanted him to at least imagine it.

'I can't feel anything,' he said. He let his hand rest. He too needed human contact. Hope's slowly distending stomach was soft and warm.

'It's probably wind,' he said. He knew that Hope was challenging him in some way and he wanted to gain the upper hand.

'It's not.'

Michael winced. Hope had said this with disconcerting certainty. He pulled his hand away.

But Hope wasn't to be so easily set aside. She grabbed his hand, gently yet forcefully, and pulled it back to her stomach. She needed Michael to touch her, to connect with her.

'Is everything OK?' Hope asked, still circling, edging closer to her concerns.

'Yeah, sure,' he said.

It was too quick. Too much like a rehearsed answer. He was being evasive again.

'You seem a bit . . . preoccupied?'

She phrased it as a question, prompting Michael to affirm or deny. This time he didn't answer straight away.

'I'm just tired.'

'Tired? Tired of what? Tired of me?'

Hope's anxieties spilled out. She felt tired. Her energy was being sapped, redirected towards the life growing inside her. How could Michael find her attractive now?

'No, no. Just tired. I'm fed up with work and I haven't seen anyone for ages. I just feel a bit stuck. Maybe I should look for another job or something?'

Not tired then, but restless. Restless, yes, and a bit lonely? He needed to see his friends. Maybe they should get everyone together again, another party perhaps? But the thought of a party, with everyone present, made Hope realize just how far she'd travelled since her birthday. Then, she'd looked forward to seeing everyone, but now she dreaded the idea. She felt unlovely and lacked the energy to do anything about it. And she wasn't even halfway through her pregnancy yet. Yet if a party would help Michael . . .

'Why don't we get everyone together for a drink on Friday? We're becoming a pair of recluses. We should get out more. When the baby's born . . .'

Hope pulled herself up short. She was about to suggest that when the baby was born, they might not have the freedom that they currently had and so they should take advantage of that freedom now, while they still could. But in truth, Hope had no real idea of just how much the baby would impact upon their lives. She thought little of the future, locked as she was in a constantly evolving biological present. She expected some disruption to her life and career during the last stages of her pregnancy and in the first few months after the birth. But beyond that, as far as she could see, her life would normalize.

But through her concern for Michael, she perceived an alternative future, one in which the baby wrought more radical changes than she'd imagined. She'd always known that the process would come to an end, that the baby would be born and she'd get her body – and her life – back. But for the first time since she'd conceived the child, she confronted the possibility that, even after the child was born, she might find herself still trapped in its world, unable to escape back to her own life. The thought was dizzying. She burst into tears.

Michael was taken aback. He'd momentarily lost himself in his own troubled thoughts. Suddenly, faced with Hope in tears, concern for her welled up in him, overriding everything else. He turned and put his arms around her.

Later that night, after they had made love, they whispered together like children with secrets. They whispered about marriage, the baby and their friends until, drained of energy, they fell asleep in each other's arms. Michael dreamed of butterflies, and a long journey. Hope dreamed of the baby, and of the woman who had helped her after her fainting fit. In her dream, the woman had a name. It was Klara, the name at the bottom of the letter.

10

'Are you sure you want to do this?'

Hope and Michael stood in front of Preston's house – an inter-war semi in a tree-lined suburban street. Beneath the trees, shadowed from the glow of the street lamps above, cars were parked bumper to bumper. Three hooded shapes drifted along the pavement opposite, coolly regarding the two strangers. It was now just over three weeks since Preston had been discharged from the hospital and he'd not yet returned to work.

Michael stood looking at the house, recalling the faces of Preston's parents in the hospital: the deep resentment which Preston's father had made no effort to conceal. When he'd phoned to speak to Preston since, Preston's mother had always been curt and unfriendly, and Preston had always avoided coming to the phone. Was it that he didn't want to talk to anyone, or was his mother preventing people from talking to him?

'Michael, *are* you sure you want to do this?' Hope asked.

It had been her idea to doorstep their friend. She'd been stung by Michael's complaint that he hadn't seen any of his friends for a while, and she felt responsible, as though her evolving pregnancy was somehow to blame for this. She glanced at Michael's apprehensive face.

'Fuck it. Let's do it,' he said, grimly.

They walked up the short path to the front door where Hope rang the bell. The hall light was on, and when the front door opened, Preston's mother stood silhouetted in the hallway, frowning in her effort to recall who these people were. Over her shoulder, Michael saw the door at the opposite end of the hall open by a few inches. The face of Preston's father appeared in the breach. Seeing Hope and Michael, he retreated stealthily, as though trying to hide the fact that he'd been there at all.

'Yes?' If Preston's mother recognized Hope and Michael, she made no attempt to show it.

'Is Preston in?' Michael asked.

Preston's mother hesitated before answering, as though quickly weighing up a number of possible responses. There seemed to have been no easing of the tension since that night at the hospital. 'Y'better come in.'

It was said with resignation, as though she could find no convincing reason to turn them away.

'Wait here,' she said, before slowly climbing the stairs. She seemed old, a tired old lady worn down by an intolerable burden. For a moment, the only sound in the house was the muffled blatting of a TV set. Minutes trudged by, and still there was no sound from upstairs.

'I don't suppose we'll get a cup of tea,' said Michael, who had to say something. Saying nothing seemed only to increase the tension.

'She'll probably come down with a shotgun to see us off,' said Hope.

'What are we doing here?' said Michael, baffled by the situation.

At last they heard movement upstairs, and finally Preston appeared, followed by his mother. He was dressed, but looked dishevelled, as though he'd slept in the clothes he was wearing. Preston had always had energy, but now he moved slowly as though he'd run out of steam. From the bottom of the stairs it looked as though his head was still bandaged, but as he drew nearer to Hope and Michael, they could see he was wearing a pale-coloured knitted hat pulled low over his forehead and ears.

'Is this your Craig David look?' said Michael, at a loss for anything else to say. To his surprise, Preston smiled. Preston's smiles were infectious, a call to arms for enjoyment. This wasn't his usual boundless grin, but it was a smile all the same and it made Hope and Michael feel a little less uncomfortable.

'Thought I'd try out a new image. In here.'

They followed him through a door into the dining room and sat on upright chairs around a bare dining table. They sat in silence, conversation stifled not only by the strained atmosphere but also by weeks of absence. Michael felt let down; he couldn't understand why Preston had been avoiding him – if in fact he'd been avoiding him – and he didn't know how to break the silence between them. He couldn't do it sitting there in that house, in that atmosphere. Michael had to get Preston away from there.

'Let's go out somewhere for a pint.'

As Michael rattled out his suggestion, panic flickered in Preston's eyes and his entire body shrank away from his visitors. Hope immediately changed the subject.

'Your bruises have cleared up nicely.'

Preston relaxed a little, and in this safety zone they talked for a while about his injuries. But when Michael asked whether or not the police had found the thugs responsible for the attack, Preston became guarded. Again, Hope changed the subject.

'So when are you going back to work? Michael's missing you, you know? And you must have over a thousand emails to deal with by now.'

Preston smiled, but his facial expression was at odds with his mouth, and when he spoke he did so with difficulty.

'I . . . I can't . . . I don't think I can. I mean, I've been having trouble . . .'

Suddenly, and to their astonishment, Preston was crying. Not just crying, but sobbing deeply, thickly, as though he'd been saving it up for weeks. Michael had never seen Preston upset like this before. And before he could work out how to respond, Hope also burst into tears, sobbing along with Preston. Michael felt himself welling up but with an effort he battened this down, telling himself that someone had to stay calm. He knew that he should say something to them both, words of comfort, but what those words should be, he wasn't sure. Then a phrase tumbled out. 'Shall I make a cup of tea?'

The sentence was utterly familiar to him, and he instantly recognized its source. As the words spilled from his mouth he heard them, not in his own voice, but in the composite voices of his mother and father. Tea: it was their solution to any crisis. Hope turned to Michael with an incredulous look on her face.

'Tea?'

For a moment there was silence, and then Hope was laughing through her sobs. Preston looked from Michael to Hope and back, and then he too began to laugh. Michael sat looking at the two of them laughing and crying at the same time, and he felt foolish and left out.

'Sorry,' said Preston, reaching for the tissue that Hope was holding out to him. 'Jesus, this is embarrassing.'

'Don't apologize,' said Hope. 'You should get it out of your system.'

'The problem is that I can't *stop* getting it out of my system. I seem to be crying all the time.'

'I know what you mean,' said Hope ruefully. 'I can't seem to stop crying either.'

Without thinking about it, Hope placed a hand on her stomach. Preston noticed the move, and suddenly remembered that Hope was pregnant.

'Oh Jeez, I'm sorry. Hope, how are you? I totally forgot. I'm sorry . . . I can't seem to get my head on straight . . .'

Preston sank his head into his hands. When he lifted it again to look at them, Michael saw on Preston's face the same weary expression he'd seen on Preston's mother's moments before.

'Look,' said Preston, clearly struggling with himself. 'Let's go out for a drink. Somewhere quiet. I can't talk here.'

Neither can we, thought Michael.

'We can drive out of the city if you want,' said Hope.

'I'll get a jacket,' said Preston.

They found a pub on the edge of the city, hemmed in by trees but with fields visible in the distance. The glow of the city they had left behind filled a quadrant of the sky, burnishing the underside of the low cloud bank. As they walked across the car park, they could hear the distant roar of city traffic, competing with the wind-ruffled trees, gossiping overhead. The bar was busy, so they headed for the quieter lounge and tucked themselves into an alcove. Preston hadn't removed his knitted hat or changed his clothes. He sank back with his drink, as though his body were too heavy to hold upright. The effort of making himself go out with his friends seemed to have drained what little energy he had left.

After his first pint, Preston seemed to relax and, when Michael came back from the bar with a second round of drinks, he found him trading anecdotes about health with Hope. As Michael sat listening to them, he noticed that while Hope talked about things internal to her body – the various manifestations of pregnancy – Preston tended to avoid talking directly about his injuries, focusing instead on his encounters with various medical professionals. Michael wanted Preston to talk about his injuries – Preston still hadn't told him what happened on the night of the attack – and although he accepted that his friend might not want to relive that evening, his curiosity was unsated.

And he wanted to know about the hat. Michael remembered clearly the image of Preston lying in his hospital bed. The scar on Preston's cheek was still visible, but no longer angry – and the swelling and bruising that had so disfigured his face that night was all but invisible now. But Preston's forehead had been swathed in bandages, and with the knitted hat pulled down low, the bandages might just as well have still been there.

As the evening wore on, Preston grew steadily more at ease. He talked about how anxious he'd been since the attack, and how difficult it still was to venture out in public. He was on medication for his nerves, and although he knew that getting back to work would be good for him, he couldn't face up to it yet.

Momentarily exhausted of conversation, all three fell silent. Then Preston spoke. 'Ben's been really supportive.'

'Ben?' said Hope, puzzled.

'Ben?' said Michael, wondering who Ben was.

'What? Ben? *Library* Ben? Ben who works with me?' This was the only Ben that Hope knew.

Preston looked embarrassed, as though he'd broken a promise, or let something slip that he shouldn't have.

'Ben, at your birthday party?' said Michael, looking quizzically Hope, then at Preston. '*That* Ben?'

While Michael turned over the question as to why Ben, who worked with Hope, was being supportive to *his* friend, Hope suddenly understood what Preston was telling them.

'*Ben*? You and *Ben*?' Hope looked astonished, though she laughed too, seeing how difficult it had been for Preston to say what he'd just said. 'Preston, you sly fox!'

Preston, embarrassed, covered his face with his hands. Through his fingers, his eyes regarded Michael, trying to judge his reaction. But Michael hadn't yet caught up.

'What's Ben being supportive for? You only met him at Hope's party didn't you?'

He looked from Preston to Hope, who stared back in disbelief at him.

'Michael! Wake up!' She laughed, and looked again at Preston. 'You and *Ben*! I would never have guessed in a million years. I can't believe it!'

At last Michael understood what Preston was saying to them. He was dumbfounded. Michael had known Preston for the entire four years he'd worked at Farsight; they'd even started there on the very same day, had been friends from the first moment they met. How could Preston possibly have kept this quiet all that time? How could Michael not have guessed? He watched Hope and Preston chatting and laughing together, completely at ease with each other, and felt bewildered. He didn't know what to do; didn't know what to say. He knew, intellectually, that there was nothing wrong with being gay, but he felt uncomfortable all the same and he wasn't really sure why. He didn't really know what it *meant* for Preston to be gay; but also he didn't know what it meant for *himself* and for their friendship. He didn't know how he should *be* with his friend now.

And something else nagged at Michael too. He felt *hurt*. He could understand why Preston, traumatized, hadn't wanted to see him over the past few weeks. But to learn that Ben had been permitted to be 'supportive' while he – Michael – hadn't, felt like a snub. Confused and resentful, he wished now that he'd not made the effort to call on Preston at all.

'So why the hat then?' The question was snapped out, and although Preston didn't pick up on Michael's tone, Hope did. She looked at Michael with a directness that felt like a slap on the cheek. 'I'm only asking,' he said to her, checking himself.

Preston looked thoughtful for a moment, as though weighing something up, then lifted the knitted hat from his forehead. In the dim light of the lounge, and against Preston's dark skin, they could see a series of deep scars, almost healed but still clearly visible. The scars seemed not to be random, as though his attackers had tried to carve a pattern into his skin.

'What is it?' said Hope looking closer. 'It looks like . . . writing?'

Preston pulled the hat back down over the scars.

'It is,' he said.

'What does it say?' said Michael, horrified at the mesh of cuts. Preston hesitated, struggling with himself again.

'It says *QUEER*,' he said.

Later that evening, Preston talked about the events leading up to the attack. He admitted that he'd found himself attracted to Ben at the party, and had begun to suspect that Ben might be interested, too, especially when Ben agreed to share a taxi into town after the party. In the taxi, Ben had asked Preston if he fancied going on to a club and Preston had said yes. The attack had happened shortly after they left the club together.

'Poor you,' said Hope. What happened?'

'There was a gang of them. You think you're going to be all right in the gay quarter. I mean, it's kind of home turf, isn't it? You think you're safe through sheer weight of numbers. You get a lot of tourists, if you know what I mean? Men and women, all sorts. But that's OK. The clubs and pubs are lively even if you're *not* gay; I mean, you don't have to be gay to have a good time, do you? Anyway, you know the area – a two-minute walk and you're away from the bars and clubs and it's all warehouses and car parks. But you still feel safe. You just don't expect anything to happen nowadays, do you? I mean, it's not like it's the Dark Ages or anything.

'So Ben and I walk off into the night. Ben's got an apartment down by the canal basin. Not far. Walkable. And it's a lovely evening. You remember? We sat out in the garden at your party? Anyway, we heard them coming behind us. But they were just a bunch of guys, laughing, having a good time. They'd followed us from the direction of the club. I mean, why would you think anything's going to happen?'

Preston stopped talking and looked down. Hope leaned forward and touched his hand with hers. She wanted Preston to go on; could sense that he needed to go on. But she could see that a change of direction would help.

'Didn't they do anything to Ben? I mean, he seemed OK.'

'They kicked him a few times, but they were more interested in me. From the language they used, I think my skin colour probably had something to that. Anyway, they dragged us both into a car park to start with. There must have been four, maybe five of them? Ben managed to get away and ran. A couple of them chased him. I didn't see any of this – he told me later; I was down on the ground having the shit kicked out of me. As soon as Ben'd shaken off the guys chasing him, he headed back up to the quarter and found some cops. By the time they found me I'd no idea where I was.'

'Ben didn't say anything about any of this,' said Hope.

'Well, he likes to keep his private life private, if you know what I mean.'

'So what's the story with your mom and dad?'

Preston explained that his parents had overheard a doctor discussing the attack with two police officers at Preston's bedside. The doctor hadn't noticed Preston's parents standing just beyond the curtains.

'Mom's OK with it – well, not OK, but *resigned*, I guess. But Dad's really having a hard time getting his head round it. For some reason he puts it all on Mom, as though it's all her fault. And he won't talk to me. It's like I don't really exist for him any more. He wants me out of the house.'

'Outed a second time,' said Michael, trying to lighten the mood. Whatever Michael thought about his friend's sexuality, he'd been moved by what Preston had been through. No one deserved that kind of beating, whatever their sexuality, or race. Preston, for his part, saw what Michael was trying to do and smiled.

'I guess it's time, really. I'm twenty-eight and I'm still living with my parents. It's time I got a place of my own.'

'Have they caught them?' said Hope, unable to contain her curiosity. Preston paused, look down. She could see that he'd reached another barrier.

'Sorry Preston, if you'd rather not talk about it . . .'

'No, it's all right. I guess I need to really. I mean, I suppose I should and all. But no, they didn't. They checked CCTV and everything – even got some images – but the quality was shit. I don't think it's going to be on *Crimewatch*, if you know what I mean?'

At the end of the evening, they dropped Preston home. As they parked up outside his house, Hope felt tired and low. Preston's story had reminded her of the violence that seemed always to be scratching at the edge of her life. She wanted desperately to steer the conversation towards the light and away from the dark, and to leave Preston on an optimistic note.

'Listen Preston, you remember the painting that Evette gave me for my birthday? Well, I decided that I'd start cleaning it up the other day.'

Hope explained to Preston about the letter, which she'd found sealed into the back of the painting. Michael sat in the back seat, hearing the story himself for the first time.

'Ben said something about getting something translated,' said Preston. 'Some friend of his teaches German or something.'

'He'll be back in a couple of weeks. I don't suppose I'll find much out, but it'll be interesting all the same.'

They said goodnight, and Preston disappeared into the dim light of his parents' hallway.

As Hope and Michael were driving home, Michael was thinking about the letter and why Hope hadn't said anything to him about it before. For the second time that evening, Michael felt that he'd been excluded by someone very close to him.

11

After ebbing away for such a long time, the tide had begun to turn in Michael's world. He sat at his desk, looking at an inbox with emails from Jeffrey and Evette. Michael hadn't had any contact with Evette for several weeks now, though he thought of her often. He read her email first:

Subject: Invite
Michael, are you free next Friday? J away in London all
day. Take me to lunch
   Evette
   xx

Michael read it over a second time, and then a third. He was excited and intrigued. It was odd enough that, out of the blue, Evette would invite him to lunch, but why would she also mention that Jeffrey wouldn't be around? Was lunch a pretext for something else? If Jeffrey was away in London, then the house would be empty and, well, who knew what might happen after lunch? What might dessert turn out to be? The winking icon at the end of the invite and the two kisses below her name seemed to invite Michael to read between the lines in this way. He replied briefly – *Where? What time?* – not wanting to name a place in case the whole idea of lunch was a pretext for just going back to her place. In his diary for the Friday ahead he wrote: *Meeting Re Stock Levels: 12.30 p.m.* – a precaution in case Hope saw it.

He moved then to Jeffrey's email: did Michael want to meet this evening for a drink? Pushing thoughts of Evette aside for the moment, and stifling as best he could the briefest tremor of guilt – Jeffrey was his best friend, after all – he replied that he did. Having reactivated his social calendar, Michael settled down to work.

It was two minutes to ten, and Parmjit was going to be late for her lecture. As she hurried across campus, a strong wind gusted in her face. A voice, carried on the wind, called her name and, as she turned to see who it was, she slipped on the mulch of wet leaves covering the pavement. Papers scattered from her shoulder bag on to the ground.

'Shit!'

Gyorgy appeared at her side. He began helping her to gather the silted papers. 'My fault,' he said, with a look of concern. 'Please. I pick them up.'

'You'll be late for the lecture,' said Parmjit, crossly.

'So will you,' said Gyorgy, calmly and factually.

As instantly as her anger at Gyorgy flared up, Parmjit accepted that the rain and the wind weren't his fault, nor that she was late and in a hurry. She knew that it wouldn't matter if they both arrived late anyway; there was always a drift of students into the room during the first fifteen minutes of the lecture. She stood up, responding to the calmness in Gyorgy's voice. It was as though he'd placed his hands on her shoulders to steady her.

'Look,' she said, making a rapid decision. 'We shouldn't arrive late for the lecture. Shall we get a coffee instead?'

Although Parmjit was enjoying the ideas she encountered in her studies, she was less impressed by the experience of university education. The lectures were interesting, but the lecturers seemed to be engaged in a constant battle to stem the mounting cacophony of student conversation, trilling mobile phones and the interruptions caused by the steady stream of wilfully late students. Week after week, tutors prefaced their lectures with requests to the students to turn their mobile phones off and to keep the noise down, but since barely half of them were in the room at that point it couldn't even be said that these requests fell on deaf ears. Moreover, the lectures were often interrupted for vox pop sessions which were usually dominated by the most self-confident students. Unfortunately, the level of self-confidence could not always be equated with the level of intelligence, and so lectures regularly descended into banality.

'I have to listen to enough empty-headed nonsense when I'm driving my cab,' said Parmjit.

They were sitting in the Student Union café, drinking tea. Gyorgy was interested in Parmjit's several jobs. 'It is good that you work,' he said, fiddling with the cigarette he wanted to light but couldn't – they were sitting beneath a NO SMOKING sign.

'What do you mean?' she asked.

This was the first time that Parmjit had been alone with Gyorgy since the start of term. A small group of students who were attending 'Introduction to Politics' had taken to going for lunch together after the weekly seminar session. Because of her various commitments, Parmjit spent very little time on campus, and so found these lunchtime sessions valuable in getting to know her fellow students. Gyorgy didn't chat readily – he seemed to dislike idle banter – and his aloofness was construed by some as rudeness. But his contributions to their discussions were always intelligent and sharp.

'Work is good. You are contributing to society. It is good for the soul.'

'You should be driving my taxi at chucking-out time,' said Parmjit, ruefully.

'But you are helping people get home. Drunk or not, they need you to help them.'

'They may need a taxi, but they don't need *me*,' said Parmjit. 'Some of them make that quite clear.'

'How do you mean?'

Gyorgy's apparent naïvety surprised Parmjit. 'Well, my family is Gujarati and I'm a woman. So I get insulted for my race and my gender. Last Friday, for instance. I pick up four lads outside a pub in town. They're big lads, and very drunk, but they want a curry, and so they ask me to take them to an Indian restaurant. So I say, 'which one?' and they say, 'you tell us, you Paki bitch, your dad probably owns one.' Now, I'm used to these kinds of insults but I don't really want to have these lads in my cab, so I drive them about a quarter of a mile down the road to a restaurant that they could've walked to if they'd been bothered, or sober. I know that the restaurant has a good reputation for dealing with drunks so I know that they'll be able to keep a lid on any trouble. But then the lads won't pay me for the journey. Personally, I'd have been happy to just let them out and leave them to it. But they start to ask me for, well, sexual favours in return for the money. My money. I mean, I didn't drive them far but I still drove them. I *earned* that money.'

Gyorgy looked concerned. 'What happened?' he said.

'It was OK. The restaurant had a couple of bouncers who came over to see what was going on. I knew one of them. When the lads saw these guys – and they're big, strong guys – they paid up and got out. All in a night's work.'

'Why do you do it?' said Gyorgy.

'Because I'm contributing to society. Because it's good for my soul.'

Gyorgy smiled and looked sheepish. He realized in an instant that he'd been naïve. But, though Gyorgy didn't know it, Parmjit had meant what she said.

Hope walked across the campus in search of a sandwich for her lunch. As she walked past the window of the Student Union café, she caught sight of Parmjit in animated conversation with a stocky, blond-haired student. They were so engrossed that Hope decided not to interrupt them. But as she passed the window Parmjit glanced up and broke off her conversation. She motioned at Hope to wait, left the young man sitting at the table, and joined Hope outside.

'How are you? I haven't seen you in a while.' Parmjit looked at Hope's face closely. 'Wow! Look at your cheeks! Being pregnant suits you!'

'I wish I could believe that,' said Hope. 'I look like I fell asleep under a sunlamp.'

'No, it doesn't look bad at all. Join us for a cuppa.'

Parmjit motioned towards the table where Gyorgy sat, still playing with his unlit cigarette. Hope remembered how they'd looked together moments before, and didn't want to intrude.

'No, I'm rushing. I just ran out for a sandwich while the rain's not too bad.'

They made a tentative arrangement to meet during the next week, and then Hope left Parmjit to Gyorgy and his cigarette.

In the supermarket checkout queue, Hope stood thinking about Parmjit and the man she'd been sitting with. There was an intimacy in the way they talked together, she thought. Or perhaps she was reading too much into a situation that she'd only really glimpsed through the window.

A voice broke through Hope's reveries. The person at the head of the small queue was speaking to the assistant. Immediately, Hope recognized the voice as that of the

Scandinavian woman who had helped her to her feet on the day she'd fainted. Hope desperately wanted to talk to her, but she could see the woman leaving the supermarket. Ahead of her, a customer was trying to pay for a basket of goods with a card that the store's machine was unable to read. As the cashier tried again and again to take the student's money, Hope dithered: should she put the sandwich down and follow the woman, or should she wait a few moments longer to pay? Immobilized by her indecisiveness and cursing herself for failing to seize the moment, Hope realized that she'd already lost the woman among the flood of students pouring out of lecture theatres across the campus. All she could do was look out of the window at the rain that was now belting down.

12

Later that same night, Michael met Jeffrey in a bar in town. Jeffrey, dressed in a long black leather coat, black turtleneck sweater, black drainpipe trousers and winkle-picker boots, looked like he'd just come from an audition with the Velvet Underground. All he lacked was a pair of shades. They took their drinks and settled at a table.

'So Preston's a shirtlifter then?'

Jeffrey's opening sentence took Michael by surprise. He was used to Jeffrey's casual sexism and racism and tolerated it when it was general in its focus. He'd always thought it was something of a posture, a desire on Jeffrey's part to appear provocative. To hear Jeffrey refer to his friend in this way made him immediately uncomfortable.

'He's not a shirtlifter, Jeffrey.'

Michael snapped this out, and immediately regretted it. After all, Jeffrey was his friend too, and Michael hated confrontation. Unexpectedly, Jeffrey apologized.

'Sorry. Shouldn't say that. Don't want to offend the political correctness lobby, do we?'

Jeffrey's sarcastic tone of voice told Michael that it was

only a qualified apology. He also realized that Jeffrey was including him in the 'political correctness lobby'.

'I'm not being politically correct. I just think it's not very nice.'

'Look, Michael, it's just a name. If these people have had a sense of humour bypass that's not my fault. It's amusing, a joke. I expect that . . .'

'Amusing?'

Jeffrey and Michael both looked up. The voice was Hope's.

'Telling jokes? I could do with a laugh. Come on. Share.'

'I thought you were meeting Alex,' said Michael. He was pleased to see Hope, not least because she would be more of a match for Jeffrey than he was.

'I was. I have. She's at the bar. Do you need a refill?'

As Hope went to the bar, Jeffrey spoke quietly, the previous discussion apparently forgotten. Jeffrey checked his mobile phone and then sat back in his seat, lost in thought. It was as though he'd forgotten that Michael was there. He was looking off in the direction of the bar when Michael spoke.

'How's Evette? I haven't seen her for a while.' Michael was thinking of the email he'd received from her that morning, inviting him to lunch next Friday while Jeffrey was in London. He was about to ask Jeffrey what he was off to London for, but remembered just in time that Jeffrey had not yet mentioned he was going.

'Here's the womenfolk,' said Jeffrey, ignoring Michael's inquiry about Evette.

'Well now,' said Alex. 'I hear you boys are telling jokes.'

Two hours and several drinks later, the conversation between all four of them had become a dialogue between Alex and Jeffrey. Alex was baiting Jeffrey about his political views. Earlier in the evening Jeffrey had grandly announced to his friends the launch of the Chancredy Multimedia Collective's website. Intent on mischief, Alex had picked Jeffrey up on his use of the word 'collective'. Politically, Jeffrey was an instinctive libertarian who saw any form of collectivism as a threat to personal freedom. Moreover, he had time and again proved himself incapable of collaborating with anyone else (even Michael had worked with him for a time, swept along on the tide of Jeffrey's oceanic enthusiasms, until almost engulfed by them). Jeffrey was as radical an individualist as it was possible to breed, so why describe Chancredy as a collective?

Jeffrey was in expansive mood. He saw himself, he explained, as a freedom fighter, engaged – along with fellow libertarians around the world – in a grand ideological struggle against the secret machinations of Corporate Interests and World Capitalism which, controversially, served the interests of a secret communistic cabal. He cited Lenin on this point, for it was that great Soviet leader who had pointed out that liberal democracy was 'the best possible political shell for capitalism'.

'Ask yourself,' he said. 'What could possibly be the best political and economic shell for communism?'

It was a rhetorical question; he didn't expect anyone to answer it. He paused before delivering the answer.

'Capitalism! It's obvious!'

'Oh come on, Jeffrey, you can't be serious,' said Alex.

But Jeffrey was. He explained at length how it was that the capitalist system and its associated political structures had been subjugated to the will of a communistic elite.

'Look,' he said earnestly. 'The signs are all around you. Think about the Chinese in their Mao suits and their *Little Red Book*. Now think about us in our Gap trousers and Nike trainers, our Calvin Klein underpants and our Ellesse tops, eating McBurgers and Kentucky Fried Shit and drinking Coca Colonic. Instead of the *Little Red Book* we have *Captain*

Corelli's Mandolin and the Third Way. We have faceless, processed music by endless niche-marketed boy bands and we have female liberation in the form of Ginger Spice's 'Girl-Power' and Madonna in a basque. We have so-called reality TV which is actually nothing more than a reflection of our real lives. *Big Brother* is nothing more than a rendered-down version of our surveillance society, with its ever-present CCTV cameras tracking our movements everywhere, our locations pinpointed by our mobile phones, our consumer profiles mapped and monitored by supermarket reward cards, our emails and phone conversations stored on central databases which sell information about us to anyone who can pay or who can manipulate the legal system to get what they want, and our citizenship rights in hock to the whims of the Government bureaucrats who want to introduce identity cards so that they can even more thoroughly monitor us. Our lives are increasingly plastic and packaged, preformed like IKEA furniture, and like IKEA furniture we dutifully assemble the ideology for ourselves because it's what we've been trained to do. From birth. We don't have individuality, we have the *illusion* of individuality.'

But Alex wasn't buying it.

'You don't think that you might be misunderstanding communism here, Jeffrey? I thought it was all about who owned the means of production, or something? You know, class struggle? That sort of thing.'

'All I'm saying is: look around you. The signs are all around us.'

'But when I look around,' said Alex, determined not to let Jeffrey off the hook. 'When I look around, I may see a McDonald's on every street corner, but I also see dozens of small, *non*-corporate restaurants too. Walk in any direction from here and within five minutes you'll come to an Indian restaurant. Nothing corporate there. And if someone wants to go through life drinking nothing but Coca Cola, then good luck to them. But you don't have to. And even if they did, why's that anything other than their business? Anyway, you're happy enough to sit there drinking corporate beer. And look at what you're wearing, for heaven's sake. You're dressed head to toe in clothes bearing exactly those labels you say you despise.'

To this last jibe, Jeffrey had a polished response: purchasing such things made no difference to the system whatsoever, whether you opted in or out. Refusing to buy consumer goods wasn't going to bring the system crashing down: for a start, you'd never get enough people to give up buying this stuff. No, he – Jeffrey – worked against the system in other ways: by using his creativity to explore the weaknesses of the system, and exposing those weaknesses in his artworks. In this task, he was aided by the system itself which continually revolutionized the means of artistic production, allowing Jeffrey, and those like him – 'the "invisible collective" if you will' – to critique the system. In pursuing this goal, it didn't matter that the 'collective' – the disparate individuals across the globe with whom Jeffrey aligned himself – wasn't guided by a central committee. It was distinctly to their advantage, he argued, that they were thoroughly decentralized and radically unorganized, since this made it impossible for the enemy to focus its counter-attack. It didn't matter that these 'freedom fighters' did not know each other, or even know *of* each other. (Jeffrey, for example, wasn't interested in anyone else's work.) Nor did it matter that, had they known each other (whoever they were), it was unlikely that they would or could agree as to what should replace capitalism. It was not for Jeffrey, or those like him, to write recipes for the cookbooks of the future. What unified the collective, if anything did, was the channelling of the creative urge to hasten the demise of the system which ensnared everyone.

'We oppose organization with lack of organization; centralization with decentralization; intelligence with instinct;

production with creation; uniformity with individuality; so-called "civilization" with the creativity of madness.'

'Brains with bullshit?'

'We're like viruses,' continued Jeffrey, oblivious to Alex's interjection, 'attacking the body of the system from within.'

He sat back triumphantly. But Alex wasn't beaten yet. 'So let me get this straight – you're going to bring the system crashing down using poetry and music and video installations? You're going to chant down Babylon? Is that it?'

'Yes, Alex. That's exactly what we're going to do.'

'Jeffrey, you're bonkers.'

Hope and Michael had sat through the exchange, but they'd now had enough. 'Time to go,' said Hope, standing up. 'A woman in my condition shouldn't be out this late.'

'It's only nine-thirty,' said Jeffrey. 'The night is young.'

'Work in the morning,' said Michael, also standing up.

Jeffrey looked at Alex. 'Leaving?'

'Maybe a quick one, for the road?'

'Always like a quick one,' said Jeffrey, winking theatrically. He stood up, feeling for his wallet.

'Right,' said Hope, leaning down to kiss Alex. 'See you both soon.'

13

Michael and Hope arrived at the hospital in plenty of time, and were pointed towards a waiting room with cool blue walls. There were several padded, vinyl-covered chairs, a coffee table covered with a pile of dog-eared women's magazines, a grey metal waste-paper basket and a noticeboard full of information leaflets. Hope's eyes kept drifting back to a leaflet which advertised a bereavement support group under the heading LOST YOUR BABY? NEED TO TALK?

Michael's eyes kept returning to a poster which announced the MEN! IT'S YOUR PREGNANCY TOO! programme of group-therapy sessions. Michael had no desire at all to talk to other men about his experience of being the partner of a pregnant woman, but sitting there in the blank utility of the room, he did find himself wondering what being a father would be like.

Casting around in his mind for a possible role model, the first thought that came into his head was his own father, followed swiftly by the absentee father of his sister's children. Neither seemed especially inspiring. Linnie's husband was a waste of space and that was that, but was his own father any better? All Michael really saw him do nowadays was sit in front of the TV set. He no longer seemed to have any interests or enthusiasms, hobbies or passions.

If there was energy and enthusiasm around his parents' home, it came from his mother. She was always doing something, whether in the house – cleaning, tidying, cooking, sewing, knitting, doing her puzzles – or in her beloved garden. She may not have been inventing a cure for AIDS, or debating politics with her local MP, or solving the riddle of the Sphinx, but she was always engaged with life. It seemed odd to admit it to himself, but all things considered, his mother was the kind of father he would like to be.

'I'm dying for a pee,' said Hope, interrupting his thoughts. 'I can't hold on much longer.'

She'd been told that she'd need a full bladder for the scan. The idea was that the full bladder would push the womb upwards, making it easier for the radiographer to scan the foetus. But to Hope it felt as though the opposite was happening: her womb and its tiny occupant were bearing down on the swollen bladder.

'I'm going to have to go and let some out if they don't hurry it up.'

Hope stood up to ease the pressure and Michael noticed that her bump was now visible, pushing the top of her trousers and the bottom of her T-shirt apart. He looked at the thin slash of taut skin revealed, and suddenly became aware that he was both aroused by the sight and that he felt uncomfortable with being aroused. Attractive as the glimpse of flesh was to one half of his brain, to the other half – the half steeped in the rhetoric of horror movies and twilight zone X-files TV shows – Hope's protruding belly looked eerily like a giant eye slowly unlidding itself. In an irrational sweat of instant paranoia, Michael felt as though he were under scrutiny from the strange creature growing inside Hope. It was as though it knew – it just *knew* – that were he not here at Hope's side in this grim hospital antechamber, he would almost certainly now be meeting Evette for lunch, or something more; for this was the day Jeffrey was away in London.

Michael hadn't realized when he'd read Evette's email just a week ago that this was also the day of Hope's first ultrasound scan. Reluctant as he'd been to cancel his liaison with Evette, he knew that he couldn't let Hope down.

'You must be Hope.' The radiographer stood in the doorway, smoothing down her uniform as though she'd just put it on. 'And you must be . . . ?'

'Michael,' said Michael, assuming that she wasn't really interested in who he was. Hope followed the woman out of the room. Michael remained seated. Seconds later the woman's head appeared around the door. 'Coming?'

Michael followed her to a room with an examination couch on which a long strip of what looked like blue paper towel had been draped from top to bottom. Beside the couch was a large machine painted the colour of sallow skin; in front of this was a chair.

Hope handed her coat to Michael and climbed up on to the couch, worrying that she might tear the paper towel. Michael sat on to the chair as the radiographer made ready for the private screening. As Hope rustled self-consciously around on the couch, Michael thought ruefully of Evette in her shapely suit with its short skirt, her copper fringe, those eyes. The grim utility of the hospital wasn't Evette's world, though it was now Hope's. And, Michael realized with regret, it was now his world too.

Lying on her back, all Hope could think about was the pressure on her bladder. 'You'd better get on with it,' she said. 'Or I'm going to have an accident.'

'Won't take long,' said the radiographer, smiling.

Lying on the couch, her pregnant stomach exposed to this stranger, Hope suddenly felt vulnerable. She reached for Michael's hand.

The radiographer switched switches and adjusted things, and finally seemed happy that everything was ready. She produced a tube of lubricating jelly and squirted a dollop on to Hope's distended stomach. 'OK, Hope, this is just a routine procedure. It won't harm your baby in any way. The gel helps me to move the probe around. Can you see the screen all right?'

As Hope turned to look at the black screen, her sense of vulnerability gave way to fear – would there be anything there? The waiting room poster came back to her: LOST YOUR BABY? She gripped Michael's hand. If the scan revealed that the baby had died inside her, would she feel devastated, or would she feel relieved? Hope stood on the edge of an unknown future – a future in which she would have to face up to one fact or another: either the baby was there and doing well, or it had died and she would be freed from its imperatives.

For his part, Michael was fascinated. He couldn't believe the amount of gel that had been dripped on to Hope's belly. As the woman smeared the scanner across it, the device left a thick track in the translucent jelly. He felt Hope's hand tighten around his own as abstract grey shapes smeared themselves across the small black screen, shadowing the movements of the radiographer's hand. The images on the screen could have been the bottom of the ocean for all he could make out.

'Well now,' said the radiographer. 'Let's see what we've got.'

All three of them now focused on the tiny screen. The woman's sweeping movements slowed as she began to look more carefully at the images.

'Well, there's your baby.'

The speed of the announcement took them both by surprise. Hope craned her neck to look at the screen; Michael leaned forward, peering closely. Nothing there looked at all like a baby.

'Where?' said Hope, a tremble of excitement in her voice. 'I can't see it.'

'There. Look. That's its head . . .'

It was certainly a round shape, but it could have been a kidney for all Hope could tell. Or her painfully distended bladder. The woman twisted the probe slightly.

'. . . and there's the spine . . .'

Another twist.

'. . . and a little arm. Can you see it? Just there.'

The woman traced a tiny curve on the screen with her finger. Hope and Michael peered intently and as they did so the thing they were looking at jerked violently.

'Oops! It's on the move!'

The radiographer was laughing, but Hope and Michael were confused.

'What happened?' said Hope. 'Is it OK?'

'Yes, yes. It's fine. Look, there's a leg . . .'

Another indistinct curve.

'But I didn't *feel* it move,' said Hope.

'They're always on the go, one way or another. You don't always feel it.'

As she spoke, the woman continued to move the scanner around.

'. . . and there's the placenta . . . good. Everything looks OK.'

Hope heard the words but she still didn't quite believe them. Michael was simply bewildered by the images. The things pointed out to him – the head, the arm, the spine, the leg – just didn't look like what they were supposed to look like. The sense of anticlimax Michael felt surprised him; he hadn't realized how excited he'd been at the prospect of seeing their baby for the first time.

The woman turned to Hope and Michael, smiling. 'Well, everything seems fine. Your baby's growing normally. Would you like a picture? You'll need to make a donation if you do.'

Hope lay back. She felt on the verge of tears, but didn't know why. The scanning started again in order to find a clear image for printing, and as the printer made the picture, the radiographer wiped gel from Hope's belly. The pressure reminded Hope of her distended bladder.

'I have to pee,' she said and, jumping down from the bed, she hurried out of the room.

In the toilet, it took her an age to finish. It took longer for the tears to stop falling from her eyes. She didn't know why she was crying. Was it relief at finding that the baby was alive and well, or grief for the child-free life that she could no longer have? Was it the confused sadness that she knew was mixed up, in some complex way, with her anger at her parents, who would never see the grandchild she was bearing them? Or was it simply relief as she finally emptied her bladder?

There was a knock at the door. It was Michael. 'You all right in there?' he called.

Hope said that she'd be out in a minute. She was glad that Michael had come with her to the hospital, that he was able to get himself out of the meeting he'd got scheduled. She re-arranged her clothes, washed her hands and checked her face. She knew that she wouldn't be able to hide the fact that she'd been crying, but there wasn't anything she could do about that. The face that stared back at her from the mirror looked tired and sad; the eyes were bewildered.

'Why aren't I happy?' she whispered, but the face that stared back at her had no answer.

As Hope and Michael stepped through their front door, the phone was ringing. It was Alex. Michael watched Hope shuck her coat off one arm and disappear into the lounge to talk with her friend, then went to the kitchen to make tea. He felt low.

He could see that Hope had been crying and he'd thought they might be tears of happiness, or at least relief, at seeing their baby for the first time, even if it did look indistinguishable from the Loch Ness monster. But on the journey home she'd barely spoken, though she'd held on to him throughout the journey.

He heard Hope's voice as she headed up the stairs. He took his tea into the lounge and settled on the sofa, sipping morosely at his drink. Life seemed to be swirling around him, out of his control. He could usually have relied on Hope to stabilize him when he felt this way, but now she was caught up in the whirlwind too. Life was shifting into another gear, or passing into another dimension – something was happening from which there would be no going back. He felt in his pocket for the ultrasound picture of their baby. The flimsy bit of paper was covered in black, smudged here and there by white flecks, like clouds in a tempest. He could just about recognize that there was a baby there – the radiographer had pointed out the head, the arms and the legs – but it too looked to be caught up in a dark, swirling universe. Other than this, he felt no connection with the strange, dappled creature in the picture.

Michael's gaze drifted to the painting propped against the wall on the mantelpiece. It reminded him of Evette in the second-hand shop and the birthday party when Evette had given the painting to Hope. He remembered his drunken encounter with Evette on the kitchen floor, and the conversation he'd had as he knelt with his head over the toilet-bowl, and from there his thoughts returned to the ultrasound photograph that lay on the coffee-table in front of him. The dark, shadowy world in which the baby floated reminded him of the forest where he'd encountered a naked Evette, beset by a hallucinatory swarm of butterflies.

Something about the butterflies resonated with him. He thought of the Monarchs who would now be settling into their Mexican mountain roosts in preparation for the long winter ahead and, as he pondered the resilience and beauty of these butterflies, he once again found himself staring at the painting on the mantelpiece. Hope had been so quiet in the car. She always was these days. He looked again at the landscape on the mantelpiece, and his gaze fastened on the enigmatic device – the butterfly-shaped signature – etched in the corner of the painting.

14

Parmjit sat in the university library reading and making notes for an essay, due in January. The Christmas vacation had begun and the library was quiet, though it wasn't empty. Here and there, students worked at PCs, nestled among piles of books and journals, taking advantage of the end-of-term quiet.

'A student studying in the library. That's what we librarians like to see.'

Parmjit looked up. Hope stood there, holding several journals in her hand. 'Oh hi, Hope. How are you? You're looking well.'

Parmjit had meant what she said, but Hope was having none of it. 'No I'm not. I've got bad hair, bad skin, a stomach that's beginning to stick out like a beach ball. I'm beginning to lose track of myself. I don't feel much like me these days.'

'No, you look great. Really, I mean it,' Parmjit insisted.

'How goes the studying?' Hope was keen to turn the focus of the discussion away from herself. 'Are you fitting it in with all your other jobs?' Across the aisle from Parmjit, Hope noticed the blond-haired student she'd seen before, drinking coffee with Parmjit. He was engrossed in a book and seemed not to notice Hope.

'Trying to. Got deadlines creeping up and Christmas'll be busy.'

'Christmas? But . . .'

'I'm a cab driver,' said Parmjit laughing. 'I won't be celebrating Christmas myself. My family's only religious when it's good for business.'

'Listen, we might be meeting later for a drink if you want to come along. I haven't seen you for ages. It'll give us a chance to catch up.'

'Can't later. I have to work. But we must meet.' Parmjit was earnest; she liked Hope and didn't want to seem diffident. 'I'll check when I'm free and text you.'

As Hope rearranged journals on the 'Recent Editions' stand, someone touched her shoulder. It was Ben.

'Gareth's back,' he said.

Hope looked blankly at him.

'Gareth? The German translator? He's back from his study leave thing.'

'Oh right,' said Hope. 'Should I give the letter to you to give to him?'

'Give it to him yourself. He's in his office now. I'll take you over there if you like.'

Hope didn't have the letter with her, so Ben agreed to arrange a drink with Gareth later in the week. Hope preferred to give him the letter herself.

'I've told him the story. I hope you don't mind,' said Ben. 'I tried to intrigue him so he'd agree.'

That was all right. Hope didn't know why the letter meant so much to her, and though she knew that it might only contain gossip, she nevertheless felt on the threshold of something momentous.

That evening, Hope arrived home first. As she sat watching the evening news, she heard Michael let himself in. He appeared in the doorway of the living room, still in his coat, and stood looking down at Hope. A smile stretched across the width of his face.

'What?' His smile was infectious, and Hope felt herself smiling in return. 'What is it?'

Michael paused, relishing the drama, then spoke. 'Guess what? I think I've found your artist!' Hope looked baffled so Michael prompted her, nodding towards the painting. 'You know. Your watercolour man.'

'What? How? Who is it?' Hope had hardly begun to investigate this herself; had no plan other than getting the letter translated. So how had Michael done it?

He sat down on the sofa beside her. 'His name is Schmetterling. Or rather, it was – he's dead; died in the war.'

'Which war?' This wasn't the question that Hope wanted to ask, but it spilled out before she could properly collect her thoughts.

'Second. World War, that is. He's supposed to have . . .'

'*Schmetterling?*' Hope thought of the envelope that had contained the letter; recalled the difficulty she'd had in deciphering the scrawled name of the addressee. Schmetterling would fit.

'It was the symbol,' Michael went on. 'Karl said that it looked like a butterfly. Well, you said the letter was written in German, so I looked up the German word for butterfly and typed it into Google along with "artist" and "watercolour" – to narrow the search field a bit.'

'The German word for butterfly?'

'Yes.' Michael was beginning to get frustrated now. He wanted to move on with his narrative in a linear fashion, but Hope kept making him loop back on himself. 'You said the symbol on the painting looked like a butterfly. I remembered that Prince changed his name to a symbol . . .'

'*Prince?*' Hope was lost now. She just wasn't getting it.

'Yes. Prince. The musician, pop star, whatever. Look, Prince changed his name to a symbol, a squiggle or something. Your artist didn't sign his painting with a *name* – he used a symbol like Prince. A butterfly. I thought that this might be significant. The letter you found was in German. I thought – *we* thought – he might be a German artist. The German word for butterfly is Schmetterling – so I typed this into Google, and he came up. He didn't sign the painting with his name, but he used a symbol that represented his name. There wasn't much, but it all fits.'

Michael held out a sheet of A4 paper towards Hope. It was a printout of a web page, from the *Deutsche Kunstenzyklopädie*. Although the various frames, links and strap lines were in German, the text in the central frame was in English. Hope read it slowly.

Schmetterling, Johannes A (1868–1943)
Austrian artist best known for his landscape paintings in oils, pastels and watercolor. Studied under von Lindstrom of Nuremburg from 1883 to 1886. Travelled extensively throughout Europe during which time he refined his watercoloring technique. Met with some initial commercial success. Took up teaching posts in Koblenz and Wurzburg before accepting post at Academy of Fine Arts in Vienna in 1902. Returned to teaching post after military service 1914–1918. Made Professor in 1924. Was removed from post in 1936. Died 1943. There are works in Amsterdam (Rijksmus), Dresden, Geneva, Vienna.

The information was thin – the bare bones of a life – but it was enough to give Hope a sense that there was a human being behind the painting. Schmetterling had touched the public world at several times and in several places. He'd left markers, traces that could perhaps be thickened up and blocked in with colour, if Hope were to pursue them. The thought struck her: perhaps he'd been important enough a public figure to warrant a biography? Maybe there was even an autobiography, or a diary kept by the artist. If there was, the mystery of the letter might find a solution in its pages. The thin paragraph before her said nothing of his private life, the life in which the letter would have found its purchase. This life was still beyond her, but the paragraph was at least a start. Michael smiled broadly as he watched Hope. He could see that he'd pleased her.

'Michael, this is brilliant! What a piece of detective work!'

'It wasn't that brilliant,' said Michael, honestly. He knew that his hunch had required little more than the ability to solve a crossword clue. But it was an achievement in Hope's eyes and he always appreciated her praise.

'Well,' he said. 'I don't need to worry about a Christmas present for you now, do I?'

PART THREE

THIRD TRIMESTER

JANUARY 2003

16th July, 1898

Dearest J –

I don't know what to say to you after such a long time. I don't know, after ten years, whether or not you still think of me. I haven't heard from you in all those years. I don't blame you for this. I know that you had to leave and that I had to stay. I knew that would be so from the day I met you. I loved you then, and I love you now. I have carried you inside me, in my heart, all those years. I hope that you have carried me in your heart too.

Yesterday I saw a painting of yours in a gallery in Linz. I knew that it was yours as soon as I saw it. I could see you in every brush stroke. I knew just by looking at that painting that you had got on with your life, with your great struggle to show the beauty of the world through your painting. It was as though I could see your beautiful hands at work on the canvas. Your hands! Those strong and tender hands of yours. Whenever I think of you I think first of all of your hands. You will find this odd, I know, but it is true. I am glad that you are still painting.

I, for my part, remain his wife. He knows nothing of us, and has never suspected. His job was everything to him, and while he worked I could live my life with my children. Now he has retired from his job and he does not find us good company. We have moved a lot recently. He moved sometimes with his job, but lately it is restlessness. He cannot settle, and he does not seem to like the children. I am not sure that he likes me. Still, I am his wife, and my place is here with his children. Sometimes though, it is hard to breathe when he is around.

I thought of you when I saw the painting, but I think of you everyday when I look at little X – he has your eyes, and he has your hands too, your beautiful artist's hands. I see you so strongly in him that I fear my husband must one day suspect. But why should I care? To have brought him into the world is enough. He is so strong and full of life. I have not been lucky with my husband's children. But little X has survived. Angels watch over him, I think. And he has your hands!

He will be an artist too, like you. He already has your love of nature – our move here has awoken this in him and he spends hours roaming the countryside. I have never seen him happier. You will laugh when I tell you that he has recently started collecting butterflies! I cannot believe that this is not, in some way, connected to you! He has his net and his killing jar, and he has quite a collection already. He draws and paints too, which my husband does not understand and does not encourage. I dream that one day you will take him under your wing, and help whatever talent is in him to grow. Is this really only a dream? I hope that you will not let it remain so.

I miss you every day of my life. I know that we shall never meet again. I am older and the burden of life has worn heavily on me. I wouldn't want you to see me now. I would rather you remember me as I was, that night on the hill under the stars. I wouldn't lose that memory for anything, and I am thankful that I have little X to keep it alive. But I would ask you to think of little X too. If he is to be a great artist, his talent must be nurtured. Please keep him in mind. And please keep me in mind too as I keep you,

Always,

Klara

15

It was a bright January morning, ten days into the New Year. It had been a quiet Christmas. Jeffrey and Evette had gone to stay with Jeffrey's parents in Cheshire – they alternated every year between his folks and Evette's – and hadn't come back until New Year's Eve. Alex had gone to stay with her brother's family in Yorkshire. She hadn't seen her brother for over a year; he worked in computing and had got a new job which took him abroad a lot. When Hope and Michael had met Alex for a drink early on Christmas Eve, she'd seemed both nervous and excited. She was going to drive up to Yorkshire later that night, and so hadn't been drinking.

'Don't worry,' she'd said. 'I plan to make up for it while I'm there. The downside of this new job is that it takes him away from his family. The upside is that it pays fuckloads of money, so my evil plan is to drink him poor in the few days I'm there. Wish me luck.'

Hope and Michael had spent Christmas Day with Michael's parents, who'd also invited Linnie and her children. They'd lasted until eleven o'clock before Michael cracked and phoned for a taxi.

Now, ten days into 2003, Christmas seemed a distant memory. It was Friday today; Hope had been back at work for almost a whole week. She was also five months pregnant, and felt it. She was sitting in the Arts Centre café with Gareth, reading the translation Klara's letter.

'Is it all right?'

Gareth wanted some response from Hope, who sat frowning at the document in her hand.

'Sorry. Yes. It's fine. I just don't know what I was expecting.'

Gareth wanted to talk about his approach to the translation, wanted Hope to admire his work. 'It wasn't easy – the handwriting was difficult to read. I might have elaborated here and there to get the sense of what's being said. A translation is never straightforward . . .'

'It's kind of florid,' Hope said, scanning the letter a third time. 'It could have been written by a lovesick teenager.'

'Well, she's clearly not a teenager. She talks about children in the plural. And her husband must have been getting on. She talks about him retiring. Let's say she was a young bride . . .'

'A very *very* young bride.' Hope wasn't serious, but Gareth didn't register this. He spoke thoughtfully.

'. . . even if we allow a twenty year difference in age, then let's say she's in her thirties when her husband retires. That makes her in her twenties when she has her fling with Schmetterling.'

The word 'fling' jarred with Hope. As florid as the prose might be, Hope – to her surprise – responded to the intensity of Klara's love for the young artist. Ten years was a long time to carry a torch for anyone, and especially for some itinerant artist who had apparently impregnated her before abandoning her to her husband.

'I think the prose style probably owes more to the kind of novels she might have been reading at the time. I've tidied it up as best I could – but she's clearly not used to writing. These are not refined sentiments.'

Gareth was sounding increasingly pompous. Hope needed to change the direction of the conversation.

'You've used X for the child's name?'

'She doesn't actually name the child. She uses a kind of squiggle whenever she refers to it.'

Hope picked up the original letter and peered closely at it. Gareth leaned over and pointed to an instance where Klara referred to the child, and immediately Hope recognized the butterfly motif with which Schmetterling had signed his painting.

'It's Schmetterling's butterfly!'

Not being able to read German, Hope had never scrutinized the letter closely enough to have noticed this before. Gareth hadn't seen the painting in which the letter had been concealed, and although he knew that the artist's name translated as 'butterfly', he hadn't made the connection with this symbol.

'Are you saying that she named the child "Butterfly"? I find that hard to believe. Even from the little that we know of the husband, it's unlikely he'd put up with one of his sons . . .'

'It's a code!' said Hope, suddenly getting it. 'The child wasn't called "Butterfly", but she *did* name it after the painter.'

'You mean Johannes rather than Schmetterling? It's possible . . . I mean, there's no way of knowing for sure, not unless we can identify who Klara was.'

'Or who the husband was?'

'Or the child,' said Gareth.

Hope thought about this for a moment. It seemed a long shot, but in the desert of possibilities, focusing on the child might well be the most fertile source of hope. It was certainly one that Hope hadn't yet considered.

'Maybe he did go on to become an artist like his father, after all,' she said.

Michael sat at his desk, reading Hope's text.

news abt butterflyman. meet later in town 4 drink? ask preston, jeffrey etc

Michael replied that he would. He knew that Hope was seeing Gareth today, and he assumed that Hope's news had come out of this meeting. He wasn't all that interested in Klara and her painter boyfriend, but he was always glad of an excuse to go drinking after work. And if he invited Jeffrey along, then maybe Jeffrey would invite Evette too.

Michael turned his attention back to his computer and, reluctant to return to his stock control duties, checked his email. Among the several work-related messages there was one from the Chancredy Multimedia Collective announcing yet again the launch of the CMC website. To his surprise the link was at long last a live one. Text slurred around the screen in a holding page while the website loaded up; words morphed from patches of colour, forming the words CHANCREDY MULTIMEDIA COLLECTIVE until they hung shimmering in metallic-bright colours before gradually fading away, leaving in their place a graphic which represented the ground-floor plan of a building. A series of animated arrows led the eye through the front door into an area labelled 'Reception', and from there through a series of interconnected rooms each with its own designation: 'Design Department', 'Administration', 'Publicity', 'Sales'. It looked like an animated game of *Cluedo*, the arrows disappearing through one door only to reappear in another room as though they had traversed some secret connecting passage.

Michael clicked on 'Sales', and the blueprint shimmered away to reveal a statement from the Chancredy Sales Team:

Welcome to the Sales arm of the Chancredy Multimedia Collective. Although no product is available as yet, the Chancredy Sales Team aim to bring you a range of

ethically-credible, non-exploitative goods put together by its globally-based team of innovative and resourceful procurement agents.

As you read this, concern for the environment and for fair-trade terms and conditions are being written into contracts for the supply of a unique range of goods and services which the Chancredy Collective will shortly make available to you. This is not about cool, or hip, and it is not about nostalgia for colonialism – we're not going to bring you Balinese raffia place mats so that you can feel good about owning some ethnic artefact or other.

It's about getting the most interesting goods and services to you while avoiding being fucked over by capitalism. And our ethical sourcing policies ensure that you're not complicit in fucking our suppliers over too.

In addition to this, the Chancredy Multimedia Collective will be making available to you products made by and for the collective by its own creative team.

Watch this space.

Michael was impressed. He'd no idea that Jeffrey had put together such a team. He navigated back to the main page, and noticed that the stairwell in the centre of the floor was a link to other levels of the virtual building. He clicked 'down' to basement level. As the page loaded, the arrows marched from the stairwell and began their circuit of the new level. This was largely the music floor, with rooms labelled 'Live Studio', 'Digital Mixing and Recording', 'Media Production Suite' and 'Café/Bar'. Michael clicked on 'Live Studio':

This is the Chancredy Musical Collective's live studio. It is a fully baffled, air-conditioned space, wired for sound. There is an acoustic drumkit (see below for specifications) and a range of analogue amplification currently installed for bass, lead and keyboard.

*There is a computerized digital keyboard programmed
with over 150 keyboard sounds, and we also have a full
range of voice amplification, effects (phase, echo, etc.) and
percussion instruments.*

*The studio is available for rehearsals at competitive
rates.*

Again, Michael was impressed, but by now also a little curious.
As he read down the list of musical instruments available for
hire he recognized them from Jeffrey's home studio. It dawned
on Michael that the virtual building he was touring was in
fact an idealized rendition of the 1930s suburban semi that
Jeffrey shared with Evette. There was certainly a recording
studio complete with all the instruments that Jeffrey claimed
to have, but it was in the upstairs back bedroom and not
in the basement, which was really a cellar, too damp to
be useful and hardly big enough to store more than half a
dozen bottles of wine and a variety of fungi. To describe the
studio as 'fully baffled' and 'air-conditioned' seemed to be
stretching a point, too. The baffling amounted to large sheets
of polystyrene suspended from the picture rail, while the air
conditioning consisted in opening the window slightly and
keeping the door ajar to ensure a through draught.

Out of curiosity, Michael clicked on 'Café/Bar', and read:

*Creative work – like any other form of socially useful
production – needs to be balanced with adequate rest
and recreation. The Chancredy Collective therefore can
provide a wide array of recreational activities with which
to supplement the creative process. There is a fully-stocked
bar . . .*

This would be in Jeffrey's living room then, thought
Michael.

. . . and tea and coffee-making facilities . . .

And that would be the kitchen.

. . . as well as a range of snacks and sandwiches, carefully prepared by Chancredy staff who are sensitive to your unique dietary requirements . . .

Michael somehow couldn't imagine Jeffrey making sandwiches for the musicians using the studio and so he presumed that this must be Evette's role.

There is a multimedia centre on which you can watch the latest films . . .

Jeffrey's DVD player and his DVD collection.

. . . or you can chill while playing a variety of computer games . . .

Jeffrey's X-Box presumably?

. . . or simply watch any of dozens of channels beamed to our high-resolution flat screen TVs.

That would be Jeffrey and Evette's subscription to satellite TV called into service for the 'Collective'. Michael was beginning to feel a little odd about Jeffrey's apparent desire to translate himself into a one-man corporation – or was it two-person, if Evette was on board with all this?

Michael was puzzled. Jeffrey's Chancredy enterprise was being presented in a way that made it look remarkably like those corporations he claimed to despise. Michael felt oddly uncomfortable about seeing his friend's house presented as though it were some glass-and-steel-clad, state-of-the-art office complex. Once Michael had twigged the re-description process, he roamed over Jeffrey's website, fascinated to see how the rooms he was familiar with were being rendered in the corporate Chancredy world. He wondered, too, what Evette thought of all this.

I'll be there. Looking forward to it! Will bring a friend if that's ok xx

The text was from Parmjit. Hope was still buzzing from her meeting that morning with Gareth, and wanted to share the news with her friends. It was another step in the direction of solving the mystery and she wanted her friends to be as excited as she was about this. To this end she was arranging to meet everyone in a city centre bar later that evening.

Hope turned back to her desk. She felt bloated today, and was experiencing a fluttering sensation just below her ribcage. She knew it was the baby swimming in the secret sea inside her. The bloated sensation had been explained to her at her monthly antenatal clinic: as her baby grew in size, so vital organs would be pushed upwards to accommodate whatever her stretching belly could not. But knowing the cause of her discomfort didn't make her any more comfortable. She placed a hand over the top of her belly, a mute form of contact with her child.

Uncomfortable as she felt, Hope had reached a kind of plateau in her pregnancy. For a long time she'd felt disoriented by the biological changes, the unfamiliar cocktail of hormones that had washed through her and sent her skittering between depression and elation. They had transformed her hair from a lustrous embellishment to a lank embarrassment, had given her spots the size of which she hadn't seen since her teenage years and the ruddy complexion of an eighteenth-century milkmaid.

But lately she'd felt calmer and more composed, and something approaching normality had returned to her hair and skin. She'd also rediscovered the joy of sex with Michael – a part of their lives that had been cordoned off while she struggled with her self-esteem in the face of the biological tempest she'd had to weather. Hope wasn't a woman obsessed by her body – she didn't diet or think herself 'fat' – but the physical presence of her rounding belly had seemed, in her darker moments, to be just another mark of her unattractiveness.

Hope was at last coming to terms with the unfamiliar and unwanted shape of her body. It helped that Michael seemed to be taking more of an interest in her, too; at least *he* didn't seem to think of her as a frump. She took comfort in the fact that he seemed to find her newly-rounded shape desirable. Because of this, she felt more confident than she'd done for some time, and was looking forward to seeing her friends later.

Michael walked through the offices of Farsight Plastic Mouldings plc towards Preston's desk. He'd last seen Preston on New Year's Eve, in a bar in town in the company of Ben, Alex, and Jeffrey. Hope hadn't felt up to an evening in a smoke-filled, crowded bar and had gone to see the New Year in with Michael's parents. Michael had left the revellers early to do the same. On the bus out to his parents' house, he'd wondered why Evette hadn't been in the pub and, being drunk, had sent her a text wishing her a Happy New Year. He'd signed off with a single 'x', telling himself that Evette would take it as an affectionate kiss from a close friend. But a knot of excitement had twisted inside him as he'd sent the message, for as the bus wound through the city streets towards the New Year, a part of him hoped that Evette might read a little more than just affectionate friendship into this slightest of gestures.

Preston swivelled his chair around.

'Mikey! Happy New Year, my friend. How goes it?'

Michael glanced without meaning to at the scars above Preston's eyebrows. Under the harsh fluorescent lighting the scars looked as bad as they possibly could – a dull, but faint purple against Preston's chestnut skin. It was impossible now to make sense of them as a word, unless you knew what that word was. Michael told Preston that he was meeting Hope later.

'Come along,' he said. 'Bring Ben if he's not doing anything.'

In spite of himself, Michael felt self-conscious as he said this. It was just over two months since Preston had come out as gay, but Michael was aware that this was the first time he'd acknowledged to Preston that he and Ben were partners. Seeing Ben and Preston together, as he had on New Year's Eve, wasn't quite the same thing.

'Nice one. I'll give him a bell. When and where?'

Later that day, as Hope made her way into the city centre, she thought of Klara's letter. Her day had been haunted by the sense of longing – and loss – that emanated from the letter. Before she'd had it translated, it had occurred to Hope that it might have been a love letter. But she'd not expected Klara to be married, or with children, and had certainly not expected an unhappy marriage, as the letter seemed to suggest. How had she put it? *He doesn't find us good company; he doesn't like the children; I don't think he likes me.* Klara, in her own words, had been 'unlucky' with children and Hope knew what this meant. Perhaps this lay behind her husband's attitude to her? Maybe he was disappointed with her; maybe he held her responsible for failing to provide him with strong children? But how many had she had? How many had she lost and how many had survived? Klara had her butterfly child, but she also seemed to have other children too. Wouldn't this have mitigated her husband's attitude towards her? Hope was aware that she didn't really know what that attitude was, beyond Klara's resentful and personal account of it, and she recognized that Klara could have been over-emphasizing his cruelty in order to prick the conscience of her artist-lover. Perhaps Klara was manipulative, overdramatizing her situation in the hope of a more exciting, bohemian life than her husband provided. Was the *husband* the victim?

But this seemed unconvincing to Hope. Assuming that Klara was telling the truth about the child – that it had been fathered by the itinerant Schmetterling ten years earlier – then surely she was the victim, and twice over at that; locked into a loveless marriage (was Hope now overdramatizing?) with a boorish, ignorant husband, then seduced and abandoned by a wandering artist and left to fend for his child.

As Hope's bus drew near to the city centre, she realized that, if she'd had those thoughts about Klara a few weeks ago, she would have been a snivelling wreck by now. Things were definitely improving.

16

Alex sat in the busy pub, in the small section which had been cordoned off for smokers. Wisps of smoke from a lone cigarette stub twisted upwards from the ashtray on the table in front of her. The pub was long and thin, little more than a corridor along one side of which stretched a bar. A window ran along the other side, so that the staff looked out across the bar on to the bustling street of shops opposite. It was now half-past five, and through the massive window the Lowryesque drift of people in and out of the vividly lit shops showed no signs yet of letting up. Alex sipped her drink and watched bored shop assistants gaze longingly across the street to the bright beer taps. She watched one shop assistant hover outside the door of her place of work, bored and shivering, pulling quickly on a cigarette before stamping it out on the street and fading back into the crowded store.

Alex checked her watch; she was meeting Hope later. She was pleased that Hope had got through the maelstrom of emotions of the past few months. Alex had begun to wonder whether or not Hope could cope with the responsibility and sheer hard work of being a mother. Hope was much calmer of late, though Alex wondered how long this would last. The baby would arrive soon enough, and Hope's world – and Michael's too – would change forever. For the better, Alex hoped, but there were no guarantees. None at all.

As the pub continued to fill with punters and the noise level rose, Alex found herself increasingly unable to keep at bay the tide of fear and loneliness that always threatened to overwhelm her. She felt panic rising inside her like a riptide. The air surrounding her seemed to become viscous. The half-smoked cigarette in her hand seemed a great distance away. The hand was shaking, and she felt that if she could only get it to her mouth and inhale the cigarette smoke, she'd be able to calm herself down. But the hand wouldn't move.

Echoing in her memory came her father's voice, whose love and attention she'd actively sought in the daylight hours, a desperate compensation for the pain and bewilderment he'd brought to her in the night. She remembered again just how much she'd loved his daytime hands, the hands that held her like a father should, that cupped her own hand as they walked together to school or to the park. She never saw his hands in the dark of her bedroom. The stench of alcohol in the bar was the smell of her father's breath, falling like a stifling blanket across her as she lay frozen in her bed. He never smelt of alcohol during the day, so she'd told herself that it wasn't him in her bedroom at night; it was someone else, a monster, the devil. She told herself this even now – *it wasn't him* – but she could no longer make herself believe it.

She'd realized that the fear he'd instilled into her had made it almost impossible for her to hold on to those things she loved; how, in order to breathe, she needed to break out of the relationships that she desperately wanted to work but that inevitably brought on suffocating panic. The longer a relationship lasted, the closer to the pain of betrayal she moved. Alex had come to some sort of uneasy terms with this until, three years before, she'd found herself pregnant. And she knew – knew it with a sureness that even now stunned her like a punch in the face – that the decision to terminate her pregnancy had been shaped years before, by the fear and despair fashioned for her by her father.

Alex looked again at the watch on her trembling wrist. She'd arranged to meet her lover for a drink before going on to meet Hope at seven. He was late. Alex forced herself to stand up. Her legs barely supported her, but she knew she could not stay. She needed air, and fewer people. With an effort of will, she left the pub as quickly and as furtively as she could, leaving the twisted stub of the cigarette behind her. A thin curl of blue smoke tried to climb free of the ashtray.

Michael sat on a sofa in the wide lounge of the pub in town where Hope had suggested they meet. He was early. He sipped his drink and took out his phone: no messages, but he'd missed a call from a number he didn't recognize. Just as he was about to dial the number to find out who it was, Alex walked through the door. Michael waved her over.

'You're early,' he said. 'What do you want to drink?'

She looked pale, and crumpled down into her seat as though she were exhausted.

'I'll have a very large gin and tonic, please.' Alex's voice trembled a little as she spoke. 'You're early too,' she continued, as though she'd only just realized this.

'I walked in with Preston. He's gone to meet Ben.'

'Ben?' Alex looked bewildered.

'You know . . . *Ben*.' Michael didn't know how to say exactly who Ben was. He'd hoped that Alex would know. He was *sure* Alex knew, but she looked absent, lost. 'Alex?'

'Sorry, Michael. *Ben*. His partner.'

Partner. That was the word Michael wanted. He was not yet comfortable with 'boyfriend' or 'lover'.

'Alex?' She was away again.

'Sorry, Michael. Gin and tonic. Large. Please.'

'Alex? Is everything OK?'

'What, generally?' Alex laughed slightly, almost not at all. 'Well, the health service is in crisis and we're about to go to war in Iraq. And it's starting to rain and I haven't brought an umbrella with me.'

'No, I mean . . .'

Alex seemed suddenly to gain her composure. Her whole body seemed to lose its slackness, and instantly she was the Alex that Michael recognized.

'I'm OK, Michael. Really. Except I haven't got a drink.' She smiled, and her eyes flirted with him from under her long lashes, as they often did in that playful way she had with him, enjoying the sense that she might be making him feel uncomfortable. Michael smiled back, relieved that the Alex he knew had returned.

'A large gin and tonic. Right,' he said, and sprang out of his seat for the bar.

Preston stood on the station concourse, watching the arrivals board carefully. Several people stood alongside him, eyes turned upwards to the board. Ben's train only had to travel two short stops from the university where he worked, but even so it was running fifteen minutes late and Preston was already beginning to lose his nerve. Still uncomfortable in public places, he'd decided that meeting Ben from the station would be another step towards his recovery. He was comfortable now at work with people that he knew and trusted, but standing there in that wide-open public space filled with people, any one of whom could be one of his attackers, was proving to be much more difficult than he'd anticipated. He was beginning to sweat, and the scars on his forehead seemed to pulse like a police siren, as though they were drawing attention to him. The more he tried to blend in with the crowd, the more self-conscious he felt; and the more self-conscious he felt, the more he seemed to stand out from the crowd. He just couldn't find the right balance; couldn't get himself on an even keel.

He tried to look up at the arrivals board, but he couldn't help dropping his gaze to catch eyes turned accusingly towards him. 'You brought it on yourself!' they seemed to say, and 'You should be ashamed of yourself!' And Preston *was* ashamed of himself, for his weakness, his failure to cope with his trauma. His father was right to throw him out. Not because he was gay, but because he was *weak*, incapable of standing up for himself. Preston felt his head start to swim. He was going to faint now, in front of all these people. He didn't need anyone to beat him up to remind him of his weakness; he could do it all by himself. His father was right . . .

'Hey you. Are you OK?'

Ben's voice was familiar and soothing, and with an effort Preston focused himself. He looked in Ben's eyes, and saw an echo of what he was going through. Ben understood. All those people weaving around them, making their way home, oblivious to the violence he and Ben had suffered, none of them understood. But Ben did. Preston's mouth felt dry, and he felt a little residual shakiness. But looking at Ben he no longer felt weak. Ben would look out for him, and he would look out for Ben. And as for the people who'd attacked them – who the fuck did they think they were? They could just fuck off back to the swamp they'd crawled out of. And his father? Well, he could just fuck off too.

'You're late. I was worried.'

'I'm glad to hear it,' said Ben, returning Preston's smile.

'I need a drink though, like *right now*.'

'You see,' said Ben, turning towards the exit. '*That's* why we're so right for each other, because *I* need a drink *right now* too.'

They left the station for the pub where Hope and Michael would be waiting for them.

Jeffrey sat down in the smoking area and looked out of the long window at the street and the shops beyond. He took a drink from his glass and dragged on his cigarette. He was relieved to have started smoking again. He'd managed to go for nearly a year without a cigarette, so that when he started again he was able to tell himself that he'd done so because he *wanted* to, and not because he *needed* to. He was a free agent, and not an addict. His friends, of course, took a different view, and ribbed him for his weak will. But Jeffrey wasn't worried about what they thought.

He looked around the crowded pub but could see no one he recognized. He checked his watch – it was now six-fifteen and he was due to meet Michael and Hope at seven. Jeffrey took out his phone. There'd been no calls and there were no messages. He quickly composed a short text – where r u? was i late? – and sent it off into the ether.

It was almost seven and Hope's bus was approaching town. Earlier that evening, lying in a hot bath, she'd watched her belly dancing before her eyes. They were only small flicks, but they made tiny ripples in the bathwater, and one movement had caused the bulk of her stomach to shift from left to right, as though the baby had rolled over from one side of her womb to the other. Hope had noticed that the baby generally seemed most active at the end of her working day; perhaps only because she had more leisure time in which to notice it.

She took out Gareth's translation of Klara's letter and read it again. She was struck once more by the love Klara clearly felt for the young artist, and for his child. It was as though, in the absence of Schmetterling, she'd channelled all the love she held for him into the child they'd made together.

Hope wondered if Klara had loved the children of her husband with the same passion that she seemed to have for Schmetterling's child. From the evidence of the letter, her lover's child was favoured over the others. Had her husband's children suffered as a result of this? Would Hope ever really know for sure?

'So, if I make love to Hope, but I'm thinking about, say, Kate Moss when I . . . you know . . .'

'Come off?' said Ben, helpfully.

'Shoot your load?' offered Preston.

'Pop your cork?'

All three men turned to look at Alex.

'*Pop your cork?*' repeated Ben, quizzically.

' . . . whatever,' said Michael, pressing on. 'So, let's say I *pop my cork* – as Alex would say – and I impregnate Hope . . .'

'*Impregnate*. Good word,' said Preston.

'Well-chosen,' said Ben.

'You're saying that if I'm thinking of Kate Moss at the exact moment I impregnate Hope, then when the baby is eventually born, it'll look like her? Kate Moss, I mean.'

'That's the idea,' said Ben.

'And the Victorians believed that, did they?' Michael looked incredulously at Ben, who'd initiated the discussion.

'Well, not all of them, obviously,' said Ben.

'So in effect, I'd be busted? I mean, Hope would know I'd been unfaithful?'

'Hardly unfaithful,' said Alex. 'After all, it would have been Hope's bones you'd been jumping and not Kate Moss's.'

'And presumably it would look like *baby* Moss, and not *adult* Moss,' said Preston.

'What's your point?' said Michael.

'Well, at that age all babies look the same, don't they?'

'It'd be an odd-looking baby if it *did* look like a supermodel on the day it was born,' said Alex. 'No, by the time it was old enough to look like Kate Moss, cheekbones and all, you'd be clear.'

'Phew!' said Michael, pretending relief. 'But hang on, does it work the other way round?'

'How do you mean?' said Ben.

'Well, suppose that I'm staring lovingly into Hope's eyes with no thought for anyone else while *she*'s lying there thinking of, I dunno, Johnny Depp or someone. Would our baby grow up to look like *him*?'

'Hadn't thought of that,' said Ben.

'Only if Hope pops *her* cork,' said Alex. 'And if what she tells me about your technique is true there's not much chance of that.'

Michael turned to hit Alex, pretending indignation.

'What if Michael *is* thinking of Kate Moss when he pops his cork, but the baby that gets born is a boy? Would he still look like Kate Moss when he grows up?'

All eyes turned to look at Preston. There was a pause as all four thought about this, then Michael ploughed on.

'Suppose we both pop our corks at the same time. Suppose that *I'm* thinking of Kate, while *Hope* is thinking of Johnny . . .'

'It'd grow up very confused about its identity,' said Alex. 'A therapy-rat.'

'Knowing the Victorians, as I do,' said Ben with false pomposity, 'the male fantasy would take priority over the female.'

'No change there, then,' said Alex.

'Evening, pop-pickers. Anyone need a drink?'

All four turned to find Jeffrey standing beside their table.

Hope walked as quickly as she could, driven by excitement about her news. People drifted past her, but in her haste they remained unformed shadows around her. As she approached the entrance to the pub, two of these shadows detached themselves from the drifting mass and fell in step beside her. Hope didn't notice until one of them spoke.

'Hope?'

She turned, and found herself looking at Parmjit's familiar, smiling face. Beside Parmjit walked the young man with the strikingly blond hair.

'I'm sorry,' said Hope. 'I was miles away.'

'Hope, this is Gyorgy. He's from Russia.'

Gyorgy extended his hand.

'Gyorgy,' said Hope, shaking hands. 'I've seen you on campus, haven't I?'

'Yes, you have,' said Gyorgy. 'And I have seen you.'

Hope wasn't sure exactly what it was about Gyorgy, but she knew immediately that she liked him. His handshake had been firm, but not aggressive. He looked at her in a frank and level way, not in the least intimidated by the strangeness of a first meeting. He seemed confident and nobody's fool. In this way, he reminded her of Parmjit.

'Well,' said Hope. 'Shall we go in?'

'My country is shit. For centuries it was fucked by Czars. Then it was for years fucked by Communists. Now it is fucked by Capitalists. All that is left is for religion, and then God Himself would fuck my country too.'

Gyorgy spoke flatly, his tone unemotional.

'There's always nationalism,' said Jeffrey, provocatively.

Gyorgy responded without missing a beat. 'Then the people would fuck themselves.'

'So, will you stay in this country when you've graduated?' Hope sipped her orange juice and waited for Gyorgy to answer. She watched Parmjit and Gyorgy as they sat together. Were they friends, or lovers? She couldn't tell from their body language.

'No,' said Gyorgy, after a moment's reflection. 'I have thought about it, but I will not stay long. It will be three years by the time I graduate. That will be long enough, I think.'

'Will you go back to Russia?'

Gyorgy looked at Ben, who had asked the question. 'Of course. But I will travel first. I wish to see other countries. The US, of course, if that is possible for me. More of Europe. And India.'

Gyorgy looked at Parmjit as he said this. She smiled and looked down at her drink.

'Why go back to Russia if it's as bad as you say it is?' said Alex.

'Believe me, it is worse than I say it is,' said Gyorgy, smiling, 'and I wouldn't live there if I hadn't been born there. But I came away to see it differently. To see . . .' Gyorgy seemed to struggle for a moment to find the right words. He tried a different tack. 'I want to find a way to help my country. It is shit, but I will find some way to help it. To make it a good place to live. For my family. For everyone, not just the criminals.'

'I'll drink to that,' said Jeffrey, and he finished his pint. 'Are we having another, or are we going to eat?'

'You can't eat yet. I've only just got here. I need a drink.'

Jeffrey turned to find Evette standing behind him. She was wearing a short black skirt, a deep-purple silk and lace bodice and neat court shoes. She wore no stockings or tights, and her faintly golden legs didn't need any. Her copper hair, with its trademark fringe, was immaculate as ever and she wore only a suggestion of make-up, an accentuation of tones. The only exception was the deep red lip gloss she wore. Michael, watching her from the sofa, could have walked up to her and kissed her there and then.

The pub was crowded and noisy now. It was hard for the friends to talk as a group, and so smaller cells had formed. What linked all the groups was the translation of Klara's letter, which Hope had handed around. Jeffrey was the last to read it as the others sipped their drinks.

'Well,' said Jeffrey, finally. 'She needs to get over it. Move on.'

'Oh come on, Jeffrey,' said Preston. 'Isn't there something to admire in holding on to love for that long? Ten years, wasn't it?'

'Exactly,' said Michael. 'Hope thinks it was written on the anniversary of when they parted.'

'When they shagged, more like,' said Jeffrey. 'The husband sounds a real dullard. No wonder she couldn't forget those young artistic hands all over her body. It's well known that those of an artistic bent make better lovers. More imaginative.'

Preston laughed, but Michael, who knew Jeffrey better, wasn't sure that he really meant it as a joke. Gyorgy, who knew nothing about Jeffrey, ignored the comment altogether.

'She would stay out of duty to husband,' he said, stating a fact. 'That is what she would do.'

'Ah,' said Jeffrey. 'A good old German stereotype. The dutiful hausfrau!'

This response seemed, to Michael, to be rather sharp. He sensed dimly that Jeffrey didn't really like Gyorgy. But if Gyorgy sensed this, he didn't show it.

'Not a stereotype,' he said carefully. 'The date is . . . ?'

'1898,' said Michael.

'If it is stereotype, then is pan-European, not German alone. The place of women then wasn't what it is today.'

'Ah,' said Jeffrey again. 'A *Victorian* stereotype!'

'That,' said Gyorgy, 'cannot be.' He spoke now directly to Jeffrey. 'Victoria was *British* monarch, not German. Different countries, though same patriarchal culture. And this woman, Klara, was Austrian, not German, though Austria would be German soon enough, for a time.'

At this reference, Michael remembered the brief biography of Schmetterling that he'd found online. Schmetterling, it had reported, had died in 1943, two years before the war had ended. A casualty of that war then? A good German soldier perhaps? According to the same biography, Schmetterling had served in the First World War. Whom had he fought for? Had he crossed the border to fight for Germany? Beyond the simplistic notion that the Germans fought the British, Michael had no idea who fought whom, or why. Perhaps Schmetterling had joined up again in the later conflict? An exemplary German soldier indeed, thought Michael.

17

Rain lashed the window of Hope and Michael's bedroom. Hope slept soundly on her side, knees drawn up, arms enfolding her belly. Beside her, Michael had slept only fitfully. He was haunted by the idea that children came to resemble whoever the father was thinking of at the moment of conception. He thought again of Evette, and the night he first came to believe that she was attracted to him. Hope was sure this was the night their child was conceived, and he knew that, as he pushed himself into Hope that night, he'd been pushing himself into Evette. He'd looked down through his closed eyes at Evette's face beneath him, her copper fringe falling back from her forehead to reveal her wide-open eyes looking up at him. Her lips – he saw them now with the red lipstick from last night – had been parted in ecstasy, the tip of her tongue visible in the depths of her mouth, promising even more pleasure. But as he lay in bed, unable to sleep, he couldn't get past the fear that their child, when it was born, would look like Evette. He knew how ridiculously superstitious this idea was, but he couldn't stop himself from thinking it all the same.

Hope stirred beside him, got out of bed, went to the bathroom. On her return she pulled her dressing gown from the floor and draped it around her.

'Michael?' He pretended to be stirred from sleep. 'Do you want tea?'

Michael dearly wanted to be asleep so that he wouldn't have to face his anxieties but he knew, hungover as he was, that he wouldn't be able to drift off now. It was nearly eight in the morning.

'Please,' he muttered, as sleepily as he could manage to sound.

As Hope's footsteps receded, Michael pulled the bedclothes around him. But there was no relief from the needling of the raindrops against the windowpane and the bitter fantasies that assailed him.

Hope leaned forward, resting her arms on the work surface while she waited for the tea to brew. In this posture, she felt the weight of her belly hanging beneath her. She wondered about her aquatic passenger, suspended in its gurgling, pulsing world. With all that noise going on inside her, how did it manage to sleep so much? The photocopy of Klara's letter lay on the work surface where she'd left it the night before, and Hope read it through one more time. It was clear from what Klara had written that the love she'd felt for Schmetterling hadn't been diminished by an absence of ten years. How many more years had that love endured? And what of Klara's child, what had happened to it? Had it ever found out who its real father was? Had Schmetterling ever responded to Klara's plea to help the child to become the artist she believed him to be? Hope's friends had offered many suggestions for how she should go about looking for answers to these questions. She needed to gather her thoughts, develop a strategy for going about her investigations. She would talk to Michael about it; after all, he was the one who'd identified Schmetterling for her.

how's the head?
  throbbing
  am throbbing too. head's fine though . . .
Alex wearily absorbed the innuendo. She put her phone back on the bedside table and wrapped herself in her duvet. She wasn't especially hungover, in spite of what she'd said in her text, but she was profoundly tired, as though a grave illness had sapped her strength. She lay still, listening to the rain, monotonous and insistent against the window, like the hissing of static on a radio. The noise filled her mind, as she hoped it would, keeping at bay the memories of the previous evening. The weekend stretched ahead of her, and she didn't want to think about how she would spend the time.

Her phone signalled the arrival of another text. Without reading it, Alex reached over and switched the phone off.

Later that afternoon, a pale Michael sat on the faded, two-seater sofa in the cluttered living room of his sister's flat. The room was bigger than his own living room but it didn't feel it. Besides the sofa there was a matching armchair where Linnie sat, aimlessly smoking, and an enormous flat screen TV which filled the corner of the room. Behind the sofa loomed a scuffed wall-unit where blurred and grainy photographs of the children, framed in gold-lacquered plastic, were shouldered aside by piles of videos and DVDs. In the space behind the armchair there was a dining table, pushed against the wall. To Michael's knowledge, it had never been used as such, since the family ate on the sofa in front of the TV. A substantial clearing operation would have been required to free it for its intended use. It was covered with layers of magazines, children's toys and washing – some folded, some waiting to be folded.

The children had barely acknowledged Michael as he entered the room. Jade, lying prone on the floor, her head propped up on her hands, had briefly taken her eyes from the screen as Michael stepped over her to sit down. Kyle, sitting beside Michael on the sofa, had craned his neck as Michael passed between him and the TV, but neither he nor his sister had uttered a word to their visitor. Linnie had let Michael in and so could hardly fail to acknowledge him, but she'd settled back down to watch the film as soon as he'd entered the flat. The electric fire seemed to have been turned up full and, within minutes of sitting down, Michael felt stupefied by the heat. He found himself pressed back into the sofa by the weight of his own body, staring at the knife battle taking place on TV.

With an effort, Michael managed to dredge his voice up from the airless depths of his chest. 'What's this?'

'Something their dad sent them,' said Linnie, without taking her eyes from the screen. 'He sends them videos.'

'*DVD*s, Mom,' said Jade, speaking at the TV screen.

'It's *Killer Zombies From Hell 3*,' said Kyle, also speaking at the screen.

'I wish he'd send games,' said Jade.

'Dickhead,' said Kyle. 'We don't have a console.'

'Dickhead yourself, tosser,' retorted Jade. 'If we had some games, Mom'd *buy* us a console, wouldn't you, Mom?'

Linnie ignored Jade, but Kyle didn't.

'Who you calling a tosser, shagbag?' said Kyle, extending a leg barely enough to tap Jade on the shoulder with his foot. Jade reacted with a violent shrug.

'Leave me alone, wanker.'

'Fuck off, shitface,' snapped Kyle, administering a sharper kick to Jade's shoulder. This time Jade responded with a smack to Kyle's outstretched leg. Neither took their eyes from the TV as this exchange developed between them.

Because of where he was sitting, Michael found himself caught in the middle of this altercation. He looked at Linnie in desperation. She seemed not to have noticed what was going on. It was only when she caught Michael's eye that she seemed to wake up to the developing scrap.

'Kyle, Jade? Stop it now or you'll get a smack.'

Linnie said this without moving her body and, having exercized her authority, she dragged deeply on her cigarette and returned her gaze to the screen.

'She started it,' said Kyle.

'No I didn't!' shouted Jade, finally taking her eyes from the TV to deliver a full-blooded thump to Kyle's leg.

As the argument escalated, Michael felt panic rising in him. He couldn't bear it; it was like being locked in an insane asylum. He stared desperately at the small window, trying to escape the room and its bickering occupants by looking outside – but it was misted on the inside and he couldn't see out. He felt tired and ill and wanted to leave, but felt duty-bound to stay longer than the few minutes he'd been there.

As Kyle and Jade squabbled, he remembered that he too had argued with Linnie as a child. He remembered the ease with which Linnie could make herself cry, a final and frequently successful manoeuvre in the competition to enlist their mother's support. It was a move that Michael could never match. He was a boy, after all, and crying would in itself have marked his defeat. But his arguments with Linnie had hardly ever been serious, and they'd never had the vicious undertow that those between Kyle and Jade seemed to have. Kyle and Jade's arguments never seemed designed to enlist their mother's support, on one side or the other. In fact, the children were largely oblivious to Linnie, ignoring her whenever she remonstrated with them, though it was a different story when they wanted something.

In spite of their youthful rivalries, Michael had fond memories of his childhood with Linnie. She was three years older than him – and to the younger Michael her life always seemed so much more exciting and interesting than his own. But when she hit her late teens, the gap between them seemed to expand to infinity. Her life shifted gear into an adulthood that was wilder and more liberated than the adults he knew. She started going to pubs and clubs, coming home late and drunk, and she started smoking, too. The tension in the house increased, and Michael retreated to his room to do his own growing up.

But as his own life became more complicated, Linnie and the tensions she brought home with her were less important. He was always out of the house and so he saw her less and less. She married, though her husband stayed only long enough to father Kyle and Jade before disappearing out of her life. And left alone, Linnie seemed to wither, as though the children had sucked her dry of life.

Michael looked at his sister, pale and exhausted, sucking on her cigarette as though drawing some sort of strength from it. Perhaps she'd loved her husband, perhaps she loved him still, but unless she made more of an effort to make a life for herself he would be the last person she ever loved. Slyly regarding his sister out of the corner of his eyes, the claustrophobic heat of the room began to confuse his senses – and, for a brief, arresting moment, he could swear that it was Hope sitting there, tired and defeated, hollowed out by her parasitic children and by Michael's desertion.

18

'We'll need to be seeing you every two weeks now.'
Something unintended in Hope's expression urged the community midwife to offer reassurance. 'Don't worry, it's not you,' she said. 'We see all of you mothers more often, now that you're nearly there.'

The label 'mother' sounded odd to Hope. Mothers had babies which they wheeled around in pushchairs and did things for. All Hope had was an ever more incongruous bump sticking out in front of her.

'Have you given any thought to your birth plan yet?'

Hope hadn't.

'You must, you know. You're getting near that time.'

Hope said that she would, but the midwife persisted.

'You want to get everything sorted in your mind before those contractions start! You won't have time to think about it when baby's on its way. Try and have it with you next time you come. We'll go through it together.'

'I will,' said Hope. 'I promise.'

Hope left the room and walked into the reception area where Dr Dangerfield was standing at the counter, chatting with one of the receptionists. She turned, and smiled in recognition.

'It's Hope, isn't it? How goes it? Any more attacks of the vapours?'

Hope reported the midwife's positive comments.

Dr Dangerfield seemed genuinely pleased at the news. 'Good, good. Well, you're looking very well. Whatever it is that you're doing, keep on doing it.'

Dr Dangerfield turned back to her receptionist. Hope left the surgery and emerged into a glowing, sunlit world.

The lounge bar was busy with lunchtime revellers, suave in their shirtsleeves and ties, suit jackets slung over their shoulders or draped across the backs of chairs. There were also more crumpled escapees from stuffy, non-air-conditioned offices, like Michael's. Jeffrey sat at a table, with two pints of beer in front of him. Michael sat down and took a long drink from one of them; he'd had a tedious morning and the prospect of more of the same that afternoon depressed him.

Or rather, it depressed him *further*, since he'd been living under a cloud for several days now. He couldn't say for sure that any one thing had caused this state of mind but there were plenty of possible reasons, including the feeling that his life was going nowhere. He was bored with his job, and the house he shared with Hope seemed cramped and claustrophobic. And Hope's increasingly obvious pregnancy served as a constant reminder to Michael that his life was about to change drastically, and not necessarily for the better. He ran movies in his mind of life with a baby in their midst. There they were, Hope and Michael, in their already-cramped home, the dimensions of which had been made even smaller by the presence of the alien gestating in Hope's belly.

He remembered the explosion of clutter at his sister's flat on the arrival of Jade, her first. In drawing its first breath, the child had sucked the walls and ceiling of the flat inwards. Linnie had never been an especially tidy person, but once Jade was born she seemed to lose all control of her surroundings. From that moment on she looked to have been fighting a losing battle against apathy, one she was too tired to care about. Was that to be Hope and Michael's fate? Exhausted in the service of the child? Too tired to tidy up, living on takeaways, and never going out? Not having a life any more?

'You're quiet today.' Jeffrey sipped his beer as though to mask the foray into personal territory.

'Sorry mate, just tired. Work's pissing me off.'

'Don't go back. Stay here and get pissed instead.'

Michael drained his glass. He stared down at the dregs swirling there. 'I'd better go back. Lots to do.'

Fatherhood was going to be like this: work before pleasure; duty before leisure. He was already resenting the life he was about to inhabit, a life he hadn't chosen for himself. He looked at Jeffrey, draining his glass and anticipating another. If he wanted to carry on drinking all afternoon, he could; Jeffrey's only responsibilities were to himself.

'Oh, fuck it,' said Michael. 'Let's get pissed.'

'Now you're talking,' said Jeffrey

'Well, I couldn't let you drink alone, could I?' said Michael, rising in the direction of the bar.

'Am I late?'

Alex looked as though she'd rushed to meet Hope, who was sitting at a table in the university's Arts Centre complex. She'd chosen to sit on the mezzanine, from where she could survey the comings and goings on the main concourse below, and also watch for Alex when she arrived. Alex settled herself down with her coffee and her sandwich.

'So, how'd it go?' Alex was referring to Hope's antenatal appointment.

'It was all right,' said Hope brightly, still basking in Dr Dangerfield's sunlight. 'The midwife seemed to think I'm doing OK.'

'Glad to hear it,' said Alex, glancing up at Hope. 'You've been a bit up and down lately.'

Hope could tell that Alex was inviting her to talk about what had been troubling her for the past few weeks, but she was experiencing a kind of euphoria as she sat there, surrounded by the hubbub of voices and movement. The noise was like the rush of life itself, the very essence of what it was to be alive, in all its restless contrariness. She found it difficult to recall, at that moment, why she'd felt so low recently. She deflected attention back to Alex, who had herself seemed out of sorts over the past few weeks.

'Hormones. They're my excuse for everything these days. How's things with you?'

'What do you mean?'

Hope was surprised by the defensive tone of Alex's voice. The sharp glance Alex gave Hope confirmed the impression.

'Well, I mean, you seem to have been a bit low yourself of late.' Hope found herself struggling to find a diplomatic form of words. 'Not *low* maybe . . . more *distant*. I mean, is everything all right, you know, with your bloke?'

Alex had still not talked with Hope about her latest relationship. This wasn't unusual: Alex didn't always let on about her relationships, not least because many of them lasted just as long as the time it took for Alex to get bored with the sex, and sometimes that meant no more than one night. But this one seemed to have some longevity, at least by Alex's usual standards, and Hope found herself wondering if Alex's secretiveness was born from a superstitious desire not to jeopardize a relationship that Hope could only surmise was working.

'Yes, everything's all right,' Alex said, but without looking at Hope. 'But he's not really "my bloke" though. It's not that serious.'

Hope could sense from Alex's evasive demeanour that there was more to this than she was letting on. Hope pressed on, determined to get to the bottom of things.

'What's he do? Where'd you meet him? Does he work at the uni?'

But Alex was having none of it. 'Look Hope, it really isn't serious. He's just someone to keep my bed warm now and again.' She gave Hope as frank a look as she could muster in an effort to shut down the enquiries.

But Hope's euphoria made her bold. 'Just a clue, Alex. Please! Something to keep me quiet. Does he work on campus? Do I know him?'

This last question brought another sharp glance from Alex, but this time Hope didn't notice; she'd just caught sight of Parmjit on the concourse below. It gave Alex time to regain control of herself. She quickly fed Hope some crumbs.

'All right, all right, you pest!' Alex's tone was deliberately light. 'He doesn't work on campus. He works in the city, in an office. I met him in a bar.'

'Go on,' said Hope, with the eagerness of a schoolgirl hearing of her friend's first experience with a boyfriend. 'You can't stop now!'

'Yes I can,' said Alex, flatly. She knew that she would have to give Hope a little more information to finally stifle her questions. 'Look, he's all right, we get on OK, he's good in bed etcetera etcetera . . .'

'But? It sounds like there's a "but" coming.'

Alex made herself look reticent. 'OK, but this is strictly between you and me, because I'm not proud of myself. I don't make a habit of this . . .'

'He's married, isn't he?' interjected Hope, suddenly realizing what was coming. A twinge of prudishness cast a slight frown of disapproval like a shadow over her face. Alex noticed it immediately, and moved quickly to reassure her friend.

'Actually, no he's not,' said Alex. 'But he's in a relationship.'

'Long term?'

'Several years.'

Hope didn't know what to do with this information. She sipped her cold tea thoughtfully. Alex, unsettled by Hope's silence, tried once more to reassure her. 'If you must know, I'm trying to break it off with him.'

'Trying?' said Hope, not quite understanding the difficulty.

Alex hesitated before speaking. 'He won't take no for an answer,' she said. 'He sends me things – flowers, chocolates, theatre tickets. Champagne, too. And he phones me – all the time. Or sends me texts.'

'I wish Michael would send *me* flowers and champagne!' Hope was trying to be light-hearted – she could see that Alex was upset by this man's unwanted attention. 'You've talked to him, obviously?'

'Yes, but we just go round and round. I say, leave me alone, and he says, why? We just end up arguing all the time. But I think he'd be happy to go on arguing with me forever, because then he would have my attention forever. While I'm arguing with him, I'm not with anyone else. I've tried silence, too, but I think he just takes silence as, I don't know, some sort of a challenge. It's as though, if I don't say anything, he can interpret the silence as anything he likes. I can't win. I don't know what to do to make him stop.'

Alex stopped talking. Hope could see the strain on Alex's face.

'It sounds crazy, I know,' she continued. 'I mean, I can't believe that I'm sitting here saying this stuff. There are people who'd probably kill for this level of attention. To outsiders it must look like a wonderful relationship. They'd probably think I was the mad one.'

'He sounds in need of help,' said Hope. 'Does his partner have any idea?'

'I hope not,' said Alex, sharply. 'At least, I don't think she does. He doesn't talk about her much.' She glanced at her watch. 'Damn. Got to get back to work. And I need a cigarette too.'

'I'll walk over with you.'

Both women rose from the table, and passed slowly through the crowd together.

Michael was browsing the Monarch Watch website again. He knew that there wouldn't be much happening as the Monarchs would still be hibernating in their roosts, high in the mountains of the Sierra Madre. But soon the warmer weather would return, thawing their chilled wings and freeing the Monarchs to mate, and then begin their thousand-mile journey home.

Michael settled back in his chair, daydreams of butterflies interspersed with thoughts of Jeffrey. They'd sunk three pints each before Michael decided that he really had to return to work. He was now buzzing from the effects of the alcohol, and he was restless, not at all interested in work. Jeffrey had spent lunch outlining his latest plans for the Chancredy Multimedia Collective. To Michael's surprise, Jeffrey had announced that he was in the process of organizing what he described variously as 'an event', 'a happening' and 'an installation'. The plan was to create a 'walk-through space' in which the Chancredy collective (i.e. Jeffrey) would create a 'sensual engagement' with a series of 'tactile and tactical' images and objects. It would be 'subversive' and 'challenging', but most importantly, it would be entirely under the control of the Collective and not some capitalist, profit-oriented corporation.

'So you're not going to charge anything then?' Michael had asked.

'Not a bean,' said Jeffrey. 'It's going to be a truly accessible event; it'll be the people's event – I'll just be the instigator, the facilitator.'

Jeffrey's eyes had glistened with a manic passion as he described, in broad outline, the various elements of the event/happening/installation. Michael had found himself briefly swept along on the tide of Jeffrey's enthusiasm and the beer he'd been necking too quickly. But now, running over Jeffrey's account only induced weariness. Michael wasn't really interested in Jeffrey's plans at all; he was tired of other people's enthusiasms which only served to emphasize his own lack of them.

Michael wanted to sleep. He wanted to be in his own bed, and to shut his eyes for a very long time. He felt annoyed with Jeffrey, a diffuse annoyance which seemed to have no specific cause. He looked at his computer, where the phrase SUCCESS BEGINS WITH THE DECISION TO MAKE THE ATTEMPT was tumbling around the screen. The stupid optimism of the motto annoyed him too. So when did failure begin, he wondered? The motto peddled only a fantasy of control, the dream that success or failure in life lies in your own hands. Michael knew that this was rubbish, that no matter how hard you worked, no matter how committed or single-minded you were, no matter how smart or sussed you were, your fortunes were driven by chance, by luck, by a random collision of events that thwarted your hopes and dreams more than it ever fostered them.

He thought of Hope, who he'd met at Jeffrey's birthday two years before. Hope hadn't met Jeffrey before that night, and was only there because a friend of his had coaxed her reluctantly into going. She and Michael hadn't noticed each other until Michael, turning to say something to a friend, had collided with Hope, spilling the contents of a glass of wine down her back. He'd stood dumbfounded, looking at the colossal stain spreading down Hope's blouse and not knowing what to do.

She'd admitted later that her first instinct was to slap him. But something about Michael's helplessness and bewilderment had appealed to her, though she didn't fully realize it as they stood there facing each other. It was only later, when Michael had plucked up the courage to apologize, that they had begun to talk as friends.

Michael considered the series of events that gave rise to that moment, the sequence of happenings that had prepared the ground for their meeting. Each element was explicable on its own terms: Michael was there because he was Jeffrey's friend; Hope was there because she'd argued with her boyfriend of the time and, still angry, had accepted Jeffrey's friend's invitation to spite him; Michael had collided with Hope because he'd been drinking and had turned too quickly; Hope was standing on that exact spot because she was talking to her friend. Each of these events had its own discrete genealogy, its own chain of cause-and-effect explanations which could be traced back through their lives.

But the conjunction of events could not be explained in the same way. The molecules moved purposefully, but the organism itself had no real direction, no real purpose. Michael had been delivered up to his fate by millions of tiny decisions and actions, mistakes and accidents, errors and omissions. He felt giddy at the thought. He felt like a crowd-surfer at a rock concert, suddenly hoisted up above the heads of the crowd and handed this way and that, never knowing where he was going to end up, out of control on a sea of other people's enthusiasms. He had to find some way to steady himself amid the chaos that was enveloping him. The world had dissolved into fragments, shards of orange light spinning around him, looking for all the world like the orange butterflies he loved so much. Thousands of them seemed to swarm around him, side to side, above and below, as though he were suspended in mid-air. Michael shook his head, trying to pull himself back to the world. The giddiness confused him; he hadn't had that much to drink, had he? What was happening?

The harsh fluorescence of the office came slowly back into focus, and Michael found himself staring again at his computer screen. He was trembling. Was it hunger? He hadn't eaten at all that day. Perhaps he was more drunk than he realized. Still searching for something to steady himself, he thought of the swirl of butterflies that he'd imagined a few moments before. And then he thought of Evette, eyelids sheathing her dark, feral eyes like butterfly wings shielding a flower from the sun. He'd had almost no contact with Evette since Christmas. Feeling less faint than he had a few moments before, Michael sat back in his chair, breathing steadily and deliberately. As he leaned back, the screen saver reactivated itself and once more the words bounced around the screen: SUCCESS BEGINS WITH THE DECISION TO MAKE THE ATTEMPT.

As though the faintness had been a mysterious, trans-formative force field through which he'd just passed, the phrase now seemed to hold a key to Michael's malaise – perhaps it was true, after all; perhaps he'd allowed himself to be buffeted by life for too long. It was time that he took control of the forces that seemed to be assailing him. He could go on being pushed this way and that by the caprice of circumstance, or he could exert himself over the events that shaped his predicament and find some sort of stability among the chaos. He felt his heart pounding as he waited to see what he would do next. His hand reached slowly for his mobile phone.

Hope was working at a desk on the third floor of the Learning Centre, checking the stock. As Alex and her mysterious lover ghosted through her mind, they were joined by another couple

– Johannes Schmetterling and Klara. Hope hadn't really made much progress investigating Schmetterling, so wrapped up had she been in other matters. Breaking off from work, she once more searched for Schmetterling in cyberspace, and quickly found a site with reproductions of several of his more influential paintings – though there was no more biographical information than she'd already got.

'Hello there.'

Hope jumped, momentarily embarrassed at being caught doing something other than the job she was paid to do. Turning, she immediately recognized the Scandinavian woman who had assisted Hope when she'd fainted.

'Sorry. I didn't mean to disturb you.'

'No, no. Don't worry about it,' said Hope, smiling and touching her distended belly. 'I don't think you've sent me into labour.'

The woman smiled at Hope. 'How is everything going?'

She was dressed in exactly the same neat, blue outfit she'd been wearing on the day of Hope's fainting fit. Her platinum-grey hair was meticulously cut and smoothed flat to her head, exactly as it had been. Under the harsher fluorescent lighting of the Learning Centre, her face looked slightly older than Hope had remembered it. 'I like that very much,' said the woman, who had noticed the reproduction of one of Schmetterling's paintings on the computer screen. 'Who is it?'

The question surprised Hope, since it was asked with an air of authority, as though the woman either knew who the artist was and merely sought confirmation, or would at least recognize the artist's name if Hope were able to give it. Hope felt a surge of excitement at the thought, a surge so forceful that it felt almost as though her baby had kicked her.

'Johannes Schmetterling.' Hope said it clearly in order to give the woman plenty of time to recognize the artist's name, and to recall any information about him that she could. The woman's response wasn't quite what Hope was looking for.

'Interesting. His name means "butterfly" in the German language.'

Hope felt foolish. It was evidently too much to expect, that a stranger would provide her with the information she needed.

'I know,' said Hope, crestfallen. The change of tone in Hope's voice registered with the woman.

'Are you all right?'

'Yes, yes, sorry. I . . . I don't know. I thought, for some reason, that you . . .'

'The painting?'

'Well, the artist really. Schmetterling. I'm trying to find out about him, but I'm not having much luck.'

'Nothing on internet?' The woman looked at the screen, puzzled.

'Not much,' said Hope. 'Not enough anyway. It's more his private life than his work that I'm interested in.'

'May I ask why?'

The woman seemed genuinely intrigued. Hope explained briefly about the painting she'd received for her birthday, the letter found tucked into the back of the painting, and the love affair and the love child the letter revealed.

'She apparently named the child after the artist,' said Hope.

'What, Schmetterling?'

'No, well . . . possibly. The letter doesn't say. She uses Schmetterling's signature-symbol in the letter, in place of the child's name.' Hope scrolled down the computer screen until the small, butterfly-shaped symbol in the bottom right-hand corner of the picture became visible. 'So I guess she might have named him Schmetterling. My money's on Johannes though.'

'Yes. Butterfly would have been an unusual name. It would have drawn attention. Perhaps even suspicion. Look, I have to go to tutorial now.'

'Of course. You're a student.'

'*Postgraduate* student. I have already a degree from Krakow.'

'Polish,' said Hope, finally fixing the accent. Not Scandinavian at all, then.

'Kolinsky. Magda Kolinsky. Pleased to meet you . . . ?' She held out her hand, waiting for Hope to introduce herself.

'I'm Hope, and I'm pleased to meet you. Again.'

They shook hands and Magda turned to leave but then turned back to Hope. 'Look, I have many, many relatives. In Poland, but also in Germany and Austria. I will ask questions. They are intelligent people. Perhaps at least they will find something out about this Schmetterling. Sound good?'

Hope was caught off guard by this offer. 'Really? Do you think they'd want to help?'

'Of course! Send me an email with whatever information you have. I can't keep it in my head. Age, you know.' Magda stooped, and wrote her email address on Hope's notepad.

'Then, yes. That would be brilliant.'

Smiling, Magda turned and headed for the stairwell. Hope slumped down into her seat. She would have to return to her work now.

Michael shut down his PC and arranged the papers on his desk, ready for tomorrow morning. He put his coat on and left the office by the back stairs. He didn't want to run into anyone who might want to go for a drink with him. Nervous as he was about where he was going, he might just have invited them along as a safety net against his own recklessness. Not that he was doing anything wrong, of course. He was only going for a drink, and a quick one at that. At the bottom of the stairwell he took out his phone and, for the hundredth time that afternoon, checked the text he'd received in reply to his.

where? when?

Michael checked his watch. He'd arranged to meet Evette at six, which gave him half an hour to get from Farsight Plastic Mouldings plc to the quiet bar he'd chosen on the edge of town.

He quickly sent Evette a text to let her know that he was on his way, then sent Hope a short message telling her that he was going for a quick drink after work. Hope's reply came almost immediately.

ok have fun xx

Michael carefully deleted Evette's message before stepping through the door on to the street beyond.

19

'Is it me? I mean, maybe it's me, or my hormones, or something?'

It was mid-morning, and Hope was sitting with Parmjit in the small cafeteria beneath the Learning Centre.

'Don't make it about hormones if there's something else bothering you,' said Parmjit. 'Don't make it about you, either. If people are messing you about, they're the problem, not you.'

Hope had confided in Parmjit that Michael seemed distant, that he wasn't interested in her at the moment. She'd tried to sit down with him several times to work on her birth plan and Michael had barely been able to sit on the sofa with her, let alone concentrate on the plan. But because Parmjit's cool and candid response clearly implied a criticism of Michael, Hope became immediately defensive.

'I know. But he's under a lot of pressure at work, and his dad's not been well. He suffers from angina, and it gets worse at this time of year. And I don't think he's really looking forward to being a dad himself. Not that he hates the idea, if you see what I mean; he just doesn't know what it's going to be like. He's probably anxious.'

'He's an adult,' said Parmjit. 'He's not stupid. It's not like he's the first bloke it's happened to.'

Hope searched inside herself for more excuses, but she'd run out of them.

Parmjit realized that she'd driven Hope into a corner. 'I'm sorry, Hope. Would you like me to talk to him? I will if you want me to. I can be diplomatic. When I try.'

Hope quickly changed the subject and asked Parmjit how her studies were going.

'Apparently they're going very well, if my grades so far are anything to go by. Not so well, if you listen to my family. I think dad might have thawed a bit though, believe it or not,' she said. 'It was when he saw the essays – the grades and the tutors' comments. I think he realized they were important, that my studies were serious and not just a fashion thing. He's very conservative. I think he thought that going to university was a feminist thing, that it was somehow a criticism of him.'

'It isn't then?'

'I suppose it is really, in a way. It's not him so much as what he represents. It's the value system that he endorses. I love him – he's my dad – but I don't agree with his politics. Or his economics, come to that.'

'Is it the marriage thing?' Hope felt embarrassed as soon as she said it. She knew very little about Parmjit's background, but she'd assumed that part of her problems with her father probably turned on Parmjit's eligibility for marriage.

'How do you mean?'

'You know. Marriage.' Hope didn't want to say it herself. She wanted Parmjit to make the connection for her.

'What? Arranged marriages? That sort of thing?' Parmjit was smiling incredulously at Hope, who could feel herself blushing.

'No, no. It's not like that at all. I mean, he'd like me to marry well, into a good family – what father wouldn't? But this isn't culture, it's just plain old-fashioned sexism. He just thinks women should know their place. Stick to what nature's designed them to do – cook, clean, breed, you know the sort of thing. When I think about how he treated my mom when she was alive . . .'

Parmjit's voice thickened as she spoke. Hope could see how raw Parmjit's memory of her mother was, and changed the subject. 'So what will you do when you've got your degree?'

Parmjit turned from the past. She thought carefully for a moment before speaking, drawing strength from a future not yet made. 'Kammi wants to be a human rights lawyer. He wants to go back to India to fight the good fight. I might go with him when I've got my degree. I've never been.'

'Human rights?'

'It seems to me that people back home don't want more culture – they've got culture by the lorry load. What they need is more human rights, more equality, more social justice. I know it sounds a bit pretentious, but I think that people like me – like me and Kammi – well, we're the bridge between the old culture and the new. The old culture's all about inequality, you know? The caste system, corrupt politics, conservatism, sexism, all that stuff. I'm all for progress and change. I don't hate my dad, but I don't want to live in his world any more.'

Hope found Parmjit's idealism energizing, admired her investment in a vision of the future. She'd come a long way since that night last year when Hope and Michael had climbed into her cab.

'What about Gyorgy?'

The question spilled out before Hope realized what she was saying. Parmjit thought for a moment, and then answered matter-of-factly.

'I don't know. It's two years before we have to make any decisions. I think he'd like to come too, though.' Parmjit glanced at her watch. 'I need to get back,' she said. 'Let's meet up soon, when I've more time. Do you want me to talk to Michael? I will if it'll help.'

'Thanks, Pam. But I guess it's really my job to talk to him. I appreciate the offer, but I think it'd be odd coming from you. I am the mother of his child, after all. No offence.'

'None taken,' said Parmjit, smiling.

They embraced, and parted.

Michael scrolled through his emails. There was a bulletin from the Monarch Watch newsgroup informing its readers that the mountains where the Monarchs roosted had been much colder than normal this winter and as yet showed no sign of warming up. Until this happened, the Monarchs would remain dormant in their mountain hideaway. Michael wondered whether or not this was the fault of global warming; though he'd no idea why a climate described as *warming* should cause the opposite of this in Mexico.

As he pondered this, he opened an email from Jeffrey. It reminded his mailing list of the date for what he was now calling a 'Terrorist Art Raid'. The title seemed to be asking for trouble in the twitchy, paranoid, post-9/11 world – but Michael presumed that Jeffrey knew what he was doing.

He checked his emails again, but there was still no reply to the email he'd sent Evette earlier that morning. He'd met Evette for drinks several times over the past two weeks, each time straight after work and for a couple of hours only, allowing them both to get home at a reasonable time. On each occasion Michael had lied to Hope about who he'd been with. He told himself that he'd no intention of breaking up either his own relationship with Hope, or Evette's relationship with his best friend. But he knew that these sly meetings with Evette couldn't continue without some change in their relationship. Something would have to happen soon.

Michael looked out of the office windows at the lowering skies beyond. It was midday, and a storm was brewing.

It was now after noon, and Hope was leaving the surgery where she'd just had her antenatal check-up. As she walked in the direction of home, clouds gathered overhead. She could feel the storm approaching, feel it viscerally. Even the child in her belly seemed agitated by the change in weather. She sent Michael a text.

checkup ok. wot time u home 2night?

His reply came almost immediately.

going 4 drink. wont b late. c u later

Hope sat looking at the reply – yet again Michael was going for a drink with his friends after work. He hadn't even acknowledged that her check-up had gone well. It was becoming clear that she – and the child she was carrying, *their* child – were very low on Michael's list of priorities. She cradled her distended belly in her hands, feeling clumsy, unwieldy, child-heavy. In spite of the careful diet she adhered to, she was tired and had very little energy. But she didn't want to go home to their empty house, at least not until Michael had got home. She needed human contact. She turned back towards the bus stop and headed into town for some retail therapy.

Later that afternoon, Michael sat in the pub with Preston. On the table in front of each stood a pint of beer, and beside each pint lay a phone. Evette hadn't replied to Michael's email, or the several texts he'd sent her during the course of the afternoon. Preston, meanwhile, had fallen out with Ben two days ago, and had heard nothing from him since. They'd rented a flat together only a month previously, and now Preston was alone again. He was worried about Ben – didn't know where he was – and he was anxious on his own in the flat. He needed to talk to someone, and had asked Michael out for a pint. But, sitting in the pub, neither seemed inclined to talk. Each watched his phone expectantly, while trying to give the opposite impression, but both phones remained stubbornly silent.

Parmjit sat in the Learning Centre, Gyorgy diagonally opposite. She was glad he was there; she felt comfortable with him, freed of the cultural burdens she felt in other areas of her life. She knew that Gyorgy was concerned about her taxi-driving, but he understood why it was that she needed to do it. She knew that he admired her willingness to make sacrifices to get what she wanted, and she knew that he endorsed the value of what it was she wanted.

She, in turn, admired Gyorgy's seriousness towards his studies, but also his seriousness towards life, his concern for others in a world shot through with injustice and corruption. She believed that Gyorgy would devote his life to challenging these evils, to making a difference in the world. Gyorgy was the first grown-up male friend she'd ever had.

She compared him to Michael. A nice bloke, fairly good-looking and with an easy sense of humour – but, as far as Parmjit could make out, no real interest in the world around him, no engagement with it. Gyorgy struggled to make the world a better place, to feel his responsibilities as a human being, to himself and to others. He had a sense of movement between past and present; a sense of a future yet to be made. Hope was pregnant, and yet Michael seemed to have no sense of movement, no sense that there was a future into which their child would be born and one day have to make its way.

Michael closed the door behind him. The house was empty and so he slumped down on the sofa and switched on the TV. He was hungry but too distracted to bother finding anything to eat. Evette had still not replied to his texts, and he didn't know where Hope was. He couldn't text Evette now – she'd probably be at home with Jeffrey – and he wouldn't want her to text him now because Hope might walk through the door at any second. He reached for his phone and called Hope.

'Where are you?' he said.

'At your parents'. I came here after my check-up.'

She was terse and made no attempt to fill the silence that followed.

'How's Dad?' he said, just to be saying something. Michael's father's angina had been getting worse in the cold February air.

'He's OK.'

Michael paused. 'Tell him I'll see him soon. And Mom.'

'OK.'

'See you later?'

'OK.'

And then she hung up.

Alex sat in her flat waiting for the knock at the door. She knew it would come; two messages on her answerphone and two texts had warned her that it would. Even so, the three hard raps in quick succession startled her. She sat immobile. Three more hard raps and then the phone started to ring. The answerphone kicked in, the tone sounded, and then he spoke.

'Alex? Pick up. I know you're in.'

How did he know? Had he followed her home? Alex waited, almost forgetting to breathe.

'Alex? Alex?'

The phone went dead and the rapping started again. Her mobile sounded this time, and Alex realized that whoever was standing at the door could hear it too. The rapping resumed, insistent, a muffled voice accompanying it. 'Come on, Alex. I know you're in there. Stop playing hard to get. Open the door.'

It was useless. She knew that she'd let him in eventually. She'd talk to him, as before, and he'd pretend to listen, as before. But nothing would change and they'd end up in bed, because that's what always happened. Why did she find it so hard to turn him away? Had the trauma of her childhood made her so weak? She fixed her gaze on the Turner painting above the fireplace, needing to lose herself in the brooding, swirling colours. And slowly, the painting began to work its strange magic on her. The more she concentrated, the faster the vortex seemed to revolve, and the faster it revolved the more it grew, consuming her field of vision until nothing of the room was left and she too had disappeared along with it.

Hope had gone to bed, leaving Michael sitting in front of the TV. She felt tired and her back ached. She was fed up of struggling to hold her belly up as she clumsily navigated it through a world hostile to her condition. Her lunchtime shopping expedition had turned into an obstacle course as she squeezed herself between racks of clothing so tightly packed together she could barely move. She'd stopped at a shop in town to buy food for their dinner, and her bulging belly had made it almost impossible to bend over the freezer chests to pick things out. On the crowded rush-hour bus out to Michael's parents, not one of the seated passengers had stood up to let her sit down. She hated being pregnant. But at least she was in good company, for everybody else in the world seemed to hate her being pregnant too. Now, lying on her side in the foetus position, her whole body wrapped protectively around her belly, Hope fell into troubled sleep.

Michael needed to go to bed too, but wanted to wait until Hope was asleep. With half an eye and half a brain he watched the news, mostly given over to heightened tensions between the US-led 'Coalition of the Willing' and the United Nations. It was looking increasingly likely that Bush would launch a pre-emptive war against Iraq, whether or not the UN endorsed this.

The familiar, smiling face of Saddam Hussein flashed up on the screen, and for some reason his trademark moustache reminded Michael, at that moment, of Joseph Stalin. The rich growth of hair on the upper lips of these two dictators brought to mind the comical moustache favoured by Hitler. Three dictators; three moustaches. What is it, thought Michael, about dictators and moustaches? Of course, Mussolini hadn't had a moustache; but then he hadn't been a particularly successful dictator by the standards of the other three. Castro had a beard, which included a moustache, but was he really a dictator? And General Franco, had he been a dictator too? Michael couldn't recall what Franco had looked like anyway, so he couldn't be counted.

His memory store of dictators exhausted, Michael's attention drifted to the fruits of Hope's research into Schmetterling, lying on the coffee table in front of him. He poked idly among the papers. Klara's letter lay there, together with its translation. Michael read the letter now with interest. Whatever it was they'd had together, and however brief it had been, the affair had clearly been a profound emotional experience for Klara.

Steeped in desire for Evette, Michael found himself wondering about his relationship with Hope. He loved Hope, didn't he? Yes, of course he did, though he had to admit that his desire for her had waned a bit of late. But wasn't this to be expected in *any* relationship after a while, after the first rush of desire had subsided? Surely you can never recapture that rush, in any long-term relationship? Even if you could, Hope was massively pregnant now, and while some men might be turned on by this, Michael wasn't. And to make matters worse, Hope's pregnancy had clearly had an impact on *her* desires too. Sex between them was hit and miss these days; sometimes she felt like it, and sometimes she didn't. He was doing his best to understand her shifting moods and everything, but he found it very frustrating all the same. After all, whether or not they were as strong as they used to be, he did *have* desires still.

Of course, Hope wouldn't be pregnant for ever, and their relationship could get back to normal. But as the example of his sister's children showed, that wouldn't happen – children changed a relationship rather than restored it to what it was. On the other hand, his desire, his feelings (as he preferred to think of them) for Evette, had strengthened during Hope's pregnancy. Evette was an uncomplicated life force Michael could draw upon. She always looked and smelled lovely; she was always smiling; life never seemed to bear down hard on her. She came and went in his life like the lightest beating of a butterfly's wings in the stillness of a summer's morning.

Thinking of butterflies brought Michael back to the letter he was holding. He remembered the conversation he'd had about Schmetterling in the pub back in January, standing with Jeffrey, Preston and the Russian guy. Ever since that discussion, Michael had pictured Schmetterling in a soldier's uniform, a fighter who'd died for the Reich: Johannes A. Schmetterling, Iron Cross First Class, awarded posthumously, his grave, some anonymous corner of a foreign field, his body never recovered, his family distraught but proud of their decorated, war-hero son. The image had a certain romanticism about it.

He looked at the letter again, and noticed the date – 1898 – in the top right-hand corner. This pulled him up short. If Schmetterling had died in 1943, and he was having his affair with Klara . . . what, forty-five years earlier? . . . then he must have been how old when he died? But 1898 *wasn't* the year of their affair, was it? Klara's letter was written on the tenth anniversary of that date, so there were fifty-five years between the date of the affair and Schmetterling's death. Michael began to realize how absurd his idea was, that Schmetterling had been a soldier in the Third Reich. Assuming that the artist must have been at least sixteen years old when he'd had the affair with Klara, then by the time he died in 1943 he must have been . . . what? Michael worked out the simple calculation on paper and sat looking at the figure – Schmetterling must have been seventy years old by the time he died. Michael realized at last that, whatever had happened to Schmetterling during the Second World War, he surely hadn't died fighting for the Reich. Not at that age. His Schmetterling hunch lay in tatters. Peevishly, Michael replaced Klara's letter on the table and sloped off to bed.

20

Hope looked at herself in the mirror. She could see Michael behind her, getting himself dressed. Jeffrey's 'Terrorist Art Attack' was due to open that morning.

'Will I do?' she asked Michael's reflection, which paused to look at her.

For the first time since she'd become pregnant, Hope had decided to wear a maternity dress rather than her usual slacks and top. She felt extra-conspicuous, the dress somehow exaggerating her condition in a way that the close-fitting garments never had. Michael was genuinely impressed: Hope looked beautiful, womanly, and very pregnant. He was surprised at just how pregnant she looked, despite having seen her naked belly many times before.

'Wow,' he said. 'You look huge!'

The last remnants of Hope's self-esteem crawled into a corner to die. Michael was too busy looking at Hope's midriff to see the look on her face.

'That's it,' she said. 'It's going back to the shop.'

She started to pull the dress up over her head.

'No, no!' Michael realized what he'd said. 'I mean, you look great! Don't take it off!'

The discarded dress crumpled on to the floor like a deflated balloon. Hope sat down on the bed. 'I'm not going, I feel like a frump. I'm never going outside again.'

Michael found himself kneeling on the floor in front of Hope, his arms embracing her girth, his head resting on the exposed flesh of her breasts. She smelt of flowers, the dark, secret perfumes of his mother's flower garden. But not just flowers; there was also the salty tang of sweat – an undertone of human flesh, like desire made into a scent. He rested there, breathing deeply and slowly, intoxicated and aroused.

A kick woke him from his reverie. A small limb had raked against the wall of Hope's belly, and Michael felt it. He pulled up sharply, just in time to see the weight of Hope's pregnant tummy shift slightly, from left to right. Instinctively, Hope's hand reached up to steady the dome of flesh and comfort the increasingly impatient occupant. She felt the movement in the form of an uncomfortable pressure under her diaphragm. She shifted her weight to ease the pressure as much as she could and took a deep breath.

'Are you all right?' Michael watched as she struggled to get herself comfortable. He didn't know how to help.

'Give me a minute,' said Hope. She stood up. Breathing more easily, she looked down at Michael. She could see the concern in his face and placed a hand on his head, comforting him.

'I'm all right,' she said. 'I think junior's nearly ready though; it's getting very lively in here.'

Michael looked up at Hope. Her hair was lit from behind by the bright sun through the window, a halo of gold framing a face that glowed with its own secret source of light. She seemed at that moment to be immensely powerful, a force of nature made flesh, bathed in ethereal light. For a brief moment he felt as though Hope's gaze was infiltrating every pore in his body, dismantling each individual cell, seeking out and exposing the smallest, darkest and most sinful thoughts he'd ever had, or ever would have.

'Are you going to stay down there all day?' she said. 'Jeffrey's expecting us to put in an appearance sometime today.' She reached for the dress she'd discarded minutes earlier and turned to face the mirror, leaving Michael bewildered and foolish.

Preston sat on the edge of the bed watching Ben, dressed only in underpants and socks, rooting in the wardrobe for something to wear, their argument of the week before forgotten. It was Hope who'd interceded with Ben and brought about their reconciliation. A couple of days later, a bouquet of flowers had arrived by courier for her. The card, signed by Ben and Preston, contained a brief message: 'Hope, you'll make a great mother, if our experience is anything to go by!'

Ben turned around, holding a pale roll-neck jumper in one hand, and a denim shirt in the other.

'Which one says: "Art Terrorist"?'

Preston looked at Ben and felt his stomach knot with desire so forceful that for a moment he could barely speak. He could only laugh, as though he were being tickled from the inside.

'What? What's funny?'

But Preston's chuckling was infectious, and Ben began to laugh too, though partly out of embarrassment.

'What? Tell me!'

He threw both shirts at Preston, who tried to dodge them. Then Ben was on top of Preston, pretending to wrestle the information out of him. And then they were making love.

'We're going to be late,' said Preston.

'So stop then,' said Ben.

'All right,' said Preston, making as though he was about to get up.

'Don't you dare,' said Ben.

The doorbell rang, and Alex jumped, though she knew that it would be Hope. Minutes later, she was behind the wheel of her car, Hope sitting beside her, Michael and Parmjit in the back. Gyorgy had been invited but couldn't make it, and Hope realized how odd it was nowadays to see Parmjit without him.

'Do we know where we're going?' Michael waved the email containing directions but Alex grabbed it from him and gave it to Hope. 'Will you navigate?' she said, throwing a theatrical frown at Michael. 'I'd like to get there today.'

'I'm a taxi driver,' said Parmjit. 'Let me.'

Alex handed the instructions to Parmjit, who squinted at them, trying to fit them to her mental map of the city.

'Bloody hell,' she said. 'This is out in the sticks, isn't it? Is it a gallery or something?'

Michael explained that Jeffrey had hired a venue rather than mount the event/happening/installation thingy in what he disparagingly referred to as an 'establishment art house'.

'He says he's taking art into the real world. He calls it an "intervention", whatever that means. You know what he's like.'

'An intervention into what?' said Hope. 'What's he intervening in? Michael – you must know. He talks to you about this stuff.'

'Is it political?' said Parmjit, also to Michael.

But it was Alex that answered. 'He's intervening in people's lives, like the self-satisfied self-publicist he is.'

Hope was struck by the bitter tone in Alex's voice and stole a glance sideways at her friend. Alex was staring ahead through the windscreen and looked drawn, as though she'd not slept for some time and had tried to cover it up with too much foundation.

'Left here,' said Parmjit. 'So what is it, if it isn't a gallery?'

It was a shed, or so it seemed at first glance. They'd driven up and down the road twice before they realized that this was the place. The road they'd found themselves on had clearly once been a busy high street, but the business had ebbed away, leaving only the jetsam of better times. The shops that had been vacated and boarded up outnumbered the shops which were still trading, though even these seemed to be running out of steam. An old man in a drab, crumpled raincoat and a flat cap shuffled past the car, towing behind him a reluctant, emaciated mongrel on a frayed leash.

'Jesus,' said Hope, in disbelief. 'This can't be the place, can it?'

'Have we got the right address?' said Michael, incredulously. 'Pam?'

'This is the address on the paper,' she said, scrutinizing the sheet just to make sure.

'Well,' said Alex. 'I suppose the revolution's got to start somewhere.'

As they stepped from the car, they realized that the shed, a wooden construction which they'd thought was the venue itself, was in fact only an anteroom, a glorified entrance hall to a more substantial single-storey brick building which had been obscured by the overgrown bushes growing either side. A faded, hand-painted notice to the right of the entrance, partly obscured by bushes, announced the building as THE KINGDOM HALL OF THE FRIENDS OF THE SAVIOUR. MEETINGS TUESDAY 7PM; SATURDAY 7PM; SUNDAY 10AM, 6PM. Nothing about the venue indicated that within these neglected walls Jeffrey had launched his revolutionary, anti-capitalist, anti-socialist, art-terrorist event/happening/installation thingy.

'Are we going in?' said Hope. 'I can't see anyone about.'

She looked around for some sign that this was really the right place. Preston and Ben stepped from the street behind them.

'Is this it?' said Ben, laughing nervously. 'We're in the middle of nowhere.'

Hope pushed cautiously at the door, which opened by a few centimetres. She peered into the gloom beyond.

'We should go in,' she said. 'We've come all this way.'

They stepped through into a darkened space. The windows had been blacked out, though here and there shards of light jabbed through splits in the blackout material. Faint coils of smoke oozed lazily through the thin slivers of light and a strangely familiar but not unpleasant scent greeted them.

'What's that smell?' whispered Preston.

'I think it's patchouli,' said Hope.

'Joss sticks,' said Alex. 'How very twenty-first century.'

As they moved slowly forward into the space, they became aware of two zones of faint luminescence, like the after-image of light on a retina, one at each end of the room. As though triggered by their movement, a mechanical whirring sound revved up and sent images – faint and indeterminate – flickering across these luminous zones.

'Jeffrey wants to sort out the focus on his projectors,' whispered Ben. 'I can't tell what I'm looking at.'

'Maybe you're not supposed to,' said Preston. 'Maybe it's abstract.'

Gradually, the images came into focus, stationary panoramas of city streets across which shadows of people drifted to and fro. The images were grainy, the colours exaggerated as though the buildings were bleeding light. A low rumbling sound reverberated about them.

'Is that an earthquake?' said Parmjit.

Grinding industrial noises now seemed to clamber up out of the rumbling noise, like a race of primordial machines emerging from the bowels of the earth, or at least from the creaking wooden floorboards beneath their feet. The whirring of the cine-projectors slotted into place amid the rising industrial cacophony. What sounded like a reversed drum kit slewed across the soundscape, accompanied by a screeching sound, like an electric guitar fed through the stretched neck of a balloon. The speakers were arranged so that the sound seemed continually to be circling them, as though mechanical wolves were prowling the edge of the darkened room.

'Jesus Christ!'

Everyone turned towards Michael. He was struggling with something that had become tangled in his hair.

'Are you OK?' said Hope, concerned.

Something nudged her from behind. She turned, and came face to face with a dark shape, bobbing eerily beside her. At that moment, the door opened, flooding the room with light. Ben stood holding the door wide so that they could see more clearly what was attacking them. Hope's assailant turned out to be a large inflatable object made of some crumpled foil-like material. She pushed it gently and it bobbed lazily away, its crazed silvered surface catching crystals of light from the projectors. There were other shapes, some floating above their heads, others scattered and drifting across the floor. Michael had become entangled in ribbons dangling from one of these floating balloons.

'What's that all about?' said Preston, no longer whispering.

The intrusion of daylight had broken the spell; suddenly they were just a group of people standing in a room filled with balloons.

'I mean, are we supposed to do anything?'

'Fucked if I know,' said Michael, finally getting clear of the trailing ribbons.

'Where's Jeffrey?' said Hope. 'If he were here we could ask him.'

Behind their heads and in front of their eyes, the projectors continued to throw out images on to the screens as the music churned and hummed, screeched and thudded towards another mini-climax.

But the images had changed. Instead of buildings and a stationary camera, there was now a sensuous rolling landscape, like sand dunes, across which the camera voyeuristically panned. Warm earthy tones flooded the screen, broken only by the occasional dark patch of vegetation.

'What's that?' said Preston. And then: 'Is that what I think it is?'

Ben closed the door again, sharpening the images on the screen.

The camera seemed to track from vegetation into a deep valley, passing briefly and rapidly across what looked like a cleft in a sandy rock face.

'What *do* you think it is?' said Ben.

Behind them, similar scenes played out on the other screen while around them synthesized human voices moaned like the damned in hell against a lush wash of swirling synthetic strings.

The camera swooped down, and then twisted through the valley, following the cleft out on to a smooth plain.

'Goodness me,' said Hope, suddenly understanding what Preston meant. 'I think you're right.'

'Oh my god,' said Ben, also getting it.

'Oh no,' said Alex, and this time Hope detected a note of panic in her voice.

'What? What am I looking at?'

Michael was still baffled by the images.

And then suddenly he wasn't. The camera tracked around again and this time it ranged across what were clearly a pair of breasts. Visible, too, was the hollow of a woman's throat, and above that her chin and her lipstick-covered lips. Vivid, red lipstick.

'Who is it?' said Ben. 'Do we know?'

Michael knew immediately who it was. He'd spent many long months fantasizing about those lips, that mouth, and those breasts which he now saw unclothed for the first time.

He couldn't believe it. He felt betrayed. Worse – it was as though Evette were taunting him by sharing her body with everyone else, forcing him to see how unexceptional he was in her life. He was just another voyeur, standing in the crowd with all the other voyeurs.

'I know who that is,' said Ben. 'It's . . . what's her name? Jeffrey's girlfriend.'

Hope was watching Alex out of the corner of her eye. Throughout the morning she'd watched Alex's reactions to various events; had sensed how uncomfortable Alex was entering into Jeffrey's world. She knew now that Jeffrey was Alex's mysterious and troublesome lover. For a brief, uncomfortable moment, she'd even thought that it might be Alex's naked body up there on the screen. Alex bit her lip and watched in silence.

A change in the tone of the music signalled a change in perspective on the screen. The sound became rhythmic, pulsing like tribal drums. Electronic shrieks scratched through the rhythm, accompanied by what seemed to be heavily reverberating but very distant animal cries. They could have been anything, from bats to cats to hyenas, but they could as easily have been Jeffrey undergoing primal scream therapy. On screen, the image was now fixed, the camera mostly stationary, but juddering occasionally, as though responding to movement elsewhere in the room. The scene was warmly lit, but still indistinct, as though deliberately set out of focus. All the same, they could make out a woman's naked body lying on a bed. But this time another body entered the frame.

'Is that Jeffrey?' said Parmjit.

They all leaned forward, squinting.

'I don't know,' said Hope, bluntly. 'I've never seen his arse before.'

The couple on screen began to fondle each other theatrically as the image became more distorted, the colour more exaggerated. The scene was intercut clumsily with amateur film of planes crashing into the twin towers of the World Trade Centre, 'smart' missiles blowing up buildings in Iraq, and other images of explosions and fires. As the animal shrieks and howls became more violent and grating, it slowly became clear to the group that the couple interwoven with the violent images were making love.

'Go for it, Jeffrey! Go on, my son!' It was Ben's voice, and there was suppressed laughter in it.

'We don't know that it is Jeffrey,' Hope reminded him.

'This is pornography,' said Preston. 'What's Jeffrey think he's up to?'

'I've had enough of this.' It was Alex's voice, and there was no trace of laughter in it at all. She peeled away from the group and walked quickly towards the door. Michael, who'd silently been wanting to tear down the screens, turned and followed her out.

Just as they got to the door, it opened. An old woman stood there, framed by the doorway and silhouetted against the daylight. She wore a checked overcoat and suede ankle-length boots. A scarf covered her head and was tied underneath her chin. She held a bulging carrier bag in each hand, and these almost touched the floor either side of her. She seemed oblivious to the images on-screen, and to the primitive techno-racket going on around them.

'I'm sorry,' she said. 'But Mr Jeffrey's been held up. He asked me to come and keep an eye on everything.'

Alex and Michael sat together on the wall outside the Kingdom Hall of the Friends of the Saviour, Alex smoking a cigarette. Neither spoke. After a little while, the others joined them.

'Phew!' said Ben. 'Totally fucking weird!'

'Mikey, Mikey,' Preston could hardly contain his mirth. 'You left just at the best bit. The old woman got herself a chair and sat down . . . with her knitting! She's sitting there by the door, knitting! It's priceless.'

'Do you think Jeffrey arranged it like that?' said Ben, seriously. 'I mean, is she part of it?'

'I can't believe Jeffrey's hired a little old lady as a security guard!' Preston was laughing now.

'I can't believe the place was open when we got here,' said Hope. 'I'm surprised Jeffrey's stuff wasn't swiped.'

Hope spoke to everyone, but she was watching Alex who, lost in thought, dragged bitterly on her cigarette.

'Nobody knows it's here,' said Ben. 'Look. There's no advertising, no posters. Nobody knows about it unless they've come across some reference to it on the net.'

'Poor old Jeffrey,' said Preston. 'He'll be disappointed if no one comes.'

'*We* came, didn't we?' said Ben. 'It's not a complete disaster.'

'Yes it fucking well is,' said Alex. 'It's typically arrogant of him to imagine anyone would want to come to see that pile of derivative, half-baked bullshit.'

'It all seemed a bit, well, *lo-fi* to me,' said Preston. 'I thought Jeffrey was a bit of a techie, you know? His website and everything? I was expecting something a bit more hi-tech than joss sticks and balloons.'

'And cine-film too. Whatever happened to digital projection?'

'Well, maybe that's the point.' Hope's instinct was to explain away Jeffrey's idiosyncrasies. 'You all know what Jeffrey's like. He sees himself as working against the dominant trends, doesn't he? Isn't that part of his art-as-authenticity thing?'

'But he spends a fortune on hi-tech stuff,' snapped Michael, who wasn't in the least bit inclined to join Hope in defending Jeffrey. 'Their house is full of it.'

'I think Hope's on to something,' said Ben. 'I don't know him as well as you lot, but from what I can gather, Jeffrey can be wilfully perverse at times.'

'Exactly,' said Ben. 'Maybe for the purposes of this particular event Jeffrey's refused to engage with technology.'

'But why?' said Parmjit, joining in. 'Technology aside, I just didn't get it. I can't see what it is that he's trying to say. Is it a critique? If so, what's it critiquing?'

Michael's phone sounded. It was a text from Jeffrey.

'Well,' said Michael, sullenly, 'if we want to know what it's all about we can ask him about it in person. He wants to meet us for a drink later.'

Hope, whose attention had been taken up by Alex, only now realized how annoyed Michael seemed. She was surprised, not only because Michael was usually indifferent to art, but also because, as his closest friend, she'd assumed that Jeffrey would have kept him informed about what he was planning.

Having arranged their day around Jeffrey's event/happening/installation thing, they all now found themselves at a loose end. With the afternoon stretching before her, Hope decided that she'd like to call in at the university to sort out some unfinished paperwork. Parmjit decided that she'd go with her; there were deadlines looming and more reading to be done, and little enough time to do it. Michael, Preston and Ben decided to head into the city centre. They would meet up with the others later on. Alex wanted to go home. She wasn't sure she would be joining them that evening.

2 I

In the city centre, Michael left Preston and Ben to their shopping and headed for the bar they'd arranged to meet Jeffrey in later that evening. He felt as though everything was smeared with violent red paint; he needed a drink to help him sort his thoughts out.

As he sat supping his first pint, he thought about Evette's naked body up there on the screen. Michael considered himself no prude, but he simply couldn't get over the shock of seeing his best friend, and the woman he so desperately wanted, not only naked – shocking enough in itself – but also shagging each other in front of the camera. In public. In full view of everyone. How could they – how could *she* – have done it? And to make matters considerably worse, he realized that he would probably have to face Evette later, if she turned up with Jeffrey. And he'd have to face Jeffrey too; how was he supposed to deal with that? Almost before Michael knew what was happening, he was at the bar ordering his second pint.

How could Evette have done it? Michael pictured her naked body on the screen with painful desire; the body that he'd spent months fantasizing about. Evette would never be his now because she was everyone's. She'd squandered her beauty on anyone who cared to wander in off the street. Michael felt betrayed. His meetings with Evette over the previous few weeks had hinted at something more intimate. He'd begun to feel that a slow-burning process had been set in train between them, with Evette in full agreement, even if she never actually came out with it. He'd really come to believe that she wanted him. He knew now that he'd been kidding himself. Once more, he found himself at the bar, ordering another pint.

He was a fool. During their conversations together, Evette had mostly talked about the trials and tribulations of living with a creative person like Jeffrey: the restless energy which Jeffrey had for his various projects, and which all too frequently she found exhausting; the time he spent alone, working in his studio, so that she barely saw him from one day to the next; the drain on their finances as Jeffrey sank his wages into the latest bit of studio technology or computer software, leaving them to survive on her relatively meagre wages. Michael had taken these conversations as a sign of Evette's discontent with her relationship with Jeffrey, but he saw now that they hadn't been complaints at all. In fact, he realized, they were signs of Evette's *devotion* to Jeffrey; she'd been using Michael as a sort of counsellor, a means to clear her head of the frustrations and doubts that would inevitably arise in the course of submitting herself to Jeffrey's world view. Evette had simply not looked at Michael in the same way that he'd looked at her.

And the reason was simple – Michael was useless and boring. He didn't have a single creative bone in his entire body. He hadn't written anything longer than a greetings card since he'd left school; he couldn't draw to save his life, and had never had the urge to anyway; he was no Schmetterling either – he couldn't paint, had no eye for colour, and no sense of co-ordination. It was Hope who chose the decor of the house; she even told him what to wear. The closest he'd ever got to creating something was the Airfix models he'd made as a child. There was no getting away from it – compared to Jeffrey, Michael was dull and uninteresting.

But it wasn't just creativity. Michael didn't even understand what was happening in the world around him. He wasn't well-read, had never been to university and couldn't claim to have a specialist knowledge about anything – except maybe the stock-control procedures of Farsight Plastic Mouldings plc, and no one, not even Michael, was interested in that. There was the Monarch Butterfly, of course, but even there he didn't have the kind of specialist, scientifically-trained knowledge that would have got him into the famous black leather *Mastermind* chair, and if he had he would have screwed up in the general knowledge section. He understood so little about what was going on in the world. How was it that Saddam Hussein had suddenly become global enemy number one? Wasn't that supposed to be Bin Laden or something? He didn't know. He didn't even understand close-up things. How had he not known that Preston was gay? How had he ended up in a relationship heading towards stability and fatherhood? How had he so misread Evette's intentions towards him? How would anyone ever find him interesting? Never mind Evette – how could *Hope* find him interesting? He was pointless and stupid. He knew so little about things. But at least he knew where the bar was.

Michael sat down with his fourth pint and a large whisky to go with it. The only thing he wanted at that moment was the alcohol, which at least took the sting out of his self-loathing. He downed the whisky, and with renewed spirit his thoughts returned to Evette. But this time they took a different tack. In a moment of inebriated clarity, Michael realized that Jeffrey must have *forced* Evette to do it. She'd acted under duress. She must have done – there was no way the Evette he knew would've allowed herself to be used in that way, to have her beautiful body exploited for such a crude enterprise. It was Jeffrey who was the villain here. He'd made her do it.

The exact mechanics of how he would have made her do it didn't trouble Michael at all. He knew that women were exploited all the time by the sex industry. Somehow, in some way, Jeffrey – manipulative, Svengali-like Jeffrey – had forced Evette to debase herself before them all. It was Jeffrey who'd done it, and who the fuck did he think he was? Someone needed to take him down a peg or two. Someone needed to stand up for Evette – poor, naked, exploited, beautiful, vulnerable, naked, lovely, naked Evette.

Michael began to feel less hollow. His sense of worth rose from the bottom of the sea of despond, buoyed up by his chivalrous thoughts concerning the helpless, child-like Evette. Michael saw, albeit in a rather hazy way, the path he must take. He suddenly remembered one of the many mottos that Farsight Plastic Mouldings plc provided him with on his company PC:

SUCCESS BEGINS WITH THE DECISION TO MAKE THE ATTEMPT

Michael had always hated these stupid slogans, but now he realized just how wrong he'd been; this one at least made perfect sense. Drawing strength from this obviously very important truth, Michael remembered another Farsight motto:

NEVER UNDERESTIMATE THE IMPORTANCE OF 'A LITTLE LOOKING OUT FOR THE OTHER FELLA'

He would do it! He – Sir Galafray of Camelot (or was it Gallagher of Camelot, or Gollum? He couldn't recall) – would look out for Evette. Though of course she wasn't a little fella. Obviously. Goes without saying, that. He'd just seen the proof of that after all, he thought, chuckling to himself.

Another Farsight motto tumbled forth from the dark recesses of his alcohol-befuddled memory:

A JOURNEY OF A THOUSAND MILES BEGINS WITH BUT ONE STEP

How true, he thought drunkenly, how very, very true that was! But if you're going to journey for a thousand miles, he told himself, you need a drink first. And the thousandth drink begins with a single step. In the direction of the bar. Wherever that was.

Hope left Parmjit in the Learning Centre and headed for her office to check her emails. Two in particular caught her interest. The first of these was from Gareth – the translator of Klara's letter. It had been sent at five-thirty the previous evening, and read:

Hope – how goes the hunt for Klara? Something puzzles me about the letter (I kept a copy – hope you don't mind). Could we meet to talk sometime – soonish if poss – I'm off to Germany again for a week. Working trip. Would really like to talk before I go. Think it might be important.

This intrigued Hope. Klara was one of the only things anchoring Hope in her increasingly unstable world. Whatever had happened to Klara, Schmetterling, and their love child, it was all now in the past, and the facts of their affair – whatever they were – would now never change. For better or worse, Klara's life was now fixed in space and time, as Hope realized her own would be, one day.

The second email had a subject line: *Greetings from Germany.*

I am told that you look at knowledge of Schmetterling artist. I have brief monograph but in German language. Send me your address by return and I will journey it to you. My regards to you.

It was signed by someone called Oskar Krause, presumably a friend of the Polish woman, Magda. Hope was delighted by the thought that a book existed about her mysterious artist, even if it was in German. She immediately replied to Oskar Krause with her address; then, too excited to settle down to work on her report, she went to drink tea until it was time to meet Parmjit and head for the city centre.

The friends met in the pub at the agreed time, though neither Jeffrey nor Evette were there. To everyone's surprise, Alex had joined them after all. Hope was appalled to find Michael visibly drunk, his eyes glassy, and his head lolling about as though it were attempting an awkward docking manoeuvre with his shoulders. She remonstrated with him, and he seemed to understand her, though he also carried on drinking as best he could. As they chatted and waited for Jeffrey to arrive, they realized how awkward they all felt about the images they'd seen. They were pretty sure that it had been Evette – the images had been digitally manipulated and were not as clear as they might have been – but they were less sure that it had been Jeffrey. An uneasy consensus was reached among the group that it *must* have been Jeffrey. Bizarre as it was to admit that two of their close friends had been filmed romping in the buff for public consumption, the idea that Evette might have been constrained to perform with someone other than Jeffrey, while he filmed them, was even more bizarre.

Jeffrey arrived, a little breathless. It could have been nerves, or excitement, or that he'd been hurrying to get there at the time he'd promised – the group couldn't tell. His eyes shone, however, and he had a broad grin on his face. He was also minus Evette. He spent the first quarter of an hour getting everyone a drink. Eventually, he sat down with them, and raised his glass in a toast.

'To you lot, for turning up today. Cheers!'

They all joined Jeffrey in raising their glasses, except for Michael who seemed to be having difficulty focusing.

'How do you know we actually turned up?' said Ben, a wicked grin creeping across his face.

'Betty told me you were there.'

Betty, it transpired, was the caretaker for the Friends of the Saviour hall. For an interminable minute, no one spoke. Jeffrey sat looking at the group; he didn't want to ask them what they'd thought of it, but they all knew that he expected them to tell him anyway. Hope broke the awkward silence.

'It was very . . . erm, *fragmented.*' Jeffrey was a friend, and Hope was trying to be non-judgemental. 'Very, I don't know . . . the images were . . . well, *interesting.*'

'Bastard!'

Michael opened his defence of Evette with a finely-honed insult. Unfortunately, no one could understand the indistinct, guttural noise that emitted from his throat. Oblivious to his own incoherence, he took another drink, and jutted his chin at Jeffrey, waiting for a response.

Everyone ignored him.

'So what's it about then?' After Hope's generous pre-varications, Parmjit's directness was striking, and Jeffrey turned immediately to engage.

'I can't answer that,' he said, his tone now serious, earnest. 'It's not *about* anything. I have my own theories, but I'm not going to tell you what they are.'

'But why?' It was Preston this time.

'Why?' Jeffrey turned now to confront Preston. 'Why should my interpretations of my own work interest *you*? *I'm* more interested in what *you* think.'

'So it's OK for you to hear our theories, but not for us to hear yours?' Alex scythed her way into the discussion.

'It's *so* fragmented though.' Hope sensed immediately the hostile tone of Alex's voice, and tried to pull the conversation back towards calmer waters. 'Couldn't you just give us some clues as to what it's about? A thread to follow . . . ?'

'But it's *all* clues,' said Jeffrey, who began to sense that a lynch mob was developing among his friends. He recognized Parmjit as the enemy. Her forthrightness had emboldened the others. He needed to assert himself over her if he was to maintain his credibility. 'Don't you get it? All I've done is give you clues. You have to try to make your own interpretation from what I've put before you.'

'But surely . . . I don't know.' Hope again. 'I know it sounds a bit waffly, but aren't we – I mean, the audience – supposed to be interested in what you – the artist – have to say? I mean, aren't we *supposed* to be interested in your judgements about the material? Aren't we supposed to be interested in what you're challenging? If you're challenging anything, I mean.'

'Yeah.' Ben this time. 'Aren't you supposed to be commenting in some way?'

'Aren't you supposed to be *committed?*' Parmjit's insistence was beginning to annoy Jeffrey. She was definitely the ringleader. That there was no leader, and no ring, didn't occur to him; at that moment, he felt under siege from a group of people he liked and trusted, led by a bloody Asian woman who he knew almost nothing about. Who did she think she was?

'Yes, Jeffrey. A non-committed artist is boring . . . uninteresting.' Alex rejoined the mob and again Hope noticed the tone in her voice. Parmjit's forthrightness seemed based on a genuine curiosity, but Alex's challenge to Jeffrey seemed to be fuelled by anger. Or was Hope imagining it?

Jeffrey scowled at Alex. Was she – were they all – wilfully misunderstanding him?

'Yes. And a non-judgemental one's a coward,' said Parmjit, her jibe accompanied by a confident, level stare. So, it had come down to name-calling, had it, thought Jeffrey.

'An empty vessel,' continued Alex. 'And your unwillingness to come clean is not only cowardly; it's also elitist.'

'Look,' said Jeffrey, 'commitment and judgement, well . . . they're inappropriate terms here.'

He paused to think how best to proceed, but even before he could begin to process his thoughts, Alex had jumped on them.

'And the appropriate term is?' Alex was clearly not going to let Jeffrey off the hook. 'I can think of quite a few terms right now.'

'The term I prefer to use is . . . well . . . *reserved*.' Jeffrey was on the defensive now. 'I reserve the right to judge. I reserve my judgement.'

'What? Pending ours?' Alex snorted derisively at Jeffrey's evasiveness.

'Look,' he said, frowning thoughtfully at her, 'I'm trying to turn the tables here. You all seem to look to me for guidance, or for instruction. It's like you expect me to be some sort of oracle, laying out the bones of the world so that you can see it for what it really is. But *that's* cowardice – on *your* part. *You* should have the courage to make your own judgements about my work. Don't expect *me* to tell you what my work means – it means something different to each and every one of you. I can't legislate for you all. You have to interpret this work for yourselves. If I gave you an interpretation you'd have to interpret *that* for yourselves too! You call me "the artist" and an elitist, but I want *you* to be the artist – each and every one of you. I'm not an artist, I'm just a facilitator. In the act of interpreting my work, *you* become the artist, each of you, individually. That's not elitist. That's . . . well . . . *democratic*.'

Jeffrey finished by jabbing his finger at the group. There was an embarrassed silence. It was clear now to all that Jeffrey had reached the point where he was taking their desire for clarification as a personal insult. Drinks were sipped as each of them reassessed the situation and wondered how – or whether – to proceed. No one wanted outright confrontation with Jeffrey. No one, that is, except Alex.

'You pretentious twat.' There was no tone of mollification in Alex's voice. As soon as she spoke, the others – Jeffrey included – knew that Alex was going that extra mile for conflict. 'What a fuckload of bollocks!'

'Alex!' Hope, who could immediately sense the tension in Alex's voice, spoke softly but firmly, hoping to deflect Alex from her target. Alex heard and understood Hope, but she was in no mood for conciliation.

'Oh come on, Hope,' she said before turning back to face Jeffrey. 'Ever since we met, we've all had to put up with your pompous neo-liberal nonsense, your pseudo-political waffle about capitalism and communism, about how terrible everything is, about how corporations conspire to rule the world and how we're all slaves of the consumer economy. Jeffrey, you're *not* a cyber-warrior using multimedia technologies to destroy a global corporate empire; you're a coward who would rather create a virtual empire of your own than get out there and tackle the *real* world, where the *real* injustices are, and where people are *really* exploited. Good grief, we're about to embark on a bloody war that no one wants, and which is going to be fought in our name by a bunch of fucking cowboys. But as far as your "art" is concerned this might as well be happening in a galaxy far, far away. Pam's right, Jeffrey, you're a coward because you won't take any responsibility for your actions. In your virtual multimedia empire you don't have to take responsibility for anything, because nothing ever happens there that has any consequences. For you or anyone else. And we've already heard how, when you venture outside of your virtual world to engage with the real world, what you do isn't your responsibility anyway. No! It's ours! The reason *your* art is a failure is because *we* refuse to do the work required to make it a success! Good grief!'

The word 'failure' hung in the air between them, palpably, like static electricity before a thunderstorm. It was Jeffrey's turn now to try to defuse the situation. He seemed to recognize that Alex was out to shoot him down and so he sought to enlist the others in an effort to stifle Alex's mounting anger. He gave a gesture of exasperation to the rest of the group in an effort to solicit their sympathy.

'Jesus!' he said, turning his attention back to Alex. 'Is it that time of the month already?'

The men and women present reacted differently, but both genders reacted. Preston groaned, and sank his head into his hands. Ben's head remained upright, but an exasperated 'Jeffrey, you prat!' escaped his lips before he even knew he was saying it. Even so, Ben's terse judgment couldn't compete with the more vociferous insults being levelled at Jeffrey by the women.

'What?' said Jeffrey, affecting innocence. 'What did I say?'

Unfortunately for Jeffrey, this only made things worse.

'Bastard!' muttered Michael incoherently, but again no one paid any attention to him.

But Michael's comment went unnoticed for another reason. For, to everyone's astonishment, Alex stood up and violently threw the remains of her drink in Jeffrey's face. There was a moment during which none of the group moved, while beer dripped in slow motion from Jeffrey's chin. Then Alex's trembling voice broke the spell.

'You're an arsehole, Jeffrey. A fucking arsehole. Disappear up yourself and stay out of my fucking life, you prick!'

Jeffrey seemed to blush slightly, but otherwise remained impassive in the face of Alex's tirade. He seemed not to notice the remains of her drink dripping from his hair down his face and on to his chest. Alex cracked her glass down on the table and walked off, leaving the group stunned into silence. Jeffrey, at the centre of the storm, sat placidly, as though none of the previous few minutes had happened. But for the first time that evening, and possibly for the first time since she'd known him, Hope thought she could see a shadow of self-doubt ghosting across Jeffrey's face.

'Good to see that your art gets a reaction anyway, eh Jeffrey?' said Preston, with a nervous laugh.

'I'd better go after her,' said Hope.

She started to rise, clumsily negotiating her bulk to the front of the seat, but before she could get herself airborne Michael stood up. The machinations of his own drunken mind had ground on independently of the group's discussion with Jeffrey, but the conclusion of his addled thinking had coincided with Alex's dramatic exit. On his feet, he swayed blearily, muttering incomprehensible insults in Jeffrey's direction. He staggered backwards slightly as he raised his fist, then tottered forwards as he tried to swing for his former friend. A vision of Evette – beautiful, naked, innocent, wide-eyed – rippled through his swimming mind, a siren urging him on, calling him to action. The time had come to avenge this beautiful woman, to make Jeffrey pay for abusing her innocence and for visiting his sick fantasies upon her. So drunk was Michael, and so besotted with Evette at that moment, that he half-believed her to be watching him as he advanced towards his nemesis. She would see Michael thrash Jeffrey to within an inch of his life; she would realize at last that Michael was her champion, the man who would save her from the squalid existence into which the wicked, manipulative Jeffrey had lured her. When at last Jeffrey lay beaten and disgraced at Michael's feet like the cur he was, Evette would run into his arms, press her lips to his, thrust her tongue into his mouth, tear his clothes off and . . .

PART FOUR

THE LIGHTENING

MARCH 2003

22

' There now. Are we awake yet? And how are we doing?'
Somebody was fondling Michael's thighs, and it wasn't
Evette. Nor was it Hope, come to that. Wherever Michael
was, he found it difficult to focus because of the bright
light shining in his face and the bag of cement someone
had placed on his head. The noise – metallic clattering and
drunken voices shouting belligerently – made it difficult to
concentrate.

'We've done ourselves a bit of damage here, haven't we?'

Again, the hands on his thighs. This, however, only
momentarily grabbed Michael's attention before he felt his
gorge rising.

'Sick.'

He barely recognized his own voice. Panicking, he sat up to
find himself on a hospital bed in what seemed to be a corridor
of some sort. A nurse in crisp white uniform busied herself
about him. She turned and started as she realized what was
about to happen.

'Hold on now. Here we are.'

Swiftly and expertly, she managed to get the cardboard
bowl under Michael's chin as he heaved up the contents of

his stomach. Sweat poured off him as he retched helplessly, over and over again. Spent of vomit and energy, he slumped back down on the trolley-bed, blinking up at the neon tube above his head, trying to orient himself. He knew he was in a hospital, but had no idea how he'd got there. He was also experiencing a considerable amount of pain. The nurse had been doing something to his thighs, where the epicentre of the pain was, but he couldn't imagine what he might have done to that part of his body. And then he didn't care anyway – he was on the verge of vomiting again. He tried gulping air down, but found himself retching into another bowl placed at his side by the nurse. He lay back again, feeling dizzy, his extremities buzzing with excess oxygen.

He felt along his thighs and realized that he wasn't wearing his trousers, though his thighs were covered in a cloth of some kind.

'How are you feeling?'

Michael recognized Hope's voice immediately and tried to focus his gaze on her, but the harsh white glare hurt his eyes and the jackhammer in his head made any thought processes difficult. He spoke with effort, through a thick curtain of alcohol.

'What am I doing here?'

'Being a drunken arsehole, that's what you're doing here.'

Hope's voice sounded hard and unsympathetic. Michael knew that he'd done something stupid but had no idea what it might have been. He tried again.

'What happened?'

'You fell over, mate.'

This time it wasn't Hope's voice, but Preston's. Again Michael tried to open his eyes.

'All right, Preston. How's it going?'

While Michael felt he could be as pathetic as he wanted – or needed – to be in front of Hope, he didn't feel this way about Preston. He tried to perk himself up and affected a more bantering tone.

'Where's Ben? Would someone get my shoes? I think I'm OK now.'

Michael tried to sit up, a gesture of normality for Preston's benefit, but no sooner had he raised himself up than his head began to swim alarmingly and he found himself retching into yet another cardboard bowl. He lay back, defeated, the pain in the front of his thighs was increasingly raw.

'My legs,' he said, panic in his unsteady voice. 'What happened?'

'You were legless, mate,' said Preston. 'But they managed to sew them back on!'

Preston's light-hearted tone gave way to Hope's more serious manner.

'You fell across a table full of drinks. You've got broken glass in your thighs. They've got as much out as they can but they think there might still be some they can't find.'

'A table?' said Michael, bewildered. 'Where? What was I doing?'

'We met in the pub after Jeffrey's art thing,' said Preston. 'You remember, Evette and Jeffrey naked for art's sake?'

A sharp pang of memory brought something of the day's events into focus for Michael. He suddenly felt exhausted.

'You looked like you were trying to hit Jeffrey, for some reason,' said Hope. Drunk as he was, Michael realized that Hope was cross with him. 'I mean, what the fuck were you thinking of? Suddenly you're an art critic?'

'It was spectacular, man,' said Preston chuckling. 'I wish I'd recorded it. Jeffrey could have used it in his installation. He could have called it "interactive". The Arts Council funds would've rolled in!'

Michael could just about recall his internal debate concerning Evette and Jeffrey as he'd sat drinking in the city centre bar, though the details remained unclear. He knew that he'd thought about hitting Jeffrey but he couldn't believe that he'd actually tried to do it. He had no memory of it at all. He sank back on to the bed, his eyes closed, but unable to stop him from seeing himself for the fool he'd been. Though his memories of the evening were vague, he remembered clearly the reason why he'd soaked himself in alcohol. He knew as he lay there that the world he'd built up carefully over the past several months – a world in which Evette had become the solar centre – had collapsed under the weight of its own absurdities.

He didn't blame Jeffrey – he knew even under the lash of his hangover that none of what had happened had been Jeffrey's fault. Nor had it been Evette's. If they wished to parade around naked in their films, then who was he to stop them? The whole affair had been a figment of his ludicrous and limited imagination. He glanced briefly at Hope, her face a fusion of concern and anger, and at Preston smiling down at him, and he couldn't understand why they were there. Why did they persist in their concern for him? He wasn't worth it.

But he was profoundly glad they were his friends. As he lay there, empty, exhausted and in pain, he suddenly thought: *Where's Jeffrey?*

'Hope. Hope.' The urgent tone of Michael's voice broke through Hope and Preston's hushed conversation. 'Hope? Did I really hit him?' he said. 'Did I land the punch?'

In the early hours of the morning, in silence, Hope took Michael home. His injuries weren't so bad that he couldn't walk, but he was far from comfortable. He wanted sympathy but he knew that he wasn't going to get any. He wasn't really sure why she was so cross with him. After all, he hadn't actually hit Jeffrey, though he'd certainly taken a swing in his direction. Perhaps he'd said something about Evette as he'd attacked Jeffrey, or maybe he'd insulted Hope in some way. He'd have to ask someone what happened. Not Hope – it would give her an opportunity to have a go at him and he didn't want that. Nor Jeffrey – it would be too embarrassing. Preston was the obvious choice. He would phone him later that day, but for now he was tired, sore and hungover and needed to go to bed.

Hope sat on the sofa, the TV flickering away unwatched in front of her. The child in her belly was restless, unsettled. The previous day had started well with its party-like atmosphere, but by its end all that had changed. Michael had tried to hit his closest friend, and Alex, who she was now convinced was involved in some way with Jeffrey, had actually thrown her drink over him before fleeing the bar. Was it coincidence that Jeffrey was the epicentre of these two events? Were they connected? It wouldn't be surprising to find that Michael knew about Jeffrey's relationship with Alex. Perhaps Jeffrey had boasted to Michael about his conquest, and Michael had managed to keep his disapproval to himself until alcohol lowered his guard. Or maybe it was Alex who had confided in Michael in an attempt to get him to persuade Jeffrey to leave her alone. Perhaps Michael's drunken act was misguided chivalry, brought on by frustration from failing to persuade Jeffrey to leave Alex alone.

With both Michael and Alex seemingly bent on attacking Jeffrey, Hope found herself wondering what Evette would have made of the evening. She pictured Evette's naked body on screen and wondered if she'd been too embarrassed to show her face in pub. In that moment, Hope realized how little she actually knew about Jeffrey's partner. She had no idea at all if Evette would be embarrassed at exposing herself in this way. In the two years that she'd known them, she'd never met Evette when Jeffrey wasn't with her, and even then it tended to be Jeffrey's wild enthusiasms that dominated the conversation. Evette always seemed content to let Jeffrey have the floor, as though his firework display provided enough sparks and explosions for the both of them.

Hope felt the baby kick slightly and she touched her belly again. She felt the taut expanse pushing out the clothes she was wearing, and she thought again of Evette's naked body – lithe, tanned, her belly flat, her waist clearly defined. She pulled up her jumper and looked at the stretched, pale flesh, a latticework of faint blue vessels beneath the luminous skin. It was ugly; it wasn't her. She wanted to be attractive like Evette, but not like Evette: she wanted to be her old self again. She wanted her body back.

As Hope stared at what used to be her belly, she remembered the journey to hospital with Michael earlier that evening. Michael had been rambling something about Evette, which Preston had witnessed too, though neither could decipher the peculiar drunken language Michael was using. But the taut beauty of Evette's naked body, contrasted with her own bloated frame, suddenly provided a key to decode Michael's slurry of words. How could she not have seen it before? How could Michael not find Evette desirable when night after night she confronted him with her own pale, exhausted, slowly deforming body? How could she possibly compete in his affections with someone as perfectly formed as Evette?

In that brief, dreadful moment, Hope realized that Michael was in love with Evette. Maybe it wasn't love proper, the kind of love that keeps relationships going through all the trials of life, the kind of love that Klara felt towards Schmetterling. She hoped it wasn't. Maybe it was just an infatuation which would pass quickly. Maybe it was just lust. How could she bear it if Michael was unfaithful to her? Maybe nothing had happened yet, and maybe it never would. But the thought that it might was hard enough to bear. She felt weak, on the verge of fainting. She had no idea what to do. Should she confront him? If nothing had happened, what would she be confronting? To accuse him of something that hadn't happened might be more damaging than silence. Hope felt a sudden impulse to check Michael's phone for incriminating messages, but she remained seated, immobilized by the weight of her own suspicions.

23

She lay across the bed, her naked body dishevelled by sex and sleep. The quilt under which they'd kissed and teased each other only a short time before was crumpled on the floor at the base of the bed. The curtains were drawn, but the room was bright with afternoon sunlight. Michael lay on his side, propped up on one arm, gazing at her slender body. She lay on her side, her back towards him. He ran his hand lightly along her thigh and over the gentle curve of her hip towards her waist, trying to feel the delicate, downy hairs that covered her skin. Each tiny hair seemed, to Michael, to capture and hold the sunlight, making her entire body appear luminous. He reached across her and cupped a breast in his hand, held it softly. Even though she was asleep he felt the nipple tighten against the palm of his hand. He wanted to wake her, but she looked so peaceful that he also wanted her to sleep on. He didn't move, but she woke up all the same.

'Hello you, did I nod off?' Evette turned her head and blinked at Michael through a smile. She rolled from her side onto her back, and seemed not to notice his hand on her breast. Feeling awkward, he took it away. 'What's the time?' she said. 'Was I out long?'

It was just over a week since Michael's unplanned visit to hospital. In the meantime, Hope had confided her suspicions about Alex and Jeffrey to him. Michael had been righteously shocked at the news. He'd no idea that Jeffrey had designs on Alex, or that Alex had any feelings for Jeffrey, and the revelation reawoke Michael's insecurities; he'd been left out of the loop yet again by a close friend, and he'd been too stupid to notice something that had been going on right underneath his nose. He resented the fact that his best friend had told him nothing of his feelings for Alex, and this revived his indignation on behalf of Evette. As soon as he was able, he'd sent Evette a text asking her to meet him for a drink. They'd met later that week – a Thursday – outside a bar in town after work. Emboldened by his anger towards Jeffrey, and by the fear of losing Evette for good, Michael, without saying a word, had recklessly pulled her towards him for a lingering kiss. It was a make-or-break gesture, as shocking and unexpected to Michael as he believed it must have been to Evette. Aware that what he'd done could be construed as an assault, Michael waited anxiously for Evette's reaction. She would either slap his face and have him arrested, or she would tumble submissively into his arms. In fact, she did neither of these things.

'Well!' she said, obviously surprised. 'Goodness me! Who'd have thought it? You naughty man, and you with a pregnant girlfriend too. Well!'

Michael was embarrassed, though Evette was smiling and obviously relishing his embarrassment. 'Sorry,' he said. 'I mean . . . Hope. I know. I shouldn't . . .'

Michael could feel himself blushing.

'Well,' said Evette again, her eyes sparkling and playful, 'what should we do with him?'

'I'll go,' said Michael. 'I shouldn't have . . .'

But he didn't move, as though he was waiting to be dismissed from her presence.

'Maybe we should tell his girlfriend?'

Michael's face dropped, to Evette's evident amusement.

'Or maybe we should tell Jeffrey?'

'Please, Evette . . .' Michael wanted to wake up at home, on the sofa, with Hope, watching TV. He wanted to be anywhere rather than here at this moment. He couldn't believe that he'd thrown himself at Evette. He'd crossed a line, and desperately wanted to find a way back.

'Or should we take him home and fuck his brains out?'

'Huh?' He'd been so wrapped up in his own embarrassment that he thought at first he'd misheard her. She stood regarding him from under her copper fringe, her eyes empty now of all light, inviting Michael to fill them up with his own. In that moment, Michael's embarrassment evaporated. Hope and Jeffrey, along with all their mutual friends, became pale shadows on the borders of his consciousness. He was alone in a world with Evette, at last. Not that he knew what to do next.

It was Evette who broke the spell. She reached for Michael's arm and turned him towards the entrance to the bar. 'I think first of all we'd better buy him a drink!'

Relieved and exhilarated, Michael thought this was a very good idea. He allowed Evette to steer him through the door and into the crowded bar beyond.

That evening, over drinks, their conversation had been as it always was – no more and no less intimate than any other drink they'd shared together. Evette's proposition wasn't discussed, though Michael was aware that at some point in the evening it would have to be. He knew that nothing would happen that evening; Hope was expecting him home, and not too late either. As he and Evette talked innocently together, he wondered where Jeffrey was; the last thing he wanted was for Jeffrey and Alex to walk into the same bar in which he sat. As he and Evette talked, he stole nervous, furtive glances around the bar, hoping to make a quick exit should they arrive.

They left early, at eight-thirty, and stood facing each other on the street outside.

'So,' said Evette. 'You'd better come round to my place, hadn't you?'

'What, now?' Michael was surprised.

'No, you idiot! What about Tuesday? Afternoon is best. Jeffrey won't be home until after five. Can you get the time off?'

Michael said that he would try. He felt as though he were arranging an appointment at the dentist, so mundane was the administration of their impending affair. They parted with a friendly, passionless hug, and no kiss goodbye.

And now here they were, in bed together. Michael, pleased with himself, nevertheless began to fear that Jeffrey might, at any minute, walk into the room. He sat up sharply, checked his watch again.

'Rushing off?' Evette levelled an amused gaze at Michael. 'Eats, shags, and leaves?'

'No,' said Michael, with a hint of indignation, though that was exactly what he wanted to do. It wasn't that he didn't want to be with Evette, but he'd have preferred neutral ground somewhere – a desert island, perhaps, or an anonymous hotel room, in an anonymous city, far away. Not knowing what to talk about, he began slowly stroking Evette's body again. He looked down at her eyes. Her eyelids flickered across the dark pools of her pupils, and he found himself thinking of the Monarch butterflies he loved so much. They would be waking themselves up now in their mountain roosts as the warm air thawed out their wings in readiness for their marathon journey northwards. The same warm air would also be igniting their desire to mate, bending them towards the biologically driven desire to replenish the species. He would have to check the Monarch Watch website again, as soon as he could get to a computer. But staring down into Evette's eyes, Michael could feel his own desire reigniting. The butterflies would have to wait.

Hope sat on the sofa staring at Schmetterling's painting: a simple landscape by a minor artist. But if what Gareth had just told her was true, it was much more significant than anyone had realized.

She'd met Gareth earlier that day to pass him the monograph on Schmetterling her email contact Oskar Krause had faithfully sent her. Gareth had promised to read it and translate anything he thought might be of interest, but he'd really wanted to talk to Hope about an idea he'd had.

Perhaps the idea would never have come to consciousness if Gareth hadn't been watching the news on TV about the developing situation in Iraq. Bush had declared his intention to invade Iraq, with or without the backing of the United Nations. Frustrated by the seeming inevitability of the invasion, Gareth had begun channel-hopping. On one of the cable channels devoted to popular history, he'd come across yet another documentary on the rise of Nazism prior to the Second World War. This particular programme had focused on Hitler's personality, trying, in pop-Freudian fashion, to understand the psychology of the man through an examination of the traumas of his childhood.

The programme had acknowledged that information on Hitler's youth was scant, but some facts were clearly relevant to the thesis that Hitler's megalomania was rooted in an unhappy childhood. The family had moved home regularly, driven by the ambition of Hitler's overbearing and sometimes violent father. This restlessness must have been unsettling, argued the programme, so that when the family finally settled near Linz following the father's retirement and subsequent sudden death, Linz had become Hitler's symbolic birthplace: the birthplace of the dictator, if not of the man himself. Small wonder, the programme pointed out, that Hitler had later toyed with the idea of eventually making Linz the capital of the Thousand Year Reich.

It was the connection with Linz that had first stirred Gareth's interest, for he remembered that the letter he'd translated had been inspired by Klara seeing a painting in a gallery window in Linz. But it was when the programme turned to the subject of Hitler's mother that Gareth really began to pay attention; for, as the programme reminded him, Hitler's mother's name was Klara too. Could Klara, the lover of the artist Schmetterling, have been Klara Hitler?

Gareth's critical faculties came into play. It would be crucial to establish whether or not the date of the alleged affair, and the date on which the letter had been written, were dates which could be fitted plausibly into Klara Hitler's life. Even if the dates could be made to fit, Klara must have been a very common name at that time. But, as he recalled details of Klara's letter, the coincidences mounted up. Klara had said something in her letter about her husband moving around a lot because of his job. Hitler's father, the documentary pointed out, had been a civil servant of sorts; an ambitious man who'd moved frequently in order to secure promotion. Hitler's father had been aggressive, sometimes violent, towards his wife and children; the letter too had said something about the husband 'not being kind' or 'not being nice', words to that effect. Was this an indication of aggressiveness, a code for violence?

Even as Gareth thought about this, the programme moved on to the youthful Adolf's artistic aspirations. Pursuing its Freudian agenda, the programme made the young Adolf's choice of artistic career a symbolic killing of the father, a rejecting of the bureaucratic ambitions he'd harboured for his son. The young Adolf had applied twice to the Vienna Academy of Fine Arts, though he failed to gain entrance on both occasions. The embittering experience of rejection was, for the programme-makers, another key moment in the construction of the Führer mentality.

Gareth recalled Klara's account of her child's emerging artistic talents, her plea to Schmetterling to take an interest in fostering those talents, as her husband would never have done. By this time, Gareth was having to work hard to resist the conclusion that the Klara of Hope's letter was in fact Klara Hitler. As soon as the credits rolled, he ran upstairs to locate his own copy of the letter.

As they sat together the following day in the Arts Centre café, Hope listened to Gareth's extraordinary hypothesis.

Gareth had dutifully cautioned her that, in the absence of cross-checking, correlation, textual support and so on, his hypothesis was unproven. But he clearly wanted to get on the case straight away. Hope found herself excited as much by Gareth's glistening, nervous energy as by the idea that her Klara might be Adolf Hitler's mother. She also felt a little deflated that her quest to find Klara might have been so speedily resolved, and by a third party too. But she could see how startling the revelation would be, were it to be proven.

'Do you see?' Gareth was saying. 'It would make Hitler the illegitimate child of some itinerant painter! Extraordinary! This could radically alter our view of the man!'

'Well,' said Hope, surprised to be the one exercising caution. 'We're not sure it's a fact yet.'

'No, no, of course not. The first thing I want to try is to see if we can match Klara Hitler's handwriting with the letter's. I'll get on to it later today. But the dates look good, see?'

Gareth pushed a sheet of paper across the table. It was a list of dates, with notes alongside. Gareth pointed to the relevant dates as he spoke.

'The letter's dated 16th July 1898, and Klara tells us that she's writing it ten years after the affair. So, the affair took place on or around July 1888. Now, Klara Hitler married Alois, Hitler's father, on 7th January 1885 – three years before your Klara's affair. Klara Hitler was twenty-four years old when she married Alois, so if they are the same person, then she was twenty-seven when she had her fling with Schmetterling.'

'And thirty-seven when she wrote the letter,' said Hope, filling in the gaps.

'Yes, but now the really interesting stuff. Look, Adolf Hitler was born in April, 1889.'

Hope cradled her bulging stomach as she leaned forward to look at the list of dates more closely. She saw almost immediately the significance of what Gareth was saying.

'Nine months. It is, isn't it? July 1888 to April 1889. That's nine months!'

'Yes!' Gareth could barely contain his excitement now. 'Nine months between what we assume to be the date of Klara's affair and what we know to be the date of Hitler's birth! It's too good to be true! It all fits!'

Hope stared at the list of dates. Gareth was right; there did seem to be something of a match between the facts, as they knew them, of Klara Hitler's life, and those contained in Klara's letter to Schmetterling.

'My God,' said Gareth, calling Hope to attention. 'You'd better look after that letter. It could be worth a fortune!'

Gareth was moving faster than Hope through the ramifications of the letter actually having been written by Klara Hitler.

'Slow down, Gareth,' she cautioned. 'We're not sure of anything yet. All this evidence is still only circumstantial.'

Hope wanted Gareth to draw back. His enthusiasm was clouding her judgement, and his own too.

'You're right, Hope, of course. Nazi Germany's not really my field of expertise. However, I do know a couple of people who *are* experts in this area, if you're OK with me approaching them. But if my hunch about Klara is right, when this goes public you won't be able to move for experts; they'll be beating a path to your door.'

Hope recoiled at the thought of Klara's letter 'going public'. Whoever Klara was, Hope felt a connection with her, an intimacy. She was entering into a deeply personal inner world, a private emotional space which Klara herself had never made public. She felt protective towards Klara, a responsibility towards her. She began to wish that she hadn't involved Gareth in this affair in the first place.

24

Michael sat at his desk, staring at his computer screen. He couldn't concentrate. He'd slept with Evette only yesterday and was already torn between elation and self-loathing. Whenever he thought of Evette – of her naked body lying there on the bed, his for the taking – he felt the raw beat of desire. It was all he could do to stop himself phoning her there and then, and inviting her to join him in some hotel or other. But he *did* stop himself, because in spite of the urgency of his desire for Evette, something was holding him back. For all his chest-out blokish pride at finally getting the girl of his dreams, it was the reality of his relationship with Hope that kept pulling him back down to earth. Even as he knew that the slightest crook of Evette's little finger would make him drop everything and go to her, he also knew that he was being a complete and utter shit to Hope.

He'd really enjoyed his afternoon with Evette, but he'd come away from the house confused and at odds with himself. After they'd slept together, Evette had driven Michael home. They'd stopped on the way for a drink in a quiet bar, where they'd sat facing each other across a table, making small talk. The fact that they'd just had sex together didn't come up at all. Michael found their post-coital drink unnervingly cordial, especially when Evette had asked coolly about Hope's pregnancy. In the months leading up to their afternoon together, Michael had come to see his as yet unconsummated affair with Evette as something completely separate from the rest of his life. Michael had been living in two worlds – a dream world in which Evette was the centre, and the real world in which Hope was the centre. In asking about Hope in this casual way, having just spent the afternoon having sex with her boyfriend, Evette had set these two worlds on a collision course, and Michael was caught in the middle. The prospect of imminent catastrophe sharpened his thoughts considerably.

After Evette had dropped him off near his home, it hadn't taken him long to realize that, for all her beauty and elegance, for all her sexiness and charm, his prospects of a deeper, more lasting relationship with Evette were counting down to zero. He knew now that he would never settle down with Evette, knew that they had no future together. Having spent months living with Evette in his head, this knowledge left Michael hollow. His dreams about Evette were rapidly dissipating, replaced by a more mundane, available Evette; no less beautiful, elegant, sexy or charming, but someone he would now only ever meet in rooms, during the afternoon, routinely. The prospect of sex was enticing, but sex was all it would be from now on.

But as Evette diminished in his imagination, so thoughts of Hope began to fill the void. As though he were waking from a long sleep, he began to remember things about Hope he'd forgotten. He remembered the night, way back last year, when they'd gone for drink to celebrate a year of living together. He remembered his stupid scientific experiment with the stones and his socks, and the way Hope took the piss out of him about it. He remembered her pushing him over the wall and grabbing his crotch, and how embarrassed he'd felt.

But what he really remembered most of all, what tied all these memories together, was the feeling that at that moment the two of them were alone in the world, together. They were in the middle of town, but they were alone. Everyone else was a shadow. What did it mean, remembering this stuff now?

That evening he'd sat on the sofa thinking about these things, and watching Hope out of the corner of his eye. She was sitting on the sofa too, legs drawn up, cradling her belly as usual. She was unusually quiet; barely said a word all evening. Was she annoyed at him? Did she suspect anything? She often seemed to know what Michael was thinking, even before he knew it himself. But she hadn't said anything, and eventually Michael had gone to bed.

But sleep had eluded him, and in the darkness of the bedroom his anxieties came out to play. What if Hope *did* know something? What if she'd guessed what was going on between him and Evette? Of course, he knew that if she did know anything, she wouldn't be sitting downstairs watching TV; she'd be smashing up the furniture, or cutting his balls off, or she'd have gone round to Jeffrey's to kill Evette.

Or would she just leave him? And if she did, could he survive without her? If Evette dumped him tomorrow, he knew he'd get over it. But with Hope it was different. In spite of his desire for Evette, whenever he was with her he felt awkward and inadequate. With Evette, he felt he had to keep on his toes. But with Hope he felt at ease. She made no demands on him that he couldn't meet; she never made him feel small because his conversation lacked finesse, or subtle wit, or even intelligence. Was Evette really worth losing all this for?

And what of Hope? If she ever found out, what would it do to her? Hope was a strong woman – the backbone of their relationship, his mother was always saying – so if she ever found out about Evette, maybe she'd be OK. But pregnancy seemed to have exhausted her, beaten her down. If she found out about Evette now, it might crush her.

And then there was the baby. If Hope left him, what would it do to their kid? Another memory pushed itself up from Michael's subconscious. He recalled the night of Hope's party, on the floor of the bathroom, his head hanging over the toilet bowl. The voice he'd imagined had warned him to stop running around after Evette. It had told him to start thinking about the future, or words to that effect; told him to start acting like a responsible adult and to think about the consequences of his actions.

Lying there in the dark, assailed in equal measure by doubt and desire, Michael thought it might be a good idea to start taking his own advice.

The phone rang on Michael's desk, shaking him from his reverie. It was work-related, and when he'd hung up, his anxieties returned. Morosely, Michael touched his keyboard and surfed to the Monarch Watch website. The site was alive with speculation and comment: there had so far been no sightings of the Monarchs in any of the places they would usually have been passing through at this time of year on their long journey north. Under normal circumstances, the Monarchs would emerge from their long hibernation sometime towards the end of February. It was now almost two weeks into March, and there was still no sign of them. One of the website's scientists – Beth Allen – had posted a report pointing out that there had been an unusually long winter that year, and the warmer weather, which acted as an alarm bell to the sleeping butterflies, had yet to arrive. Michael read some of the comments posted by members of the public.

Thanks Beth, but explain how global warming lengthens the winter down there rather than shortening it! – Lennie, Texas. 03-11-03: 11.45

Not my field! I'm strictly a butterfly girl! – BA. 03-11-03: 11.58

Not so tough to explain. Effects of GW are not necessarily uniform. Consider: GW melts the ice caps; ice fields collapse into sea; mean temperature of sea falls; Gulf Stream cools; Gulf Stream washes/warms s. coast of Britland; if Gulf Stream cools, s. coast cools too. Result? Goodbye Cornish Riviera. Counter-intuitive, or what? – Mainman, England. 03-11-03: 12.04

So, lemme get this straight, y'all – it takes one butterfly flapping its wings somewhere in Peking to bring about storm weather over New York. So which butterfly where flapped its wings and caused the freak coldspell in Mehico, amigos? – Jonnyfartpants, Oregon. 03-11-03: 12.21

Maybe it was a Monarch!? Or is this too chicken-and-egg . . . – Annieloo, Cal. 03-11-03: 12.23

Cool! They did it to themselves! – MontyPronty, Toronto. 03-11-03: 12.26

The last exchange cheered Michael up a little. He was familiar with the so-called butterfly effect, and he liked the idea that the Monarchs might themselves have brought about the weather that now prolonged their hibernation. He left the window open on his screen desktop as he worked so that he could keep up with any developments; it was the nearest he could get to seeing the Monarchs for himself, though he'd promised himself that one day he'd make the journey to one of the Monarch hot spots in the United States. This would most likely be Texas, where Monarchs funnelled in their thousands through a corridor roughly two hundred miles wide, stretching from Wichita Falls to Eagle Pass. One day, Michael would be there to witness the orange wave as it rolled, like a strange liquor, down the thin throat of the United States. Maybe he would even make the journey into the Mexican mountains, to see for himself the spectacle of the Monarchs as they clung in their millions to their high mountain roosts.

Hope's stomach felt taut, stretched beyond its capacity. She was constipated and made uncomfortable by wind she couldn't get rid of. It was as though the entire contents of her overstuffed belly were being forced upwards through her diaphragm. On top of all this, her back ached and she felt listless, worn down by the sheer effort of carrying her belly around in front of her.

She sat naked in front of the mirror in her bedroom, looking at the ridiculous, bloated figure in front of her. Her breasts had ballooned in solidarity with her belly, and they slumped across the top of the spacehopper that was her stomach. Her nipples already resembled the teats on a baby's bottle and pale blue veins radiated out from them across the watery skin of her breasts. She seemed, in the past few weeks, to have put on a layer of fat across her entire body, so that her arms and legs looked thick. They were pasty too, like uncooked French loaves. Her ankles were swollen, puffed up by liquid that seemed to have drained there for want of anywhere else to settle. She could no longer see her pubic hair, unless it was reflected back at her in a mirror. Hope felt imprisoned in her own body, and she no longer had the energy to get herself free. The child growing inside her had taken control of the ship and had arranged for all her energy to be directed to itself.

She was hemmed in further by her fears and suspicions about Michael. He'd obviously been for a drink before coming home from work last night, and although he hadn't been late, he'd been vague about who exactly he'd gone drinking with. She'd been bursting to share Gareth's revelations about

Klara's letter with him, but when he arrived home he was in a foul mood and had gone to bed early, giving her no chance to tell him.

And now this morning she felt remorseful for being suspicious of him. On top of everything else, she was losing her ability to trust even the people she loved.

Michael went straight from work to visit his parents. He'd had a text from Jeffrey who needed to talk to Michael urgently about something – could they meet after work? Michael had seen Jeffrey several times now since the evening of the art event, when he'd tried to punch Jeffrey. Michael, of course, had done his level best to avoid Jeffrey since then, out of sheer embarrassment. But when they did eventually meet, and Michael bashfully tried to apologize, it turned out that Jeffrey had no recollection whatsoever of Michael trying to sock him one.

'You were trying to *hit* me? Why, for fuck's sake? Was the installation *that* bad?'

'No, no. I really enjoyed it,' said Michael, lying. 'I can't really remember why I wanted to punch you, if that's what I was trying to do. I mean, Hope *says* that's what I was doing, but I don't really remember. All I remember is that I came to in hospital with my thighs in bandages.'

'I saw you fall over the table of drinks. But that's all I saw. I was a bit distracted, having just had a pint emptied over my head by one of my critics.'

'Anyway, sorry if I did try to attack you.'

'Apology accepted, old man,' said Jeffrey. 'Water under the bridge and all that. Just wish I knew why you wanted to hit me in the first place.'

But now Jeffrey had a reason to hit Michael. Was this what Jeffrey wanted to talk to him about? Had Jeffrey found out about his sleeping with Evette? So soon? Maybe Evette herself had told Jeffrey; after all, he didn't know her well enough to trust her not to tell him. And he knew how devoted to Jeffrey Evette really was, even though she'd embarked on an affair with Michael the day before. Whatever it was that Jeffrey really wanted, Michael couldn't meet him in this panicked state. And his creeping guilt about Evette meant that he didn't want to go home to Hope just yet. He knew that he wouldn't be able to avoid Jeffrey – or Hope – for ever, but for now at least he was off the hook, back in the changeless refuge of his parents' house.

When he arrived, his father wasn't in his usual place in front of the TV. He wasn't even in the house, which was odd. Michael found his mother in the kitchen, making herself a cup of tea. She explained that he'd gone for a walk to Linnie's flat and would be back shortly.

'He doesn't usually visit Linnie,' said Michael, wondering if Linnie had managed to get herself into one of her periodic predicaments with debt.

'He's not visiting Linnie,' said Doreen. 'He walks to her flat and back, every evening.'

'Why?'

Michael's mother paused, and in the stark fluorescent light from the strip above her head, Michael suddenly saw a weariness in her face that he hadn't noticed before. She looked old, and tired. Something was wearing her down. Was it just age, Michael wondered? When she spoke, it was with resignation, as though she no longer had any choice whether to speak or not.

'Your dad's not well,' she said, and as she spoke she seemed to Michael to rally herself. It was as though the worst admission was over; the rest would be mere elaboration.

'Not well how?' Michael knew that his father suffered from angina, but he could sense that this was something different.

'It's his heart. They say he's had a mild heart attack. They say he was very lucky; he might have died. Funny, I remember him complaining of indigestion. Very bad, you know, not just a little bit of heartburn. He thought it was something he'd eaten. He's always joking about my cooking. Anyway, he stuffed himself with Rennies and went to bed. He was sweating so much I gave him an aspirin in case he had a fever. They said I probably saved his life. I made him go to the doctor's the next morning. You know what he's like – he'd never take himself there. The doctor told him to go straight to the hospital. Even phoned for an ambulance. They kept him in for tests. Turns out it wasn't indigestion at all.'

'He was in hospital and no one told me?' Michael was shocked and angry. Once again, he'd been left out of the loop. 'Did Linnie know?'

'We didn't want to worry you.' She tried to elaborate. 'It was your dad, really. He said he didn't want to worry you, you know, with Hope the way she is. And he didn't want you to see him like that, in a hospital bed and all. The machines and things . . . he was all wires and tubes, and he looked . . . he was all . . .'

Michael's anger evaporated instantly as his mother broke down, struggling to describe the scene. Michael stepped forward to hold her, on the verge of falling apart himself. He held himself in, breathing deeply. He wanted to appear to be strong for his mother's sake.

'He looked so helpless, so old,' she continued. 'It's funny how you joke about it with each other; you know, growing old. But I never really thought of him as old until I saw him in that bed. He looked grey all over. And when he dozed off he was so still, I thought he'd gone.'

Michael almost said, 'gone where?' He hadn't actually considered the possibility of his father dying.

'Is he all right now?' he asked, with some trepidation. Doreen had recovered herself a little, and was blowing her nose on a sheet of kitchen roll.

'He's all right. But it scared him. And me. They told him at the hospital that he'd got to change his lifestyle. I said, "but he doesn't have a lifestyle." They laughed at that.'

And so did Michael, relieved to hear his mother cheering up a little.

'They said he's got to exercise more . . .'

'And you said "more than what?"' said Michael, stepping into his mother's shoes.

She smiled. 'Well, I didn't. But he does spend too much time sitting around the house. I said to him we'd better get rid of the telly.'

'What did he say?'

'He said all right.'

'And will you?'

'Not bloody likely,' she said, laughing. 'He's not the only couch potato in the house, you know. I don't spend all my life in the kitchen.'

No, thought Michael to himself. You spend it in the garden.

The front door slammed and there was a rustling of clothing as Ernest took his coat off in the hall. He came straight to the kitchen, seeing the light on. Michael knew that he didn't have to mention his father's heart attack, and his father knew by the look on Michael's face that Doreen had told their son about it.

'All right, Dad?'

'I'm all right, son. You?'

'I'm OK.'

'Hope?'

'She's OK.'

'Good.' He turned his attention to Doreen. 'Any chance of a cuppa, love? It's bitter out there.'

Familiar with his routines, Doreen had already poured him a cup. The three of them sat drinking their tea as though nothing at all had changed.

25

The phone rang. It was nine o'clock in the morning, and Hope felt groggy. A woman, sounding as though she'd been awake for hours, spoke clearly and economically. She confirmed Hope's name, and then announced that she had Professor Nicholas King on the line.

'May I call you Hope?'

Professor King's voice sounded rich and complex, as if seasoned by fine wines, aged brandies and good cigars; it was assured and authoritative.

'Yes. If you like,' said Hope. 'Is anything wrong?'

Hope assumed that the call was work-related. It didn't occur to her that Professor King might not even work at the same university as she did.

'Call me Nicholas, won't you? My secretary probably mentioned that I head up the Modern History Research Programme here at Sheffield.' Still surfacing from sleep, Hope couldn't immediately recall what the secretary had said to her. Professor King moved briskly forward. 'You're probably wondering why I'm calling you. Let me get straight to the point here, so that I don't take up too much of your day.'

He left a practised pause, to allow Hope to catch up. Hope began to resent being played like a fish on a line. 'Go ahead,' she said, sharpening herself up so as to gain some standing in the conversation.

'I shall. I had a conversation yesterday, a very interesting conversation, with an old colleague and friend of mine, a mutual acquaintance of ours. I believe that you've been discussing some very interesting . . . *material* with Dr Gareth Williams.'

Hope wasn't used to hearing Gareth's full name. 'This is about Klara's letter, isn't it?' she said.

'Yes it is,' said the Dundee-cake voice. Professor King went on to explain that Gareth had called him yesterday evening, at home, to outline his thoughts about Klara's letter. Gareth had explained to Professor King how it had been found and had faxed through a copy of the letter with his translation.

'Needless to say, I'm intrigued by the document,' Professor King concluded. 'I take it that you have it somewhere secure?'

Hope had slipped it into a folder which was, at that moment, tucked underneath the sofa in the living room. 'I think so,' she said. Her heart was sinking; she knew that she was about to lose Klara to the world.

'The thing is,' continued Professor King, 'I can only do so much with Dr Williams' photocopy. I really need to begin the process of examining the veracity of the actual document. We need to run tests . . . the *Hitler diaries*, you recall? If this letter should turn out to be in any way *problematic* . . .'

'I know,' said Hope.

'If I may, I'd like to have someone collect the letter from you. We shall give you a receipt, of course, and the letter shall remain your property. But if it is as important as Dr Williams thinks it is, we can't have you risking it in the post, quite frankly.'

'I know,' said Hope, the resignation palpable in her voice.

Having made her arrangements with Professor King, Hope threw on some clothes and went downstairs to the sofa. She picked up the folder and took out Klara's letter. Holding the document in her hands, she felt an immediate connection with Klara: this was the actual letter that she'd written all those years ago. Hope had no idea what had happened after Klara had sent the letter; she didn't even know if Schmetterling had read it. Maybe it had been returned to sender. Maybe the painting was Klara's and she'd hidden the letter in the back rather than destroy it on its return.

Hope looked over the letter again. Ten years; a long time to carry a torch for someone. Ten years of yearning and hope. Here was the evidence, in this letter, in the single word with which she'd ended her plea: *immer* – always. Such a small word in which to invest so much hope, so much love. In ten years' time, would Hope still love Michael as much as she did now? As much as Klara loved Schmetterling?

Did Klara direct all the love she couldn't give to Schmetterling to his child instead? The letter seemed to suggest as much. But how could all that love lead to so much hatred, so much evil? It simply couldn't be true. The letter couldn't have been written by Klara Hitler, whatever Gareth or Professor King might think.

But suppose it were true; was Klara responsible for what the child became? Perhaps love didn't matter as much as people thought it did. There were so many other things that could shape a child's character. The world was chaotic, a billion things happening all at once. Parents – mothers – did what they could, but weren't they really helpless in the face of all this chaos? In the end, who could really know what created Hitler?

The child in her belly moved, a small kick. It was only a few weeks away from its entry into the world. What would become of it, she wondered? Boy or girl, it could as easily be a saint as a sinner, a Martin Luther King or a Saddam. Would she – or Michael – really make any difference to what it would become? *Could* they make any difference? The child kicked again. It was restless today; it was frequently these days. Eager to get born. *Immer.* Whatever happened between Klara and Schmetterling, whatever it was that had driven them apart, Klara had held on to her love, like faith. Maybe that was all you could do: hold on and have faith in the future and in those people you loved.

She lay Klara's letter beside her on the sofa, and got herself ready to go out. She didn't want to go to work, but she knew that she couldn't sit around the house. The child's restlessness was infectious.

'They're going to war, and that's that!'

Parmjit could barely contain her anger. The seminar was about Britain's role in international politics, and the discussion had inevitably turned to the mounting crisis over Iraq's alleged weapons of mass destruction.

'Bloody good job too!' said Paul, a Politics and War Studies student who was taking the class alongside Parmjit, Gyorgy and the others. 'If the Frogs and the Krauts can't take the heat, they're better off out of the bloody kitchen! Bloody cowards!'

'Steady on now, Paul. We mustn't use such derogatory . . . I mean, we must keep our prejudices –'

Ed Frampton was trying to keep the seminar under control, but he was struggling, and Paul cut his plea short.

'I'm sorry Ed, but they *are* bloody cowards. They've done nothing but protect Saddam from what's coming to him!'

'I rather meant "Frogs" and – '

This time it was Parmjit who cut Ed short, though her comment was directed squarely at Paul.

'You still talk as though Bush cares about the UN. That he's somehow disappointed in it. But he's already said – on prime time TV, no less – that he'll go to war without UN backing. Bush doesn't give a toss about the UN. I think he's always planned to go to war with Iraq. He wants to finish what his father started.'

'If that's true, why would he send Powell to the UN to plead the case for war?'

'He doesn't like the UN but he'd like the legitimacy that comes with its support. He doesn't want America to seem like an out-and-out imperialist power, if he can help it. Isn't it better to have the support of the UN than not, even if, at the end of the day, it serves American interests?'

The Scouse accent was Emily's, and they all turned to face her. She shrank back in her seat. Ed Frampton gallantly attempted to come to her rescue.

'A very good point, ah . . . Emily.'

Ed Frampton was pleased with Emily's contribution. He hoped that the all-too-palpable tension between Paul and Parmjit would be diffused by the interjection of a third voice. But Parmjit wasn't going to be sidelined so easily.

'Hang on,' she said. 'First, we should care what Bush's reasons are for seeking UN approval, shouldn't we? I mean, it matters whether or not he's really interested in involving the UN in the decision. There's a difference between really believing in the UN and using it as a means of legitimizing American foreign policy, isn't there?'

'Who cares why Bush wants UN approval for his policies?' Paul rejoined the discussion, again directing his comments at Parmjit. 'You damn him if he doesn't go to the UN, and you damn him if he does. Who cares what his reasons are? Isn't it enough' – and here he turned to acknowledge Emily's point – 'that his desire for legitimacy gets him to the UN?'

'No, it's not enough,' said Parmjit, calmly, 'because it's merely an instrumental reason. What lies behind it is an implicit threat to undermine the credibility of the institution by ignoring it anyway. In fact, it's not even implicit any more, is it? Bush is quite open about his contempt for it.'

As the participants thought this over, Ed Frampton looked at his watch and realized that the seminar had run over by a full five minutes.

'Goodness,' he said, barely able to contain his relief as he slid towards the door of the room. 'Well, doesn't time . . . a very interesting . . . lots to think about . . . next week, perhaps.'

And he was gone, leaving an animated, chattering group behind him. They would head for the coffee bar, as they did every week, and the discussion would continue there. Parmjit looked around the group and thought of her first experience of a university seminar only six months ago; the arguments they'd had, both inside and outside of the seminar room, since then; the anti-war protests she'd attended with Gyorgy. She thought of how far they'd travelled as a group of individuals since then, how much they'd grown in confidence and in ability. Parmjit was only a sixth of the way through her studies, but already she knew that this was what she wanted to do for the rest of her life. Having struggled so hard to get here, she didn't want to leave university ever again.

It was getting on towards noon, and Hope was almost ready to leave. Michael had told her the previous evening about Ernest's heart condition and she wanted to call over to see him and Doreen.

Ready to leave, she sent Michael a text to let him know where she was going. As soon as she pressed send, she heard the muffled tones of Michael's phone coming from the living room. Knowing that her message would be useless to him when he eventually arrived home that evening, she decided to delete it from his phone. She found the phone tucked down the side of the sofa where it must have fallen out of his pocket that morning. She deleted her text but noticed another one, unopened. Had it been from Jeffrey or Preston, Hope would have ignored it, but it was from Evette. Why, she thought, would Evette be texting Michael?

It took Hope a moment to realize that the sensation she was experiencing was her heart beating rapidly and not the baby kicking. She opened the message and read:

njoyed tues. nxt tues poss but not cert. will let u kno

Hope read the message over and over again, as though its meaning would gradually become clear. But it didn't. What had they done last Tuesday? Had they met for lunch? If they had, Michael had said nothing about it. She tried to remember what she'd been doing on Tuesday, what Michael had been doing. As far as she knew, he'd been at work all day, then gone for a drink, then come home. Nothing unusual in that. But if he'd met Evette for lunch, then it *was* unusual for Michael not to say anything. Maybe he'd just forgotten; maybe he'd been distracted by the news of his dad's illness, or something. But Evette wanted to meet Michael *next* Tuesday, too. Why? What were they meeting *for*?

Through the living room doorway, Hope caught sight of herself in the hall mirror. Even in her coat she looked fat, bloated, unattractive. The face staring back at her looked tired, puffy, pale. Who'd want *that* when they could have someone beautiful like Evette?

The heat drained from Hope's body. She felt dizzy, as though she might faint. Her hands were shaking as she reached for the arm of the sofa. She had to sit down, get control of her breathing and her thoughts. It couldn't be true. Could it? Not Michael. He couldn't do that to her, could he? Not while she was pregnant with their child. The word Klara had used came back to her now – *immer*. Always. Hope now felt the full force of this word for herself. For the rest of her life Klara had held on to her love for Schmetterling. But Schmetterling had deserted her; left her holding the baby. Would Michael do that to Hope? Was Hope facing now what Klara had faced all those years ago?

This couldn't be happening. There *must* be an explanation. She would ask Michael straight out, this evening, as soon as he got in from work. She would get it all cleared up there and then.

Regaining some control and breathing more steadily, Hope pushed herself up from the sofa and realized she was still holding Michael's phone. She reread Evette's message. It was all so vague, so tentative. Had she got it all wrong? Had she got Michael all wrong? She knew that he was low, a bit depressed; like herself, in fact. But was that enough to drive him into someone else's arms, someone else's bed? Once more the bloated figure staring back at Hope from the mirror in the hall answered her question. She sat down again, unable to stand. Her limbs seemed to give way as she realized that *she* was the problem, not Michael. She'd let herself go, let her pregnancy drag her down; the child inside her had drained her of everything. She no longer knew who she was. She wished it had never happened, that it was all over.

Now the idea of confronting Michael only increased her anxieties. Suppose he'd done nothing wrong; how would he react to being accused of having an affair? Would he come clean about meeting Evette? And if he was having an affair, would he walk out? Leave her? Would she want him to stay? If he'd done nothing wrong, then accusing him might push him away for good. She wouldn't even need to accuse him; he'd know that she'd read his messages, know that she'd spied on him.

Hope watched her fingers delete Evette's message from Michael's phone, watched her hands tuck the phone back behind the cushion where she'd found it. As she stood up to leave, she saw her reflection once more in the hall mirror. The face staring back at her looked drained of energy, of spirit, of hope.

It was just after midday, and Michael sat in a busy pub in town, waiting for Jeffrey. He sipped at a pint and quietly practised masking his anxiety. Much as he now wanted to avoid Jeffrey, he couldn't put him off any longer. Although he couldn't shake off the idea that Jeffrey knew something about his affair with Evette, if Jeffrey *didn't* know anything, then avoiding him might look odd and arouse his suspicions.

'Same again?' Michael hadn't noticed Jeffrey come in, but he noticed him now. He was wearing a long, black trench coat over a black polo-necked sweater. He wore slender black trousers, with thick-soled buckled shoes protruding from the bottom. His blond hair fell in artistic wisps around his shoulders. He looked as though he'd stepped from the science-fiction future of *The Matrix*, or *Equilibrium*, an impression enhanced by the designer shades he was in the process of removing. For all that he looked like a hit man from a proto-fascist future, Jeffrey's blue eyes, once unveiled, sparkled with geniality. To Michael's relief, he didn't look like a man who was about to confront his girlfriend's lover, and he immediately asked Michael what he was drinking.

Jeffrey returned a few minutes later carrying two pints, and after some initial banter, he seemed to decide that the time had come for the serious point of the meeting. 'Look, Michael, I don't know how to say this so I'll just come out with it.'

Jeffrey leaned closer to Michael, a conspiratorial gesture that baffled Michael. Nevertheless, he too leaned towards Jeffrey, meeting him halfway.

'I think,' said Jeffrey, 'Evette's having an affair.'

Michael could feel two things happening simultaneously, which was odd because they seemed to be contradictory reactions. He felt the blood draining from his face at the same time as he felt himself blush wildly. His body was conspiring to betray him to Jeffrey. It had written 'Guilty' all over his face in a red-and-white marbling effect. Michael dragged his eyes to meet Jeffrey's and waited for his friend to hit him. But Jeffrey was staring into his pint, seemingly lost in thought.

In the course of the morose monologue that followed, it transpired that Jeffrey had read a text to Evette before she'd had a chance to read it herself. He'd thought nothing of reading the message, for after all, as he reminded Michael, there were no secrets between Evette and himself. Michael knew this to be a lie on more than one front. But at this moment, this was the least of Michael's concerns. Surely Evette's phone would have identified the sender of the message? He felt himself simultaneously blanching and blushing again.

'So, what did it say?' he asked tentatively, expecting the worst.

Even as he spoke, Michael racked his brain, trying to recall the various messages he'd sent to Evette over the past few days. Instinctively, he reached for his phone to check.

'It said,' and Jeffrey hesitated. This was clearly painful to him, and Michael could well understand why; accusing a good friend of sleeping with your girlfriend was undoubtedly a difficult thing to do. And it was painful to Michael, too, watching his best friend struggle like this. He saw clearly what he must do – the game, after all, was up. He could end both Jeffrey's pain and his own by owning up – he would do the decent thing and confess to Jeffrey, and let the chips fall where they may.

'Look, I never meant . . .'

But Jeffrey wasn't listening to Michael. His inner struggle had come to an end and he picked up where he'd left off.

'It said: "I want to lick you all over and fuck you like a machine."'

'What?' Michael was stunned. He couldn't remember sending any such text to Evette. His search for his own phone became more urgent.

'It said,' repeated Jeffrey, 'I want to –'

Michael cut him short. 'But I never sent that!'

'Steady on, Michael,' said Jeffrey, surprised by his friend's reaction. 'I'm not accusing *you*. Christ, I know you well enough to know that it's not you.'

Michael realized his gaffe. But while he appreciated Jeffrey's reaffirmation of their friendship, he was still bewildered by what his friend was saying to him.

'But who did? Send it, I mean.'

'That's partly why I wanted to talk to you,' said Jeffrey.

At these words, Michael once more experienced the peculiar ice/fire sensation. Jeffrey had been toying with him; Michael *had* sent the message in a drunken stupor, and Jeffrey was about to deliver the killer blow. Yet, in spite of Michael's impending fate, his mind couldn't help but find room to explode another landmine as he slowly realized that he hadn't got his mobile on him. *Where was it? Had he lost it?*

'I wrote the number down.' Jeffrey placed a slip of paper on the table between them with a phone number written on it. Michael looked at it. For all he knew, it could well have been his own number; all mobile phone numbers looked the same to him. He stared down at the number.

'I know it's a lot to ask,' continued Jeffrey. 'But I want you to phone that number for me. Find out who it is, if you can.'

Had he left it in the office? Dropped it in the pub toilets?

'Sorry, Jeffrey. You want me to . . . ?'

'Just give it a call. Pretend you're, I dunno, the police or something.'

Had he used it at all that morning? Maybe he'd left it at home?

'What, *me*? Pretend to be the police?'

He'd sent Evette a text before leaving for work that morning. But where had he been when he sent it?

'Something else, then. A taxman maybe. Use your imagination.'

Unfortunately for Jeffrey, Michael's imagination was already overburdened trying to remember his movements that morning.

Then a cup of tea for Hope in bed. Downstairs again. The kitchen. Toast. Tea. To the living room . . .

'Not now, of course,' prompted Jeffrey. 'Don't ring from your own phone. Use your work's phone.'

Bag. Phone in bag. Sit on sofa. Tea, toast on coffee table. Sofa. Phone. Message. Sofa. The sofa . . .

'Shit!'

'What? What is it?' Jeffrey looked concerned at Michael's outburst. 'Do you recognize the number?'

Michael's mind was reeling. He'd left his phone on the sofa where Hope could find it. He was sure he'd deleted the text he'd sent to Evette before he'd left for work this morning, but had Evette replied to the text? More importantly, would Hope have read Evette's reply? Jeffrey brought him back to his immediate environment.

'What? No, sorry. No, I'm just a bit shocked, that's all. I mean, Evette, you know . . .'

'I can't believe it myself,' said Jeffrey.

'So, who sent it then?' said Michael, as intrigued now as Jeffrey was.

'If I knew that, Michael, I wouldn't be asking you to find out, now, would I?'

Jeffrey sipped his pint and sat back, looking much more relaxed. He was on top of the situation now, reasserting his control over events. Michael, for his part, wanted to be out of there. He needed to get to his phone before Hope did, just in case Evette had replied to his text.

'So you'll give it a go then?'

'Sure,' said Michael, downing the last of his drink and standing up to leave. 'No problem.'

'Hello Hope, love. Come in.' Ernest stepped back from the door to allow Hope to enter. 'Doreen's out the back. I'm just off for me walk. Tell her to have a cup of tea ready when I get back.' He said this with an indulgent wink. He was wearing his new tracksuit and a pair of white trainers. He stepped out through the door, closing it behind him. Hope made her way through to the kitchen and out into the garden. She found Doreen standing over her border, gloved hands pulling gently but expertly at plants, snipping here and there with a pair of secateurs.

'Hi, Doreen,' said Hope.

Doreen turned, shielding her eyes from the sun with a forearm. A warm breeze fluttered through the bushes at her side. Behind her, four unusually early cabbage white butterflies scattered like confetti, then came together and swooped around each other like the tail of a kite. For a brief moment they formed a ragged halo around Doreen's head, then broke off and cast themselves along the tops of the bushes like empty paper bags caught in a breeze.

'Hope, love. How are you?'

Hope stood at the edge of the lawn, the sun warming the back of her neck as it rose over the rooftops behind her. The brilliant light seemed to ignite the colours of the plants and bushes: vivid greens; hallucinogenic yellows of daffodils; fluorescent mauves, reds, and oranges of tulips; crocuses like multicoloured tongues of fire spitting from the earth. And in the middle of this psychedelic scene stood Doreen, serene in her pale yellow overalls, orange gloves and green gardening shoes, the biggest flower of all at the heart of the garden. Hope could feel the garden coming alive again after its winter hibernation; she could feel the restlessness of the plants as they tried to force their leaves out.

A single bee droned past and the faint sound stirred an image from Hope's past. She stood now in her parents' garden. Her father sat on a blanket on the beautifully tended lawn, his back both to Hope and to the sun that picked out his shadow across the newspaper he was reading. The scent of recently cut grass hung powerfully on the still air. The plants in the border were as neatly trimmed as any in Doreen's garden. At the end of the garden, Hope's mother knelt, gloved hands working away at the border.

Hope knew exactly where she was and what would happen next: she was about to announce her decision not to try for a place at Cambridge. She knew even then how much her parents wanted this for her – after all, they'd both studied and fallen in love there – and she knew that telling them would be deeply disappointing to them, and an argument would follow. Her relationship with her parents was difficult enough at the time, and about to suffer a blow from which it would take years to recover. All because of her selfishness. And now Michael seemed to be retreating from her. Was this her fault too?

Hope was back in the present, standing in Doreen's garden with tears streaming down her face.

26

Michael was depressed – his life wasn't going according to plan. No, that wasn't it; he didn't actually have a plan. So what was it, then?

The first reason was impending fatherhood: Michael wasn't looking forward to being a father, though there was a clear expectation among family and friends that he should be. The only role model he could find around which to organize his thoughts was that of his sister and her fiendish, selfish spawn. He'd seen Linnie sucked dry of energy, joy, ambition, *life*, and Michael knew that the same would soon be happening to him.

The second reason was that Hope was heavily pregnant and she'd put on weight. It wasn't just her stomach, which was now as distended as an overinflated balloon; it was her whole body. It wasn't that Michael found her physically unattractive – he wasn't repulsed by her body at all – but when he looked at her, he no longer saw a desirable woman; he saw something gynaecological, as though Hope's pregnancy had transformed her into a giant Petri dish for the sole purpose of cultivating the parasite that was growing inside her. The more it grew, the more her whole body seemed to become colonized by it:

complexion, hair, desires – it seemed to be draining her of all but the ability to service its increasingly agitated demands for more living room.

Finally, there was his anxiety about Evette. It was now just over a week since he'd gone to bed with Evette, and since then he'd had no response to the five or six texts he'd sent her. On the two occasions he'd phoned her, his call had been diverted to her answerphone. He'd left 'innocent' messages on both occasions, but Evette hadn't responded to either of them. And then there was Jeffrey's revelation that Evette was having an affair with someone else, someone who clearly wasn't Michael. Could this explain Evette's evasiveness, Michael wondered? He found it hard to believe that she could have started a second affair in the few days between sleeping with him (Tuesday) and his meeting with Jeffrey (Friday). Surely she couldn't have dropped Michael *that* quickly? Perhaps the message intercepted by Jeffrey had been a hoax of some sort; a colleague of Evette's had sent it to wind Evette up, not expecting Jeffrey to read it.

But then why was Evette ignoring him? A dark thought occurred to him that he could not banish from his mind: perhaps he'd failed to please her in bed. With his scrawny, pale body and his tiny penis – his *minuscule* penis – how could he ever have believed that he could measure up to a beautiful woman like Evette? He suddenly saw clearly that Evette was too good for him: too beautiful, too intelligent, too much in command of herself to be doing with the likes of him. What a fool he'd been. Whenever Michael thought of Evette she was always clearly defined, the image in his mind as sharp as the razor-edged fringe across her forehead. Whenever Michael thought of himself, he always saw himself blurred at the edges, like a photograph taken on a cheap digital camera. A *very* cheap digital camera.

At least, thought Michael, now desperately searching for something to shore up the last remnants of his self-esteem, if his brief affair with Evette was really over, if it really had been nothing more than a one-night, or one-afternoon stand – well, at least Hope knew nothing about it.

Ernest sat at the small kitchen table, a bowl of cereal barely touched in front of him. He stirred his mug of dark tea slowly. Doreen stood with her back to him, washing up at the sink. She was lost in thought, staring out into the garden. It was a lifeless day outside. There was no breeze, and in its stillness the garden seemed to have arrested its spring growth. Doreen sighed deeply. She moved wearily, as though the garden's lack of life was holding her in check.

Ernest, startled out of his reverie by Doreen's profound sigh, looked up at his wife. Framed against the luminous window, she looked beautiful, stately, like a duchess or queen. She still had something of her figure: shapely hips, and good shoulders; she was a strong woman in every respect, and nobody's fool. But he knew that, beautiful as she looked standing there, it was in the garden where Doreen really looked her best. Ernest had no real interest in gardening – unless it was one of those garden makeover TV shows. But Doreen, in her garden, was a force of nature.

Ever since his heart attack, Ernest had seen Doreen differently, more like he used to see her when they were first courting. He was in awe of her then, but the years had dulled his appreciation of her and his thoughts about her had become routine. All that had changed now. The thought that he might die in a month, a week, a day, an hour, a minute, *this* minute, had sharpened his perception of the world. And the sharper his perception became, the more he knew that he wanted to hold on to that world for as long as he possibly could. And on to Doreen. More than anything, on to Doreen.

And the new grandchild too, Michael and Hope's first. Difficult as he knew they could be, he loved his grandchildren, Jade and Kyle. And he loved Hope like a daughter, and he wanted everything to be all right for her and Michael. He didn't know what help he could be to them, but whatever he could do, he wanted to be around to do it. Ever since Hope's visit last Friday, he'd seen that all wasn't well between her and Michael. He couldn't put his finger on it, and neither could Doreen. Hope had deflected Doreen's inquiries, saying that it was just exhaustion: the pregnancy wearing her down. But Doreen knew that Hope was being evasive. Since that visit, Ernest and Doreen had heard nothing, and the silence had increased their anxieties.

Ernest stood up. 'Well, I think I'll go for my walk.'

'I'm going to ring her today.'

'You said that yesterday, love.'

'I know. It's stupid, but I don't want to seem to be interfering. I told her that we were here if she needed to talk.'

'Whatever it is, I'm sure they'll work it out. They'll be all right.'

Ernest said this partly to comfort Doreen and partly to comfort himself. But he knew that he really didn't know one way or the other. He gave Doreen a kiss and a hug and went to the foot of the stairs to put on his trainers.

Doreen came to the door behind him as he stepped out. 'You're a bit early today,' she said. 'You don't usually go this early.'

'I just fancy a walk after my breakfast. A bit of fresh air.'

'Don't overdo it, now,' she said.

'I'll be all right.'

Doreen watched him stroll off down the street, waiting for him to turn and wave to her before she closed the door.

Michael sat at his computer, listlessly switching between his stock control programme and the Monarch Watch website. He wanted to talk to Hope but didn't want to give her another opportunity to sound pissed off at him, so he'd sent her a brief text asking her how her day was going. She hadn't replied. Jeffrey, on the other hand, *had* sent a text asking if Michael had investigated Evette's mysterious lover yet. Michael hadn't, and so didn't reply. He could feel the tension mounting. The baby – his child – was due in just a few weeks. Hope seemed increasingly testy with him and he didn't know where this would end; it was getting harder to ignore Jeffrey, and Evette still hadn't got in touch with him; a war was about to start in Iraq; the Monarchs still hadn't left their wintering sites. Where were they? Were they dead, or still in suspended animation? Michael imagined the butterflies, frozen in their millions to the branches of the trees, like the scales of an exotic fish. And he saw himself suspended there with them.

He glanced at the clock on the screen. It was almost midday, but it seemed as though several mornings had been crammed together, stretching out the minutes into hours. He tapped a few more keys, and then the phone on his desk rang. It was reception.

'Michael? Your father's here at the desk. He wants to know if you're going for lunch yet?'

Hope arrived at her front door just as her phone trilled. It was a message from Gareth.

need 2 meet. can u do lunch?

Hope was in no mood for socializing, and so ignored the message. She noticed that she'd also missed a call from Gareth. She switched off her phone and stepped through the doorway into the cosseting stillness of the house. For a moment she stood motionless, so as not to chase the quiet away. Then the phone in the hall rang. Freed by the sudden noise, she stepped on into the kitchen. She heard the answering machine kick in, and then a voice spoke.

'Hope? It's Gareth here. I've been trying to contact you on your mobile; left voicemail, blah blah. Listen, it's really important that I talk to you. Nick's on my back about the letter. Nick King? He spoke to you? He says . . . well, I'll tell you when you call me. OK. Call soon. Bye. Call my mobile, OK? Bye.'

Hope knew immediately what Professor Nicholas King had been on Gareth's back about. She'd so far managed to avoid giving up Klara's letter, in spite of Professor King's efforts to obtain it from her. For reasons she couldn't articulate to herself, she just couldn't bring herself to let it go yet. And it wasn't just the letter she couldn't let go; she'd also not yet told Michael about her conversation, over a week ago, with Gareth.

Hope made herself a drink and took it into the living room. Besides Gareth's message, there were two others on the answering machine. The first was from Professor King – and Hope immediately noticed that he'd made the call himself and not, as usually happened, through his secretary; a sign of his increasing frustration. His voice, however, was calm, almost apologetic. His strategy was clearly to take responsibility for failing to obtain the letter, rather than risk alienating Hope by pointing the finger of blame at her. As in her first conversation with him, Hope felt herself being played like a fish on a line by a man used to getting people to do what he wanted them to. It wasn't that Hope resented this – she knew that people like Professor King were respected in part for their ability to motivate people to get things done. She knew, too, that the letter was important, and that Professor King's interest in it was legitimate. And yet she still could not let Klara go.

The third message was from Doreen: hesitant, unsure of how to respond to a machine.

'Hope, love? It's Doreen here. I . . . hello? Are you there? No. I called to see if you're OK. And Michael. Will you give me a ring soon? I'd better go now. Ring soon. Bye, love.'

There was a silence, as though Doreen were waiting for the machine to acknowledge the end of her call. Then she hung up.

Hope settled back into the stillness of the house. She reached under the sofa for the folder containing Klara's letter and, taking it out carefully, she read it once more, trying to resign herself to letting it go.

'Are you sure you should be drinking?'

Ernest placed a pint in front of Michael and settled into a seat. Michael couldn't remember the last time he'd seen his father in a pub.

'The odd pint can't hurt,' said Ernest. 'You never know, it might do me some good.'

Michael sipped his drink, unsure of what to say. He knew that his dad wanted to talk to him about something and he didn't want to delay his saying it. The artificiality of the circumstances was solely down to this topic, whatever it was. Small talk with his father made Michael uncomfortable – and he didn't want to prolong the discomfort, not least for his father, who seemed equally ill at ease.

'How's Mom?'

'She's fine, son.'

Another awkward silence. It was Ernest who eventually broke it; he'd spent the entire journey to Michael's workplace going over in his mind what it was that he wanted to say.

'Listen, son. I'm not good at this sort of thing, but, well . . . no one knows how much time they have left. I could drop down dead in the next five minutes, or I could live until I'm ninety. So, anyway, I'm going to say this, because, well, it's upsetting your mother.'

Michael knew from the way in which his father skirted around the issue that Michael was in for a telling-off of some kind, though he'd no idea what it could possibly be for. His father, however, had come to the point.

'Look son, it's Hope. Your mother's worried about her. We, your mother and me, we don't think she's happy.'

'Dad, she's massively pregnant. I wouldn't be happy carrying that weight around in front of me.'

Ernest didn't notice the immediately defensive tone in Michael's voice, and ploughed on.

'No, it's not that. I know she's pregnant, and that's a lot to cope with when you're so young. But it's something else. When your mother was pregnant, she sort of blossomed.'

Having broached the difficult topic, Ernest was feeling more at ease in his fatherly role. He was departing now from his script.

'She had a tough time with Linnie, tougher than with you; she was the first you see. It never really got her down, though. She was tough, your mother. Being pregnant, the trouble she had, it never really defeated her. You could always tell that, underneath it all, she wanted Linnie, wanted everything to turn out OK. There was never any question of that. And it was the same with you. She had her rough times, but she was . . . *resilient*; you knew she'd see it through. She's been a good mother to you both.'

Michael couldn't disagree with that. He sipped his beer, but kept his silence.

'But Hope's not like that. Not now. Your mother saw it . . . sees it. I'm not as sharp as she is; I didn't see it at first. But I do now, son. She's not happy, and I don't know what I'm good for any more, what with my heart and everything, but I want to help you to sort it all out with each other.'

Michael knew that his father was right; Hope wasn't happy. She'd been distant since the time of Jeffrey's art event. She barely spoke to him at the moment. Yes, he'd slept with Evette, but whatever he may have wished for, it had only happened once, and he'd been careful to conceal it from Hope. He was sure that she knew nothing about it. So what was it then? Maybe it was something to do with him getting so drunk on the day of Jeffrey's art thing. Had he said something to offend her? He couldn't remember. His thoughts were chased away as his father continued.

'I don't know what it is that's going on between you. But something is, and if you want to talk about it, then you know where we are. That's all I want to say. If you don't want to talk to your mother about it, then talk to me. I'm not saying that I'll know what to do, or what to say. I'm not very good with this kind of thing; your mother's better at this stuff than I am. But I know that sometimes you can't tell women everything. So, if there is anything . . .'

Before Michael could unpick what it was his father was saying to him, the memory of Evette's naked body filled his mind. He felt himself blushing, as though he'd involuntarily projected the image on to a screen in front of them both. He sipped his beer and tried to blink the image out of his mind. He suddenly had the impression that his dad knew exactly what the problem was between himself and Hope. He wasn't sure precisely what his dad knew, though it seemed to be more than he was letting on. But how could he know anything at all? No one knew about him and Evette, other than Evette and himself.

Or did they? He suddenly remembered the day he'd accidentally left his phone at home; the day he'd met Jeffrey and found out about Evette's other affair, if that's what it was. He remembered he'd sent Evette a text earlier that morning, which he'd routinely deleted from his phone just in case Hope looked at his messages. He'd left home before

Hope, accidentally leaving his phone behind. He'd worried at the time that if Evette had replied, then Hope might have intercepted and read that reply. But when he got home that night, his phone was tucked behind a cushion, and not in plain sight. So, even if Evette had replied – which she hadn't – then Hope couldn't have read it. Could she?

'Are you all right, son?' Michael realized his father was talking to him. 'Only, you look a bit peaky.'

'Sorry, Dad. I'm all right. Honestly. Tough morning at work.'

He sipped his beer, to be doing something ordinary. If Hope *did* know about him and Evette, why had she said nothing? Unable to figure this out, Michael's thoughts took a different route; suppose that she'd spoken to Evette instead, confronted her, warned her off. That would at least explain Evette's silence, her reluctance to reply to any of his messages. And if Hope knew, this would explain her moodiness towards him, too. He felt sick, as though he'd been punched in the stomach. The idea that Hope knew about him and Evette appalled him. What had he done? He felt ashamed of himself. How could he go home and face her?

He looked up at his father, who was lost in thought himself. Suddenly, it all fell into place. Of course Hope knew, and what's more she'd shared this knowledge with his mother, his own mother! And now his father was here, to warn him off the affair. News of Michael's guilt was spreading outwards like ripples in a pond. He wondered who else knew?

'Your mom and I haven't always seen eye to eye, you know.'

Michael's attention sharpened. Something had changed in the tone of his father's voice.

'We've had our . . . *difficulties* . . . too, you know.'

The word 'difficulties' seemed to burst at the seams with a welter of emotions – pain, anger, sorrow, regret, melancholy

– like a dam that was no longer capable of holding the weight of water behind it. His father faltered and fell silent. Michael was astonished. He could see, as plainly as anything, that his father had had an affair himself, a long time ago perhaps, but, as they sat there together in the pub, Michael could see also that the emotions it had inspired were as close to the surface as they must have been at the time it happened. He thought his father was going to cry. Instead, he reached for his pint and took a long drink. He put the glass down.

'Ah well,' Ernest said, not taking his eyes from the glass. 'Water under the bridge.'

Michael watched his father closely: this elderly, ailing man with his failing heart. How, he wondered, could you have known someone all your life, and yet know so little about them? This was the man who seemed to spend his entire life sitting in front of the TV; the man whose sedentary lifestyle made him as much a part of the furniture as, well, the furniture; the man who, Michael often jokingly suggested to Hope, could be put to bed simply by having a sheet draped over him as he sat in his favourite armchair; to wake him up the next morning you'd pull the sheet off him, place a cup of tea beside him, and switch the TV back on.

But now Michael could see that there was more to him than this; he could see that there was a life here, a life that was as rich in its own jumbled, confused tragicomic experiences as his own. And he realized with a shock that it was a life that would one day cease, and that when this happened, all those experiences would be lost forever.

Hope sat for a long time looking at Klara's letter, immobilized by indecision. Part of her wished that the letter had remained tucked into its hiding place at the back of Schmetterling's painting, and part of her wished that, having found it, she'd had it translated by someone indifferent to the content. But it was too late now, and she knew that she could no longer prevent Klara's intimate thoughts from being scrutinized by people like Professor King. She believed the emotions which Klara struggled to express were of no importance whatsoever to people like him.

Hope knew that the time had come to talk to Michael about Klara. She hadn't told him yet about Gareth's speculations or Professor King's interest in the letter. Her suspicions concerning Michael had stalled her feelings for him – though she had to admit that, since the day she read Evette's text, Michael had given her no reason to think that there was anything going on between them. He'd not been evasive or sly, so far as she could tell (and she'd been watching especially closely) and he'd arrived home when he was supposed to. He didn't act like a man who was having an affair, though Hope wasn't naïve enough to think that this meant he *wasn't*. She was also aware that she herself was the one who had been changed by the suspicion she harboured about Michael. She knew that she'd withdrawn from him; put her emotions into neutral until she could be sure one way or the other. But now she felt the cold; the need to reconnect. Klara was pushing her back towards Michael. Hope decided that she'd talk to him that evening and would try to arrive at a decision concerning the fate of Klara's letter once and for all.

Michael sat on the crowded bus, homeward bound. He felt hollowed out. It had been a strange day, unsettling and inconclusive. Hope had still not replied to the text he'd sent that morning, nor to the one he'd sent after meeting his dad for lunch. His initial fear that Hope knew about his fling with Evette had subsided. After all, she hadn't really given any indication that she knew anything about it. And if she did know something, then she would have said something by now. He was sure of that. He'd panicked earlier, yet in that brief moment of panic he'd come to a dim realization, which he'd tried to make clear to himself over the rest of the afternoon, of just how much he depended on Hope: how much he relied on her, how much he wanted to be with her. If she'd found out about him and Evette, what would she have done? Would she have dumped him? He'd surely deserve it; he'd been unfaithful to her, and while she was struggling so hard with being pregnant, carrying their child.

And then there was the strange meeting with his father; what had that all been about? Michael kept coming back to his father's mention of the 'difficulties' his parents seemed to have faced at some point in their relationship. As far back as Michael could remember, his parents had been exactly as they were now with each other, so these 'difficulties' could have occurred before he was born, or while he was still too young to remember or to notice. Maybe Linnie, who was older, knew something about all this. He would have to ask her sometime.

A thought occurred to Michael: if his parents had split up before he was conceived, he wouldn't have been born at all; wouldn't be sitting here now, on this bus, on his way home to Hope. He wouldn't have met Hope, who wouldn't now be pregnant with his child. Unable to get off the train of thought, Michael started to track backwards through events in his life, extracting himself from them. He wondered just how different the world would be if he hadn't been born. Would it really be any different? If he hadn't existed at all, would anyone really have noticed? Would anyone really have cared?

Michael arrived home to animated voices. In the living room, a man he'd never seen before was standing in front of the fireplace, speaking excitedly to Hope. She was sitting on the sofa, arms folded across her belly. She saw Michael and stood up. But before she could introduce the stranger, he stepped forward and offered a hand to Michael.

'You must be Michael. I'm Gareth. I translated Klara's letter for Hope?'

Michael shook the hand. He sensed excitement in the air and waited for an explanation. Hope told him about Gareth's speculations concerning the identity of Klara, and the interest that Professor King had since taken in the letter.

'Nick King's one of the world's most eminent historians of Nazi Germany,' said Hope, her voice trembling slightly.

Michael was, by now, astonished at the news he was hearing for the first time. 'Hitler?'

'I know. It sounds ludicrous, doesn't it? My Klara, Hitler's mother.'

'And Schmetterling?' Michael was still struggling to assimilate the information.

'Hitler's real father,' added Gareth, confirming the story Hope had relayed moments before. 'But there's more to come, as I've just been telling Hope. Michael, I think you'd better sit down for this.'

27

It was dawn and Hope and Michael had barely slept. The long, intimate night had wrapped them up and nurtured their excitement, and they had found themselves lost in each other, as much as they were lost in the startling series of revelations which Gareth had breathlessly recounted to them the previous evening. Like children with a guilty secret, they'd gone over Gareth's incredible story again and again: the child conceived all those years ago on a hillside under a canopy of stars by two lovers who would never meet again.

Gareth had read the short biography of Schmetterling which Oskar Krause had sent to Hope. It was largely an appreciation of his art, but several incidental statements had caught Gareth's eye, statements that, had he not already embarked on his speculations concerning the identity of Klara, would have passed without comment. In particular, two pieces of information seemed especially important.

The first concerned Schmetterling's career trajectory, for he may have been an itinerant artist when Klara knew him but by 1905 he was a state-employed Professor at the Vienna Academy of Fine Art. Schmetterling, according to the book, was born in 1863, which made him two years younger than Klara when they had their tryst, and forty-two years old when he was appointed to his Professorship. It didn't escape Gareth's attention that the Vienna Academy was the very institution to which Hitler himself had applied as a prospective student in 1907. Hitler, in October of that year, had withdrawn his inheritance and moved up to Vienna, where he'd sat the two-day entrance exam hoping to gain admission to the Academy. At that time, Hitler clearly saw himself as an artist. Unfortunately, the Academy disagreed, and turned him down. It was a bad year for Hitler – not only was he rejected by the Academy, stalling his ambitions as an artist, but in the December of that year Klara, the mother whom Hitler had loved so deeply, died of lung cancer.

All this was well known to those acquainted with Hitler's early years. What interested and intrigued Gareth, however, was the idea that Johannes Schmetterling had been an employee of the Academy at the time of Hitler's application. It was perhaps not surprising that Hitler would see the prestigious Academy as the place where best to develop his artistic talents. But, Gareth wondered, was this the only reason for Hitler choosing to study there? Had Klara, her burden lightened by her husband's death four years before, and faced with her own impending death from the cancer eating away at her body, finally broken the news to Adolf concerning the true identity of his father? Had this knowledge played any part in Hitler's decision to apply to the Academy?

It had occurred to Gareth that, following her husband's death, there might well have been some communication between Klara and Schmetterling. Had Klara, for example, written to Schmetterling to let him know that Adolf, his son, was intent on pursuing his career as an artist? Had she tipped him off that Adolf would be applying to the very institution where he, Johannes, taught? Perhaps she'd hoped that Schmetterling would be able to put in a good word for their son, to smooth his passage into the Academy. And if

Schmetterling had indeed played any part in the admissions process, why had the young Adolf found himself rejected not once but twice? Perhaps Schmetterling was ignorant of the young man's identity as Klara's child. But more intriguingly, perhaps he *wasn't* ignorant of the young man's identity, and it was precisely this knowledge that had led Schmetterling to reject him.

Gareth was almost certain that, barring any more letters hidden in the backs of Schmetterling's paintings (and he was sure that there would be a thorough search of all Schmetterling's works once the news of Hope's letter broke worldwide), there would be no way now of establishing the truth of these speculations. Evidence of Hitler's time in Vienna had surely been explored more thoroughly than that of any other person in history. Could there really be any more information to be discovered about his time there? If any new insights were going to be gained, they would have to come from Schmetterling, whose own life would surely now be scrutinized in intense detail.

That Schmetterling's and Hitler's paths might at some point have crossed was intriguing enough in its own right, but it was the second piece of information contained in the short biography that had really shaken Hope and Michael. So startling was this revelation that Gareth hadn't told anyone else, not even Professor King. For the book had mentioned briefly in the introduction that Schmetterling had died in 1943, at the age of seventy-nine, in Dachau concentration camp.

'Of course,' said Gareth, as he waited for Hope to draw out the implications of this briefly stated fact of some long-dead artist's life, 'it doesn't follow that he was Jewish. I mean, he might have been a communist, or homosexual. Or even a Gypsy, for all we know.'

'But he *might* have been Jewish?' said Hope.

They looked at each other: Gareth standing by the fireplace barely able to keep from punching the air, an exuberant grin stretched across his face; Hope trembling on the edge of the sofa, her eyes shining with excitement.

'Yes,' said Gareth. 'Savour the moment, Hope, because when this gets out it'll be like a nuclear bomb going off.'

Michael got up to make tea, leaving Hope lying in bed. The child in her belly lay quietly too, as though it too were exhausted by the previous evening's excitement. She lay on her right side, in the position that had become second nature to her – knees drawn up under her belly, her right arm folded under her head. Her left arm rested gently across her bulge, sensing the slightest movement, the fluttering limbs inside her confirming the presence of life. For all the previous evening's excitement, she felt herself strangely cocooned; the warmth from the duvet was amniotic, and her limbs seemed to float in the air trapped by the down. She felt perfectly relaxed, almost fluid; she could have been floating in a giant immersion tank. The room itself was full of the shadows of morning, the still-drawn curtains keeping the light of the world outside at bay.

Michael returned with their tea. Hope sat up and took her cup.

'I'm not going into work today,' said Michael, climbing back into bed beside Hope. 'I'm too tired. I hardly slept last night.'

'I know. There's been a lot to take in.'

'Do you believe it all? I mean, Klara, Hitler . . . it all sounds so far-fetched.'

'I don't know. Part of me doesn't want it to be true. Part of me wants Klara to slide back into history, to be left alone with her memories of her lover. I'm not sure I want her life to be raked over by people like Nick King.'

'But if she does turn out to be who Gareth says she is, then surely it's important that we know?'

'Why? What does it matter? She'd no idea what her son would turn out to be, if he did turn out to be you-know-who. She saw him as an artist, not as some future mass murderer. All that stuff – world domination, the concentration camps, genocide – all that came later. After she'd died.'

'I suppose so,' said Michael. 'But you can't absolve her absolutely, can you? I mean, she was his mother after all. She must have played *some* part in making him the man he was, mustn't she?'

Hope was silent. She didn't want Klara to be responsible in any way, but she also knew that Klara must have played some part in shaping the adult her son became. She thought again about her teenage struggles with her own parents. She'd believed at the time that her rebellion was justified because of the apparent lack of interest her parents had shown towards her, palming her off on nannies and minders. She still believed this, though she understood better now why they did it. But she couldn't deny that they'd shaped the person she now was, for better or worse. When her own child was born, would she be a better parent to it than her parents had been to her?

They sat together in silence, sipping tea and listening to the rain. Michael's thoughts drifted to the previous day and the conversation he'd had with his father. What exactly did Hope know, if she knew anything at all?

Michael's speculations began to spin out of control. Assuming that his parents suspected something, that made five people who might know what he'd been up to. Maybe there were more. Perhaps Evette had by now told Jeffrey; maybe Hope had shared her thoughts with Alex; maybe his parents had told Linnie. The circle of shame grew wider and wider.

But really, what was the big deal? Michael had slept with Evette only once, and that was hardly an affair, was it? Nothing to feel too ashamed about. Except that Michael did feel ashamed. While he was involved with Evette, he never thought of himself as having an affair as such; he saw it instead as another life, another Michael, another dimension he could step into when he wanted to, and then step out of again. It wasn't that he wanted to hurt or deceive Hope, nothing like that. He didn't even want to lay claim to Evette; all he wanted was for her to be there, waiting for him when he stepped back into their life together, just as he would be there for her when she wanted him. But now the two dimensions had spilled over into each other, muddying his world.

He looked sideways at Hope. If she looked at him now she would surely read the guilt that must be written all over his face. He knew that he couldn't go on concealing what he'd done. He would have to tell her; get it off his conscience. If she wasn't going to forgive him, better get it over with now rather than later.

At that moment, Michael woke up to the fact that he'd made a decision. He realized that he really was going to tell her, and that he couldn't stop himself now. 'Hope?'

Michael turned towards her but still couldn't look directly at her. She could sense immediately – the body language, the tone of voice, the expression on his face – that he was about to say something to her that she wouldn't want to hear. She could sense the struggle he was having to find the words to tell her what she already knew.

'Hope, I think I've done something stupid.'

She watched him as he stared at nothing, debilitated by his ineptitude in the language of emotion. The thought that he might pull back from the brink flickered momentarily, but died as he spoke again. She could see that he was pushing himself to get it out.

'I'm not sure how . . . I mean, I don't know. This thing . . .'

As Michael approached the threshold of his truth, he glanced over at Hope, needing to know that she wanted him to go on. She sat rigid, unmoving, her face pale. Her arms, which had been folded across her taut belly, had dropped to her sides. Her eyes fixed him and he faltered as he noticed how shocked she looked.

And she was. For no matter how much she'd anticipated, imagined, and feared this, it was now clear to her that she'd been right: Michael had slept with Evette. The sob that broke from her brought Michael up short, but in a nanosecond Hope had caught the emotion and regained control over herself. She sat as rigid as before, but her eyes were wider now with the effort of not crying.

'Hope . . . ?'

Michael spoke out of concern for her. He hadn't actually said anything of substance yet, but looking at her now he realized that she wasn't only listening to him; she already knew what he was going to say.

The revelation seemed to free Michael from his struggle for words. He realized that he didn't need to find a special vocabulary for what he needed to say. He resolved therefore to just say it.

'Look, Hope. I have to tell you this. I have to get it off my chest . . .'

'Why?'

The abruptness of her reply surprised them both.

'What?' said Michael.

'I said: "Why?"'

'Why, what?'

Michael was caught, unsure if she meant 'Why did you do it?' or 'Why do you have to get it off your chest?'

Hope looked at the confused face before her, then looked away. She knew, in a way that Michael never would, that those closest to you were capable of hurting you the most. But she also knew that they only hurt you the most because you were closest to them. She couldn't decide to stop loving Michael – she knew that now – and she wanted to believe that Michael loved her. Maybe he did. But that was for the future. If they were still together in ten years' time, then good. But here and now, they had to edge forward moment by moment. The baby was due in just a few weeks' time, and Hope needed to give all her strength to getting through those few weeks. She'd no strength left to deal with Michael's guilt.

'I know what you want to tell me, Michael. Or I think I do. I mean, I could be wrong, but I don't think I am. But I don't want you to say any more. I know it sounds stupid, but I'd rather not know what it is you want me to know.'

Hope paused. She wasn't getting it quite right yet. It was her turn now to struggle for the right words. She spoke slowly, carefully formulating her thoughts.

'I think what I mean is this. Some people, in this situation – in *my* situation – would need to know every last detail. They'd need to know names, times, places, how long, were there others, and so on. A million questions. And each answer would probably throw up more questions. And the more I found out about . . . whatever it is you've done . . . the more I learned about it, well, that would make me realize how easily I was deceived; and then I'd feel the need to mistrust you in order not to get taken for a ride a second time.'

Hope paused, still not sure that she was getting it right.

'Look, I know that some people in this situation, *my* situation, would still need to ask those questions. But Michael, if I did, I think I'd make a cage for myself. I don't think I'd ever be able to free myself again. My fears would burrow into me and corrupt me; and my biggest fear of all is that I might end up hating you because of this. And I don't want that because, well, because I love you. I honestly do. And I can't do anything about that except to protect myself from anything that might threaten how I feel about you.'

Hope paused again, still unsure whether or not she was making sense. She pressed on.

'Your face. I love your face. I love the *familiarity* of your face. It's so familiar to me that it could be my own face, if you see what I mean. I know it like I know my own face – that kind of familiarity. But I think if I sat here and let you get it all off your chest, like I think you want to, then this moment would become my image of your face forever, and I'd hate that. Do you see?'

Hope's arms lifted as she spoke, and Michael watched as they enfolded her belly in the now-familiar way she had. He wanted to say something in response, but thought better of it. He could see she wanted to continue.

'Maybe at a different time I'd react differently. But here, and now, inside this moment, this is how I want it to be. I want your assurance that it's over.'

Michael moved to speak, but Hope cut him dead.

'Not now. I don't want you to give it to me because I ask for it. But I want it all the same. And that's all I want. What's done is done, and I want it to pass out of memory. With luck, our baby, the baby we've made, will pop out of here in a few days, and a whole new life will start. But when it arrives, it'll mean a new life for us too. It'll be a fresh start for us, and what I don't want, what I *really* don't want, is for what's happened in the past to poison our future.

'I know you think I've been a bit crazy about Klara these past few months, but I can't stop thinking about her. I know that people like Gareth and Nick King look at Klara and all they see is Hitler's mother. But I see a woman whose life drained away because she lost the one person she really loved. I don't know if that played any part in creating Hitler's character, any more than it created the Treaty of Versailles, or the Wall Street Crash.

'But I don't care about any of that. Michael, I don't want to lose you. And whenever I look at you, or think about you, I don't want to always see this thing you've done as well. So if you love me too, you're going to have to swallow your need to confess, OK? I don't want to know. What you do with your guilt is your problem, OK? Bury it. Cut it out. But whatever you do, don't make me share in it. I want to draw a line under the past. I want to have our baby, and then I want the three of us to get on with making a future for ourselves. What happens then is what happens, for better or worse. OK?'

Hope sank back on to the bed, eyes closed, arms still enfolded about her belly. She looked pale and spent.

Michael barely had time to take this in before the doorbell sounded from below.

'What time is it?' said Hope. She looked at the clock on the bedside cabinet. It was nine o'clock. 'Shit, it's Gareth. I told him he could pick up Klara's letter this morning. I didn't want him to take it last night.'

Hope was out of bed and throwing clothes on. She left the bedroom as the doorbell rang a second time. Michael dressed slowly, trying to figure out if Hope had forgiven him or not. Bewildered, he followed her downstairs. She and Gareth were in the kitchen, mugs in hand, when Michael joined them. Klara's letter lay on the work surface between them.

'I know it's asking a lot,' said Gareth, 'but Nick thinks it might be a good idea to let him have the painting too. It might help in the authentication of the letter, you know, where it came from and so on. I mean, are you sure the painting actually is a Schmetterling?'

Hope said she couldn't be sure, although Schmetterling's butterfly signature was on the painting. 'I suppose it could be a copy. Was he famous enough to have had forgers?'

'If he wasn't famous before, he soon will be. At the very least you'll get to know whether it's an authentic Schmetterling. And with its history, the letter and all, you'll probably find that it'll be worth a small fortune. It'll be an investment for your old age!' Hope didn't seem particularly overjoyed at the prospect, but Gareth ploughed on, oblivious to Hope's lack of enthusiasm.

'And the letter too. It's yours, and once we're finished with it you'll have to think about what to do with it. You could donate it to a museum or archive. Or you could sell it.'

Michael noticed the change in Hope's demeanour, though Gareth didn't. She turned her body defensively and her fists seemed to tighten, as though she were about to be pounced upon. 'I'll get the painting,' she said, and fled to the living room.

'And you'll be able to sell your story to the media, too.' Gareth had raised his voice now so that Hope would be able to hear him while she was out of the room. 'There's going to be a lot of media interest in this. If I were you, I'd think about getting myself an agent. Opportunities like this don't fall into your lap every day of the week, you know. You want to make the most of it.'

Michael, half-listening to Gareth, wondered why it was taking Hope so long to fetch the painting. He left Gareth and went into the living room. Hope stood by the fireplace, staring at the picture between her hands. The bottom edge of the frame was resting gently on the top of her distended belly.

'Hope?' Michael spoke quietly. He felt as though he were intruding. As he drew to Hope's side, he could see that she was pale and close to tears. Her hands seemed to tremble as they held the painting, though it could have been because of the lively occupant of her belly.

'Hope? Are you OK?'

'I don't want all this,' she said, as though to herself. 'I don't want the money. I don't want the attention. I don't want a fucking agent, for fuck's sake!'

Michael put his arm across Hope's shoulders. He remembered what Gareth had said last night, and at last realized that he'd been right; Hope's actions in the next few minutes could change their lives forever. He touched her belly, and felt the baby scrape a limb across the taut skin. It was almost time for the child to get itself born. Their lives were changing anyway, whatever happened to Klara's letter and Schmetterling's painting.

'Hope, you said to me upstairs that you saw how important this might be. Maybe Gareth's got it wrong, but if he hasn't then it's important that people get to know about it, isn't it? I know how important Klara is to you, but haven't you just been telling me how important it is to put the past behind us and get on with making a future for ourselves?'

A noise behind them caused Michael to turn around. It was Gareth. He stood gingerly in the doorway, aware that Hope and Michael were discussing the painting and the letter, still talking themselves into letting them both go.

'Everything all right?'

It was Hope who answered, marshalling herself. She spoke without turning around, not wanting Gareth to see how upset she was. 'I haven't got anything to wrap it in. Will it be all right?'

'I've brought some bubble wrap and a packing case. In the car,' said Gareth, relieved that Hope seemed to have made her decision at last.

Professor King phoned the following morning to let Hope know that both the letter and the painting had arrived safely. Hope thanked him.

'There is one other thing,' said Professor King, his voice almost conspiratorial. 'We'd prefer this didn't leak out to the media just yet. We'd like to be sure of ourselves before we go to press, so to speak.'

Hope pointed out that she'd no intention of speaking to anyone else about it, but Professor King pressed on.

'It's very important that we keep this under wraps until we've done our stuff. It will be so much more difficult if we're having to deal with media speculation. It makes life very' – he paused, almost theatrically, to choose the right word – 'messy.'

Hope assured Professor King that she understood and that she planned to talk to no one.

'You may not know this – why would you? – but we happen to be approaching the anniversary of the Great Dictator's birthday and, quite frankly, there are always a host of fresh stories concerning various aspects of his life circulated around this time, many of them put about by those who are, shall we say, *sympathetic* to the Nazi ideology.'

'Hitler's birthday?' said Hope. Although she'd often thought of Klara and her child, she'd never actually considered the physical process of bearing and giving birth to that child. Sitting on the sofa with her belly resting in her lap, Hope felt a sharp pang of identification with Klara, and in that instant realized that she too was approaching the birth of her own child, just as Klara must have been all those years ago. A thought occurred to Hope. 'When exactly is that?'

The question seemed to take Professor King by surprise, as though Hope had unwittingly strayed from a script he'd prepared in advance.

'What?'

'Hitler's birthday. When is that?'

'It was the twentieth of April, 1889. Why do you ask?'

Professor King's question was met with a startled silence; the twentieth of April was the date on which Hope's own child was due.

'So, let me get this straight.'

Preston sipped his pint of lager, and tried to get his bearings. He was having difficulty taking in the extraordinary story that Michael was relating to him.

'You're saying that the woman who wrote the letter . . .'

'Klara, yes.'

'You're saying that she's Hitler's mother?'

'Yes.'

Jeffrey, who'd joined them in the pub for lunch, intervened. 'And this artist, Schmeichel or whatever . . .'

'Schmetterling.'

'Whatever . . . he's Hitler's father?'

'His *real* father.'

'His real father. As opposed to . . . the bloke who everyone *thinks* was Hitler's father.'

'Alois,' said Michael, who was actually enjoying the sensation of being privy to a secret of such proportions as the one he was now sharing with his friends.

Jeffrey paused to sip his beer, and Preston took up the baton. 'And Schmetterling turns out to be Jewish?'

'He *might* be,' stressed Michael. 'We don't know for sure. But it seems he died in a concentration camp.'

'It doesn't follow that he's Jewish though does it?' said Preston. 'I mean, he might have been gay.'

Jeffrey and Michael looked at Preston.

'What?' said Preston.

'Nah, he wasn't gay,' said Jeffrey, authoritatively.

'How can you be sure?' said Michael, a little peeved at having the initiative taken away from him.

'Hello?' said Jeffrey. 'He shagged wassername, didn't he? He fathered a child? This doesn't scream "gay" to me!'

Preston gave Jeffrey a resentful look.

'Not everyone who's gay "screams", as you put it,' he said, pointedly.

'Sorry, mate,' said Jeffrey. 'I didn't mean it like that.'

'Maybe she was trying to straighten him out,' said Michael, helpfully.

'But the Nazis banged up communists and Gypsies too, didn't they? I mean, they banged up anyone who got in their way, didn't they?'

'Jeffrey, I hardly think the phrase "banged up" captures the appalling nature of what the Nazis did to them. Starved, them. Enslaved them. Tortured them. Murdered them . . .'

'All right, all right.' Jeffrey scowled at Preston. 'You know what I mean.'

With his two friends bickering, Michael sat back and sipped his beer, thoroughly enjoying himself.

Hope stepped through the entrance to the Old Varsity Tavern and looked through the lunchtime crowd for Alex. She was sitting at a small table by the window, in the modest non-smoking lounge, reading a magazine. A barely touched drink stood on the table in front of her.

'Am I late?' said Hope, settling her belly as best she could in relation to the edge of the table.

'Not at all. I came early so that I could have a cigarette. I didn't think you'd want to sit with the smokers. What are you drinking?'

'I'll have an orange juice,' said Hope.

Hope looked around the bar. As usual, age seemed to be the only indicator of who were lecturers and who were students, and Hope knew that even that indicator was unreliable. Above the bar, a bust of Julius Caesar gazed eyelessly across the heads of the punters, imperious in its detachment from the plebs below. Looking at the marble bust, Hope felt oddly uncomfortable. She seemed to be haunted by dictators at the moment.

'There you go.' Alex put Hope's drink on the table in front of her. 'So, what's new?'

'Look guys, all this is in complete confidence, OK? I mean, no one knows how much of this is true yet. It wouldn't be . . .'

– Michael struggled for a moment, trying to recall Professor Nicholas King's phrase, as Hope had reported it to him – '*helpful*, it wouldn't be helpful if the media got hold of this. Not yet, anyway.'

'They won't hear it from me,' said Preston.

'Or me,' said Jeffrey. 'Scout's honour.'

'I can tell Ben, though, can't I?' said Preston.

'And Evette? I can tell her, too?'

Michael had the feeling that he'd sent a snowball rolling down a mountain.

'This is a secret, OK?' Hope said, looking squarely into Alex's eyes.

'My lips are sealed,' said Alex.

They'd spent Alex's entire lunch break talking about the Klara and Schmetterling revelation. Hope had had no chance to catch up on Alex's personal life, and so she had no idea what state Alex's relationship with Jeffrey might currently be in. For all Hope knew, they might still be seeing each other, sharing a bed together, indulging in pillow talk . . .

'You can't tell *anyone*,' said Hope, trying to will Alex not to say anything to Jeffrey, while not mentioning him by name. Alex seemed to understand.

'Hope, I promise. I won't tell anyone. Not anyone.'

All the same, and much as she trusted her friend, Hope couldn't help but feel that she'd set fire to a fuse.

It was Sunday. Hope and Michael had been invited to Doreen and Ernest's house for dinner. As they arrived, Ernest was in the front room, setting out the cutlery. Hope and Michael had brought wine and took the bottle through to the kitchen where they knew they'd find Doreen. The aroma of roast chicken filled the small kitchen space. Pots simmered on the stove, sending tendrils of steam to drip slowly down the windows.

'Christ, Mom,' said Michael. 'It's like a tropical rainforest in here. Get yourself an extractor fan.'

'If you'll give me the money,' she said.

'Ignore him,' said Hope. 'It smells gorgeous, as usual.'

Someone yelled from elsewhere in the house. 'Nan! I want a drink!'

Without hesitation, Doreen turned to the refrigerator and took out a bottle of cola. 'Jade,' she said, by way of explanation. 'I've got the kids while Linnie's away.'

This was news to Michael, who'd spoken to Linnie by phone only a few days before. She'd said nothing about going away, let alone leaving the children with his parents. 'Where's she gone?' he asked.

'Gavin's taken her to Ibiza, or Majorca . . . one of those type of places. He said it was a late surprise birthday present. Linnie asked me to have them. She didn't want to leave them with Gavin's family.'

'Huh, unusual concern on her part!' said Michael, resentfully. He wasn't happy that Gavin had reappeared in his sister's life.

'Michael,' said Hope. 'You know she loves the kids.'

'Enough to abandon them with our parents, apparently.'

Doreen had finished pouring two beakers of the drink, and was returning the bottle to the fridge. 'I really don't mind. They're no trouble at all. It's not like it's forever.'

Michael was unconvinced. He didn't think that his parents should have to shoulder the responsibility of looking after someone else's kids at their age, even if they were family. Michael's father had a weak heart, after all. However, he kept his thoughts to himself.

'Would you take these drinks through? Tell them dinner will be about fifteen minutes. It's best to warn them, so it's not a shock when you tell them to turn the TV off.' This was said with a mischievous smile as she handed the beakers to Michael.

'I'll do it.' Ernest appeared in the doorway behind Hope and Michael. He took the beakers from Michael's hands. 'I'll go and see what they're up to.'

Doreen waited until Ernest had disappeared before she spoke. 'Your dad likes having the kids around. Says it keeps him young.'

'They'll put years on him,' said Michael.

Hope knew Michael's views about his nephew and niece, and about his sister. But she could also see that Doreen and Ernest loved having their grandchildren around the house. Their forbearance towards Linnie's wayward children dignified them in her eyes. 'We've got something important to tell you later,' she said, deliberately changing the subject.

'Well, I hope it's not that you're having twins,' said Doreen, the mischievous smile still on her lips.

Later that night, Hope sat in bed, sipping at a cup of tea.

'Should we have told them?' she said.

Michael hesitated. He too had wondered at the wisdom of doing so. 'I don't know. What harm could it do? They're not going to phone the papers, are they?'

'But will they tell anyone else?'

Michael thought about this for a moment. 'I don't think so. I mean, who do they know? Who would they tell? They'd probably tell Linnie, but she's not here anyway.'

'I guess so,' said Hope. She thought for a moment and then, as the memory came into her head, she spoke it. 'I told Alex.'

Michael sipped his tea and pondered. If Hope had told Alex, he reasoned, he might as well admit that he'd spilled the beans to his friends too. But Hope's reaction wasn't quite what he was expecting. 'Jesus Christ, Michael! Jeffrey *and* Preston? Why not stand on the top of the Rotunda and shout it to the world?'

Michael was taken aback by this. 'But you told Alex!'

'Michael, she's my best friend! Of course I told her.'

'And Jeffrey and Preston are my best friends.'

'Yes, but Preston'll tell Ben.'

'And?'

'Well, we don't know Ben that well, do we? And you told Jeffrey, too.'

'What's the problem with that?'

Hope hesitated, and Michael understood why. Evette still cast a shadow across their relationship. 'Come on, Hope. These people are our friends.'

Hope remained silent. Since discovering Klara's letter, she'd presided over a progressively widening pool of initiates, beginning with herself and Gareth, and taking in Professor King (and God knows who else at his university), Michael, Alex, Preston, Jeffrey, Doreen and Ernest, and probably Ben and Evette as well. And Jeffrey, with all his internet contacts and his website, too! She realized that in spite of her best intentions, the number of people who knew was about to increase exponentially and there wasn't anything that anyone could do about it.

It took almost a week. Michael was at work so Hope took the phone call. A woman's voice checked Hope's name and asked for a few general details. Hope's first thought was that Professor King was trying to reach her again. This voice, however, seemed in no hurry to give way to Professor King, and after a few moments of politely insistent questioning concerning Hope's identity, began to make its mission clear.

'My name is Lucy Osterbank, and I work for the *Sunday Telegraph*. I'd like to get your views on a matter in which I think you may have an interest.'

Hope sharpened at this. She spoke tersely. 'Go on.'

'Am I right in thinking that you are the person who discovered a certain . . . *letter*?'

It became clear in the subsequent discussion that, not only did Lucy Osterbank know all that Hope knew about Klara and her relationship with Schmetterling, but she also seemed to hint at knowledge that Hope didn't yet have. When Hope reminded her that the authenticity of the letter, and the details of the story it pointed to, had yet to be confirmed, Lucy Osterbank responded by assuring Hope that the authenticity of the letter was 'pretty secure', according to her sources.

'Which sources would they be?'

Hope quickly realized that, since the question of authenticity was out of the hands of any of the people she and Michael had revealed the story to, the source must be the academics who were researching the letter.

'Was it Nick King?' said Hope.

'I'm not sure it would be wise to . . .'

'Or Gareth?' Hope didn't expect a direct answer, though she listened for some audible confirmation – an intake of breath, an unexpected pause, an embarrassed silence – but Lucy Osterbank was a professional journalist, used to dealing with the insistent demands of high-powered Government officials. Hope was small fry by comparison. She simply ignored Hope's questions.

'Look, Hope, let me get to the point here. I'm not at liberty to tell you anything about the letter that you don't already know. You're going to find out soon enough, anyway, and from people who are qualified to know whether or not the letter is authentic. I'm only acting on a tip-off, so to speak. Nothing's on the record yet. But if my source is sound, then I wouldn't be surprised if this doesn't turn out to be one of the most important stories of our lifetime. If what you and I know turns out to be true, then we're sitting on one of the biggest stories since, well – since Hitler himself was making news.'

Hope remembered the discussion she'd had with Michael, about what the significance of Klara's relationship with Schmetterling might be. But she also knew that Lucy Osterbank was talking about newsworthiness, rather than historical importance. As Lucy Osterbank drew towards her point, Hope also remembered Gareth's advice about getting an agent.

'Before I say what I'm about to say,' said Lucy Osterbank, 'have you been approached by any other media organization?'

need to talk. v. important. meet 4 lunch x

Michael looked at Hope's text and wondered why she wanted to meet him. As he thought about this, he opened up the Monarch Watch website to check on the progress of the butterflies. There had been a considerable amount of activity since Michael had last visited the site. One posting in particular caught his attention.

I've seen them! I've seen them! Am I the first? I'm looking out my window and there's 3, poss 4 (can't tell – they're flitting about) Aren't they just beautiful?- Emilylou, Tx 03.26.03: 09.53

Michael read the message, relieved. It was as though he'd been struggling for some time to remember a particular fact and now it had simply popped into his head. One response to Emilylou's posting read:

At last! Now maybe we'll get some rain here! – Christytiger, Williamsburg, NY 03.26.03: 10.23

Michael laughed out loud at this, recognizing the allusion to the butterfly effect. He thought of the thousands upon thousands of butterflies that would now, finally, be taking to the air, stretching their wings, and beginning the arduous journey north, guided by ancient biological instincts following the imperative to reproduce. They would die in their thousands along the route, but their children and grandchildren would find their way in their place, there and back again, and again, and again. Michael saw them now, millions of butterflies, sun-dappled motes flickering among the trees, tousling the air about them, each responding to the turbulence the others had created, a secret, fathomless message uniting them all in their difference.

Hope put her phone down and stood up. Something had changed; her burden had eased in some small way. Breathing was more comfortable. She knew instinctively what was happening; the baby had shifted itself so that its head could drop into her pelvic cavity. She examined her belly, trying to feel objectively with her hands what she knew was happening inside. The midwife would confirm the extent to which the baby's head had engaged and would be able to tell which way the baby was lying. Perhaps the baby was breech? Hope didn't care. She'd made it almost to the end of her pregnancy without any major problems. Such a realization would, under different circumstances, have induced a superstitious caution – *don't count your chickens, don't speak too soon, you're tempting fate, pride goes before a fall* – but such caution now seemed preposterous. Trembling with excitement, Hope realized that the baby had begun its slow passage towards her birth canal. She had so much to tell Michael.

28

'Are we early?'
'Not at all. Come in, come in.'

Though slight of build, Parmjit's uncle was a handsome man with weathered features, as though in his time he'd worked for long spells in the open, under a hot sun. His eyes were dark brown but bright and alert, dancing with life. His hair, groomed and elegant, was almost entirely silver with only the faintest trace here and there of the colour it had once been. He wore a black suit over a white shirt, and a black bow tie. As he offered a hand to Parmjit, Hope could see elegant cufflinks at the wrist. Parmjit took the hand, shook it briefly, almost formally, and then the two embraced warmly.

'How goes it, Uncle?'

'Fine, fine. And how's my little college girl?'

'University, Uncle. I'm your little *university* girl.' This was said with ease and affection, as though it were a private running joke. The rest of the group stood awkwardly by. 'I'm very well, Uncle. How's business?'

'Ah, could be better, could be worse.' This was said with an indulgent smile, suggesting that business was actually OK. 'Well, come in then. Are you going to keep your friends hanging around by the door? They'll think you're ashamed of my restaurant.'

Parmjit turned to the group and, without hesitation, introduced them one by one to her uncle. Inside the restaurant, waiters dressed in dark trousers, dark-blue shirts and black ties moved unobtrusively among the tables. A cool raga played in the background, barely clambering above the chatter of the diners. It was almost eight o'clock and the restaurant was nearly full. There were whole families dining and chatting, a warm ambient noise.

'There's a couple more to come yet,' said Parmjit, who stood beside her uncle while the others took their seats. A waiter pushing a food trolley moved silently past Parmjit, a hand lightly touching her elbow. She turned to be met by the bright, brief smile of the young man, his teeth inordinately white under the subdued lights of the restaurant. Parmjit barely had time to return the smile before the waiter turned to the table he'd arrived at. Moments later a sheet of flame flashed into the air above it as the waiter set light to a dish. It burned for a few seconds, to the delight of the children sitting nearby, before it was captured and extinguished under the lid. Waves of subtle, charred spices rolled towards the friends as they took their places. Parmjit's uncle moved away to oversee the evening's dining.

'I'll have what they're having,' said Alex, sniffing the spice-filled air ostentatiously.

There were four vacant seats: one each for Jeffrey and Evette, one for Gyorgy, and one to spare. Preston and Ben had been invited but had reluctantly declined. A meal had been arranged for relatives and friends by Preston's mother, in part, so Preston explained, to help bring about a reconciliation between Preston and his father. Ben had been invited too, and Preston knew that turning up at the party as a couple, essentially announcing his sexuality to all those present, could drive even more of a wedge between him and his father, despite his mother's good intentions. He was nervous but he was excited by the idea.

'If it comes off,' he said, 'my life will feel different. I won't ever be the same again. No more fending off questions from my aunts about when I'm going to settle down with some nice girl, when I'm going to give my parents grandchildren. No more advances from cousin Janine. That'll be a relief!'

'You never know,' said Hope. 'If Janine knows you're gay, she might see you as more of a challenge. She'll want to straighten you out something rotten!'

'Shit, hadn't thought of that. Anyway, I'll give you a full report tomorrow if I'm not massively hungover or lying in a ditch having been murdered by my father.'

'Or humped to death by Janine!'

'Yes, can you imagine the scene at the police station? "But officer, one more shag and I'd have claimed him for heterosexuality. That's the real tragedy here!"'

Gyorgy appeared, chaperoned to the table by Parmjit's uncle. Hope surmised that this wasn't the first time Parmjit had brought Gyorgy here, judging by the familiar way in which he and Parmjit's uncle chatted together, smiling easily at each other. Gyorgy took his place at Parmjit's side. Drinks were ordered and menus arrived, followed by plates of poppadums and trays of pickles and sauces.

Michael loved Indian restaurants. He loved the insidious smell of the spices which rolled in exotic waves from the kitchens or, as now, drifted in sharp tendrils from the flaming pans at tableside. He loved the food too, the sulphurous tang of the masala, the charred sweetness of the meat from the tandoori ovens, the pillows of naan bread. Michael rarely used a knife and fork; he loved the tactile pleasure of eating his food using only the bread provided. As a child, his favourite part of Sunday dinner had been sopping up the rich gravy with chunks of white bread. He still enjoyed this, at Sunday dinner with his parents, but that was nostalgia. Once he'd savoured the rich, complex sauces of the Indian subcontinent, there was no going back.

They ordered starters while they waited for Evette and Jeffrey to arrive.

'Jeffrey's just sent me a text,' said Hope.

'What's the delay?' said Parmjit.

'Doesn't say,' said Hope.

'Ah well,' said Michael. 'Best not let these go to waste.'

And they all fell upon the poppadums.

As they were eating, Alex's phone rang. She turned her back to the others and spoke softly into it. With Evette and Jeffrey about to arrive, Hope was keeping a keen eye on both Alex and Michael. She strained to hear what Alex was saying; was she talking to Jeffrey? Alex put her phone away and turned towards the others. 'I just need to step outside for a minute. Won't be long.' She got up and left the restaurant.

'Cigarette break,' said Michael to the others. Hope wasn't so sure.

Before Alex returned, Evette and Jeffrey arrived. Jeffrey stood proprietorially, looking down on the group ranged along the table. Evette stood beside him, smiling, her copper hair and razor-sharp fringe immaculate as usual. She didn't meet Michael's sheepish gaze.

'I see you've tucked in without us. Good, good. Don't hold back on our account.' It was meant light-heartedly, as everyone understood.

'Don't worry Jeffrey, we won't,' said Michael, coming to. 'Where's Alex?'

Hope expected them to have met Alex outside the restaurant but Jeffrey's query told her that this wasn't the case.

'She's gone for a cigarette,' said Michael, helpfully. 'You must have walked right past her.'

Evette and Jeffrey settled at the table. Hope couldn't see whether or not Michael had made eye contact with Evette, but she was trying her best not to care anyway. She wanted to enjoy this meal because the past few weeks had been stressful in ways that she could never have anticipated. It had taken her a long time to make a decision to sell Klara's story and her role in it to the *Sunday Telegraph*. Lucy Osterbank had courted Hope politely but insistently in much the same way that Professor Nicholas King had done, and Hope liked being played in this way by Lucy Osterbank no better than she had in Nick King's case. In spite of her insistence, Hope had managed to keep Lucy Osterbank at bay for over a week before making a decision. In that time she'd talked over the offer with Michael, and with Alex and Parmjit too. But it was Doreen's advice that struck Hope as the most sensible.

'I don't know much about all this,' Doreen had said, 'but I know that you're pregnant and that, God willing, you'll soon have a child to look after. If you and Michael are at all like me and Ernie, you'll want to do your best for the child. It's a harder world now than when Michael and Linnie were kids. We had an NHS worth the name in those days, and dentists to look after the kid's teeth, and hospitals that didn't send you home more ill than when you went in. An education was an education too, and if you wanted to go to university you didn't have to get yourself into all sorts of debt to do it. And you know yourself how difficult it is to afford a place of your own these days. I don't suppose it'll be cheaper when the kids are grown up. And everyone has to have a car these days, and clothes and foreign holidays. It's all money and expense. You don't want it to be like that but there it is. You try to teach kids that there's more to life than money, but everything they read in their magazines or watch on the telly tells them the opposite. And you resent it, but at the same time you want your kids to have what they want; not *everything* they want, but you don't want them to feel left out. Ernie and I, we've tried to do our best by Linnie and Michael, but we're old and life's not getting cheaper for us old folks either. When I look at the way Linnie's struggled with her kids . . .'

Doreen paused, lost in thought for a moment. When she spoke again, it was as though she'd made the decision on Hope's behalf.

'Take the money, Hope. If this newspaper is daft enough to want to give it to you, then take it. Whoever Klara was, she's gone and the world has changed. Maybe if she'd had a windfall like this, she could have bought her child a place at art school and we'd never have had the concentration camps. Nobody knows. You've got to do what's best for your child. You've got your head screwed on; you're not going to be stupid with the money. Michael, well, you'll sort him out; you're the brains of the operation. It'll be all right. Take the money, Hope. You don't owe Klara anything.'

Hope phoned Lucy Osterbank as soon as she got home that evening.

Alex stepped through the door followed by a bearded man, slightly taller than her and, at first sight, slightly older than she was. He was dressed informally, a rust-coloured jacket over an open-necked beige shirt, and a pair of chinos. His hair, arranged in a boyish fringe across his forehead, was a mousy brown. His eyes were framed by round, gold-rimmed glasses. As he followed Alex over to the table, walking easily, one hand in the pocket of his chinos, Hope caught a flash of nut-brown brogue. Something about Alex's demeanour, the lightness of her smile, drew all eyes to her. As the couple approached the table, Michael glanced sideways at Jeffrey who was studiously ignoring them.

'Everybody?' said Alex. 'This is Will.' Will raised his free hand, and nodded his greeting around the table. 'Will's from

Canada,' said Alex, 'and he's a writer. In residence. At the uni.'

'For one semester,' said Will, holding up one finger. 'Unless I can hoodwink the university into letting me stay longer.'

'What are you writing?' Hope was genuinely curious. And she wanted to make Will feel accepted, for her friend's sake. She liked the look of him, and wondered why Alex hadn't mentioned him before now.

'I'm writing about the UK.'

'Is it a history?'

'Nothing so interesting,' said Will. 'It's a travelogue. I'm basically a travel writer. You must be Hope.' As he said this, Will jutted out his stomach and rubbed it with his free hand. Alex had evidently told Will about Hope's condition. Will was introduced to the rest of the party and the couple sat down. 'Have you ordered yet?' asked Will.

'We were waiting for Alex to come back. We thought she'd gone for a cigarette.'

'She had,' said Alex. 'Let's order. I'm starving.'

'I love curries,' said Will, his eyes eagerly devouring the menu. 'I'd come to the UK for the curries alone.'

'Wouldn't you rather be eating them in India? I mean, if you're a travel writer and all.' Jeffrey managed to make the phrase 'travel writer' sound as reprehensible as 'mass murderer'.

Alex glanced across at Hope.

'Actually, I've written a book about my travels there, too.' Will spoke factually. He wasn't boasting about his publications.

'I'll look out for it then.' The unspoken addendum 'in the remaindered section' hung over the table like a spectre at the feast, but Will was unfazed by Jeffrey's baiting.

'Well, much as I love the place, and the food, I'd rather eat my curries here.'

'But they're not really curries here, are they?' Evette spoke, genuinely curious. 'I mean, it's fabricated isn't it? A hybrid cuisine, or something. Chicken tikka masala's not an authentic dish is it?'

'Ah,' said Will, the scholar, 'that's partly my point. The one thing I've learned on my travels is that *authenticity* is a weasel word. I used to wander around places looking for the authentic this and the authentic that, but I never found it anywhere. So I gave up looking, and I'm happier for it. The world seems a much more varied place than it did when I was looking for authenticity.'

There was a silence.

'I like that.' All eyes turned to Gyorgy. 'I think it is true open mind.'

'Russian, right?' said Will, along the table.

'As vodka,' said Gyorgy, smiling.

'But at the end of the day, I'm an Anglophile,' said Will. 'I love British culture, I love the British countryside, I love British curries. And I *really* love British beer. There's nowhere in the world that makes beer like you Brits.'

A waiter appeared behind Will.

'Ready to order?'

'Indeed we are,' said Hope. 'I'll have the chicken tikka masala, madras hot please.'

All eyes turned towards Hope.

'Madras?' said Michael. 'Are you sure?'

The level of noise in the restaurant had increased considerably, as though in direct proportion to the dwindling number of children dining there. Hands reached across the table, tearing at naan breads, scooping sauces from the dishes set on the warming trays, lifting drinks. Conversations eddied back and forth, carrying various members of the group until a cross-cutting wave took them off in a different direction. Parmjit and Gyorgy were now in the middle of their spring vacation, and they'd returned earlier that week from a protest outside the Houses of Parliament.

'It was on the coach home that we heard that Bush had called a halt to the fighting.' Parmjit was talking to Hope, Alex and Will. 'Twenty-six days. Extraordinary.'

Hope was sweltering from the spices in her curry, and the back of her nose tickled, causing it to run. But she was determined to finish the meal.

'But it is not over,' said Gyorgy. 'Troops will remain. Country is not stable now.'

'It seems to me,' said Will, 'that ending hostilities is one thing. Knowing what to do next is another. I'm not sure that they've really thought it through.'

'I don't think they understand what they've got themselves into. Why is it that, in spite of all their advisors, all their intelligence gathering, all their resources, they never seem to see what we can all see?' Alex's question was rhetorical, but Gyorgy answered it all the same.

'Is not in their interest to see. There is agenda for public benefit – democracy, human rights, civil society – and there is agenda for their own benefit – oil, puppet government, ally for Israeli state.'

'It looks like they're going to go for Syria next. Bush is already making the noises,' said Parmjit.

'Believe me,' said Gyorgy. 'Is only just starting.'

'She says she's going to invest it.'

'Very wise,' said Jeffrey, responding to Michael. 'But frankly, I'd put the money to good use in my studio.'

'I'd go for a new wardrobe,' said Evette. 'And the holiday of a lifetime. But definitely the new wardrobe.'

'A new wardrobe wouldn't do Hope any good just now,' said Jeffrey. 'She's about to go on a crash diet.'

'When's it due?' said Evette.

'Sunday,' said Hope. 'The twentieth. Easter Sunday. If all goes according to plan. Which it rarely does, apparently.'

'Easter Sunday, eh?' said Jeffrey, suddenly interested. 'Don't they say that the Antichrist will be spawned on an Easter Sunday?'

'Jeffrey! What a lovely thing to say,' said Evette, admonishingly.

'The twentieth of April was also Hitler's birthday,' said Michael.

'There you go,' said Jeffrey, smiling wickedly around the table. 'It's just too much of a coincidence.'

'You're just jealous, Jeffrey,' said Alex, tiring of his relentless niggling.

'Me? I tell you, I have no desire to give in to the biological imperative.'

'I think she means that you're jealous of the money,' said Evette.

Michael was now fairly drunk and hadn't been paying much attention to the exchange. He spoke anyway, trying to connect his thoughts with the conversation going on around him.

'It's a funny thing, but Hope's spent the past couple of weeks decorating. It's like she's nesting, or something.'

Jeffrey pounced on Michael's cue. 'Like I say, it's biological. She's a hormonal automaton.'

As everyone around him groaned at Jeffrey's remark, Michael realized that it was he who had fed Jeffrey the line. He wasn't yet so drunk that he didn't care.

'Coffee? Dessert?'

The waiter held his notepad expectantly. Alex and Will wanted coffee and, having placed their orders, they stepped outside for a cigarette. Michael and Jeffrey ordered another pint each.

'Michael, are you sure? You've had quite a few already.'

'Hope, I'm fine. I'm all grown up, you know? I'm thirty next week. I can have another drink if I want one.'

Michael's faintly sneering tone was proof, to Hope, that Michael had indeed had enough – but she let it go. The back of her nose was still irritated by the hot spices, and she was beginning to wonder whether or not the madras had been a good idea. But she'd stuck to her plan, half-baked as it was, and had seen it through. It was out of her hands now.

Evette had left for the toilet at the same time as Alex and Will had left for a cigarette, and now she reappeared at Hope's side, sitting in Alex's vacated seat.

'Apologies for Jeffrey's remarks,' she whispered. 'You're no automaton. You look really beautiful. Pregnancy looks well on you, it really does.'

Hope looked at Evette. Sitting this close to her, she could see just how beautiful Evette really was. It was her eyes more than anything else. Hope could feel herself being drawn into their mysterious, dark universe, and in that moment she understood something of what it was that had so attracted Michael. Hope realized, as she sat regarding Evette while the restaurant conversation wreathed itself around them, that she felt no animosity towards her at all.

'Thank you,' said Hope. 'But you're the real beauty, you know.'

'Thanks Hope, I appreciate it. But I know my limitations.'

Hope wasn't sure what Evette meant by this. But as she said it, a shadow seemed to flit across Evette's face. Was it guilt? Hope pushed the thought away. She wanted to enjoy the remainder of the evening. She forced another topic into the space between them.

'I owe you a thanks for the painting.'

'Painting?'

'Schmetterling's painting.'

'You thanked me at the time, Hope. No need to do it again.'

'No, I want to. I love the painting. I really do. I can't explain what finding Klara's letter has meant to me.'

'What? The money? Good luck to you, I say.'

'No, I didn't mean the money. I meant . . . I'm not sure what I mean, really. It's Klara. I can't really explain it, but she's changed my life somehow. Across all these years, she's made me see the world differently. She's made me . . . she's made my pregnancy somehow *matter*. That sounds stupid, I know, but that's what it feels like. My pregnancy, our child, matters to me in a way that I don't think it would have if Klara hadn't tumbled into my life.'

Hope looked at Evette, who was smiling with genuine affection, wanting to understand what it was that Hope was trying to say.

'I'm not explaining myself very well, am I?' Hope felt embarrassed at her inability to make herself clear.

'Maybe,' said Evette, 'you'll be able to explain it better when the baby's here. It's all still a bit up in the air at the moment, isn't it?'

At that moment the coffee arrived, and Will and Alex were standing at the table. Hope looked up at them. They seemed to be radiating light, each glowing like a neon tube in the presence of the other's electricity. Evette leaned over and, taking Hope unawares, kissed her lightly on the cheek before vacating Alex's seat. It was a small gesture but Hope was moved by it, and oddly relieved, as though it somehow helped to draw a line under that part of the past she wanted to forget.

'So,' said Will, smiling across the table at Hope as he settled into his seat, 'Alex tells me that you're the one who discovered the truth about Hitler's father.'

Hope wasn't especially keen to discuss the matter any more. She'd had enough of the topic, and anyway she was feeling strangely light-headed. Her belly felt odd, too, in a way that she couldn't quite describe. Fortunately, Michael responded to Will's prompt.

'He might not have been Hitler's father. Schmetterling, I mean. The artist. Even if she did have an affair with him, it doesn't follow . . .'

'No, I appreciate that,' said Will, humbly.

'They think they've established the authenticity of the letter,' said Hope, talking to distract herself from the odd sensations assailing her. 'But they can't conclusively establish that Hitler and Schmetterling are related.'

'Can't they do DNA tests, or something?'

'Yes,' said Parmjit, joining in. 'At least, they're trying to find DNA to test. Hitler's body was burned at the bunker, after his suicide. Or so it's claimed. No one seems able to say for certain. And Schmetterling's body must have been disposed of in the camp.'

'They'll find some. And they'll prove that Schmetterling was Hitler's father.' The voice was Jeffrey's. He'd obviously heard the exchange from the other end of the table. Alex's derisive snort at Jeffrey's intervention only seemed to goad him on.

'Michael?' Hope spoke quietly, but Michael was too busy trying to follow the exchange between Will and Jeffrey to hear.

'It's obvious,' continued Jeffrey. 'The propaganda coup that this would create, it would be too good an opportunity to miss. Mark my words, if they can't find the evidence, they'll manufacture it.'

'Who are "they"?' said Will, genuinely puzzled. 'I mean, if this is going to be a conspiracy, whose interests is it going to serve?'

'Michael,' said Hope more forcefully, though again he didn't hear. It was Parmjit who noticed that Hope was trying to attract Michael's attention.

'Hope, are you OK?'

In the half-light of the restaurant, Hope looked drawn and pale; her eyes were wide, as though she were on the edge of panic. Michael, alerted by the tone of Parmjit's question, turned to look at her.

'Michael,' she said, 'I think I've wet myself.'

Michael was bewildered. What did she mean? 'Hope, are you OK?'

He looked at her face, into her eyes which were filling with tears he could not understand. For a brief, pinprick of a moment, he thought that she might be dying, and in that moment he felt as though he himself had died. His breathing stopped, his heart stopped and all thought halted within him. He was helpless. And then, as though rushing to fill a vacuum, he was overwhelmed with the thought of the child in Hope's belly; if Hope died, the child would die too and he would never see it, or Hope, ever again. Parmjit's voice broke through the wall of Michael's inertia.

'Michael, I think her waters have broken. Don't panic. I'll phone for an ambulance.'

Glad that someone was taking control of the situation, Hope relaxed, resting her head on Michael's shoulder while she waited for things to happen around her. Parmjit left the table to make the phone call. Michael reached for Hope's hand. It was trembling, and he held it tightly.

'Are you OK?' he whispered.

A small cramp gripped the lower part of Hope's abdomen, almost as though the baby had kicked one last time before beginning its journey into the world. It eased almost as quickly as it had started.

'It's on its way,' said Parmjit, referring to the ambulance.

'It's on its way,' echoed Hope, and closed her eyes.

Hope lay on the bed, empty and exhausted, tears streaming down her face with relief and gratitude. The pain, even dulled by huge gulps of gas and air, had been excruciating. Antenatal classes had simply not prepared her for the sheer, physical urgency of the pushing. At the beginning of the evening she'd fretted about maintaining decorum in front of the midwife, but she'd ended labour in a place beyond all pretence of decency. Legs splayed, fluids leaking from her slowly but remorselessly tearing vagina, she'd cursed as never before, pouring a torrent of insults on the heads of both Michael and the midwife – like an angry Old Testament God raining down water on a corrupt humanity. As her labour approached its climax and the contractions intensified, she was so overwhelmed by the urge to expel the child from her that she was no longer in control of herself. The contractions, when they came, passed through her like a primal force of nature, earthing through her body. By the time the baby sluiced into the hands of the midwife in the final act of expulsion, she'd lost all sense of where her body was. It was as though she'd turned herself inside out.

But it was over.

She lay spent and evacuated. A nurse worked away between her legs. Neither Hope nor Michael really knew, or cared, what she was doing.

'What is it?' said Hope, drunkenly, her head swimming with excess oxygen.

'It's a . . .'

Neither Hope nor Michael heard what the nurse said. Hope found herself lying with the baby on her chest, awkwardly cradling the child to herself, not sure how to hold it; not sure even how to look at it. She would have been happy to fall asleep there and then, but the nurse lifted the baby from Hope to clean it up and deal with the umbilical cord, the first moment of true separation. Michael stood holding Hope's hand. She gripped it without seeming to be aware of what she was doing, taking comfort from it in a curiously detached way. Just at that moment, she had too little energy left for emotion.

'Michael, what is it?'

The midwife turned and handed Michael a bundle wrapped in a white towel. 'There you are, Dad,' she said.

Michael looked down at the wrinkled thing wrapped in its white towel. Something that looked like a shrunken head squirmed from side to side, eyes barely able to keep themselves open. Every so often, a half-hearted bleat emanated from the bundle, as though a kitten had got its head stuck inside a tin can and wasn't sure whether or not it cared. One tiny, clenched hand appeared beside the face, rubbing a cheek with the smallest thumb Michael had ever seen. The head nodded instinctively in the direction of the fist and the mouth opened, latching on to the soft knuckle. Immediately, the head relaxed, the eyes closed, and for a moment the only movement was an involuntary trembling of the tiny lower lip. Michael stood in wonderment, watching the clumsy manoeuvre. The nurse between Hope's legs stepped back, holding a stainless steel dish containing a bloody mass.

'It's sucking its thumb,' said Michael, 'Hope, it's sucking its thumb!'

'Michael, please, what is it?'

Michael was enchanted and bewildered by this strange creature in his arms. Hope's question filtered through into his consciousness and he tried, as best he could, to process an answer for her.

'It's a baby, Hope. It's a baby!'

About the Author

Alan Apperley is a Senior Lecturer in Media Studies at Wolverhampton University and a member of 1980s cult post-punk band The Nightingales, who played more Peel sessions than any other band excluding The Fall. The Nightingales re-formed in 2004, with Alan on lead guitar. He lives in Staffordshire with his wife and children.

Acknowledgements

Many people have helped in the writing of this novel. In particular I would like to thank my long-suffering wife, Helen, my children Joseph and Catherine, Dee Dyal and the members of the Little Aston Reading Group, and my colleagues, Gaby Steinke, Mark Jones and Aidan Byrne. I would also like to thank Alan Mahar, Luke Brown and all at Tindal Street Press for their support and guidance throughout the publishing process.